... and funny and poign...
...und it as refreshing as a breath of sea air'
Nicola Cornick

Readers love

How to find Love in the Little Things

'Fabulously glorious, funny, uplifting and feel good . . . The best
book for those hot summer days' Karen W

'A beautifully written novel full of humour and pathos' Ann G

'A warm and fuzzy read! Relatable and real characters' Prachiti K

'I loved all the characters, found it funny, heartwarming, sad,
nostalgic and I galloped through the book to the end which came
as a total surprise' Lucy D

'What a beautiful book, the setting is just lovely and the gentle
humour is great fun to read' Claire L

'Highlights that age doesn't stop you from embracing life
and love . . . Loved it' Alys G

'A lovely read with a few surprises thrown in' Julie H

Virginie Grimaldi grew up in Bordeaux and wanted to be a writer for as long as she can remember. She wrote her first novel aged eight in a green notebook with multiplication tables in the back. It was about love and the sea and featured a thirty-page-long sunset . . .

How to Find Love in the Little Things was first published in France in May 2016 and became an instant bestseller, translated into multiple languages.

You can follow Virginie on Twitter: @GinieGrimaldi and Instagram: @virginiegrimaldi

VIRGINIE GRIMALDI

TRANSLATED BY ADRIANA HUNTER

REVIEW

First published in Great Britain in 2018 by
HEADLINE PUBLISHING GROUP

1

Cataloguing in Publication Data is available from the British Library

ISBN 978 1 4722 5008 7

Typeset in 12.5/15.5 pt Baskerville MT Std by Jouve (UK), Milton Keynes

Printed and bound in Great Britain by Clays Ltd, Elcograf S.p.A.

Headline's policy is to use papers that are natural, renewable and recyclable
products and made from wood grown in well-managed forests and other
controlled sources. The logging and manufacturing processes are expected
to conform to the environmental regulations of the country of origin.

HEADLINE PUBLISHING GROUP
An Hachette UK Company
Carmelite House
50 Victoria Embankment
London EC4Y 0DZ

www.headline.co.uk
www.hachette.co.uk

For William

Prologue

It was just another Saturday evening. Not destined to be engraved on my memory, and yet I remember every detail. That's a prerogative of traumatic experiences, apparently. They embed themselves so deeply in our brains and bodies that we keep on reliving them afterwards, like endlessly watching the same scene of a film.

Marc's stomach was acting as my pillow, we were watching *Game of Thrones*, episode nine of season three, we'd eaten takeaway sushi, the fan was whirring, it was nice. If I were a cat, I would have been purring.

When my phone rang, I sighed. Who'd disturb me at this time of night?

When I saw 'Mum' on the screen, I grumbled. She knows perfectly well it worries me when she calls late.

I wish I hadn't answered. I wish it hadn't happened.

That was six months ago, and I still feel like I've had my heart wrenched out.

February

'Our greatest glory is not in never failing,
but in rising up every time we fail'

– Ralph Waldo Emerson

Chapter 1

Monday, rain, February: a winning combo for a shit day.

The further my car travels along the road, the further I want to get away. I fork off down the lane and a sign on a tree tells me it's straight ahead. Maybe no one will notice if I turn back. I come to a small car park dotted with trees and flowerbeds that clearly haven't seen a gardener in a long time. I drive around it and park in front of the big building.

'OCEAN VIEW U SING HOME'

If even the cast-iron lettering is packing in, I should be worried. Or what if the job offer had the typo, and this *isn't* a nursing home and I'm really going to find myself in some kind of residential glee club . . . To be honest, that sounds much more fun than what's in store for me.

The last few footsteps between me and the front door take for ever.

One step. I could still leave.

Two steps. I'd only have to get back to the car.

Three steps. No one would ever know, after all.

'Do come in, we've been waiting for you!'

I don't have time to get to the door before a woman appears in the entrance. She's tall and solid, and her hair's so frizzy she can hold a pencil in it. I scour my mind for an escape route, an excuse to run away, but nothing comes to me. So I smile politely, proffer my hand and follow her towards the next eight months of my life.

Chapter 2

Her high heels make a loud click-clacking on the white floor tiles. She walks briskly and I follow, respecting the appropriate distance. Two tiles, and I'm too close; four, and I'm safe.

What I'd like, in no particular order or all at once, is to disappear, become invisible, die, disintegrate, do a U-turn or rewind. Yes, there, that's it. Could we rewind, please? Let's meet up a little way back, when everything was fine. When my life didn't feel like a horror film with me as the girl who's slashed a hundred times with a chainsaw and gets back on her feet each time. Let's meet before every-thing turned upside down, before everything fell apart. Before I told myself it would be the brainwave of the cen-tury to reply to this ad.

What the hell am I doing here?

We come to a stop by a white door and my guide puts a key in the lock. I look up at a small sign which reads:

Anne-Marie Rouillaux
Director

So this is the person I've spoken to several times on the phone. She goes in, walks around her desk and sits down in her chair.

'Close the door and sit yourself down.'

I do as I'm told while she opens a file and studies the documents inside it, screwing up her eyes. A cactus standing next to her computer monitor indicates the mood. Somewhere in the background, the ticking of a clock marks out the seconds, in what feels like slow motion. Either that, or my heart's beating too quickly.

I take a deep breath and launch into my explanations.

'I'm so sorry I'm late. There are roadworks on the way into Biarritz and it took for ever to get through the temporary lights.'

She draws the pencil from her hair and jots down a few words on a fresh sheet of paper.

'It's all right this once, but I hope it remains an exception. We can't afford to keep the residents waiting, do you understand?'

'Yes, I understand.'

'Good. I'll give you the morning to settle in, look around and get your bearings. This afternoon, you'll meet Lea Marnon, who you'll be taking over from, as of tomorrow. Because of her condition, she can't stay on to train you up, but she'll try to teach you as much as she can in the few hours she has left here. That should be plenty. As I said on the phone, there aren't many residents: twenty-one exactly, including one couple who share a studio.'

'Oh, are there studios?'

'That's what we call the accommodation,' she explains, getting to her feet. 'Each one has a small bedroom, a living room with a kitchenette and a bathroom. Right, unless you have any questions, I have a meeting. Go to reception and Isabelle will show you your studio.'

I stand up, too, and follow her to the door.

'Welcome to Ocean View,' she smiles, slipping the pencil back between her curls. 'You don't know it yet, but you're going to like it here!'

As she gestures me through the door, I think I'd be more likely to make friends with a unicorn than to enjoy being in this end-of-the-road place. The woman's lost some of her marbles, for sure.

Oh god, what the *hell* am I doing here?

Chapter 3

Isabelle definitely suits the second half of her name. She'd be the belle of any ball, with her long black eyelashes framing green eyes, and a smile that could light up a decommissioned coalmine. Fairy godmothers had clearly just had a pay rise when Isabelle was born. When I introduce myself, she comes around the counter at reception and gives me a kiss on each cheek.

'We can treat each other as friends, not just colleagues, can't we?' she suggests, without really waiting for an answer. 'Everyone here does, except for Anne-Marie, and the residents, of course. But we do call them by their first names, it's less formal. So you're Julia?'

'That's right.'

'And I gather you'll be living on site. Come on, I'll show you your studio, it's in the annexe.'

She takes my hand and leads me out to the front of the building. There are ten or twelve trees and a few benches in the paved parking area. Sitting on one of them is an old lady who appears to be waiting for an imaginary bus. She has her walking stick in hand, wears the strap of her little black handbag across her body, and she's matched her lipstick to her pink loafers.

'Everything okay, Lucienne?' Isabelle asks as we walk past.

The old woman looks to see where the voice came from, eventually focuses through her tinted lenses and gives us a sketchy smile.

'Everything's fine, dear. I'm waiting for my son, to go to the market. Oh, and I finally opened my bowels this morning!'

'Well, that *is* good news!' my new colleague exclaims. 'You know what they say: "A poo before noon, the whole day's a boon!"'

I pause momentarily. My car's just a few metres away; if I'm quick, they won't see me scram. But, governed by some sort of resignation to my fate, I keep following Isabelle.

The annexe is a small, two-storey construction thirty or forty metres from the main building. Like its bigger brother, it's made of stone, punctuated with white windows and wrought-iron balconies.

'There are seven studios here,' Isabelle explains. 'The four on the ground floor are for residents' families who want somewhere to stay when visiting, and for elderly people to get a feel for the place before moving in. The three upstairs are for staff. Follow me. I'll show you yours.'

'Are the other two occupied?' I ask as we go upstairs.

'Yes, by Clara and Greg. Clara's a care assistant who's been living here since she split up with her boyfriend;

she's a laugh, but, between you and me, I find her a bit much. Greg's the activities coordinator; he's living here while he has work done on his apartment. You'll see – he looks like a god, but you and I don't have what it takes to catch his eye, if you know what I mean . . . So, here's your new home!'

Isabelle opens a white door and steps inside to give me the guided tour . . . which is quick; there are only two rooms: a dark bathroom equipped for someone with reduced mobility and a living room-cum-bedroom which is bathed in light but must have been decorated by some-one way past their sell-by date. My new habitat comprises a two-seater sofa in mustard-coloured velvet, a round table covered with a doily, a vintage-but-God-knows-what-vintage sideboard, a medieval television, a single bed pressed up against the wall and blackout curtains in burgundy velvet. I feel like crying, and not for joy.

'And now for the best bit!' Isabelle exclaims, opening the French windows. 'Come and see the view!'

I join her on the balcony. The grounds of the retire-ment home extend almost a hundred metres away, with a little white pebble path meandering between huge trees, a vegetable plot, luxuriant shrubs and wooden benches dotted here and there. The grass is so green it looks fake, like nowhere else on earth but Basque country. A fence marks the boundary at the far end of the plot. Beyond that, nothingness; and down below, the ocean, stretching as far as the eye can see.

'Isn't it just fantastic?' she crows.

'It is, it's really beautiful,' I reply, realising just how much I've missed the sea.

'There, I told you, didn't I! This place is paradise. Okay, I'll let you settle in. If you need anything, you know where to find me.'

Lost in thought, I hardly hear the door close. The view really *is* glorious, there's no denying that. But calling this God's-waiting-room of a place paradise strikes me as optimistic, to say the least. For the thousandth time, I wonder why I came here. As if I don't know . . .

Everything turned upside down one Saturday evening. The evening my father died.

Chapter 4

When I picked up, there was silence. That's never a good sign, when silence does the talking.

'Mum?'

Nothing.

'Are you okay, Mum?'

My lips trembled. As if they knew what was going on before I did.

Marc pressed Pause; I sat down and cancelled the call. My mother must have had a bad signal. Or she'd phoned by mistake. There, that's all it was. Still, I called her back to make sure. She picked up, her voice swimming in tears.

'Sweetheart, your father's had a heart attack.'

'Is he all right?'

Silence.

'Mum!' I wailed. 'Mum, is he all right? Please . . .'

'He's dead, sweetheart. He's dead . . .'

She described it all, but only the occasional word got through to me. Kitchen, roast, fell, ambulance, cardiac massage, failed, so sorry. Then we stayed on the line for many minutes, crying in silence, together. I clutched my phone tightly in my hand and wished it was my mother in my arms. In the end, we hung up, I told Marc, my future husband, he could press Play, and put my head back on his stomach as if nothing had happened. Every ounce of me refused to accept reality.

It was when I took my make-up off before going to bed, looking into the mirror, which reflected my terrified expression, that it hit me. My father was dead. He no longer existed. He would never exist again. He would never pinch my cheek again and call me Juju, never again grumble that I'm always late, never again read the sports pages of his newspaper in his green armchair; he wouldn't be walking me down the aisle now, or eating the crust off the end of a baguette before sitting down to a meal, or leaving his shoes by the door. I wouldn't see his hair go any whiter now, or hear his voice, or joke about Mum's cooking with him; I wouldn't wrinkle my nose when his beard prickled my cheeks. I'd never say 'Daddy' again. One of my greatest fears had just been realised. We'd come to it, to the moment when everything turns upside down. Nothing would ever be the same again.

My reflection distorted and an animal sound came from my throat. Then another. Then many more. I screamed continuously, until I slumped, breathless, to my knees in my little bathroom.

All I could think about was going home to my family, burrowing into my mother's arms, hugging my sister to me, being near him. But I was in Paris and they were in Biarritz; I would have to wait till the morning to catch the first train. That night, I made acquaintance with real pain.

Every now and then, just for a few seconds, I would think about something else and forget what was happening. And then reality would strike me brutally. My father was dead. I'd been lying peacefully on the sand, but a wave had come crashing down on me. The next few months saw a succession of these violent waves. My father, my boyfriend, my grandmother. I was drowning. So, when I read this job offer last week, what I saw was a lifeline. A retirement home in Biarritz urgently needed a qualified psychologist for maternity cover. On-site accommodation was available. The prospect of working with the elderly enthused me about as much as kissing a spider, but it was a question of survival.

The cold wind makes me shiver. I cast a last glance over my new home before going to fetch my bags. A sunbeam breaks through the clouds, sending a shaft of light down on to the ocean. In a burst of optimism, I see this as a sign and find myself believing I may have made the right choice. A wild belief which is quickly dashed when I hear Isabelle's voice coming from the garden:

'You've forgotten your incontinence pad again, Paulette!'

Chapter 5

The psychologist is putting her personal belongings into a small crate when I join her in her office. She comes over to me, her hand outstretched, and her stomach, too.

'Ah, you must be Julia. I'm Lea, pleased to meet you.'

'Yes, that's me. Nice to meet you, too. Do you need any help?'

'Nearly done,' she says, picking up a pile of books. 'Did Anne-Marie explain why I'm leaving?'

'Well, it's for maternity cover, so I'm guessing you're pregnant?'

'Four months, and I'm already having contractions. As far as possible, I need to avoid stress, so my obstetrician's prescribed sick leave. Do you have children?'

'No.'

'We've been trying for two years,' she confides. 'So, I can tell you, I'm not prepared to risk losing this baby for work. And, it may not look it, but it's tiring working here . . . where were you before?'

'In a cosmetic-surgery clinic in Paris.'

'Wow, that's fantastic! Did you get operations for free?'

'Only the sex change.'

She pauses for a moment, struggling to keep the polite smile on her face.

'Really?'

Okay, so she's taken me seriously. I'm about to go into detail about having my penis excised, but I don't want to send her into early labour.

'I was joking. No, I didn't get a discount on operations, and there wouldn't have been any point, anyway. I've seen too many to be tempted myself.'

'I'm not surprised . . . It's a bit like that here. Spending the whole day with old people makes you want to die young. Right, that's enough chitchat, let's get to work!'

She invites me round to her side of the desk and I take out a notepad.

'All the residents' files are stored digitally,' she explains, clicking on a series of icons. 'This is where you enter the information you gather every day, but there's not actually that much deskwork. You have to see each resident at least once a week, and the sessions are held in their studios. It's easier to get them to talk in a familiar environment. Have you worked with the elderly before?'

'At the end of my degree I did my final placement in a geriatric unit, but that was a while ago.'

'It's different, you'll see. They don't think you can do anything for them, so they don't confide in you much. I basically just ask how they're feeling: mostly, they're more or less okay and, when they're not, you make sure they're prescribed antidepressants. Never have any qualms about doing that – I mean, at their age, there's not much we can do for them.'

Three cheers for the psychologist. She's about as sharp as a feather pillow.

'Really? I seem to remember the opposite, they really wanted to open up . . .'

'We'll soon see if you can do any better than me, but I doubt it. They're tricky. I'm going to be honest with you, I'm glad I'm stopping work early. If you stick it out till I get back, it'll be quite a feat. Come on. I'll introduce you to everyone, then I'm off.'

Lea hares off to the day room. Literally, like a hare. I practically have to run not to be left behind.

She's in a hurry, I get that. If I could, I'd be running for the door, too. Her gloomy forecast has wiped away the last traces of my enthusiasm. I'd pictured the minutely small possibility that the residents here would be adorable and would change my ideas about old age. I need to be realistic: that's not going to happen.

I don't like old people. To be really accurate, it's not that I dislike them, even though I can't say I actively *like* them, it's that I'm afraid of them. They're on first-name terms with death, and I prefer to keep it at arm's length. I'm so keen on avoiding any mention of it that I often used to skip history lessons, because studying the lives of people who now exist only in books bothered me so much. And, I might as well admit it, they're not very interesting. There's nothing more like an old person than another old person, a bit like babies and miniature poodles. They all have the same hair – whether it's real or synthetic – and the same stooped back, the same glasses, the same shakes and the same constant regrets.

'Here we are!' Lea announces.

The double doors are closed. She presses on the handle and pushes. I clutch my notebook to my chest, a paper barrier between me and them, and I step into the communal day room. Inside, sitting facing the door in a half-circle, twenty crinkled faces light up and cry:

'Welcome, Juliaaaa!'

I select my most professional smile and slap it on my face. How am I going to tell them apart?

Chapter 6

Lea has gone. She gave me the keys to the office, lobbed a general 'goodbye' to anyone who was listening, then cleared off with a haste I didn't find very reassuring. From now on, the psychologist at Ocean View . . . is me.

The fear must be plain to see in my eyes because a tall, dark-haired man, who I can safely assume is not one of the residents, comes over to me with a beaming smile.

'Hi, I'm Greg, the activities coordinator. Not easy on the first day, is it?'

'I'm feeling a bit lost, but I'll be okay. Thanks!'

'Don't worry, it'll be fine. I'm guessing Lea painted a terrible picture – she's the personification of pessimism. Come with me. We'll soon change that.'

He slips his arm into mine and leads me over to the residents.

He introduces me to them one by one. I shake each resident's hand, trying to remember their names, but soon give up. I do manage five: Lucienne, the woman with the black handbag who was on the bench this morning, waiting for her son; Leon, who doesn't deign to look up from his iPhone; Marilyn, who's proudly wearing a 'Miss Granny 2004' sash; Louise, who holds my hand in hers a little longer than the others; and Gustave, who asks, 'Do you like salmon, Ella?' and roars with laughter when I say my name's Julia. It takes me several seconds to understand his pun. And when I've given my last handshake, he's the one who starts slow hand-clapping and chanting, 'Spee-eech, spee-eech!', and the other residents immediately join in. Greg gives me a nod, which seems to say I have no choice. I clear my throat, dig my nails into my notebook and launch into my best airport voice.

'Good afternoon, everyone. I'm Julia, your new psychologist. As from tomorrow, I'll visit you in your rooms every week so that we can assess how you're feeling. Of course, should you need me, I'll be available at any time. I'm delighted to be here at Ocean View with you, and I'll do everything I can to work alongside you on a daily basis.'

My speech is greeted with a smattering of lukewarm applause. While the residents drift away – with or without walking sticks, wheelchairs or walking frames – Greg comes over to me.

'You need to speak up next time – lots of them are hard of hearing. Otherwise, you came off okay. Even Leon wasn't too unpleasant.'

'So, Leon's the one glued to his phone?'

'Exactly, a real geek. He never looks up from his screens, unless it's to grumble or complain. I've been trying to find his redeeming features for two years, without success. I'd have more luck looking for a bit of Madonna's face that hasn't been Botoxed!'

For the first time since I arrived here, I laugh. A little too loudly and for a little too long, but I'm struggling to stop, as if every new outburst is driving out another pocket of stress.

'I've got a bit of time before Bingo. Shall I show you around?' he asks.

I accept gladly, and not just because his smile deserves a place among the seven wonders of the world. I don't know my way around; I feel like a new pupil at the beginning of the school year and I'm very happy a classmate has offered to hold my hand. As I follow him, my notebook at the ready, I hear a quavering voice behind me:

'She's prettier than the other one but she seems even less friendly.'

Chapter 7

I almost have a heart attack when I hear voices while I'm walking through the grounds of Ocean View in the dead of night.

I'm such a scaredy-cat. There was a time when my nickname was *Boo!*, and I have to admit it suits me better than Julia. I jump out of my skin every time I come across someone unexpectedly, going down blue runs in snowplough feels like an extreme sport and I wail like a fire-engine siren if a dog so much as comes near me.

Once, I must have been about fifteen, I heard my mother scream in the kitchen. I ran to see what was going on and found her trying to control the flames billowing from a frying pan. In my mind's eye, I saw myself grab a tea-towel, run it under a tap and smother the fire with tremendous composure. But only in my mind's eye. Because what actually happened was I just managed to blurt out, 'Rest in peace, Mum,' before running, shrieking, from the scene.

Another time, when I was in the car waiting for Marc outside his office, a man knocked insistently at the window. It was dark and he had a picture of a kitten on his T-shirt – very suspect. Without even thinking, I squirted my whole canister of pepper spray in his eyes. It turned out to be a colleague of Marc's who'd kindly come down to let me know he was running late.

So now, when I hear voices in the grounds, my legs start to wobble, my throat constricts and my heart beats a David Guetta bass line.

What a brilliant idea it was to come out this late.

I couldn't sleep, too much stuff milling around inside my head. The perfect moment for a cigarette. I keep a packet in the car, so I've come out to get it and, now that I'm out, I've decided to have a little stroll in the grounds. In the moonlight, I hadn't noticed how far I've strayed from the building. It's only when I hear someone talking that I realise I'm at the far end of the garden, where no one would hear me if I screamed. I do the most ridiculous things when I'm tired.

Okay, breathe. It's gone midnight and, judging by my freezing nose, the temperature is on a par with the inside of a pot of Häagen-Dazs. It's highly unlikely anyone else is crazy enough to be venturing outside. I must have imagined the voices; that's the only explanation. I'm going to go back to my monastic studio, lock myself in, push the sofa against the door and fall into a peaceful sleep – that's what's going to happen.

In a few speedy strides, I'm back at the annexe, and I'm trying to get back inside when I hear footsteps near the main building. While I struggle to put my key in the lock (a straightforward procedure, which becomes an elite SAS mission when you're shaking like a leaf), I glance around, in the hope of identifying the source of the sound, and I almost pass out when I see a shadow sneak behind the vegetable patch. I stand there, paralysed, for a few seconds, long enough to see a person's head emerge behind the wall, turn towards me and then whisk out of sight. They've seen me. Quick, I need to get to safety. This sodding key must go into the lock eventually; surely I'm not going to die here, strangled by some lowlife in the grounds of a care home in my pink flannelette pyjamas, my puffa jacket and my cat-head slippers!

I turn the key the other way up, push with all my strength, call on the god of doors . . . but it's no good, the key's determined not to go in. Behind me, I can hear footsteps drawing slowly closer. My heart isn't just beating in my chest now, it's beating in my neck, my eyes, my fingers, my ears, my hair and the whiskers on my slippers.

So is this what it's like when you know the end is near? You turn into a giant vibrator?

My assassin is only a few metres away now; I can almost feel his hands around my neck. No, honestly, dying at thirty-two is a bit much. Especially as he only had to go a few metres further and he'd have found prey that'll soon be dead anyway. In a final, miraculous jolt of lucidity, I realise that the key I'm frantically trying to put into the lock is the one for the studio, not the building itself. I hold my breath while I grapple for the right one and give a squeak of relief when it goes into the lock. I slam the door behind me, climb the stairs four at a time, shut myself in my studio and press my ear to the door.

Forty minutes later, I'm forced to acknowledge that the only thing following me was silence.

Two hours later, my muscles have relaxed, my teeth have stopped chattering and my heart is beating normally again.

I might have got just a teensy bit carried away.

Chapter 8

'How are you feeling today?'

Louise is my first patient of my first day. Sitting in an armchair that faces out through the big picture window, she does her knitting while I settle into a chair opposite her. She's shaking slightly, all part of being old. I'm shaking, too, all part of being terrified.

Her studio is crammed with stuff. There's an accumulation of mismatched furniture, knick-knacks, framed photographs, books and knitting. At a glance, none of it looks like anything much, but each item must have some special value in her eyes. She must have carefully chosen what should come with her into her last bedroom.

'I'm getting better and better,' she says, putting down her knitting. 'I'm starting to get my bearings. Did you know I haven't been here long?'

'I saw that in your file. Three months, is that right?'

'Nearly three months, yes. First, I spent five weeks in hospital after my stupid stroke, then the doctors said I couldn't go home. So my children found me a room here; apparently, it's the best place in the area. I'm not too miserable here . . .'

'Would you like to talk about your stroke, Louise?' I ask gently.

'Oh, there's not much to say about it. I was doing my shopping in the market and *bang!*, I ended up on the ground, unconscious. When I came round a few days later, I'd forgotten the last forty years of my life. Can you imagine? Forty years gone in a few seconds.'

'How did you feel?'

'It was terrible. The year I turned thirty, there was a huge fire in the house I lived in with my husband and children. It destroyed everything – everything. We lost our home, our furniture, all our paperwork, our clothes . . . But what upset me most was losing the memories. Photos and slides of the children when they were babies, their drawings, their poems, the letters they sent from summer camp, the photos of my parents, of our wedding . . .'

She pauses and looks out of the window.

'When you don't have all those things, your memory has no right to fail. It doesn't have an understudy. Oh, what a twit! I haven't offered you anything to drink. Would you like coffee, tea, hot chocolate? My daughter's given me a very sophisticated machine. You just put a capsule in and the drink makes itself.'

You haven't got any whisky, by any chance?

'I'd love a hot chocolate, thank you. So, we were talking about your memory . . .'

'Oh, don't worry, I know!' she says, heading for the kitchenette. 'My short-term memory works well, thank goodness. I told you about the fire to explain how I felt. Losing your memories when they're material things is painful enough. But that's nothing compared to how I felt when they told me forty years had been wiped from my mind. Just think, forty years ago, my children weren't yet twenty, my husband was still alive, I was still young, my grandchildren didn't even exist . . . not to mention mobile phones, dozens of TV channels, the internet and nose piercings!'

When I read Louise's file, I almost envied her for forgetting part of her life. I'd give quite a lot for the last six months of mine to disappear. But as I watch her fight back her tears, I don't envy her at all.

'Thanks,' I say, taking the cup she hands me. 'How did you go about coming to terms with it?'

'Well, it was simple,' she says with a shrug, as if it really were. 'When they told me my memory wouldn't come back, I had two options: either I didn't accept it and was unhappy for the rest of my days, or I accepted it and lived my final years in peace. I've always had quite a taste for happiness.'

'What a wonderful philosophy!'

'I'm very lucky, you know. I'm eighty-four, and I can still hear the tiniest peep of birdsong, I can read with ordinary glasses, I even still have a few real teeth. Lots of people don't get to my age in such good shape. And, anyway, my past hasn't really gone, I just don't remember it, that's all. My children, grandchildren and friends remember it. Those forty years *did* happen.'

She gets up and takes a photo from the sideboard. In the picture, she looks radiant and is surrounded by people of all ages.

'Look,' she says, handing it to me. 'These are my children and grandchildren. That was fifteen years ago. It doesn't show my youngest grandson and my two great-grandchildren, who were born later, but it's one of the only pictures with all of us together. I have four children, ten grandchildren and two great-grandchildren, and they've shown me so much love since this happened. Please believe me when I say I don't have any reason to opt for being unhappy. Do you have a big family?'

I nod my head then change the subject.

'And if I asked for your level of happiness on a scale of one to ten?'

Louise doesn't consider this for long before replying, 'I'd say nine. I've deducted one for when I wake up – it takes me a good ten minutes to get out of bed every morning. I feel like a little piece of paper folded up tightly and I have to unfold it very carefully for fear of tearing it.'

She watches me while I write this in my notebook so I can add it to her file. And then, out of the blue, she asks me a question:

'How about you? How do you feel on a scale of one to ten?'

Chapter 9

It's bangers and mash for lunch today. The menu is written out in large, proud letters on the board. It's only just twelve and the residents are already tucking into the main course. Perhaps they think the day will be over sooner like this.

There are five round tables in the refectory, spaced sufficiently far apart for wheelchairs and walking frames to get through easily. Greg explained yesterday that all the staff take turns to serve meals. 'Versatility's the buzzword at Ocean View,' he said. So long as I don't have to wash anyone, that's fine by me.

Today, Isabelle and a short, blond-haired girl are flitting between residents, helping some of them eat. Greg waves me over, so I go and join him on what must be the staff table. There's a place set for me and I sit down while he does the introductions. I already know Anne-Marie, the director, who's too busy cutting her sausage into tiny pieces to notice me, and I now meet everyone who works here full-time: Jean-Paul, the coordinating doctor; Sarah, one of the care workers; Laura, the physio; Moussa, the nurse; and Stephanie, the admin assistant.

'And you already know Isabelle, the receptionist, and

Clara, the other care worker,' Greg adds, pointing to them as they try to convince one of the residents that yes, the mashed potato is home-made.

My bottom has hardly touched down on the chair before the barrage of questions begins. You'd honestly think these people were prisoners who haven't seen anyone new for ten years.

'I live in Paris but, originally, I'm from here; no, I don't have any children; no pets either; in a cosmetic-surgery clinic; only the sex change; yes, very pleasant; I'm not married either; Paris; I'm not at all sporty; because I liked the sound of the job; no, I'm not just saying that because Anne-Marie's here; thirty-two . . .'

I'm pretty close to asking whether they'd like to see my last cervical smear test when a male voice interrupts.

'Whoever did this, give yourself up or I'll press charges against all of you!' roars an old man standing bolt upright, like a soldier to attention.

'What's happened now, Leon?' Clara asks, rolling her eyes.

'What's happened is my dentures vanished while I was using the facilities. I put them down on my serviette and they're not there now.'

'Why did you take your dentures out?' Isabelle asks.

'I like eating mashed potato without them. I still have a right to do as I please, for heaven's sake!'

The other residents around Leon keep eating their lunch and don't say a word.

'I'm warning you,' he rails, 'if I don't get my dentures

in the next minute, I'll take this to a tribunal. This is abuse. I won't be bullied!'

'You're a pain, Leon!' Miss Granny 2004 says bluntly. 'We've had enough of your scenes. You know perfectly well where your dentures are.'

'Here we go again . . .' the nurse says, laughing.

'Does this happen often?' I ask.

'Regularly, yes. You'd think he does it on purpose . . . he leaves his things lying around and knows exactly how it will end.'

Intrigued, I keep watching. On the next table, Gustave, the joker grandpa, pushes back his chair, leans on his walking frame and makes his way slowly over to Leon. Once he reaches him, he puts a hand on his shoulder and smiles.

'So, old boy, no sense of humour?'

'You call this humour?' replies Leon. 'Give me back my dentures right now or . . .'

'Or what? You'll bite me?'

A ripple of amusement runs around the tables. Louise crams a serviette against her mouth to stifle a laugh.

'I'm waiting . . .' Leon says.

'Well, go on, take your dentures, then,' Gustave swaggers, with a broad smile.

'Where are they?'

'Can't you see?' Gustave insists, broadening his smile even further.

'Clearly not.'

Gustave brings his face closer to Leon's and draws back his lips. Isabelle shakes her head.

'Oh, no, Gustave, you haven't! Are you wearing Leon's dentures?'

The old man starts laughing about his prank, followed by most of the residents and the staff. And me, I have to confess. What with Leon's thwarted expression and Gustave's obvious pride as he grins with teeth that are too big for his mouth, my black mood is lifting.

'Hey, Julia, tomorrow's Polar Bears day. Would you like to join us?' Greg asks, pouring himself a glass of water.

'Polar Bears? What's that?'

'It's a small group of residents who get together once a month to swim in the sea, whatever the weather.'

They're bonkers.

'But would I have to swim, too?'

'Definitely. If you come with us, you go in!'

All my new colleagues have turned to look at me. They're testing me, the sadists. If I refuse, I'll look like a wimp or, worse, a snob who doesn't want to join in their activities. If I accept, I'll probably turn into Mr Freeze. Tough choice.

'I'd love to come with you!'

I don't know who said that, but I seem to recognise my voice and it came from my mouth. If even my own body's betraying me, there's not much hope for my dignity.

Chapter 10

They could have chosen a sunny part of the day, just to claw back a few degrees. But no. It's nine o'clock in the morning and it's cold, very cold, so cold that all the hair on my body is standing to attention, and yet this little gaggle of degenerates – myself included – is preparing to dive into the Atlantic.

Since arriving in Biarritz, I've had plenty of time to wonder whether dropping everything to come here was the right choice. This morning, with my feet sinking into icy sand and wearing my most forgiving swimming costume as my only protection against the wind, my teeth are playing the maracas and I've stopped wondering – I now know for sure I've gone mad. A switch has flicked inside my head: I'm disturbed, distraught, distressed, disconcerted, disenchanted, discombobulated and every word that begins with dis-.

'Are you all ready?'

Greg walks down to the water, followed by seven almost transparent figures. Gustave leaves his walking frame just before the wet sand, Miss Granny keeps her sash on, Louise holds in her tummy, Elisabeth and Pierre cling to each other's hands, Jules jogs in his polka-dot trunks, Arlette stretches her arms . . . and I join them, praying that some unforeseen event will stop us getting into those arctic waves. A hurricane, a thunderstorm, a great white shark, an attack of giant crabs, or zombies – it doesn't matter, so long as I'm spared this. I know my body; there's no way it will cope with the shock. I shower in practically boiling water – my anatomy won't understand what's happening and it'll give up the ghost.

'Okay, line up!' my tormenter says. 'Julia, because this is your first time, I'll explain the rules. I'm going to count to three, then we all run into the water. The last one in has to pay a forfeit. Ready?'

No, wait, I think I left something in my room – my brain – I need to go back to look for it.

'Ready.'

'One . . .'

I bequeath my books and jewellery to my mother.

'Two . . .'

I bequeath my make-up and my Ryan Gosling DVDs to my sister.

'Three!'

Farewell, cruel world.

I can't hear anything, and I can't see anything. I'm running like my life depends on it, emitting a series of little cries. I might even call for my mum a few times. The water's so cold it feels as if it's burning. I'm going to disintegrate (there, another dis- word) and only my teeth will be left. Children will think they're seashells and will make necklaces from them. Great, I'm going to end up as a necklace. The words on my gravestone will read: 'She was a gem.' What a way to go!

When I come back to my senses, I'm in up to my chest and I'm still in one piece. Well, I think I am. I'm half paralysed, so I can't be sure. I wonder what sort of state the others are in – they won't be a pretty sight. Legs stiff and head buzzing, I manage to turn round. It takes me a few seconds to see them; I didn't realise I'd gone so far.

I can't believe my eyes.

Lined up on the sand, nice and dry, all eight traitors are laughing so hard their jaws might drop off.

Chapter 11

'How are things today?'

Leon the Grouch's studio is about as cheerful as he is: immaculately made bed covered with a grey eiderdown, grey leather sofa, grey curtains and a smell of mothballs. The only decoration amounts to two computers – a desktop and a laptop – along with a tablet and two digital photo frames showing a series of portraits of him several decades younger.

'What does it matter to you?' he replies, without looking up from his phone screen.

Not much, to be honest. Right now, this old grump's well-being matters distinctly less to me than the pain developing in my throat. Probably as a result of yesterday's dip . . . Proud of their initiation ceremony, were they? Well, they won't look so clever when I sneeze my germs all over them. But I can't, in all decency, tell Leon that.

'Don't think that. I'm genuinely interested in how you feel.'

'Yes, because you're paid to be. No one ever worries about anyone else without an ulterior motive. I wasn't born yesterday. Maybe you can bluff with the others, but I'm too astute to get caught in your traps.'

'What makes you think I want to catch you in a trap?'

'It's so obvious. You see, young lady, all my life I've been surrounded by major players in the world. I set up and developed a company with an annual turnover you wouldn't even know how to pronounce, and all that just by using my own grey cells. So don't go thinking I can't see you coming, with the mud still on your boots from your bumpkin upbringing.'

About now would be a good time to sneeze.

'What sector was your company in?' I ask, trying to get a conversation going.

He doesn't answer. I study his perfectly combed, raven-black hair, his still-full lips and his unrealistically smooth face. The scalpel has definitely had some outings there; shame there isn't an operation to get rid of a sour character. Leon could do with a shot of affability, and without anaesthetic.

'I'm here to see you, Leon. You don't have to talk to me, I just think it could help you. It's not always easy ending up in a retirement home . . .'

'What do you think?' he snaps, still without deigning to look at me. 'I'm not like all these old wrecks who get shut away in here because they can't live on their own any more! I came of my own free will, I'm in full possession of my faculties and no one can force me to do anything I don't want. And right now, what I don't want is to be pestered by someone looking for an excuse to pump me full of antidepressants.'

'Fine, Leon, I—'

'And stop calling me Leon, in the name of God! We hardly know each other.'

There's no point going any further; he's as rigid as his own forehead. I stand up without another word, put the chair back where it came from and head for the door. Just as I'm about to close it behind me, Leon finally concedes and looks up with a forced smile.

'So, did you have a nice swim?'

Chapter 12

I'm going to die. My throat's an inferno. I'm burning up from the inside. I think the characters from *Inside Out* have all met up in my larynx and built a camp fire, and arranged for some of their henchmen to play darts in my windpipe.

I've been here three days and I've already had three near-death experiences. The cosmos is obviously sending me signs. I'll deal with that later – right now, I have an emergency: I have to put out the throat fire. It's nine o'clock in the evening, night time, the pharmacy's closed, and I'm not convinced Strawberry Softies are good for soothing sore throats. As usual, I'm certain I've never been in so much pain. In the hope of reassuring myself, I've done what I tell everyone else they must never do: I've opened my laptop and done a bit of research on the Web:

Sore throat

Very sore throat

Throat cancer symptoms

Can you die of a sore throat?

How to get revenge on people who force you to swim in icy waters in midwinter

I think I'm a hypochondriac

With the internet predicting an imminent and painful death for me, I take the courageous decision not to give in without a fight. My closest neighbours might have throat pastilles, honey, a fire extinguisher or some other accessory to get rid of this pain. First, I try the door opposite, which I seem to remember is Greg's studio. After knocking three times, I give up: he's not there. The other door is Clara's; this will be an opportunity to get to know her. She opens the door almost before my hand has reached it. She's wearing a dressing-gown and her hair is coiled up in a towel.

'Hi, Julia, great to see you at last! I was looking forward to having a neighbour to chat to. Come on in!'

'That's really kind, but I just came to see if you have anything for a sore throat, some cough syrup, or pastilles . . .'

'Yes, I can give you something that'll make you feel better. Come on, come in, I'll get it for you.'

Clara's studio is exactly like mine but the other way around. In terms of decoration, though, she's obliterated any similarities. The bed and sofa are covered in brightly coloured fabric, the walls are a riot of photos of people smiling, gurning and kissing and pictures of her doing a duckface, the table is awash with copies of *People* magazine and there's an acrid smell in the air.

'Sit down,' she says over her shoulder from the kitchenette. 'I won't be a minute. So, do you like it here?'

'I don't know yet . . . I have to say, I was picturing worse.'

'That doesn't surprise me! What were you thinking,

43

coming to work in a retirement home? I heard you were in a face-lift clinic before, kind of different . . .'

I laugh.

'Mind you, I'm happy here,' she goes on, almost shouting over the clinking of pots and pans. 'I was eighteen when I arrived. I didn't think I'd stay long, but I've been working here five years now. The grannies and grandpas at Ocean View are nice. And the staff, too.'

'Well, they certainly have a sense of humour! You must have heard about my, erm, initiation?'

'Oh, that's just tradition. I arrived here in August, so it would have been too easy if they'd played the same trick on me. They branched out: they arranged a baking session and I was chosen "at random" to taste the cake. They all pretended to be disappointed and I really thought I was lucky. I can't tell you how much I milked it as I brought the spoonful up to my mouth . . . I couldn't swallow a thing for two whole days. They'd stuffed the cake full of chilli . . . Here, this should do you good,' she says, handing me a steaming mug.

'What is it?'

'A hot toddy. I don't have any rum, so I put tequila in – I think they're basically the same. I've made one for myself, too, to keep you company.'

I wrap my hands around the hot drink. It smells good. I'm not particularly convinced tequila will do much for a sore throat, but the honey and lemon will soothe the pain.

Four hot toddies and two hours later, I know Clara's whole life story.

The summer she turned seventeen, her parents insisted she went to Biarritz with them for a holiday, when she wanted to stay in Strasbourg with her friends. She lay on the beach feeling sorry for herself every day, with her head buried in magazines. On the fifth day, she looked up and noticed that one of the lifeguards had all the necessary qualities to improve her stay.

'You should have seen his abs . . . Just as well my bikini was already wet.'

From that point on, her one mission was to get him to notice her. She swam only right in front of his lifeguard chair, she stepped into the water like a ballerina floating on stage and stopped breathing whenever he looked at her. She swam a long way out several times, hoping to hear a whistle warning her to come back in, but her own muscles always gave up before that happened. In the end, it was a weever-fish sting that propelled her into his arms. Literally. She was just practising a new chest-out-back-arched pose right in front of him when the fish, which was buried in the sand, took a liking to her foot. She howled and doubled up in pain, and it was then, when her mascara and her nose were both running, that he came over to her for the first time. He smiled, leaned close to her ear and admitted that he couldn't resist her acting talent.

'He didn't believe me, the twat! There I was, dying, and he thought I was just pretending so I could pick him up!'

A year later, Clara left Strasbourg to come and live in Guillaume's bedsit, and that's when she started working at Ocean View. Two years on, they rented a one-bedroom flat and got a cat. Four years on, they were engaged. Five years on, with three weeks to go before the wedding, he fell in love with a German tourist who'd just been stung by a jellyfish.

'The guy's got a venom fetish,' she growls. 'He deserves to come across an adder.'

'You're right,' I say, nodding solemnly. 'He deserves to be eaten by a black widow.'

She bursts out laughing, then stops suddenly and stares at me with the particular earnestness of people who've had too much to drink.

'What about you, though?' she asks. 'What did he do?'

'Who?'

'There must be a guy behind this. You don't turn up with your suitcases and a car full of cardboard boxes if there isn't a man involved.'

I don't know if it's because of the tequila, or Clara's openness, or the acrid smell that's going to my head, or maybe my fever, but before I even realise what I'm doing, I start telling her everything.

Chapter 13

I met Marc in the confectionery aisle of my local super-market. I was twenty-five, and I was in Paris with Nannynoo, my grandmother, who was there for an eye operation. I was playing nursemaid, she was playing tour guide. It was my first time in the capital and she treated me to all the classic sights: the Eiffel Tower, a *bateau-mouche* on the Seine, Montmartre, the Champs-Élysées . . . we'd rented an apartment near Place de la Nation, with a dou-ble bed that we snuggled up in at night, me reading to her and her giving a running commentary. Our favour-ite thing was bingeing on sweets when we were cuddled together like this.

And that's why I was in the supermarket that day. I was scouring the shelves in search of chocolate teddies when a tall blond guy in a leather jacket stepped right in front of me. I waited a few seconds, sure he'd realise he was in my way, but no.

'You okay? I'm not bothering you too much, am I?' I asked.

'No, it'll be okay, but you'll have to talk more quietly,' he replied, with the same sarcasm.

'Can't you see I'm trying to look at the shelves?'

'Sure I can.'

Big sigh.

'Is there some kind of problem?' I said.

'I'm afraid there is. My problem is that I've been following you for fifteen minutes and I really want to talk to
you but I don't know how to go about it.'

'Well, congratulations.' I laughed wryly. 'You did it:
we're talking! I might even be tempted to stroke your
chin *with my fist*. You should be pleased with yourself.'

He laughed. I shrugged. He put out his hand and
introduced himself. I groaned. He unleashed his I-know-
people-can't-resist-this-smile smile . . . and I think it's
about then that I began to melt.

When I finished studying, I went to live with him in
Paris. We'd waited so long for this that, for several months,
it felt as if every minute we spent apart was wasted. We
showered together, ate off the same plate, wore the same
T-shirts, read the same books, dragged on the same cigarettes, had the same urge to make love all the time. As if
we wanted to catch up on all the years we hadn't known
each other. The only places we went without each other
were work and the loo. After a few months, we'd even
sometimes leave the toilet door open if one of us was in
there. Apart from that, our fusion had given way to a bal-
anced relationship.

I was happy. When I listened to my girlfriends talking
about their relationships or their search for the perfect
man, I purred inwardly. I'd found my perfect man. Of
course, he had some flaws: he ate a lot of onions and had

trouble digesting them, he shaved his chest, he liked really trashy reality-TV shows, he could go a whole day without uttering a word if I didn't start the conversation, and he said 'pacific' when he meant 'specific', but none of these could cancel out his good points. My world was a better place when he was there, and he felt the same about me. We had no doubts: we were in the right percentile of the statistics and we'd end our days together.

The first warning sign came two years ago. I went down with a flu virus that morphed me into a wet blanket for a week. I got out of bed only to go to the toilet, every part of my body ached, I breathed like an asthmatic warthog, and had about the same level of conversation. I hardly saw Marc all week: work, meetings, visits to his parents, dental appointment – he seemed to grab at any excuse to get out of the apartment. And when he was there, he avoided the bedroom. His habits returned to normal at the same rate as my temperature. I thought he might be one of those flakey kind of guys, there when everything's going well but cowardly enough to clear out when you need them most. He was soon back to his attentive ways, though, and that swiftly quashed my fears.

The evening my father died, Marc stayed by my side till midnight, at which point he decreed I'd cried enough and it was time to go to bed.

'I have to be up early tomorrow, I've got my meeting with the Italians, remember?'

He had a lot of meetings in the days after that. So

many that he didn't come to Biarritz with me, didn't come to the funeral and cut short our phone calls as soon as my grief overran the time slot he'd allocated it in his schedule.

When I returned to Paris ten days later I saved him some time by packing up my things while he was out. I left a note on the living-room table, explaining as clearly as possible why I was leaving; that way, we wouldn't have to talk about it. It was pretty short, only about ten lines, and there's a chance a few swear words found their way in there, along with a reference to how small-minded he was; yeah, and it wasn't just his mind that was small.

'How did he react?' Clara asks.

'He didn't react. On the one hand, that was a good thing, because I could easily have caved, but it was tough.'

'I bet it was! But a man who's not there for you when you lose someone is a total fuckwit. You did the right thing. Exactly the sort of guy who goes off with the nurse if you get cancer.'

'That's it, that's so Marc. You can't just have the good times. It doesn't work like that. By the way, I'm really sorry to ask, but what's that smell?'

Clara sniffs loudly.

'What smell? I can't smell anything . . .'

'I don't know, it's quite acrid – it's stinging my eyes a bit. It's like a sort of ammonia smell. Do you know what I mean?'

'Oh, holy shit!'

She jumps to her feet and staggers to the bathroom,

muttering, 'Fuck, fuck, fuck!', then I hear water running. After a few minutes, wailing comes from behind the bathroom door.

'I'm going to come out now, but swear to me you won't laugh!'

I've already guessed what's going on before she comes back and there's a strong chance I won't be able to keep to my word, but I swear. With my fingers crossed.

The door opens slowly and a foot appears, then an arm. Then her head. I struggle to stay straight-faced, determined to keep my promise, but as soon as she's close enough for me to gauge the full extent of the massacre, any resistance gives up the ghost and I laugh till my stomach hurts.

'I just wanted some blond highlights . . .'

All around her sad little face, Clara's still-wet hair falls in soft waves, streaked here and there with magnificent flashes of green.

Chapter 14

'That lady, um, she's got cheeks just like Cookie.'

Little Heloise, aged four, is staring attentively at little Arlette, aged ninety-two, who, luckily, has forgotten to put in her hearing aid.

'Who's Cookie?'

'He's my dog! He's got dangly, drooly cheeks just like the lady.'

Heloise hasn't yet learned the art of tact, but she already has highly developed powers of observation.

Today, Ocean View is trying a new venture: children from the local nursery school have come to visit the residents. The idea came from the school's headteacher, who claims this will be as beneficial to the children as to the pensioners. When Anne-Marie asked what I thought, I immediately confirmed this.

The residents' visitors rarely bring children with them. For fear of disturbing the others with this overabundance of life, for fear of traumatising the youngsters, or for fear of being slapped in the face by a graphic illustration of the circle of life. The net result is that the old folk here are mostly surrounded by people their own age. This retirement home is like a ghetto for the elderly. Introducing a few hours of innocence, youth and life into the place can only be a good thing.

The day room is teeming with ecstatic little faces. For children, any outing is a pleasure: whether it's a library, a zoo or a retirement home, their enthusiasm for new experiences is the same. It dries up over the years and eventually gives way to a sort of weariness. It boils down to this: if you invite a child to play with pebbles and twigs, they are close to hysterical excitement; if you invite an adult to spend a week in a hotel in the Seychelles, they shrug and ask whether drinks are included. But here, this morning, before my very eyes, something surprising is happening: the children's good humour seems to be rubbing off on the grown-ups.

Louise is teaching two mesmerised kids to knit, Gustave is trying to perform magic tricks for a wide-eyed audience of three, several children are queuing up for a spin in a wheelchair with Mohamed, Marilyn is lending her 'Miss Granny 2004' sash to various little girls, and Isabelle is dashing about to catch every photo opportunity. Only Leon hasn't joined in: he let it be known that he's put up with 'too many brats' in his lifetime to be pestered with this now. 'If anyone's looking for me, I'll be in my studio.'

I move from one resident to the next to see how they're feeling, even though their faces leave little doubt that the experiment is a success.

'What a delight!' Louise whispers to me. 'I haven't been so happy since I arrived . . . It feels like I've been transported back in time to when I taught my daughters to knit. Mind you, they were a bit more mischievous!'

Her eyes are shining. I automatically put my hand on her arm and smile. This morning is special for me, too. I've been here nearly a week and I haven't felt the urge to run for the hills for several hours. I only slightly rolled my eyes when Gustave asked me, 'Do you like salmon, Ella?' I'll have to do some googling this evening. I must be going down with something.

Clara joins me with a smile on her lips and a scarf around her head.

'I did some work experience in a day nursery a few years ago, and do you know what? Babies and old people are exactly the same. No teeth, no hair, you have to change their nappies, they eat gloop and you don't understand everything they say. But we love 'em all the same!'

As if to illustrate her point, little Lucas starts walking around Gustave, trying to work out how he manages to pull all those colourful scarves from his sleeve. When he arrives behind Gustave, he suddenly comes to a stop, frowns inquisitively and prods Gustave's bottom with his finger, like someone choosing fruit.

'Are you wearing a nappy? Why've you got a nappy on?'

Gustave flushes, then looks at the little boy very seriously.

'Because I'm a baby in a grown-up's body.'

'But that's impossible! My mummy says I'm not a baby any more, so you defuntly can't be one . . .'

'Your mummy's wrong, little man. But that's probably because she doesn't know the secret.'

The child frowns, fascinated.

'What secret?'

'*The* secret,' Gustave half-whispers mysteriously. 'The biggest secret in the world. The secret of life. I can tell it to you, but you have to promise to keep it to yourself. Not everyone's ready to hear it. Are *you* ready?'

'Yes, yes! I'm ready!' the boy squeals.

Gustave sits down and takes him on his knees, almost dropping him twice.

'Well, you see, little man, everyone thinks people are different in the different stages of their lives. Everyone thinks that there are children and adults and old people, but it's not true.'

'But it is true, it *is*! I'm a child and you're *old*.'

'That's what people think. But the truth is that we carry on being babies all through our lives. We put on different costumes to hide it and to be like everyone else: there's the teenager costume, the adult costume, the parent costume . . . and then, one day, when you're too old to pretend, you take off the disguise and show everyone what you've been all along: a baby.'

'Pff, your secret's silly!' Lucas says, jumping off Gustave's lap.

'You'll see, little man. All through your life, deep down inside, you'll still need the same things: to be loved and comforted, not to be alone, to have enough to eat and drink, to enjoy yourself, to be looked after and to have someone near you who loves you more than themselves. Like a baby.'

'I like you more when you're funny!' the child says, walking away and leaving Gustave with his pack of cards, his hat with the false bottom and his coloured scarves.

He looks sad all of a sudden. The joker act crumbled when he came in contact with that child; so, old Gustave goes far deeper than the character he's at pains to portray. What if I made the most of this breach to get to know him better?

'I really like what you told that child,' I say, coming over to him.

When he hears my voice, Gustave immediately recovers his composure and beaming smile.

'But it drove him away . . . don't they say, "Out of the mouths of babes . . . "? People prefer me when I'm funny.'

'When you *try* to be – there's a difference,' I point out with a wink.

'Well, I do have to adapt to suit my audience,' he replies, laughing. 'Which reminds me, do you know the joke about the nomad?'

'No.'

'Mad!'

Now, I feel like running for the hills. That's reassuring: I'm perfectly healthy.

Chapter 15

This evening, I'm on BSO duty.

Translation a: I'm the one who gets to sit with the residents while they have their daily dose of their favourite Boring Soap Opera.

Translation b: I'm going to spend half an hour in the day room suffering mind-numbing conversations with people who can hardly hear a word.

Translation c: If asked, I think I'd opt instead for a complete bikini epilation with tweezers. Or a blowtorch.

The audience is already seated. They've all settled themselves facing the big screen in the motley crew of armchairs, a mismatched legacy from former residents. Those in wheelchairs form a short row of their own, and walking frames are parked against the wall. I sit myself down in an old, claret-coloured sofa just as the titles roll. Three pairs of eyes glower at me: apparently, I'm making too much noise. I'll hide their hearing aids, then we'll see if they give me evils.

I've never watched this particular soap, *Plus belle la vie*, but that hasn't stopped me forming a poor opinion of it. I've heard the acting's bad, that it's mawkish and that the screenplay seems to have been written by a five-year-old on LSD. If I'd known that being versatile meant undergoing torture sessions, I'd have taken more time to consider before accepting this role. It's usually Greg's job to enjoy this highly cultured experience, but Sir has granted himself a week's holiday.

8.21 p.m.: Come on, Julia. It's only half an hour. I can do it. I. Can. Do. It.

8.22 p.m.: It's impressive; they're all spellbound. I could dance naked on the walking frames and no one would notice.

8.23 p.m.: 'What did he say?' Arlette asks.

'He said, *Shush.*'

Still just as friendly, our Leon.

8.25 p.m.: Oh my word, the cast are struggling to do Marseille accents.

8.27 p.m.: Right now, there's someone called Blanche held prisoner in a cave with her hands and feet tied. She doesn't seem too thrilled about this, judging by her wild-animal screams. God help us if she ever has to do a childbirth scene.

8.31 p.m.: Eyes riveted on the screen, Elisabeth is fiddling anxiously with a hankie, Lucienne's wiping her eyes and Mohamed clutches the armrests of his wheelchair.

8.33 p.m.: Now there's someone called Leena crying in the arms of a tall, blond man. If I've got this right, she's fallen devastatingly in love with someone she met on holiday and she's distraught because she knows their love's impossible. The tall, blond guy asks her why. 'Because Luke is a priest,' Leena replies. That old chestnut.

Next to me, Gustave breaks the almost reverential silence.

'Do you know Leena's surname?' he asks me.

'No.'

'Little-Klosa,' he replies with a hearty laugh. 'Leena Little-Klosa.'

Note to self: stop answering Gustave's questions.

8.35 p.m.: 'What did he say?' Arlette asks.

'He said, *Shut up!*'

Such a sweetheart, our Leon.

8.36 p.m.: Blanche has now stopped her wailing (her vocal cords must have been threatening to kill her) because she's just noticed there's a pair of scissors not far from her. Two explanations: either her abductor loves her really, or he has the intellectual capacity of pond life.

While she goes into contortions trying to reach the scissors, I watch the residents' reactions. I don't want to be pessimistic, but we're on the verge of heart attacks.

8.38 p.m.: Leena decides to disclose her feelings to her mysterious priest. With her brows furrowed like an accordion, she dials his number. Two chairs away from me, Miss Granny 2004 is clinging to her sash like a virgin to her knickers.

8.40 p.m.: 'Are you stressed, Julia?' Louise asks me, staring at my fingers.

The fingers on my right hand are busy worrying at loose bits of skin around the nails of my left.

'Not at all,' I reply with a shrug. 'It's just a bit of psoriasis.'

8.41 p.m.: 'What did she say?' Arlette asks.

'She said everyone who watches *Plus belle la vie* is going to die, starting with anyone with mauve hair,' Leon growls.

8.43 p.m.: Currently on screen is someone called Roland, kissing a brunette. There's muttering in the audience.

'Oh no! He's cheating on Mirta!'

'Poor Mirta!'

'I'll never forgive him for doing this to her . . .'

'It can't be! Not Roland! They really are all the same . . .'

8.45 p.m.: Blanche is quite near the scissors now. She reaches her arm as far as she can, moans, stretches and finally manages to brush them with the tips of her fingers . . . just as the door is thrown open. Zoom on to Blanche's terrified face, music and credits.

Seriously? They stop the episode at the most exciting point? It's not five-year-olds who write this stuff, it's sadists! How can they leave the audience in the dark about what happens to poor Blanche? Not knowing how the priest will react to Leena's declaration? Or what will happen to Roland and Mirta? Not that I'm interested, obviously, I'm just thinking of the well-being of the residents. It's inhuman to leave them in suspense like this.

The chairs are emptying, and I'm last to leave the day room. In the corridor, I meet Anne-Marie, who's heading home.

'Have a nice evening!' she says.

'Thanks. You, too!' I reply.

I look around to check no one's listening and add in a whisper, 'If you ever need someone for the BSO slot, I don't mind sacrificing my time.'

Chapter 16

Gustave the joker's studio looks like a teenager's bedroom: the mess, the comics, the DVDs of comedy shows, the full ashtray, the sweets – it's all there. In fact, the only thing that might indicate that the master of the premises is five times fifteen years old are the posters on the walls. Not sure that posters for Charles Aznavour concerts are currently considered 'sick'.

Gustave is sitting at his table, circling words in a word-search puzzle. He gestures me towards a chair facing him and I sit down.

'So, what's being going on since last week?' I ask.

In our first session, Gustave talked about his past: his childhood in a large and not particularly happy family, how he met Susanne at a dance, the long years trying to have a baby, Françoise coming along when they'd given up hope, then Jean-Claude, his work at the funeral parlour, his extensive travelling. In the space of an hour, he confided all these memories as if they were someone else's, maintaining distance with his constant joking. He's hiding, and that's his right. But today, I'd like to know who Gustave really is.

He shakes his head as if to say, 'Nothing new, move along.' If he thinks he can get rid of me that easily . . .

'Last time, you told me about your family. Do you like to have people around you?'

'Do you know the big question about Isabelle?' he breaks in.

'Gustave, plea—'

'Isabelle necessary on a bicycle?' he says, with a roar of laughter.

He's his own best audience.

'Gustave, I'm not here to hound you. If you don't feel like talking about yourself, I completely understand, but I'd like you to say so.'

His laughing breaks off abruptly and he stares at me with infinite sadness.

'But what on earth can I tell you, my dear? You're young, you have your life ahead of you, do you really want to know that none of it makes any sense at all, that life's a fight we've all lost from the outset? Do you really want to hear that even happy memories become painful when you lose all your loved ones? Do you really want me to tell you that I was lucky, surrounded by people I loved – my wife, who I couldn't bear to be apart from for a single day; my daughter, who wrote me poems at every opportunity; my son, who always laughed at my jokes; my brothers and sisters; my friends . . . and now I'm alone? Do you want me to tell you how illness deformed my wife's body, then her face, before taking her away completely? Do you want me to repeat the words of the police officer who told me my son didn't hear the car coming? Do you want me to tell you that my daughter thinks of me only on her birthday, that all my brothers and sisters are dead, and my friends, that I have no one left? Do you want me to admit that I never understood how anyone could end up all alone, and I was convinced it wouldn't happen to me, I thought it was impossible? I had so many people around me . . . Do you really want to know all that, Julia? Well, I don't feel like telling you. Because, you see, life's a joke. Otherwise, how do you explain the absurdity of how far we can fall? Life's playing a huge practical joke on us . . .'

I can't speak. How do you reply to that? I'm the one who's so convinced talking is good for you, but now I almost regret getting him to start. What's the point? If Gustave prefers his life wrapped up in brightly coloured paper, if turning everything into pranks is his way of coping, why make him confront reality?

He's looking out of the window, jaw set. I'm wondering how I'm going to get him to shake off his sorrow when, before I have a chance to stop myself, words are coming out of my mouth:

'Monsieur and Madame Additch have a son – what's his name?'

The corners of his lips quiver and his eyes crease. He thinks for a few seconds, then gives up.

'I've no idea.'

'Doug,' I say, prouder than if I'd just presented a thesis

on the theoretical and digital modelling of the saturation of unstable Raman spectroscopy results produced by the interaction between lasers and plasma.

I'm expecting Gustave to burst out laughing, but he just looks at me, befuddled. He gives me that look people save for anyone they think is nice-but-weird. There's nothing worse than explaining a joke, so I decide to file this one, never to visit it again, and I move on swiftly with: 'So, anyway, do you like it here?'

An hour later, I leave Gustave's studio with two firm intentions: to stop and count to at least five before opening my mouth in future, and to contact his daughter. She must have a good reason for not coming to visit him, but I'd like to be sure of that and – why not? – convince her that he needs her. I'm heading to my office when my phone buzzes. It's a text from my friend Marion.

Hi babes! You need to call your mum, she's left a message with me to say she can't get hold of you, she's worried. Xxx

So I add something else to my list of intentions: call Mum. Of the three, that's definitely the one that appeals the least.

Chapter 17

It's nearly ten o'clock at night when I press the word 'Mum' on my contacts list. A photo of her laughing in my father's arms appears. I'm making the call, but I still don't know what I'm going to say to her.

My mother thinks I live with Marion. That's where I *was*. I moved into her apartment in Paris after leaving Marc. I was living in a sort of fog, devastated by so much loss: first, my father, which wasn't helped by losing my boyfriend, and then I was completely floored by losing my grandmother, too.

For several months, I slept on Marion's sofa (when I wasn't in the bed of some guy I'd met in a bar), drank too much, established that the human body has an inexhaustible supply of tears, cut my hair and burned some bridges while languishing in front of American TV series (but skipping all the scenes involving fathers, deaths and even green armchairs). I read seventeen books on happiness and how to find it, sent three thousand texts to my mother and sister, had two periods of sick leave, wore the same knickers three days running, ate five thousand cheeseburgers and bought ten million nail polishes that all looked the same, put on weight and lost some illusions.

And then, one evening, when I was trying to take off my dress without falling over, blind drunk in the bedroom of a man I'd met a couple of hours earlier, it hit me like an electric shock.

Seriously, if my father could have seen me he'd be horribly ashamed of his daughter. I pulled my dress back down and fled, forgetting, in my haste, that the staircase was slippery. When I landed on my bum at the bottom of stairs, now stone-cold sober, I gave a little smile for my father and promised to get my act together.

The next day, I came across the advert for a job at a retirement home in Biarritz: Ocean View.

I didn't say a word to my mother. *Hi, Mum, just calling to say I'm giving up my job and Paris for a temporary contract at a nursing home in the Basque country. Okay, see you!* She really didn't need that. And, from a completely selfish point of view, it suits me fine that she doesn't know I'm just a few miles away from her. I need time to get back on my feet and work out what I want to do with my life without anyone else's influence.

I'm lost in a labyrinth: every time I move forward, I bump into something so I turn back. I'm not sure where I'm going, but I have to find the way out by myself, without Ariadne's thread or a GPS. Every night when I close my eyes, the same image comes into my mind: I'm being filmed by a camera which is moving further and further away. I'm in my room, which is in the annexe, which is in the grounds; and they're in Biarritz, which is in France, which is on the planet. Growing smaller and smaller – that's how I see my life. Microscopic, insignificant, adrift. If my mother knew I was near her, she'd come to see me every day, she'd insist I move in with her and would mollycoddle me like the baby she still thinks I am. It's tempting, the thought of nestling into my childhood bed with my Spice Girls posters and my cuddly toys. But I'm thirty-two, I'm not a baby; I have to learn to cope on my own. Because if there's one thing these last few months have taught me, and Gustave's revelations have just confirmed, it's that, however many people we have around us, we alone feel the pain and the pleasure.

My mother picks up before the phone's barely rung once.

'Hello?'

Her voice is hoarse, like a goat's. She must be really worried.

'Mummy, it's me, you tri—'

'Oh, my darling!' she cries. 'I was in a complete state. I've left hundreds of messages, why didn't you call me back?'

Now I feel bad.

'I'm so sorry, Mum. I've got loads of work on, I lost track of the days. How are you?'

'If you're doing overtime, you need to make sure you're paid, my darling . . . That clinic will be the death of you. Have you still not found an apartment?'

'Not yet, but don't worry, Marion's sofa's very comfortable! How about you? How are you?' I ask again.

'Oh, you know, I'm fine . . . I have a new work

colleague – she reminds me of your sister, she never stops talking, just says whatever comes into her head – but she's nice. On the subject of Carole, I had your godson to stay last Saturday, he was a sweetheart. He did a drawing for you, I'll have to send it to you. Apart from that, it's rained a lot recently and the roof wasn't standing up to it. Luckily, the builders I had in have done a good job. It was expensive, but I wasn't planning on having a holiday this year, anyway. So, yes, apart from that, nothing new . . .'

That's my mother. She tells me about roof repairs, her colleague, my godson . . . anything so she doesn't have to talk about herself. Not a word about my father, when I know he's on her mind every waking moment. She's always been like this, wanting to spare my sister and me. As if, by pretending horrible things don't exist, she can actually make them go away.

'But, Mum, how are *you*?' I ask emphatically.

'I'm fine, as I said,' she says, with the little laugh she always uses in awkward moments.

'Last Tuesday wasn't too hard, was it?'

'What was last Tuesday?' she asks innocently.

'Mum . . .'

'You mean your father's birthday? It was okay, darling. It was okay. Did I tell you Madame Etcheverry has left her husband? He was cheating on her with the children's gym teacher, can you believe?'

'Mum . . . you *can* talk to me about Dad, you *can* tell me how much it hurts, you *can* talk about what happened.

I think about him all the time, you know. I'm sad – I'm *very* sad – I miss him terribly, every minute. So please don't be worried about upsetting me by talking about him because I'm already upset anyway. And what's really hard is not having anyone I can share memories of him with.'

There's a slight sniffling sound down the phone. Then a throat-clearing, followed by my mother's shaky voice.

'I know, my darling. But this time I'm not actually trying to spare you . . . I'm trying to spare myself. It's too hard. I can't do this yet.'

My throat constricts.

We sit in silence for a few seconds as we both try to find the best way to carry on with the conversation, pretending this admission hasn't been made. I get there first.

'Right, so what's this new colleague's name?'

March

'We have two lives. The second begins
When we realise we have only one'

– Confucius

Chapter 18

When I realised I'd been picked to run the Bingo session with Greg, it wouldn't have taken much for me to jump back in the ocean.

Marilyn, draped in her 'Miss Granny 2004' sash, is doing the honours, drawing the numbered balls with such professionalism she could add this to her CV. She diligently turns the handle to spin the see-through sphere, then plunges her hand in with her eyes closed – and with her spare fingers over her eyes so no one can be in any doubt about her integrity. On top of this, she banishes any sense of suspicion by regularly intoning, 'It's not me who chooses the balls, it's the balls that choose me.'

Which makes Gustave chortle every time.

Most of the residents have been sensible and are playing with only one card. This doesn't stop a succession of questions – 'Has number eight come up yet?' or 'What did she say?' and the occasional 'Are we playing for one line or the whole card?' – coming from one table or another, to the delight of Leon, who uses each one as an opportunity to complain. Which all means he must be concentrating hard to keep track: he has no fewer than ten cards spread out before him. When Clara was handing them out, she told him the limit was four per person, so he came right out and threatened to lodge a complaint for, and I quote, 'psychological bullying and mental harassment'. He announced that, as he wasn't a bedridden wreck like those around him, he wouldn't tolerate any constraint. He could 'pull strings' so, if anyone continued to harass him he would have the place closed down. I thought Greg was about to ram Leon's cards down his throat, but he controlled himself and agreed to the master blackmailer's terms, so as not to ruin the game.

Leon has been sitting alone at his table preening ever since. His strategy is working: he's already won three prizes in less than an hour. He's the lucky recipient of the anti-slip shower mat, the voucher for a blow-dry with the hairdresser who visits once a week and the tube of denture fixative.

'Twenty-six!'

'Fiddlesticks!' Gustave trills.

He indulges us with these little nuggets at regular intervals. The first time was quite funny; by the tenth, you want to have your eardrums forcibly extracted.

Greg and I are responsible for ensuring the residents' safety. In a retirement home, the most inconsequential activity can rapidly turn into an extreme sport. The danger with Bingo is the counters. In the early days, chickpeas were used to mark the numbers that had been called. These were replaced with plastic counters when one resident, who was busy trying to find the number 36 on his card, put a handful of chickpeas in his mouth and nearly choked.

'I thought they were peanuts,' he told the paramedics.

Coloured counters pose less of a risk, so long as no one drops any. A few months ago, Arlette broke the top of her femur when she slipped on a pink one. Since then, she's loathed the colour pink, and Bingo sessions have been carried out under tight security.

'Forty-four!' Marilyn announces.

'Sick on the floor!'

Leon is practically apoplectic, Louise laughs out loud and Arlette stares wide-eyed at her card and shrieks, '*Bingo!*'

Greg and Marilyn check that the five numbers on her card have actually been called. A good fifteen minutes later, it's confirmed, and the old lady has got herself a bottle of special shampoo for white hair. She looks genuinely, profoundly, excessively happy.

I don't want to get old. Ever.

The last round. And the biggest prize. Whoever fills their card first will have the huge privilege of going to a Frank Michael concert next month, with the guest of their choice.

'And what's more,' Miss Granny 2004 says, struggling to suppress her excitement, 'they're front-row seats!'

The male residents manage to contain themselves. The women, on the other hand, giggle and snigger, coo and quiver. Louise lines up her counters, Arlette adjusts her hearing aid, Elisabeth briefs her husband, each doing everything to maximise her chances of winning this coveted prize. I don't know who Frank Michael is, but Justin Bieber clearly needs to watch his back.

'Would you like to take them to the concert with me?' Greg asks.

'I don't know when the concert is, but I know I'll be ill.' He shakes his head.

'Shame, you'll be missing out. Last time, it was Michel Sardou and I had one of his songs on the brain for more than a week, but it was worth it. You should have seen them, singing at the tops of their lungs, eyes sparkling . . .'

'You like your little oldies, don't you?'

'Yup,' he replies, beaming. 'This is my family here, the residents and my colleagues. By the way, are you up for a social this evening?'

'A social?'

'Yes, Clara and I have one from time to time. We get together either at her studio or mine, have a few drinks and nibbles, put the world to rights . . . do you fancy it?'

'Yes, great idea! It'll make a change from watching TV . . .'

We're interrupted by a thundering *'Bingo!'* immediately followed by a second, quieter one. The first is from Gustave, the second from Louise. After a quick check, it's confirmed that both their cards are full.

'It doesn't matter,' Gustave says. 'I'm very happy to let you go, Louise, dear.'

'Oh, no, please! You said "Bingo!" before me,' the old lady demurs. 'You must go to the concert.'

'I certainly won't.'

'Oh, come on, we're not going to spend all day on this,'

Leon interrupts with a sigh. 'If no one's volunteering, I'll have the tickets and the problem's solved!'

'Dream on, old boy,' Gustave retorts. 'Louise will go, and that's an end to it.'

'Thank you very much, I'm really touched,' Louise says quietly.

'Does that deserve a little kiss, then?'

While we're clearing away the cards, Louise comes over and leans close to my ear.

'I pretended to remember so that I could join in the fun, but who exactly is Frank Michael?'

Chapter 19

I play host for my first 'social' evening. Clara arrives first, carrying three boxes of pizza.

'Fuck me, it's changed in here!' she exclaims when she sees my studio.

She hasn't been over since I decided I just couldn't go on living in dated, crusty, old-fangled surroundings. I wanted to hang myself with a string of doilies every time I walked into the place. So, last weekend, I did the rounds of the interiors shops and gave my room a facelift. I covered the sofa, table and bed in warm – but not really matching – colours, hung several pictures above the bed, put up some shelves, on which I've loaded books and photos of my friends and family, bought two or three pieces of furniture and an enormous TV, which almost makes me feel like I'm part of the action, but, most of all, I've added my own personal touch: mess.

The result could provoke epileptic fits but, weirdly, I like being in this hotchpotch. It feels safe.

'Are these your folks?' Clara asks me, pointing to a picture of my parents.

'Yes,' I say, putting glasses out on the table. 'That was last summer, just before . . .'

'Your dad looks like he was a great person. What was his name?'

She drops down on to the sofa and smiles. She has no idea what her words have just done to me. My breathing has stopped dead, my heart has plummeted to the bottom of my stomach and all my blood is rising into my cheeks.

No one ever talks to me about my father. Marion is careful never to mention him unless I've taken the initiative, my mother scrupulously avoids the subject, my sister would rather talk about her son's poos. That's what people tend to do. When someone dies, people no longer mention them in front of their loved ones. Your friends and colleagues become gifted in the art of finding topics of conversation that have no connection to the deceased. Probably for fear of causing pain, as if the hurt wasn't there until someone brings up the person you've lost.

Since 8 August last year, no one has mentioned my father in front of me. And then Clara turns up, with no self-filter at all, and asks me his name, as if that were perfectly normal. When I'm over the initial shock, a huge wave of gratitude washes over me. If a little knock on the door hadn't interrupted us, I think I would have hugged her.

Greg has brought drinks, and his cheerfulness. We're sitting around my new coffee table, eating salty carbs, drinking alcohol, chatting easily and laughing hard.

'Oh, by the way, I finally managed to get Gustave's daughter on the phone,' I say, taking a swig of Lambrusco.

'So, she really does exist,' says Greg. 'I've been working here nearly two years and I've never seen her.'

'Same. I've not seen her the whole time Gustave's been here,' Clara adds. 'He's the only one who never has visitors. Maybe she lives a long way away?'

'Yeah, other side of the world,' I tell her. 'About two and a half kilometres away. She must be afraid of flying, I can't think of another explanation.'

'You're joking!' Greg exclaims. 'She lives in Biarritz? But why does she never visit?'

'No idea, but I'll soon find out. I've managed to persuade her to meet me in a couple of weeks.'

'Maybe they fell out,' says Clara. 'Mind you, I'd be surprised. Gustave is as kind as they come.'

Greg nods vigorously.

'Completely agree with Clara. Gustave wouldn't hurt a fly, even if it had just crapped on him.'

It's not the first time I've noticed how enthusiastically Greg backs up whatever Clara says. And I'm not even talking about the way he looks at her, which is pretty much the way people on a diet look at lasagne and chips.

I make the most of a cigarette break on the balcony to interrogate Clara. Greg has stayed inside, mocking us smokers, who are prepared to freeze for a hit of nicotine.

'What the hell? He's gay!' Clara retorts, when I tell her what I'm thinking.

'No! Seriously, when he looks at you, his eyes say: "I want to rip off all your clothes, jump on you like a wild animal and make you scream my name!"'

Clara throws her head back and laughs.

'Maybe I look like a bloke!'

'Or maybe he's not gay after all . . . Haven't you ever noticed?'

'I've never really paid any attention,' she replies, inhaling on her cigarette. 'I'm convinced he's gay, and anyway, he once told me about his ex, whose name was Jean-Luc. He's never got over his death. But even if you're right, I'm starting to like being single, and I'm planning to make the most of it, have some fun. Don't get me wrong, Greg's gorgeous – I could happily end up on all fours on his bed – but he's a colleague. You know what they say: no knob in job!'

When the evening comes to an end, it's practically morning. Greg and Clara head back to their studios, telling each other to 'drive carefully', which makes us weep with laughter. I slip into bed fully clothed, with my make-up on and, for the first time in a long while, with a smile on my face.

Chapter 20

My weekly sessions with Marilyn have become a pleasure. If anyone had told me this over a month ago, when I arrived . . .

Wreathed as usual in her 'Miss Granny 2004' sash, she's made me a coffee and is confiding insights into her life with her customary optimism.

'Have you heard?' she asks me.

'Yes, I've heard. How are you getting on?'

She shrugs her frail shoulders.

'When they gave me the diagnosis, I was stunned for a moment, but I already had my suspicions. My grandson came to see me the other day, and I don't remember it at all, can you believe? It used to be called senility; now, they call it Alzheimer's. But what can you do? I'm not the first and I certainly won't be the last!'

'Do you feel sad, or angry?'

'Neither. I have no right. This illness has come at the end of a long life. Lots of people don't have that sort of luck. I'm frightened, though.'

'What exactly are you afraid of?'

She readjusts her sash with a more than usually shaky hand and sighs.

'I'm afraid of losing all my memories. I couldn't care less about remembering what I ate an hour ago, but I'm afraid of forgetting the intense joy I felt when each of my children was born, or forgetting how much I love to cuddle and reassure them, to see them smile . . . I'm frightened of forgetting my grandchildren's happy faces when they played under the cherry tree in my garden, or the tenderness in my own parents' eyes. I'm going to cling to these memories with all my might, in the hope that the illness will take the others first, because I know I don't have any choice but to surrender them.'

She takes a deep breath before continuing.

'I was elected Miss Granny 2004, you know! The judges were won over by my love of life and my optimism. I'm not going to change that because of some condition with an unpronounceable name. Some people say old age is like being shipwrecked, but I think it's a stroke of luck. An honour. Not everyone gets to go there. And anyway, I'm convinced there's a good reason for it to be hard.'

'And what's that?'

'If old age was too much of a pleasure, no one would want it to end. The fact that it's so tough makes life itself less of a draw. Old age was invented so we could break away from life.'

I've stopped taking notes. I could listen to Marilyn talking for hours without noticing the time go by. She has the same effect on me as having a cosy rug over my knees, a cup of hot chocolate in one hand and a good book in the other.

All at once, she gets to her feet and draws the heavy beige curtain.

'With this weather, it seems to get dark just after lunch-time . . . I can't bear it,' she sighs. 'Would you like a coffee?'

'Thanks, but I haven't finished this one.'

She frowns briefly, then dismisses this latest memory lapse with a shake of her head. Silence settles over us. Her eyes are gazing off into bygone days, where I don't exist. I give a little cough to remind her I'm here, and she looks up, slightly dazed.

'You were telling me about your theory of old age,' I say.

'Yes, my theory . . . By the way, have you been told about my illness? Apparently, I have Alzheimer's . . .'

Chapter 21

I was planning to spend the morning in my office, catching up on the admin that's accumulated over the last few days. It has to be said that procrastination is one of my strong points. I don't take an interest in my bank balance until the bank threatens me with terrifying penalties, I'm always sending 'Sorry I missed your birthday' cards, I have to cough up the late-payment fine for my taxes every year, I have a drawer full of unopened envelopes, I wait till the car's petrol tank is empty before filling up, I deal with the roots coming through in my hair when it's starting to look more as if I've had a dip-dye, the photo on my ID card is still from when I was thirteen, I'm incapable of keeping plants alive, and I collect Post-it notes smothered in lists of things that need doing, most of which begin with 'See previous Post-it'.

Good psychologist that I am, I'm aware that this behaviour stems from my fear of death. By putting everything off till later, I'm guaranteeing there will be a 'later'. It's quite a hindrance – I have a permanent to-do list in my brain – but the biggest problem with this affliction is that, if I ever get to the age of the residents here, I'll need a whole room just to house my unopened envelopes.

So, I was meant to be spending this morning in my office, but I hadn't factored in Team Granny. Every morning, I walk across the courtyard between the annexe and the main building, and every morning, whatever mood the sky is in, there they are on their bench, Louise, Elisabeth and Marilyn, debriefing on the previous night, a run-down of their news and an airing of their memories. So, every morning, I set aside a few minutes to chat to them, before my professional status demands a degree of restraint. Without realising, and certainly without expecting it, I've come to look forward to this little get-together.

This morning was no exception. Team Granny greeted me with their usual warmth.

'Did you sleep badly?' Marilyn asked me.

'No, I slept rather well, why?'

'You look terrible – you've aged ten years!'

'Or you need to change your pillow,' Elisabeth suggested.

'From a distance, I thought you were a new resident!' Louise added.

The three of them had a good laugh.

'Don't laugh too much, you'll wet yourselves,' I retorted playfully, making them laugh all the more.

Louise was first to catch her breath.

'All the same, you'll have to make an effort if you want to find a boyfriend, my dear. Men like women who look after themselves . . .'

'Good for them,' I said glibly. 'I'm very happy on my own! And if a guy ever takes an interest in me, I hope it won't be just because I've done my make-up and I'm wearing high heels.'

The three grannies exchanged looks and shook their heads.

'It's the whole package, Julia,' Elisabeth explained. 'Do you know, the first thing my husband noticed about me were my eyes, then he liked my smile, then he fell in love with my personality. We're not saying you need to transform yourself, just come out of that shell.'

'Elisabeth's right,' Louise agreed. 'It's obviously armour! Under your tousled hair and baggy clothes, I'm in no doubt you're very pretty.'

'Well, you have to scratch beneath the surface to see it . . .' Marilyn added. 'You could walk around with a STOP sign on your head and the message wouldn't be any clearer.'

I rolled my eyes. Okay, so I prefer wearing jeans and trainers to dresses and heels; okay, so I do the absolute minimum in terms of a beauty routine: moisturiser, mascara, etc.; okay, my light brown hair is about shoulder length and has no shape or style . . . but I don't think I've ever scared a child in the street.

'Is that it? Have you finished my MOT, or would you like to check the lock on my knickers?'

That set them off laughing again, but then Louise turned to her two friends.

'We could see if she'd like to come with us.'

'She wouldn't last five minutes,' Marilyn replied, shaking her head.

I was intrigued.

'What are you talking about?'

'We have an exercise class in half an hour,' explained Elisabeth. 'It's quite physical: if you're not sporty, don't even contemplate it.'

I sniggered. An exercise class for people who've exceeded their life expectancy would be a joke for a thirty-something in perfect health. Granted, the last PE lesson I had was in secondary school and I risk rupturing something in my thighs every time I climb a flight of stairs, but these women are nearly three times my age. How could they think I wouldn't cope with doing a few moves?

'I'll just nip to the office to sort out a couple of things, and I'll join you.'

That's why I'm now in the small hall used for sporting activities, surrounded by Team Granny, Gustave, Jules and Arlette, all dressed as if they're about to run a marathon. The teacher, Svetlana, is a pretty blonde with a slight accent and a smile that suggests she's as soft as triple-ply Andrex. I can't see how her class could be a problem for me.

'Right, we're going to start warming up. To your places!'

9.30 a.m.: Off we go for an hour of gentle gym. I don't know what came over me, agreeing to this, it's not like I don't have a ton of files waiting to be updated in the office . . . If Anne-Marie drops by, I'll make a case for the psychological advantages of sport.

9.34 a.m.: We've been swivelling our wrists for four minutes. I think they're warmed up now.

9.35 a.m.: If we keep this up any longer, my hands will come unscrewed.

9.37 a.m.: Hallelujah! We've moved on to shoulders. Maybe, tomorrow morning, we'll get down to some exercise.

9.40 a.m.: The music would be quite nice if it weren't drowned out by the *Concerto for Joints in D minor.*

9.43 a.m.: Now it's ankles. If I fall asleep, someone wake me.

9.45 a.m.: Maybe if I slip out discreetly, no one will notice . . .

9.46 a.m.: 'So, Julia, leaving already?'

That Marilyn is so nosy.

'Not at all. I was just checking the door was shut properly.'

9.48 a.m.: I wonder whether you can achieve take-off by flexing your ankles.

10.00 a.m.: I jump at the sound of Svetlana's voice. I might have fallen asleep for a few minutes.

10.01 a.m.: First exercise – we have to roll the top of the body down towards the floor. 'The supplest will reach the floor with their hands,' adds Miss Yogabunny.

10.02 a.m.: I'm proud of myself. My fingers are level with my ankles. Bet those three aren't so pleased with themselves now.

10.03 a.m.: I cast a surreptitious eye over Team Granny

to check they're admiring me. I told them it would be child's play.

10.04 a.m.: They're anything but admiring. In fact, they're not paying any attention to me. Louise is touching her toes, Elisabeth is skimming the floor and Marilyn has her hands flat on the mat.

10.05 a.m.: Pretend I can't see them, pretend I can't see them. I strain a bit to reach my toes. It hurts, but I won't let it be said I was outdone by octogenarians.

10.06 a.m.: It must be the osteoporosis that makes them so supple.

10.07 a.m.: Come on, try a bit harder, Julia. Don't think about the pain in the backs of your thighs. You're nearly there.

10.08 a.m.: Svetlana and her accent are inviting us to straighten up slowly, with a rounded back.

So I try to straighten up slowly, with a rounded back.

10.09 a.m.: I try to straighten up slowly, with a rounded back.

10.10 a.m.: I try to straighten up slowly, with a rounded back.

10.11 a.m.: Right. So it looks like I'm stuck.

10.12 a.m.: However hard I try to get up, my lower back has gone on strike. I'm electrocuted by a terrible pain every time I try.

If anyone notices, I'll be the butt of their jokes till the end of my contract.

10.13 a.m.: 'You can come up now, Julia. We're moving on to the next exercise.'

'No, thanks. I really like this position. I'm going to stay here.'

10.14 a.m.: While the others circle their hips, I negotiate with my lumbar vertebrae. Come on, play nice, let me back up. I can't stay like this, for goodness' sake! If you do as you're told, I'll arrange a massage for you.

10.15 a.m.: My lumbar vertebrae don't respond to bribery.

10.16 a.m.: What if I had to stay in this position for the rest of my life?

10.17 a.m.: How am I going to brush my teeth?

10.18 a.m.: All the others are carrying on with their exercises, as if I'm not quietly turning into a coat rack . . .

10.19 a.m.: All my blood's flowed into my head. It's going to explode, it'll go everywhere and no one gives a damn.

10.20 a.m.: Marilyn, who's doing the splits, is watching me with a perplexed frown. She suspects something. You don't say! A purple face is rarely a good sign.

I give her a big grin and a little wave. ALL. FINE. WITH. ME.

10.22 a.m.: I've tried everything – crouching down, pushing with my arms, praying – but nothing works. Every time, I have to suppress a howl of pain.

10.25 a.m.: In one final attempt to stand up again – and salvage my dignity – I've made a moaning sound that was somewhere between a cow's moo and a chainsaw. With the net result that there are now seven very serious faces in a circle around my backside.

10.26 a.m.: Is it possible to die of shame? Just wondering.

10.27 a.m.: Miss Downward Dog puts her hand on my back.

'Try to stand up.'

Now, there's a thought, why didn't I think of that?

10.28 a.m.: 'Push against your legs,' she insists, 'and release your sphincter.'

Bearing in mind where her head is right now, I'm not sure she really wants me to release my sphincter.

10.29 a.m.: Gustave gets me under my shoulders and unlocks me slowly. My blood starts flowing again, but the pain in my lower back makes me cry out.

'I didn't know my class was dangerous,' quips Svetlana, provoking a ripple of laughter through the group of pensioners.

This is all a good joke, is it?!

10.30 a.m.: The class is over, and the yogis leave the hall, though not without checking whether I'd like a doctor/ambulance/pain relief/hot-water bottle/help. I turn everything down, claiming – with a grimace – that the pain is already easing. Through the half-open door, I see Gustave turn around and nod towards something.

Under the window in a corner of the room, he's left me an ally: his walking frame.

Chapter 22

The other patients in the waiting room have done their best to hide their surprise. But a thirty-something doing a good impersonation of a set-square, aided by a walking frame and three eighty-somethings in perfect health isn't an everyday sight.

Marilyn, Elisabeth and Louise – my tormentors – insisted on coming with me.

'It'll do me good to get some air,' argued Louise. 'And anyway, the haberdashery is just next to the hospital, and I need some wool.'

'We're partly to blame,' added Elisabeth. 'If we hadn't encouraged you, you wouldn't be injured.'

'Are you two responsible for this?' Marilyn asked. 'How did you manage that? Poor little thing . . .'

Anne-Marie dropped us off in the minibus and will come to pick us up once I've been seen. Which I'm hoping will be very soon.

Sitting as best I can in an orange plastic chair, I leaf through a copy of *Paris Match* from March 1997. Michael Jackson is doing his *HIStory* tour, Paco Rabanne says the end of the world is nigh, Princess Diana is relishing her newfound freedom, and there's a double-page spread devoted to a strange novelty: the mobile phone.

A&E isn't littered with interesting reading material. What would be the point? The people here are so scared they'll gladly read the waiting-room rules on a loop or count the floor tiles; anything to keep their thoughts off their symptoms.

I'm not frightened right now. It's bound to be a muscle that's gone into spasm. I'll stuff myself full of painkillers and, in a few days, I'll be fine. I don't need to read the rules or count the floor tiles. But the white walls, the characteristic smell and the glint of anxiety in other people's eyes remind me of a Wednesday evening many years ago.

I had her hand in mine, and she'd never seemed so fragile. As if her fear made her vulnerable right to the tips of her fingers. We sat and waited for a long time that evening. Long enough for me to ask about a million times for Whoever's-up-there to spare them this. She'd put plasters over my grazed knees, she'd kissed things better countless times, she'd healed my childhood pains, and I felt so powerless with my constant 'Don't worry, Nanny-noo, he'll be fine,' although I wasn't convinced. And I didn't dare meet her eyes. Oh fuck, the look in her eyes. Like a frightened child, in complete contrast to her lined face. The sort of look we all hope we'll never see in the mirror. A look that says you know your world's about to turn upside down.

She'd given my name when the nurse asked if she'd like someone to be informed, and I wasn't succeeding in reassuring her. So we waited, hand in hand, for a white-coated stranger to come and deliver us from this torment.

It took just thirteen words: 'We're very sorry, we've tried everything, but we weren't able to resuscitate him.' My grandfather had arrived in a wailing van with a flashing light and he'd be leaving in a silent one with no windows. His life was over. And my grandmother's was, too, sort of. I held her tight, so, so tight, I wished I could put plasters over her heart and find a remedy for her tears, but some pain can't be kissed better.

The counsellor at the hospital was called Marie Etchebest. She had a soft voice and soothing words, she explained the stages of grief and let my grandmother cry. She was with us when we said goodbye to him. She called a taxi and went with us to see him. When my grandmother said goodbye to Marie, she said she would never forget her. I finished school a month later and signed up straight away to study psychology.

'This is taking quite a long time. My back's hurting!' Marilyn joked.

'Can I point out,' I said with a frown, 'that, thanks to you, I look like origami, so I think I've cornered the market on backache.'

Two hours and thirty-three minutes later, I'm fully versed in the long list of aches and pains experienced by Team Granny. A life-size game of Operation. I don't like to admit it, but I'd rather have lower back pain than be eighty years old. I don't like to admit this either, but

I prefer chatting to these three women to reading *Paris Match*.

We're on to Elisabeth's left little finger, which is deformed by arthritis, when a man's voice calls my name. I grab my walking frame, insist my three companions don't come with me, and drag myself over to the doctor, who leads me towards a consultation booth.

'Why are you walking with a frame?'

Because I just love it, it's a look I'm cultivating . . . do you really have to study medicine to come up with questions like that?

'My back just froze when I was doing an exercise class.'

'In a fitness club?'

'No, a retirement home.'

He looks at me as if I'm having a stroke.

'I work in a retirement home, I was at the class with the residents and I made a wrong move.'

'Okay. Take off your clothes and lean forwards.'

I resist the temptation to tell him it's a long time since anyone's asked me to do that, and do as I'm told as quickly as the pain will allow.

He comes around behind me and puts his hands on my lower back. I shiver. A man is touching me, and he's not four times my age – it's been a while. Mind you, he's got big, goggly eyes and could take the lids off beer bottles with his teeth – but a man is touching me.

'Not too hard, working with the elderly?' he asks.

'Not as hard as I thought it would be,' I reply, trying not to sound like a porn star.

He runs his fingers down my spine. I shudder.

'I don't know if I could do it.'

'I thought the same, but actually, it's okay. It can be quite depressing – you can't help seeing yourself in their shoes. Getting old is really tough . . . But it also helps you get things in perspective and make the most of every minute. It feels very strange discussing deep questions with someone who has a bird's-eye view of my knickers.'

I bite my tongue. No, really, what was I thinking, saying something like that? For him to offer to rip them off with his teeth?

He takes hold of my shoulders and straightens me up.

'That wasn't what I meant,' he says. 'I'm nowhere near old yet! But, I don't know, isn't it a bit degrading being with people who smell of urine, changing their incontinence pads, and listening to them rambling on? Plus, they think they can do whatever they like and they spend the whole time complaining. I think, if I were you, I'd be praying for a cold snap.'

The good news is he's just knocked my fantasies on the head. The bad news is I'd quite like to thump him in the face, but I'm in no state to do that.

Less than two months ago, I'd have been perfectly capable of making more or less the same kind of comments. To my considerable surprise, hearing them now produces a sort of protective instinct in me: 'Leave my oldies alone, buster.' I think I might need therapy.

I don't say another word until he's finished examining my back and given me a diagnosis: muscle spasm. I was right: hypochondriacs make the best doctors. Then I put my clothes back on, look him up and down and give him the retort I've been mulling over for several minutes.

'The problem isn't the elderly, the problem is miserable little pricks like you. Cold snap, or no cold snap.'

And I sweep out triumphantly, head held high.

With my walking frame.

April

'Being happy does not mean everything is perfect.
It means you have decided
to overlook imperfections'

– Aristotle

Chapter 23

Gustave's daughter Martine doesn't have the looks to match her personality. Large, clear eyes, made softer and sweeter by crow's feet, a mouth that smiles even at rest and cheeks so round they seem to be harbouring apples. She's the sort of woman you feel like saying hello to when you see her on the street. Except, here's the thing, when she opens her mouth, you feel more like waving goodbye.

She's been in my office for three minutes and I'm already regretting asking to meet her. 'Please be quick. I don't have all day for this,' was the first thing she said. So I'm being quick.

'I felt it important to talk to you about your daddy . . .'

'My daddy? D'you think I'm five?'

I take this on the chin and keep going.

'Right. How do you think your father's feeling at the moment?'

'I have no idea, I don't see him. But I don't imagine you've asked me here to tell me he's doing well . . .'

'Are you angry?'

Her eyes nearly pop out of her head.

'I'm not in the habit of talking about my private life to strangers.'

'Could I just ask whether it would be possible for you to visit him from time to time?'

'Yes,' she says curtly.

'Yes what?'

'Yes, you can ask me. But I don't have to answer your questions. I'm nearly sixty. Believe me, I'm absolutely *not* accountable to you.'

Come with me, we could go for a walk along the cliff edge . . .

'Madame Luret, no one's trying to lecture you. I'm very sorry if you feel that's the case. I haven't been here long, and I get the impression your father minds very much that you don't visit him. I wanted to be sure you realise that, and now I know. Thank you for coming, I won't keep you from your day any longer.'

I stand up; she has stayed sitting. Her cheeks have gone bright red, her eyebrows are meeting in the middle, her mouth has almost disappeared. I think she's undergoing some sort of transformation.

'Is *that* what you disturbed me for?'

'Excuse me?'

'You don't have any news for me – some illness, a financial problem or anything else that would explain your urgent need to meet me?'

Now she stands up and heads for the door. As she opens it, she turns around and snaps one final sentence at me:

'Don't tell my father I was here.'

She closes the door behind her clicky heels. I wonder how Gustave can have produced someone so different to himself. I understand better why he sees life as a joke: his daughter's about as civilised as the candlestick in Cluedo. I feel sorry for the old man but, at the end of the day, it might make him unhappier if he saw her regularly.

He's raking soil in the vegetable patch when I make my slow way over to him. My back is better, but it will still be a while before I'm doing somersaults.

'Hello, Gustave!'

He gives me a beaming smile.

'Hello, do you like salmon, Ella?'

'Ella and I both love it, thanks. How are you, Gustave? What have you been planting?'

'Artichokes and asparagus. I bought the plants yester-day from the local garden centre, but I should have gone to my usual supplier. Look at these horrible leaves . . . by the way, do you know what a market gardener says to his girlfriend?'

'Erm . . . no?'

'Be-troo-to me, darling!' he bellows with forced laughter.

'Did you want to tell me something?' he asks, wiping his hands on his overalls.

'No, I just came by to see if everything was all right. I often see you gardening – is it something you love?'

'I like tending things, yes. There's nothing to start with, and you have to make it all happen. You sow a seed, take care of it, nurture it, then you see a seedling appear and grow and eventually bear fruit . . . It's like life, basically. Oh, do you know the worst thing a gar-dener has to do?'

'No, I don't . . .'

'Drop his trousers to make tomatoes go red.'

He starts laughing again, and I can hear the pain behind the smiles. If he only knew . . .

'Well, I'm delighted everything's going well. I'll leave you to your vegetables. I'll see you tomorrow in your studio.'

'All right, then, see you tomorrow!' he replies, planting out a leek.

I'm a little way away when his question reaches me.

'Was she well?'

Chapter 24

It's Sunday.

Greg is keen for us to visit his new apartment, so here we are, Clara and I, ringing the doorbell outside an old building in the centre of Bayonne. She heaves a sigh.

'This is such a pain. I'd rather be lying on the beach in weather like this. And anyway, I can't really see the point of seeing a place full of building works. You watch a film when it's been made, not during the shoot.'

She's been grumbling ever since we left. It was too hot, I wasn't walking quickly enough, people were driving badly, her hair was blowing in her eyes on purpose – everything was a good excuse to whinge. There are only two possible explanations: either Leon has taken over her body or something's happened.

The door opens before I have a chance to ask her. Standing at the top of the stairs, Greg greets us with a lordly 'Welcome to my humble abode!'

Clara is right. There's no point at all in seeing an apartment halfway through building works, unless you want to stock up on dust in your lungs. Several walls have been knocked down to 'create a large living space and let the light in'; it looks as if a bomb's gone off. The floor is covered with dust sheets and the windows are filthy. It's impossible to see the potential.

'You're going to have a nice place here,' I manage, out of compassion, as he shows us the kitchen-to-be.

'I should hope so! I needed to change everything after Jean-Luc died . . . Too many memories. It'll be a fresh start! Come and have a look,' he says, leading us down the corridor. 'The bedroom's finished.'

He opens the door with a big 'Ta-dah!'

'You're right, it's wonderful!' Clara says sarcastically, nodding. 'Well, I imagine it will be, because, right now, it's hard to see . . .'

All around the bed, which has pride of place in the middle of the room and is covered with heaps of clothes, there are boxes piled up, almost to the ceiling in places. Two wardrobes are pushed up against the window and a fridge is squeezed between a partition wall and an oven.

'No, but look!' he insists. 'You can see a bit of the wood floor here – it's nice, isn't it? And here, behind the door, you can get an idea of the wall colour. I asked them to do "polished concrete". I love the stuff!'

It does look good, but that's not what I'm interested in. A big corkboard leaning up against the bedhead has caught my attention. Pinned to it are several photos clearly cut from magazines.

'Is that you in those photos?'

'Yes, my mother gave me that little shrine to my hey-day . . .' he replies, embarrassed.

'But what the hell are you doing in magazines?' Clara asks.

'It was a while ago. I acted in an ad and a TV series, and I had a minor role in a film.'

'You're joking! You're an actor?'

He shrugs.

'I wanted to be, but it's not easy getting in. I tried my luck, lived in Paris for three years, but I didn't get a break so I gave up. End of story.'

'Are you sad?' I ask.

'No, because otherwise I wouldn't have had Jean-Luc. I sometimes wonder what sort of life I'd have had if it had worked out. But, to be honest, I really love my job. I don't get the recognition of the general public, but the smiles on the residents' faces during their activities mean just as much to me.'

Clara tries to weave her way between the cardboard boxes.

'What was the ad for? This picture rings a bell . . .'

'I've completely forgotten, it was ages ago,' he says, ushering us out of the pandemonium and closing the door.

'Ohmygod, I've just remembered!' she shrieks, laughing.

When we leave the apartment, I have a smile on my face, thanks to Clara's suddenly brighter mood, although she hasn't told me anything about this mystery advert. The twinkle fades when my phone rings. The number on the screen feels like a punch in the guts. It's Marc.

Chapter 25

Elisabeth and Pierre are the only couple at Ocean View. From the start, they've wanted to have their sessions together. 'We don't have any secrets from each other.'

Sitting one at each end of the sofa, they sip glasses of Elisabeth's home-made lemonade. I will have doubled my bodyweight by the end of this contract.

Pierre isn't feeling great today.

'I'm exhausted . . . the head is willing, but my body just can't keep up with it any more. The tiniest effort wipes me out. I went to the market with Elisabeth this morning, and we had to stop several times for me to gather my strength. If only I could tell myself it was temporary . . . but it wouldn't help. No sort of training will give me my energy back.'

'It's the hardest thing,' Elisabeth explains. 'Accepting that the body's a machine that gets worn out and eventually breaks down. Every day, my eyesight gets a little worse. Soon, I'll be in complete darkness . . . unless another organ gives up sooner.'

'Does that frighten you?' I venture to ask, as if the answer weren't obvious.

'I'm terrified,' she replies. 'It's gone so quickly . . .

Yesterday, I was just a girl, and now it's nearly over. I can't stop wondering what my last moments will be like. It's difficult not making new plans, knowing we'll soon leave the people we love. We like this life. I'd much rather stay a bit longer.'

'I mind most for the little ones,' Pierre adds. 'Our children, grandchildren and great-grandchildren are very fond of us. I hope they'll get over it quickly . . . Well, I also hope they don't forget us!'

Elisabeth takes a deep breath and looks at Pierre.

'I'm frightened, yes. But I still hope I go before Pierre. In fifty-nine years, we haven't been apart more than a day. Not once! He's been by my side all through my life. He's always been there, in the day-to-day things, in moments of great happiness and in crises. I hope what they say is true and that there really is an afterlife where we can be together again.'

'And I hope *I'll* be the one to go first! Otherwise, who's going to massage my fingers to ease my arthritis?'

They both start to laugh.

Marc and I used to have the same conversation. We'd do whatever we could to go at the same time, because neither of us could cope without the other. But here I am, still alive, and, judging by his message, so is he.

I didn't pick up when he called. I hesitated the whole time the phone was ringing, but I stuck it out. I'd been waiting for his call. A long time. The first few days after I left the apartment, I was convinced he would come begging. I'd even warned Marion: I would only be on her sofa for a few days, because everything would sort itself out. Marc would realise that he hadn't stepped up, he would walk over hot coals to be forgiven. It would give him a boot up the backside and he would turn into the boyfriend every girl dreams of having.

I don't think that the boyfriend every girl dreams of having would take nine months to call back the love of his life.

'Have we already told you how we met?' Pierre asks me, before launching into the account without waiting for my reply. 'We were still living in Tunisia. I was walking along avenue de Paris in Tunis when I saw this beauty. I'll never forget it. She was wearing a scarf in her hair, like Brigitte Bardot, and a pink suit and ballet pumps. You should have seen her: a real film star!'

Elisabeth stands up, takes a photo frame from the chest of drawers and hands it to me.

'It must be hard for you to imagine. Here, this is a picture of our wedding. I really was beautiful!'

She's wearing a long lace dress and a shy smile. Her blond hair is lifted into a chignon. In her hands, she has a bouquet, and probably plenty of hopes for the future. He is wearing a dark suit and a happy smile. His arm is around her shoulders: it's happened, the pretty young woman from avenue de Paris now shares his name.

The photo completely bowls me over.

It's black and white, but it could have been taken yesterday. They were young once, too. They've been my age. They had plans, hysterical laughter and hard slogs, they made love and had parents, friends, babies. They had a life. Fifty years ago, they weren't thinking about getting old someday either.

For a long time, I thought of old people simply as old people, ignoring the individuals hiding beneath their grey hair.

Maybe one day someone will look at pictures of an old lady and realise that she was once young. That she took duckface selfies, that she liked roaring with laughter, that she had quite a lot of lovers and she adored her girlfriends. One day, the old lady in the picture will be me.

'Are you crying, Julia?'

Shit. I'm crying.

As if nothing is amiss, Pierre keeps on telling me their story. Thank you, Pierre!

'She was with her cousin Marie-Josée, who I knew. So I said hello to them and carried on walking, wondering how I could meet this Elisabeth again; she'd bewitched me. So I started running.'

Elisabeth giggles. He smiles and continues.

'I ran as fast as my legs would allow. I took the first side road and doubled back along the avenue that runs parallel to it. A few minutes later, I came across them again, as if it was perfectly normal. I was probably a bit dishevelled, but she accepted when I invited her for dinner.'

'You were perfect,' Elisabeth says coyly. 'In three months' time, we're celebrating our diamond anniversary. I don't mind telling you, it hasn't all been a bed of roses. There have been difficult times – rough patches, as the young say. You don't spend a lifetime with someone without making a few concessions. But I can now confirm: I couldn't have dreamed of a better husband . . .'

'Oh, stop now, you'll make the poor girl cry again . . .'

When I leave their studio, my head is buzzing. I'm the psychologist, but I get the feeling the residents are giving me far more than I am them.

Elisabeth's words keep ringing in my ears: 'You don't spend a lifetime with someone without making a few concessions.' In his message, Marc said he still loves me. That he's sorry. What if he was my Pierre? What if I don't find a side street to turn down and cross his path again? What if I've made a huge mistake?

Almost before I'm back in my office, I take out my phone and call his number.

Chapter 26

Sometimes, I wish I couldn't speak.

The evening they asked who would volunteer to accompany the residents to the Frank Michael concert, for example. I'd have preferred to be mute then. Or struck down in a freak harpoon accident.

Instead of which, I put up my hand and said I'd do it. What was I thinking!

That's how it is. For some reason that's completely beyond me, I'm sometimes possessed by this well-meaning – not to mention very stupid – impulse. The same impulse that convinced me, when I'd had my very first kiss at a party with a boy I'd never met before, to look him in the eye and tell him he would be the father of my children. Or that encouraged me to tell my ex-'mother-in-law' she could come over whenever she liked. Or that goes along with hairdresser's suggestions, even if that means having half my head shaved.

This time, my idiot alter-ego thought it was a good idea for me to go to a concert by some crooner called Frank – well, to be frank myself, I'd rather not.

There are twelve of us in the minibus. Louise won two tickets at Bingo and invited Gustave; Arlette, Elisabeth,

Pierre, Mina, Mohamed, Leon and Lucienne bought their own, as did Isabelle, Greg and I, who are here to look after them.

Greg is driving, and Isabelle is bordering on having a heart attack.

'Oh my God! Oh my God, I haven't seen him for five years. This is too exciting!'

'We can hardly tell,' Leon retorts, checking his camera.

'Really?' she asks innocently. 'But I'm shaking like a leaf. I think I'm going to have an epileptic fit!'

'If only . . .'

Our receptionist is impervious to the old man's sarcasm and keeps up her running commentary. Isabelle isn't usually very talkative about her private life, but she doesn't spare us a single detail now: from how this singer was the soundtrack to her childhood, to how her brother is called Frank-Michael in his honour, via her mother's collection of signed photos, all of it punctuated with shrill laughter. If she were acting, you'd think she was massively overdoing it.

The other passengers are starting to get impatient, when the minibus comes to a halt.

'It's all good. I've found a parking space!' Greg announces. 'We'll be there in a few minutes.'

Everyone claps enthusiastically. Including me, but not for the same reason. If my face is still wearing this idiotic smile, if I've tolerated Isabelle's monologue without chucking her out of the window, if I'm in a very good mood . . .

it's not because I'm about to go to a Frank Michael concert. It's because I'm seeing Marc tomorrow.

He picked up on the first ring. When I heard his voice,
the wall I'd put up between us collapsed. Fuck, I've
missed him.

I didn't tell him that. But he said he'd missed me. He
didn't want us to do this over the phone, so he's booked a
plane ticket to come and spend the weekend with me.
Then he said, 'I love you,' before hanging up.

I said, 'Me, too,' but after I'd hung up.

Chapter 27

During the second song by Frank Michael, I want to go to sleep.

During the third, I want to cry.

During the fifth, I'd even opt to die in hideous pain.

From where he is in the wheelchair zone with Mina and Mohamed, Greg mimes putting a noose around his neck. I reply by putting two fingers to my temple. Elisabeth glowers at me. I'm slumped down in my seat while Isabelle stands on hers, playing the fan girl. Or the victim of demonic possession; it's hard to tell.

She's perfectly in keeping with the rest of the audience. The men may be trying to hide the sheen in their eyes behind blasé expressions, but the women are beside themselves. I wouldn't be surprised to see granny pants thrown at the stage.

The row behind us clearly comprises the singer's most fervent fan club: a dozen sixty-something women wearing T-shirts featuring a picture of him and smiles like teenage girls having their first ovulation. I watch them, and I'm trying to imagine Marion and me with wrinkles and white hair, bellowing out the words at a U2 concert, when my heart suddenly misses a beat: over there, not ten metres away, I recognise my mother's best friend, Anna.

If she sees me, my mother will know I'm in Biarritz within a minute, and I can say goodbye to my solitary private journey. Accepting that she can't be there for her daughter in difficult times, even if it's what the daughter wants, is way beyond my mother's abilities. That and cooking.

Anna mustn't see me.

That's easy for now – she's far too busy gazing longingly at Frankie – but it will be a different story when he leaves the stage. Maybe I could borrow Lucienne's wig . . .

When the concert ends, I have a cricked neck.

I've spent more than an hour looking at the left-hand wall. If Anna has realised it's me, she can go on *France's Got Talent* with her amazing gift: recognising people just from the nape of their neck.

Isabelle is in tears, the residents seem thrilled with their outing, even Leon is clapping. If I manage to get out of here without bumping into Anna, we can call this a very successful evening.

'Let's wait till everyone's gone. It'll be easier,' I tell the group.

'Seeing how comfortable the seats are, it'll take us an hour to get up, anyway,' laughs Louise.

'You can count on me to help you,' Gustave offers.

I'll have to watch those two. I wouldn't be surprised to come across them playing strip Bingo one evening.

'I need the loo!' wails Lucienne.

'Me, too!' says Elisabeth.

'Oh yes, and me, too!' Gustave throws in.

'As if we haven't got better things to do than wait for you . . . Couldn't you have put a pad on?' grumbles Leon.

Louise gives him a winning smile.

'Pads give you a big backside. Some people take care of their appearance, even at an advanced age. You should try it – it might do you some good!'

They say that if you want to, you can. It turns out that if you don't want to, you can, too. I didn't want to bump into Anna, but here I am, face to face with her outside the toilets. Just my luck.

Maybe if I start speaking Slovakian she'll think I'm my own doppelganger?

How do you say 'hello' in Slovakian?

'Hello, Julia!' she says with a forced smile.

'Oh, hello, Anna! I didn't see you – were you at the concert?'

Call me Meryl Streep.

'Yes,' she says, glancing about anxiously.

'Is everything okay?'

'Yes, yes, everything's fine, it's just . . .' She breaks off briefly before saying, 'Basically, you were the last person I was expecting to see. You see, I thought you were in Paris . . .'

I cast around frantically for a reliable excuse. How does anyone explain going to a Frank Michael concert in Biarritz!

'Your mother mustn't know I'm here,' Anna says.

'Really?'

'Definitely not. I didn't tell her I was coming.'

'Okay. But why did you lie to her?'

Or how to turn the tables in one easy lesson.

'Because she's had a row with Pascale, and she thinks I'm not seeing Pascale either,' she whispers, nodding towards a woman who has a photo of Frank Michael on the sleeve of her T-shirt. 'I'm very fond of Pascale, but I don't want to hurt your mother . . . do you understand?'

'I understand. I won't say anything if you d—'

'Got to go,' she interrupts. 'Pascale's in a hurry, her husband's waiting up for her. You won't let me down, will you?'

She blows me a kiss and hurries off.

I didn't even have to explain why I'm here. Let alone ask her to lie.

The black cloud that's been hovering over my head seems to have floated off to find some other poor sod to torment. Good riddance.

119

Chapter 28

I'm early.

I'd rather wait than have him watch as I walk awkwardly towards him. The waiter asked if I'd like to order; I said I'd just like to hit Pause. That wasn't on the menu.

I'm scared. I'm terrified, petrified, liquified, losing my shit and flipping my lid. I was awake all night and I've been out of sorts all day. I even encouraged Mina enthusiastically when she admitted she couldn't wait to die. And to think I thought I was over Marc.

I was early for our first date, too. I'd spent the whole day getting ready. Face and body scrub, a thorough weeding of, erm, fallow land, a hydrating-restorative face mask and my hair carefully styled to look as if it hadn't been . . . I felt like a try-hard idiot when he pitched up in a crumpled T-shirt with a line on his cheek from his pillow.

After two hours, I knew I was going to love him truly, madly, deeply. Four hours in the preparation, two hours in the tasting, seven years in the digesting – it's official: my love life is a pot roast.

He has a bunch of roses in his hand and that smile I love so much: the one that makes him look like a shy little boy. I stay sitting. Then get up, and fall back down.

I didn't think he could still get me in such a state. I thought you could decide to stop loving someone, like you can decide to stop eating sugar. I've been on a Marc diet. I've weaned myself off his words, resisted wallowing in memories of him, kept myself away from his voice. And now here I am, face to face with him, ready to dive right back in. Doctors are right: if you deprive yourself too much, you always end up caving.

'It's good to see you,' he murmurs as he reaches me.

I manage to stand, but my legs are wobbling; they start tap-dancing when he puts his arms around me. I bury my face in his neck. He's wearing an aftershave I don't recognise and seems taller. It's like a first date, but also completely different.

He's hardly sat down before he launches into what he has to say, as if afraid of forgetting part of a formal speech.

'I want to apologise, Julia. I was a prick . . . I could say it was because I had work and money problems on my mind, or even my brother's new baby, but the truth is I don't have an excuse. I let you down when you needed me most, and that's terrible. I love you. I want you to come back. Please. We were so good together.'

He means it, I can tell. I can see it in the exclamation-mark furrow between his eyebrows, in his right hand, which clasps his left one supportively, in his lips, which are trembling ever so slightly. I wouldn't even have dared hope to hear these words and he's serving them up in pretty, scented wrapping paper. I should be feeling my heart bouncing around on a pogo stick or not feeling it at all, I should have to restrain whoops of happiness, I should throw myself at him and kiss him like they do in the movies, I should call Marion and squeal, 'You'll never guess what he's just said!' I'm wearing my prettiest dress, having hesitated over ten other, similar options, I rehearsed this scene in my head all night, and played out other versions where he abandons me and I'm in tears.

So why isn't this having any more effect on me than seeing it in a film? For fuck's sake, Julia, you're the heroine this time!

On our very first date, my feelings of excitement just kept on growing. I'd gone along with no expectations and, after two hours, I felt like swearing to love him till death us do part. After five hours, I let my knickers fall at the foot of his bed.

Today, it's the other way around. Two hours ago, I was shaking like crazy when I saw him come into the bar, and, as the time goes by, my excitement is melting like an Easter egg that's fallen behind a radiator.

I listen as he tells me about his friends, who were my friends, too; about what was once our apartment; about his family, whom we saw a lot; his work, which he never stopped talking about . . . and it all feels like such a long time ago. Another life.

Even physically, he doesn't feel familiar now. I hadn't noticed that his eyes are so big, his shoulders so sloping. I knew plenty of things by heart: his pout when things go wrong, the shape of his ears, his chipped tooth. I saw him with an everyday eye. Absence washes all that away.

Seven years ago, after two hours, I felt as if I'd known him all my life.

Today, after two hours, I feel as if I no longer know who he is.

Maybe we need some time.

I'm not giving up that easily. This is Marc.

'Is working with the elderly helping with your fear of death?' he asks, pushing the whipped cream off his ice-cream with a spoon.

He booked this table in our favourite Biarritz restaurant. We used to eat here every time we came to see my parents. I'm a big fan of their squid-ink risotto, even if it leaves me with black teeth every time. But this evening, I'm too busy trying to convince myself I'm happy to appreciate what's on the menu.

'I don't actually think about it that much,' I tell him. 'Most of the residents are still very independent. They're pretty full of life.'

'That's just as well! Because you used to freak out about death. You used to look away every time there was a corpse in a film. I don't know how you coped with your dad—'

'No, you wouldn't know, would you?'

Bang. There's the rub.

'Do you still hold it against me?'

No, of course not, my darling, I'm grateful to you.

I put down my spoon and wipe my mouth.

'Of course I do.'

'I'm so sorry,' he whispers, taking my hand. 'I've

changed, you know. If it happened tomorrow, I'd be there for you.'

'The trouble is, it happened then. It was then that you didn't hold my hand at my father's funeral, then that you left me to cry all night, alone in the bathroom. You should have been the person supporting me, but you were the one kicking me when I was down. Why's it taken so long for you to call? Why did you leave me on my own all this time?'

'I don't know,' he says, looking away. 'I think I was scared of how you'd react. So long as I hadn't yet tried to get you back, there was still hope.'

I try to put myself in his shoes. I swear I'm trying. I try to see how work and a few figures on a bank statement could take priority over the grief of the person you love. I'm trying. But I'm having trouble.

'Why did you agree to see me if you resent me so much?'

'Because when you called I didn't realise I did. I've done everything I can to avoid thinking about you all this time, so the anger was buried. Seeing you has brought it back . . . I suppose it's a necessary process, it'll run its course.'

'I hope so . . .'

I hope so, too.

Chapter 29

We're walking through the streets of Biarritz. It's a little chilly; Marc puts his arm around my shoulders. Every now and then, one of us tells some anecdote and the other responds enthusiastically. From the outside, we look like a perfectly normal couple. From the inside, we're more like a huge question mark.

The more time goes by, the more natural things feel, the more automatic reflexes resurface, the more relaxed we are.

'This is where I'm staying,' he says, stopping outside the Best Western. 'Would you like to come up?'

I don't hesitate for long. Because there's no way I practically dislocated my hips epilating my bikini area for nothing, and because making love would be a good way to bring us together and because I want to. Nearly three months of abstinence . . . if that carries on, I'll knock Mother Teresa off her pedestal.

We don't even put the light on.

Marc closes the door and presses me against the wall, his lips crushing mine. I always liked him taking charge – he remembers. With one hand, he grips the back of my neck; with the other, he kneads my buttock while his hips rock against mine. I slip off my jacket and remove my shoes; he takes his off, too, then rolls my tights down my legs. Then he picks me up, I wrap my legs around his waist and he drops me on to the bed. His lips move down to my breasts, he kisses them passionately and I, meanwhile, wait for the fireworks that just aren't happening. I give a few moans: maybe pleasure is like hunger, which grows as you eat.

His head moves down between my thighs, and I take this opportunity to open my eyes and quickly assess the situation. Shouldn't have done that. Wearing nothing but a pair of white socks, Marc is on all fours, mooning at the ceiling. And now I feel like laughing. Stop it, Julia, laughing during sex is *bad*. Close your eyes and concentrate on what he's doing. Actually, what *is* he doing? He never used to do whatever this is; it's borderline irritating. He must have OD'ed on porn while we were apart – I can't see any other explanation for the way he's scrubbing away at my clitoris as if he's found a dirty mark on it. Hey, Aladdin! Stop rubbing, there ain't no genie coming out of there!

I gently take hold of his head and guide him back up. He lies on top of me, pushes between my thighs and slides into me.

Two minutes later, when I realise I'm thinking about the risotto I had for dinner while he does his thing on top of me, I know that our relationship is over.

Chapter 30

He didn't want me to see him back to the station.

'It was a bloody stupid idea, coming here,' he sulks as he heads for his taxi.

Some relationships end badly. Some relationships end badly twice.

I tried not to hurt him. Just to tell him how I felt, neither upsetting him nor particularly sparing his feelings. However much I've tried to bubble-wrap my emotions in the last few months, it only took a few hours to identify my last response to Marc: anger.

I'm angry with him for not being there.

I'm angry with him for being so selfish.

I'm angry with him for not trying to hold on to me.

I'm angry with him for letting me stop loving him.

What a waste. What a shame. We got on so well. We loved each other so much. It will never come back, I know that. The way I see him has changed. Before, I saw him as he liked to be seen: kind, helpful, generous and considerate. Now, I read between the lines: I look for the flaw hidden behind the façade and imagine the deceit behind the smile. It's probably an exaggeration, but that's how he makes me feel now.

Sometimes, when years of wear damage the varnish on a piece of furniture, an even more beautiful wood appears underneath. And sometimes, you get splinters that dig so deep into your flesh you can never get them out. Try as I might, I'll never be able to forgive him.

He had no right to do that. Not to us.

He throws his rucksack on to the back seat of the taxi, and a last glance at me. I've done my best to do this right, but everything about him screams, 'My ego hurts!' He needs to injure me to ease his own bitterness, so he brings out the big guns.

'You want to know why it took me so long to call you? It's because I was having such a great time. I've been partying, shagging, getting a whole load of pussy, and not one of them was a bitch like you. I was free. I don't even know why I called you. Pity, probably. Yeah, that's it, pity at the thought of you all on your own, crying about Daddy dearest.'

I know that he's going beyond what he really feels, that he's laying it on in order to hurt me. But the splinters are digging into every inch of me. Even breathing is painful. I can't utter a single word.

'Did you really think your little revenge would get to me?' he sneers.

'But I . . .'

'You set the whole thing up perfectly – you must have asked Marion to tell me you were inconsolable. And I – out of the kindness of my stupid heart – I nearly felt guilty. Seriously, did you really believe me when I said

I still loved you? Did you really think I meant it? Poor little Julia . . .'

He turns away and jumps into the taxi. My stomach hurts, I can't breathe, my head's spinning, but there's no way I'll let him see he's had any impact. I take the two steps between me and the taxi, catch hold of the door as it swings closed and lean towards him with a big smile.

'A bit of friendly advice, if I may. When you're getting a load of pussy, as you so elegantly put it, you should avoid scouring them between their legs like you did with me last night. Sorry to ruin the mystery, but there isn't an oil spill to clear up down there . . .'

I slam the door on his stunned face and walk away, trying to control my tears. As I cut across in front of the taxi, a movement inside catches my eye. The driver, clearly very amused, gives me a thumbs-up and winks at me.

Chapter 31

Clara is shouting so loudly that even Arlette must be able to hear her.

The social is in her studio this evening. We're sitting on the rug around her low table and treating ourselves to a McDonald's, which Greg went to pick up in Anglet.

'Oh my god, what a bastard!' she rails. 'Basically, he came, he fucked and pissed off again . . . they're all the same!'

She clearly hasn't calmed down since last time. I've just told her the bare bones of the return of Marc. I deliberately omitted intimate details, but not my lack of response or his parting rant. Clara is beside herself.

'You mustn't say that.' Greg tries to calm her. 'There are good guys, too!'

'Yeah, right. Well, if you see one, give him my number. No joke, if there are any decent men, they're on the brink of extinction. There must be fewer of them than polar bears. Tell you what, I'm off to live on the icebergs!'

Greg rolls his eyes.

'What's the matter, Clara?' I ask, pulling the gherkin out of my Big Mac. 'I feel like something's been up for a while now. Do you want to talk about it?'

She eyes me warily.

'You want to give me therapy?'

'No, I really just want you to know that, if you'd like to talk, I'm here.'

'Yup, we're both here,' Greg agrees. 'If something's wrong, talk about it. You're becoming a right pain.'

Clara bursts out laughing.

'Well, thanks a bunch! Okay, so maybe I'm a bit stressed at the moment. But not with either of you. It's just that . . .'

She breaks off to take a bite of her cheeseburger.

'All right, Hitchcock, don't leave us on tenterhooks!'

'Sho, like I waj shaying, I shaw my friend Jushtine,' she says, before swallowing her mouthful with a gulp of Coke. 'Well, "friend" may not be the right word – she's really a friend of Guillaume's, my ex, and I kind of put up with her. I've always found her really fake, and she's a complete slag; she'll jump on any man who comes within ten metres. Best way to describe it is: if the roads were paved with cocks, she'd crawl to work on her arse. And plus, she's . . .'

'Come on, spit it out!' Greg says impatiently. 'I feel like I'm watching a thriller and having to wait till the ad break's done to find out who did it.'

'Okay, okay, I'll tell you! Can you believe, the stupid tart couldn't resist telling me that Guillaume's going to marry his German girlfriend. I swear she was getting off on it.'

'Who, the German?'

'No, Justine! She was over the frigging moon when she dropped this bomb on me; she must have seen I was falling apart. She even sniggered when she told me she was the bride's witness for the ceremony. Prob'ly find out he's using the same wedding ring we chose together . . .'

I shuffle over to her on my bum – hoping no penises pop out of the floor – and stroke her shoulder.

'You going to be okay?'

'Yeah, I'm all right. I'm not sad, I'm pissed off. He was meant to marry me and, in less than a year, he's managed to forget me and marry someone else. I'd like to punch his stupid face.'

'Do you want me to take care of him?' offers Greg. 'I'm quite stacked, and I once had a fight in primary school.'

We all start laughing. Clara is first to stop.

'He obviously needs to be taught a lesson, the wanker. He didn't make it easy for me, when I'd given up everything to be with him. One day he tells me he loves me and can't wait to be my husband, then *bang!* He comes straight out with it and says he doesn't want me any more. If at least he'd tried to dress it up – but oh no! In the space of a few seconds, he became a stranger, really distant, like I was his enemy. He even chucked me out of the apartment because the German didn't have anywhere to go. It was his place, I had no choice . . . Luckily, I could come and live here; otherwise, I'd have had to go back to my parents on the other side of the country. I fucking hate him.'

'When's he getting married?' I ask.

'Twenty-fourth of May.'

'Perfect. That gives us a month to arrange the kind of wedding present he deserves.'

Clara's mouth twitches.

'Really? Would you do that for me?'

'We're civilised human beings,' I tell her, 'and civilised human beings give presents at weddings. You're with us on this, Greg, aren't you?'

He pretends to think for a moment.

'Of course I'm with you! I'm a pro when it comes to poisoned presents. When my ex left me, I wrapped one of Jean-Luc's turds in newspaper, put it on the fuckwit's door-mat then set it alight before ringing the doorbell. Of course, the instinctive reaction was to stamp on the flames, and of course stamping revealed the hidden gift . . . Oh, you should have seen it!'

Greg's euphoric. Clara glances at me, disgusted. My Big Mac would quite like to resurface.

'Did you really pick up one of Jean-Luc's poos?' I ask, horrified.

'Of course! Why are you looking at me like that? Have you never played that sort of prank?'

'Nope, sorry, but I've never touched my boyfriend's shit!' Clara replies with a grimace.

Greg freezes, opens his eyes wide, then roars with laughter.

'Are you serious, girls?'

Clara and I look at each other, perplexed. Does he really think this repulsive story is funny?

'I can't believe it,' he says, taking out his phone. 'You're completely bonkers. I don't believe it!'

He scrolls through something on his phone for a while, then hands it to us.

'Clara, Julia, may I introduce Jean-Luc.'

On the screen, lying with all four feet in the air and gazing up at us, is a chocolate Labrador.

'He died last year,' Greg adds, suddenly serious again. 'I'm still not over it . . .'

Clara's eyes are in danger of popping out of their sockets.

'So you aren't gay, then?'

'WHAT?!' Greg bellows. 'Me? What a weird idea! You thought I was gay?'

'Well, everyone does, actually,' I tell him. 'I have to say, you sowed the seeds with your Jean-Luc . . .'

He sits in silence for a few moments, then starts to laugh again.

'No way! Loads of things make more sense now! I couldn't understand why Isabelle came to me for advice about her little brother who wants to come out . . .'

'You're very gentle, for a bloke,' Clara adds. 'And you take care of your appearance, you always have nice hair, you're freshly shaved, you smell great . . . and you're a fan of *Plus belle la vie*!'

'Great, thanks for the stereotype! And the fact I've been trying to come on to you since I've been living here, that never got you thinking?'

Clara flushes scarlet. Greg looks shocked that those

words actually came out of his mouth. I giggle. I love the way this conversation's going. Come to think of it, the more time we spend together, the more I enjoy these nights and being with my colleagues.

Avoiding the subject, Clara gets up and heads towards the balcony.

'Did you hear that?'

'Hear what?' I ask.

'Voices,' she says, opening the French windows. 'I've heard them several times. I wonder what the hell it is.'

'That's rubbish,' says Greg, most likely a little sore over the lack of a response from Clara. 'It's nearly midnight. I don't know who'd be wandering around a care home now.'

'I sometimes hear them, too,' I say, joining her on the balcony. 'The first time I was outside having a cigarette and I thought I was going to get chopped up in little pieces, I was so bloody scared . . . I've heard them two or three times since then.'

Leaning on the wooden ledge, we see if we can make anything out in the darkness. The grounds are lit by the moon, but nothing seems to be moving.

'You can see there's nothing there. You two hear voices and see gays all over the place – you need to take your medication, girls!' Greg snorts, heading back into the studio.

I follow him.

'No, no, there really is someone out there,' I say. 'If I were braver, I'd start my own investigations. It stresses me out, not knowing.'

'I'm no chicken,' Clara announces. 'We could go and have a look together?'

'Don't hold out any hope for me,' Greg says, attacking his sundae, 'if you're prepared to believe I'm a pansy. Anyway, I don't give a stuff who it is: in a month, I won't be living here any more.'

'How come?' I ask.

'My building contractor called me earlier: the work will be finished in a month, tops. I can go home!'

He glances over at Clara, probably in the hope of seeing some sign that she's disappointed. But he must be the one feeling disappointed because she's tucking into a brownie as if she hasn't heard a thing. Nicely done. If I weren't a psychologist, I probably wouldn't have noticed her foot jigging under the table. Maybe she's not totally indifferent, after all.

Chapter 32

'How are things today?'

I ask this on autopilot, rather than in the expectation of a proper answer. Which is obvious, anyway. Louise is smiling from ear to ear and she's put on so much jewellery I nearly mistook her for Elizabeth Taylor.

'Absolutely wonderful!' she exclaims. 'My son's celebrating his sixtieth birthday, and we've arranged a surprise party for him. My daughter's coming to pick me up at eleven; he doesn't suspect a thing. His wife and children have hired a hall, there will be about forty of us and the lunch is being done by a caterer. It's going to be marvellous!'

I blow on the hot chocolate she's made for me, as I do every time. This morning, I brought some little choux-pastry puffs to make a real treat of it.

'How lovely! You'll spend the whole day with your nearest and dearest.'

'Yes, I haven't done that since Christmas. And even then, it was just my daughter and one of her daughters. This time, all my children will be there, along with several grandchildren. The ones who don't live too far away.'

'Do some of them live a long way away?'

'Oh yes! The young don't stay very close to the nest these days, you know. Two of my children live in Biarritz, the other two in Bordeaux and Toulouse, but my grandchildren are scattered about: Marseille, Paris, Savoie, Barcelona – I even have a grandson in Australia. They're all making lives for themselves – it's good.'

I offer her another cream puff to wipe away the sadness darkening her face. She smiles.

'What about you? Are you close to your grandparents?' she asks.

'Those I have left, I try to call regularly. But the one I was closest to was my mother's mother. I always had a special connection with her. I called her Nannynoo and I think I was her favourite. She called me her "Technicolor Dreamgirl" . . . When I was little, I would go to her every Wednesday afternoon. And I still did as I got older; it was our day. She'd take me to the park, into town, to the beach; I watched her make little dresses for me, she taught me to knit and read me poems that she wrote in her pretty notebooks, she made me hot chocolate, waffles, pancakes, things with too much sugar in them that made my mother grumble, so they became our secret. But what I liked best was when the two of us sat in her old brown armchair. I'd snuggle up to her and her smell of Chanel N° 5, she'd put her lovely soft arms around me and we'd stay there a long time, sometimes hours, talking, or just sitting there. The last time was just over a year ago. I'd come down to spend Christmas with the family, and the next day was a Wednesday. We did everything just like in the old days: I had a waffle with icing sugar, heard her latest poems, and we had a snuggle in her brown armchair. I remember I cut the visit short because I was meeting up with some friends. If only I'd known . . . I miss her so much . . .'

Louise's kindly eyes feel like a warm blanket around me. I'm shocked when I realise how much I've confided in her. If there were a competition for the worst psychologist, I'd probably come second to last, just ahead of the guy playing games on his phone while his patients talk.

I'm mortified. Though I can't deny it's done me good. Missing my grandmother is like missing my father – I can't talk to anyone about it. Either people aren't close enough themselves and don't understand, or they're too close and I'm afraid of hurting them. Maybe I should get a dog.

'Your grandmother was very lucky to have you,' Louise murmurs. 'Grandchildren are a gift from heaven. They bring such joy!'

'So who's going to be at this party?' I ask, changing the subject.

She's in the middle of listing everyone – and having to start again several times because she always forgets someone – when a noise makes us both look round. A white envelope has just been slipped under the door to her studio. Louise jumps up to get it.

'Oh, it must be Elisabeth,' she says. 'She's meant to be giving me a knitting pattern she found in a magazine. I'll have a look at it later . . .'

I don't say anything, but I can't help smiling. She and I both know there's no knitting pattern in the envelope. And I can't picture Elisabeth putting a heart instead of the dot on the *i* of 'Louise'.

Chapter 33

There are a lot of people on the beach. It will be May in a few days, and the sun has arrived early. I'm not the only one who's chosen to spend Sunday on the sand. There's a group of kids gathered round a guy with a guitar, families building sandcastles and memories, couples taking salt-sprayed selfies, a brave few venturing their feet into the water then shrieking a little as they run away, teenage girls gossiping, a child dazzled by the exploits of his kite, dozens of surfers, tourists attempting to immortalise their trip to Biarritz, people sitting reading alone with their feet in the sand. Like me. I've dug mine in deep. It's quite cold, but I like feeling the grains trickle between my toes. The sand, the crash of waves, the smell of the sea and sun cream are some of the things I missed most when I was in Paris. These, and my family.

When I was little, my parents, my sister and I would spend whole days on the beach. We'd set off in the morning with the cool box and the parasol and wouldn't come home till we'd had our fill of good times. The sort of moments that feel natural when you're experiencing them and magical when you look back on them. The four of us could all have been kids when it came to running into the water, waiting for the perfect wave and diving through it just before it broke and enveloped us in foam. We ate sand and swallowed seawater, but always went back for more. I remember my father's laugh, and how we jumped on to his strong back crying, 'All aboard!!' I remember his strong hands hauling us out of the rollers when they were too powerful, the way his hair flattened on to his forehead when he popped his head out of the water, the way he put his arms around my mother, only to throw her into the waves, but there's so much I've forgotten about him . . .

In my mind, there's a 'Dad' folder that I open – sparingly – to look after it and keep him alive. But the files in it are fragile. Over time, they become worn and disintegrate. Memory is a pencil drawing. Without family videos, I'd no longer be sure of the sound of his voice. Without photos, I'd have my doubts about how he looked. We should be able to transfer our memories on to a USB stick.

At the water's edge, a little boy is playing ball with his mother. Shielded from the sun behind a baseball cap and glasses, he complains about his playmate. Every time she hits the ball, it ends up much too far away. However hard the child tries to jump, run or dive, he invariably ends up collecting the ball from where it's landed on the wet sand. There are two possible explanations: either a Martian taught her how to play or she's doing this deliberately, to have a bit of peace. Crafty. I used the same tactic in the thankless phase called 'the teenage years': when it was my turn to do the washing-up, I made sure I splashed the walls and left scraps of dried food on the plates. The day my name featured less than my sister's on the rota of chores, I savoured my victory. But I'd underestimated Carole . . . who suddenly became incapable of vacuuming properly.

Clearly infuriated by his mother's inadequacy, the little boy really belts the ball, and it lands behind her. When she turns around, I see her face. Wow, the woman looks very like my sister. On closer inspection, she really is the spitting image of Carole – it's incredible – and she's left-handed: what an amazing coincidence . . . It takes my stupid brain a good thirty seconds to grasp the fact that the two people only a few metres from me are my sister and her son.

I'm instantly torn. The sensible half of me, the one that doesn't dive into the Nutella pot when the tiniest thing goes wrong, wants to bury itself in the sand. The other half, the one that adds whipped cream to the Nutella, wants to throw itself into Carole's arms, give her a huge hug and tell her how much I've missed her and how much I need her. Thank goodness the human body needs unanimity to function: it wouldn't make a pretty sight.

I stay motionless for a moment, hiding behind my sunglasses. Seeing my sister, even from a little distance, is a sort of comfort. Like when she curled into my arms when Bambi's mother died. I was the big sister, but she was the one who felt like a comfort blanket.

I know she wouldn't breathe a word. If I explained the reasons I'm here, she'd understand and respect my decision. She wouldn't tell my mother. She'd leave me alone, which is what I want, but she'd be there if I needed her. It's tempting, very tempting, especially because I frequently just want to call her and tell her everything. Carole isn't just my sister, she's my best friend. We speak on the phone as much as possible, and I usually wish 'possible' meant more often. She knows everything about me, and I about her.

The advantage of a sister is she'll always love you. She can disagree with you, she sometimes judges you or perhaps even wishes she had a different sister, you can fall out, but there will always be a deep affection tying two people who've grown up side by side all their lives. With her, I can drop all pretence, say what I really feel, remove any shiny exterior. Be myself. A sister is an unconditional friend.

She would become my accomplice if I asked her to. But I won't. She hates lies more than anything else. I can't ask her to lie to our mother. End of dilemma.

The problem is that, what with their inept ball skills, they're now dangerously close to me. No guarantee my sunglasses will stop Carole recognising me much longer. And if I casually get to my feet, I run the risk of being spotted. I need a back-up plan.

I'll escape by turning my back to them.

Or dig a tunnel and get away by crawling along it.

Or I could hang on to the feet of the next passing seagull and hope it drops me far away.

I need to make up my mind. I'd say the first solution is the most doable. I turn my head the other way and pick up my shoes and bag, then wait till my sister's looking away before getting discreetly to my feet and scuttling off sideways like a crab.

May

'A lifetime lasts just as long,
whether we spend it singing or crying'

– Japanese proverb

Chapter 34

'How have you been since last time?'

As usual, Leon is snubbing me. I've tried everything with him. Every week, I attempt a different approach. Every week, I come up against a brick wall. He's not crazy, and therapists are for crazy people. He hasn't asked anything of anyone; he came here for some peace and quiet, and so that he didn't have to do the cooking and cleaning now that his wife is no longer around to take care of that. I'm disturbing him. In case this little speech wasn't clear enough, he then behaves as if I'm simply not there.

I've contemplated stopping our sessions. After all, if he doesn't feel he needs them, I have no reason to force him to speak to me. But the St Bernard in me still lives in hope of sniffing out the person waiting for help under the icy carapace. I'm convinced that there's some sort of anguish lurking behind Leon's sarcasm, and I'd like to help him deal with it – whatever route I have to take to achieve this.

I've planned my attack. The idea came to me during our last session, which he spent in his massage chair, surfing the net on his tablet and giving the occasional contented sigh. I left after an hour, firmly resolved to win this stand-off he'd initiated.

Half lying on his sofa, he doesn't answer my question. Everything is going to plan. I get up from the hard wooden chair he consents to offer my backside once a week and, without a word, settle into his beloved massage chair. Out of the corner of my eye, I see him look up and study me. I suppress a smile. This is working. Time to move to the next level.

I put my hand into the pocket of my tunic and ostentatiously take out my phone. Leon sits up. You'll see I can play ball, too. I turn the volume right up and touch the coloured square to start a game of Candy Crush. The screen instantly loads with brightly coloured sweets that I line up in order to score points and fill the room with all sorts of sound effects. Leon stands up. I can tell he's dying to ask me what I think I'm doing. But if he does that, he'll be breaking the pact of silence he's made with himself. What will get the upper hand? Pride or indignation?

He walks around the table and sits on the wooden chair, facing me. I don't take my eyes off the screen. He sits in silence for several minutes, his surgically lifted face turned towards the window. Then he starts to speak.

'I was adopted. My mother left me in a church porch, naked in the middle of January. I was two days old. The orphanage was no fun. There were very strict rules and lots of punishments, but no love. When I was six I was taken in by a couple who ran a bakery. I started work the day after I arrived. I had to get up at four o'clock every morning to make bread, and my adoptive father took all the credit for it. If I ever made the mistake of eating a piece, I spent the rest of the day locked in the hall cupboard with the shoes. At sixteen, I went up to Paris. I lived on the street for a while, until the day luck came my way . . . her name was Maryse.'

He breaks off. I can't get over this. If I'd known I just had to pretend I didn't care to get him to talk, I could have saved a lot of time. I'll remember: with Leon, if you want something, you have to make out you want the exact opposite. What I hadn't suspected, though, was the old man's story. He hadn't become sour as a result of privilege, not at all. Under the grumpy-old-man costume he always wore there were deep wounds. To think I've often fought the urge to string him up, but I was misreading the evidence. If this carries on, I'll be wondering whether I've chosen the wrong career.

'Maryse and I were happy,' he continues, after a long silence. 'We built up her parents' little company far beyond what we'd hoped: from a small local business, we created an international company with more than a thousand employees, and all the big directors knew we were the best when it came to special effects. We rubbed shoulders with the greats – I'm still in regular contact with Steven by email . . . Spielberg, you know who I mean?'

Of course I know. You wouldn't have Brad Pitt's number, by any chance?

'We travelled a lot,' he goes on, not waiting for my

reply. 'We handled millions of francs and had three beautiful children. Then our lucky star stopped shining. In one year, we lost our two younger children. If you knew how devastating it is to watch your own flesh and blood suffer and die . . . Maryse couldn't bear it; she joined them a few months later. I ended up alone with my older son, who was very troubled. I had to sell the company to take care of him properly.'

He wipes his eyes.

'I remarried twice, but I was never happy again. Over the years, my heart shrivelled up. I do realise I'm not easy; I know I'm grumpy, but it's my way of protecting myself. When you get fond of people, you suffer. I don't want to love anyone again, and I don't want to be loved. There are people who swear they'll never have a dog again when they lose one. Well, I swear I'll never get close to anyone again.'

'Aren't you lonely?'

'I'm not lonely. My memories are still alive. And my son comes to see me at least twice a week. Now, I'm waiting for the end . . . Luckily, time goes quickly, thanks to technology!' he says, gesturing towards his tablet.

'Well, I have to say you're very good at this. The cracks in your armour don't show at all.'

He smiles. It's the first time I've seen him smile. If it didn't pull at his seams so much, he'd look like a friendly grandfather.

'Having spent so much time with actors, I've probably acquired some ability.'

'In any case, I owe you an apology. I've been hard on you since I arrived. I was impatient. I've entertained the possibility that you weren't really the gruff person you were pretending to be, but I never imagined you'd had such a difficult life . . . Are you angry with me?'

He looks at his watch.

'The session's over, isn't it?'

'Yes, it's over for this week. I just want to check you're not angry with me and I'll leave you.'

He gets up and goes over to the door.

'I'm not at all angry with you. In fact, I'm grateful to you.'

I follow him, smiling with relief.

'I'd like to thank you,' he says. 'Thanks to you, I've just had a very special moment.'

'Don't thank me, it's my job!'

'No, no, really. I haven't had so much fun for a very long time.'

'Fun?' I ask, after a slight pause.

'Yes, fun. It was an absolute delight. If you could have seen your face while I was telling you that *Les Mis*-esque tale, you'd have laughed, too. Good Lord, you're naïve!'

I'm flabbergasted. Now I really am fantasising about stringing him up somewhere. Maybe nailing him to a wall. He'd make a very good toilet-paper dispenser.

'You invented the whole lot?'

He eyes me smugly.

'Well, look at me, for goodness' sake! Do I really look as if I've ever been abandoned by anyone?'

I grit my teeth, but this is stronger than me. It needs to come out.

'You, no, but your heart's clearly been left at a motorway service station.'

I leave his studio before I say too much. Maybe sometimes, under the ice, all you find is more snow.

Chapter 35

I've always had trouble getting up in the morning.

Even as a child, it was a whole performance. My mother opened hostilities by coming to stroke my head and whisper my name a good twenty minutes before I was due to get up. Then my father entered the arena and, determined to make an impact, pushed aside the shutters, my duvet and my deluge of groans. However much I fought and hoped that, by wanting it enough, I could make my mother, my father and the day go away for a few more hours, I always ended up losing. Morning has always beaten me.

It still does, but I haven't given up the fight. The alarm on my phone has now replaced my parents' assaults. I've set up four of them, each taking over from its predecessor after a five-minute struggle. The first alarm is birdsong. The second, Beyoncé's 'Crazy in Love'. The third, a bugle. The fourth, the music from *Jaws*. Pretty effective, I have to confess, although I'm always scared I'll see a shark when I open the shutters.

What I really love are days when I don't have to set an alarm. Leaving my brain to surface when it feels like it, taking time to stretch, sometimes going back to sleep, or staying there, doing nothing. That's exactly what I have planned this morning.

Since I've been here, I've made a point of keeping busy on my days off. I started with things that needed doing: decorating the studio, putting my belongings away, sorting out my change of address and dealing with a backlog of paperwork. Then I went for leisure pursuits: walks, films, reading, crosswords, shopping. When I thought about branching out into making figurines with clothes pegs, I realised I was avoiding something. Boredom would give my mind too much space, so I was keeping busy. Doing to avoid thinking.

I know what I'm running away from. I sometimes have a dream; always the same dream.

A car. Oh, she's quite a sight with her gleaming paintwork, flashing chrome and all-weather tyres. She's hurtling along at top speed, not taking much interest in the scenery because she has to get there: it's where everyone's going. The destination is programmed into the GPS, she's on autopilot, happy to be steered. Occasionally, she hits a rut or a pothole that gives the shock absorbers a good run for their money, but she always sets off again, all the more determined. Forging ahead.

Then, one day, a wall.

She didn't see it coming. She's blown to smithereens. It's brutal, violent, explosive. There are pieces of her all over the place. A seat to the right, a pedal to the left, the engine on fire. For a moment she thinks it's all over; part of her even hopes it is.

She stays there for a while, studying the scene as if looking at another car, then she decides to put herself back together. She tells herself someone might come to help, but no one does. So she builds herself up again on her own, piece by piece, bit by bit. It takes time; she gets it wrong sometimes and has to start again; it's a slow process.

And then she's the same magnificent car that everyone knows and loves. If you look closely, there are a few scratches, one tyre is flat and the engine makes a funny noise, but the overall impression creates the illusion. Except for one detail. In the impact, she lost one of her passengers. He's there, by the side of the road; he's stopped moving, stopped responding. She loves this passenger. She's known him since she was first built, she's got used to the feeling of him on her seats, his voice inside her. She was planning to travel further with him. She doesn't want to leave him there, by the side of the road, next to the milestone marking 8 August. She doesn't want to travel on without him. But a mechanic comes by and doesn't give her the choice: 'If you don't set off now, you'll be lost, too. That's how the road works. It's not easy.'

So she sets off again. A little more slowly, paying more attention to the scenery and watching out for ruts, bumps and unexpected walls. And, in the rear-view mirror, watching her passenger get smaller and smaller.

The year that's just passed has been a succession of walls that have compromised my bodywork. I need to find the courage to look in the rear-view mirror. I need to find the strength to keep going without worrying about every tiny pebble on the road. So when I went to bed yesterday evening, I decided that today would be devoted to that. Thinking, and crying. So that I finally accept things.

Eight months to realise that being an ostrich isn't the answer: who'd have thought I have a psychology degree.

It's after ten when I wake up. I suspect my subconscious of trying to sabotage my plans. I peel back the duvet with some regret and have a long stretch, wondering as I do how it is that in films, women stretching look like models during a photo shoot, while I look like a turkey with paralysis.

The coffee is percolating and I'm hovering between chocolate-filled biscuits and orange-filled ones when someone knocks at my door. Well, when I say 'knock', I should really say 'someone's bashing my door down'. I open it cautiously, expecting to see a battering ram, but Clara is on the landing, her cheeks flooded with tears.

I instantly know that my day of introspection has had it.

'I know you're not working today, but we're going to need you,' she says, between sobs.

'What's going on?'

She dissolves completely and manages to splutter, 'Miss Granny 2004's died.'

Chapter 36

All the residents are gathered in the communal living room and, today, that name has special significance. Those who've coped with the shock are drying the tears of those who are devastated, there's a steady stream of hugs and comforting words, yesterday's enemies are friends today. Pain has a lot of down-sides but one positive: it brings people together.

I join Elisabeth and Louise, who are at the table they share with Marilyn every lunchtime. They're inconsolable. Team Granny has suffered an amputation.

'We know this has to happen,' Elisabeth says, wiping her nose on an embroidered handkerchief, 'but I never thought she'd go before me . . . Apart from the Alzheimer's, she was so fit and well.'

Louise sits in silence, but I can see the sorrow in her eyes. At her age, she must already be acquainted with loss. No point in my trotting out the usual speech about the stages of grief. All I can do is be here, offer to listen to them and acknowledge their pain, putting my own to one side. I'm going to miss that Miss Granny.

'I've been here long enough,' Elisabeth continues. 'You'd have thought I'd be used to it. I've seen others go.

But this is more than I can cope with. I'll never accept it. We live and breathe and make plans, then suddenly we stop. Life is like a house of cards. You take ages building it up, trying to give it a solid base and working your way up through the different levels, then one day the whole thing collapses and someone puts the cards away in a box. What's the point? Can you tell me?'

No, I can't. Because I ask myself the same question. Because death is a subject that completely paralyses me and stops me thinking straight. I can't accept it either, I can't accept the fact that one day we stop feeling, hearing, loving, existing. I wonder where we go afterwards, too, and it terrifies me. So, no, I can't say what the point is because, try as I might, I can't see it.

Gustave and Pierre come over to us. Pierre strokes his wife's back and Gustave hands a cup of hot chocolate to Louise.

'I know you like it, I thought it might help.'

She tries to form a smile, but it instantly morphs into a grimace of misery and she dissolves into tears. He squeezes her shoulder and turns away discreetly.

'I'll be in the vegetable garden if you need me.'

She nods and he walks away. Elisabeth pulls another hankie from her pocket and hands it to Louise.

'We still have each other, my dear friend. We're going to stick together and keep each other company to the end. That's what Marilyn would have wanted, I'm sure of it.'

'You're right,' Louise replies in a shaky voice. 'We'll

honour her memory by staying cheerful. But I also think I've forgotten how to grieve . . . I just need a bit of time to cry.'

'Of course it'll take time! We should give her all the tears she deserves and then we'll honour her memory. And I've got an idea about how to do that!' Elisabeth says, her face brightening.

I'm about to ask her for details when the director bursts into the room and waves me over to join her. Before I leave, I remind the two remaining members of Team Granny that I'm there for them if and when they need to talk.

Anne-Marie leads me outside.

'Are you handling this okay?' she asks.

'I think so. I'm working my way round the residents to find out how they're all reacting and I'll organise some group therapy as soon as possible.'

'Good,' she says, nodding. 'Deaths are a tricky time: if you have any problems, come and talk to me.'

'I will. For now, it's fine.'

'But the hardest part is yet to come.'

'Really? What could be harder?'

She runs a hand through her curls and heaves a long sigh.

'Marilyn's family will be here soon.'

Chapter 37

Grief can try all it likes to hide, but it's still as clear as an angry red spot on the end of a nose.

I go to meet Marilyn's elder daughter, Corinne, in the car park. She looks just the same as she has done every Monday, Wednesday and Saturday morning, when she'd come to visit her mother at ten o'clock sharp and the two of them would walk around the grounds of Ocean View arm in arm. Her hair in an impeccable chignon, an affable smile, shoes to match her handbag. But if we're playing spot the difference, we might notice that, today, she doesn't take off her sunglasses and the words come tumbling urgently out of her mouth.

'My brother's on his way, he's coming from Rouen with his wife. I'll start sorting out her things on my own, then it'll be done, my son might come to help a bit in his lunch break.'

'You don't have to do it today. Take as much time as you need, there's no rush.'

'But then we'll be out of your way,' she replies, reaching for some empty boxes in the boot of the car. 'It'll be fine, it'll be fine. My mother didn't like to be any trouble. If you want to take on a new resident, I need to empty her studio. There's not much left, anyway. It won't take long.'

She freezes and stares right at me.

'Do you know whether she suffered?'

Her question feels like a punch in the jaw. Whatever age we are, we ask the same questions when we lose someone.

'You'll be meeting the doctor – he should be able to tell you – but, on the face of it, no, she won't have suffered. She died in her sleep.'

She takes a shuddering, deep breath.

'I hope she had a nice last evening . . .'

I think back to yesterday's supper. As usual, Marilyn sat with Louise, Elisabeth, Pierre, Gustave and Leon. I didn't think her any different; she was wearing her sash and teasing her grumpy neighbour. Then we watched *Plus belle la vie*. She was upset to see Luna abandoned by Guillaume, and as she left the room she made a wish that everything would work out between them. She'll never know.

'I think she did,' I say. 'At least, she was still smiling her lovely smile when she wished us goodnight.'

My throat constricts as I say these words. I'm very sad to think I'll never see Miss Granny 2004 again. I dread to think what state her daughter's throat is in.

I go to the studio with Corinne. It's the last time she'll make this journey. She puts her hand on the doorknob and looks at me. I understand what she's not saying.

'Would you like to be alone?'

'Thank you, I'd prefer it.'

'I'll be outside if you need me. I'll pop back in to see you in a bit. I hope you're okay . . .'

I walk away as she goes into the room.

I sit on the steps by the front door, dragging furiously on a cigarette and trying to concentrate on the leaves coming out on the trees, the swell of the waves, a plane flying overhead – anything rather than think about what's going on only metres away.

When I came to work in a retirement home, I was well aware I'd be confronted with mortality. The residents at Ocean View may be in good shape, but they're still human. And past eighty, a human is no longer under guarantee. It can stop working, break down with no warning. Until a few months ago, I rated the seriousness of a death by the person's age. I used stock phrases that suited my ignorant young convictions: 'Yes, but hang on, it's okay to go at eighty, you've had your fair share of time, you need to make way for younger generations!'; 'I don't understand why people cry when someone old dies . . .' as if 'The Old' were a different species, worth less in the great lottery of life.

I sometimes feel I'm not the same person.

Despite my best efforts, my thoughts keep coming back to the inside of the building. I've been through it recently, what Miss Granny 2004's daughter is doing now. I know what's going on inside studio five. She holds her breath every time she hears footsteps, in the hopes her mother will come through the door. She strokes photographs and buries her face in Marilyn's nightdress, trying to find the smell she's known since the day she was born. She smiles when she comes across the grandchildren's drawings, kept lovingly in a folder. Things are more than just objects to the person they belong to. They're memories, a comfort, a necessity, part of life. This is all the truer for the elderly, who must make careful choices about the few things they have in their last room. Putting them away in a cardboard box means accepting that this beloved person has gone. I can't stay here smoking when, nearby, someone's going through the most painful moments of her life.

When I go into the studio, Corinne is on the sofa with a box on her lap. With a nod, she invites me to sit beside her. I settle down next to her and have a quick look at the box. Grey cardboard, stickers showing the style and price, no different from any other shoe box. No different at all, except for the words written on the lid in wobbly felt-tip:

For my children.
To be opened after my death.

Chapter 38

I made us some coffee. Corinne said she didn't need it, but she downed hers in one. She rubbed her hands together, steeling herself, then opened the box. I said I could wait outside; she said I could definitely stay.

It's just papers. Silly, I know, but I felt a moment of relief, as if I was expecting to see a human ear. Two photos and three envelopes, one of which has the words 'To be read first' on it. So she does.

My dear children,

If you're reading this, then I must be gone. I've always thought that a ridiculous statement when I've heard it in sentimental films, but here I am using it . . .

First of all, I want you to know I love you with all my heart. You've been the greatest happiness of my life, closely followed by the grandchildren you've given me. I know you're sad, and I hope you won't be for too long. I'm sorry I can't put my arms around you and tell you everything's going to be all right. Failing that, I'll promise you one thing: if there really is something up there, I'm going to find myself a comfortable armchair and watch you while I wait for you to join me. Don't cry too much, otherwise I'll cry, too, and you'll complain about the weather.

The second thing I wanted to talk to you about I've never told anyone. I thought of doing it several times, but I wasn't sure it mattered and was worried about upsetting you. I could have got rid of this box, but I didn't have the strength. You're bound to find out when you sort out my things. So I owe you some explanations.

Corinne stops reading, gets up and drifts across the room.

'I'm not sure I want to know . . .'

'Do what you feel is right. You can wait for your brother. It might be easier if you're not alone.'

She shakes her head.

'I don't know. If I decide to keep reading, I'd rather do it before he arrives. I've no idea what sort of revelation she's going to make, and I know my brother – he could react badly. I'm expecting the worst.'

'Of course I didn't know your mother anything like as well as you, but I'm almost sure she wouldn't have left you with a confession that could hurt you.'

'You're right, she wanted us to be happy,' she agrees, turning her back to me to hide the tears that are threatening to spill from her eyes. 'But I'm frightened. I know she had a terrible time with Dad; he wasn't easy. He drank a lot and hit hard . . . When I was little, I could tell whether it was going to be a good or bad evening from the way he

165

opened the door when he arrived home from work. It was often bad. It's a shame; he was kind when he hadn't been drinking. I think Mum was relieved when he was no longer there to come through the door. Cirrhosis of the liver; it took him away in two months. I've hated alcohol ever since, and squeaky door handles. It took me years to stop being angry with him, and I'm worried my mother's words will reopen old wounds . . . What would you do?'

Oh, wow! If there's one thing I know, it's that family affairs are like overtight skinny jeans: it's better to keep out of them. So, like the good, neutral and dependable psychologist I am, I decide to avoid the question . . . well, for three and a half seconds.

'I think, if I were you, I'd already know the letter by heart. I'm the sort who evaluates the risks after taking action.'

As if I've just given her the incentive she needs, Corinne sits back down and starts reading again:

I'll let you have a look at what's in the box before you read the rest. I'll explain everything.

The first photo is black and white. A dark-haired young woman and a tall, fair-haired soldier smiling and holding hands. The picture is so alive you almost expect to hear the laughter they're struggling to stifle and the photographer asking them to take this a bit more seriously and look at the camera.

The second photo is more recent. In a flower-filled

garden, an old man poses in a deckchair with a smiling child in his arms.

Corinne looks at me.

'I don't know this man. But I think the woman in the first photo is my mother when she was very young . . .'

She appears to think for a few seconds, then takes the envelope that is most yellowed with age. An address in black ink is written on the front.

> *Madame Raymonde Noyre (née Pontel)*
> *7 allée des Acacias*
> *33400 TALENCE*
> *France*

I knew that Marilyn's real name was Raymonde. She told me that she'd made the change when her husband died, because a film star's name sat better with the personality she wanted to have. She was right: it suited her well.

The flap no longer sticks down, proof that the envelope has been opened many times.

Corinne reads out loud:

Berlin, 15 September 1947

My dearest Raymonde,
  I write to you with a very heavy, despairing heart.
  I've just found all your letters. I read of your love, your pain and your disappointment . . . through to your last letter.

I realise it is too late, but I want to assure you it wasn't for want of love or out of cowardice that I did not keep my word. When I asked your father for your hand, I'd never been more sincere in my life. I can imagine no stronger love than ours. Every day, I thank fate for bringing us together. Seeing you every evening was my one reason to live, in those dark times. I beg you to believe me.

I promised to come back for you at the end of the war and marry you. I didn't keep that promise, and I will suffer for that for the rest of my days.

In your last letter you announced that you were to be married. Please believe me when I say I understand your decision. You waited for me for nearly two years, with no sign of life, no reply to your letters, convinced I'd forgotten about you . . . that was so far from the truth.

For those two years, I was a prisoner-of-war in the Soviet Union, as many Germans were. For those two years, I thought of you night and day. Memories of our long conversations, your smile and the kiss you granted me on our last evening gave me the strength to carry on. The moment I was liberated, I could think of only one thing: finding you and honouring my promise. But it's too late, and I'm devastated.

I know I'll never love a woman as I love you. Part of my heart belongs to you and will always be yours. The war brought us together, the war separated us. I have no regrets. I would rather have lived those few months of happiness in your company and weep for you the whole rest of my life than never have known you.

I will leave you in peace now, but I owed you this last explanation. I hope you will be happy, you deserve to be.
  Your ever loving
  Helmut

Without a word, without betraying the least emotion, Corinne puts the letter back in its envelope and takes out the second.

I don't know how she does it. I'm gritting my teeth with all my might to stop myself breaking down.

Berlin, 4 January 2013

Dear Madame,

  I am the wife of Helmut Steinkamp, whom you met in France. I'm afraid I'm writing to bring you the sad news that we lost him last month. Shortly before he died, he told me his one last wish was to contact you. He wanted to go with a clear conscience. So I am honouring a promise I made to him.

  He told me about how you met and fell in love during the war. He wanted you to know he never forgot you. He loved you very much. I met him in 1950 and we had three children, a boy and two girls. Helmut was a good and generous man whose death has left a terrible hole in our lives. I think he was happy.

  I'm enclosing a picture of him taken last year, with our great-grandson Oliver.

You and I loved the same man, which is why I feel close to you, and I'd like to take the liberty of saying you have my complete affection. If you would like to reply, we could talk.
Yours sincerely
Veronica Steinkamp

PS My son, who teaches French, translated my letter. Please forgive me if there are mistakes, I don't speak your beautiful language.
PPS My son found your address on the internet. If this letter isn't addressed to you but you are related to Raymonde Noyre, née Pontel, please could you forward it to her.

I stopped gritting my teeth on the last paragraph. There's no point trying to hold it in: I now look like a freshly exploded water bomb. Corinne is in the same state.

What a waste! I thought this sort of story only happened in films. But in the days before Facebook helped people get back in touch, lots of paths must have diverged like this.

Corinne picks up her mother's letter again and strokes it. Patterns of ink on paper have the power to link past and present, writer and reader.

'I only ever thought of my mother as a mother,' she whispers between two sobs. 'I never tried to find out more about her, to see the woman in her. She must have been so unhappy . . .'

'I think we all do the same,' I tell her, trying to pull

myself together. 'Don't blame yourself. It's hard to see your own parents as real people.'

As I say this, I realise that I've never seen my mother in any other way; particularly when my father died. I saw her as the person consoling her daughters, the person organising the funeral, the person still soldiering on, even if she was slightly out of step. Of course I realised that life without him would be difficult for her. But I didn't see the woman who had just lost her other half, lost the man she had chosen to live her life with. I didn't see the woman waiting till night time to shed her tears in a heartbreakingly empty bed. I saw Mum, but not Christine.

Corinne makes us some more coffee and starts reading the rest of Marilyn's letter. It's the last part, her final message. Perhaps that's why Corinne reads it more slowly.

If you've read the two letters and seen the photos, I'm sure you now understand, my darlings.

I met Helmut in 1944. I was still living with my parents, near Bordeaux, at the time. They ran a café which was near a large house requisitioned by the Germans. We were not fond of them – your grandfather even started refusing to serve them. But we didn't really have a choice . . .

I noticed Helmut straight away. He had gentle eyes, which lit up whenever he saw me. We exchanged a few words, then sentences, then our feelings. We met every evening, when everyone else was asleep, and we chatted, sometimes right through the night. I taught him French and he sang me German songs. He was tender, gallant, sensitive and devastatingly kind. I often wondered what he was doing there . . . and so did he.

My parents learned to accept him, to get to know him and not see him as a Boche, so much so that when Helmut asked for my hand, my father agreed. It was the day Helmut left, and he promised to come back soon. It was both the most wonderful and the most painful day of my young life.

You know what happened after that. I waited two years for him, and I thought I would die of a broken heart. He'd abandoned me, I was sure of it.

Your father was a regular customer in the café; he seemed kind, if a little gruff. I thought that, with him, I would manage to forget Helmut and find some semblance of happiness. When I received the letter telling me Helmut had been imprisoned, I'd just found out I was pregnant with you, Corinne. It was you three who kept me going, my darlings. I so loved fussing over my beloved children, taking care of you, watching you grow and turn into wonderful people, that I have no regrets. I've had a happy life. I couldn't have wished for a better one. But every day God gave me, I remembered Helmut, with a heavy heart.

I hope that I'm by his side now. But I'm sorry I'm no longer with you. I'm going to miss you, my little ones. I hope you'll remember the one lesson I really tried to teach you: make every day a happy memory. In the end, happiness is the only thing you take with you.

I love you with all my heart.
Mum

I'm holding Corinne's hand in mine. Not one particle of me is a psychologist any more. Right now, I'm made up of 99 per cent water and 1 per cent snot. If I listened to my instincts, I'd take her in my arms and rock her like a baby. It might be just a teensy bit inappropriate.

'It's terrible,' she says, taking her four hundred thousandth tissue from the box. 'I can't take on board the fact I'll never see her again. She's the person I turn to whenever I have something important to share, whether it's happy or not. When I was told she'd died, she was the person I wanted to call to be comforted . . . I'm going to miss her so much!'

'Do you have family around you?'

'Yes, yes, I have my husband, and my children aren't far away. But it's not the same. I'm no longer anyone's daughter,' she wails, sobbing with all the more abandon. 'Losing a parent means losing your childhood. I feel no one will understand me now . . .'

I put my hand on her shoulder.

'Your brother shouldn't be long. It'll do you good to see him.'

'Yes, probably. I can't wait to see him and my sister. Sometimes I wish we were little children again, mollycoddled by our mother.'

She gets up and starts emptying Marilyn's wardrobe into a box.

'I'm sorry,' she says. 'I shouldn't be crying like this. If Mum were here, she'd say I should look on the bright side, we were lucky to have her for so long. She would be right – lots of people are younger when they lose their parents. Maybe I'll be able to get this in perspective tomorrow. But I just can't today.'

'But that's completely normal! Cry as much as you like, feel sorry for yourself, go to pieces. If you can't be unhappy when you lose your mother, when can you be?'

Someone opens the door just as her tears are spilling again. A couple in their sixties with reddened eyes come into the studio just as Corinne takes the 'Miss Granny 2004' sash from the wardrobe, the one that lived permanently around her mother's neck. She throws herself into her brother's arms. Time to leave them alone.

I slip out discreetly and close the door behind me. My legs feel like pieces of string carrying enormously heavy weights. Every step requires a superhuman effort. I've just been hit by a runaway train, and death and despair were both on board. It's going to take a while to get myself back together. But before that, there's something more urgent I have to do.

I go back to my studio, drop down on to the sofa and make the call. She picks up on the second ring.

'Hello, Mum, it's Julia. I just wanted to say I love you.'

Chapter 39

My head is spinning when I go to bed.

Earlier this evening, we met up in Greg's studio: Clara, Greg and me facing our sadness together. We had quite a lot to drink, and did quite a lot of crying, too. We told each other things usually kept for old friends, or for those sharing an ordeal.

It's at times like this that I'm really struck by the feeling that, deep down, we're all the same. Whether we live in France or Mali; whether we have curly hair, straight hair or no hair at all; whether we prefer languages or chemistry; whether we're generous-hearted or pessimistic . . . we all have the same joys, are knocked back by the same crises, feel the same pain and experience the same happiness. Emotions, that's what they're called. Universal stuff.

Greg opened up to us about his mother's illness for the first time. She's more or less pulled through now, but for many years their lives were punctuated by her spells in hospital, her chemotherapy and all its side-effects, periods of hope and times of crushing news. Clara talked about her brother, who died in a scooter accident when she was sixteen, she told us about the empty space he left, one child down in the family, and about her father, who's never recovered from it. I told them about my father, and the grief I seem to be floundering in, unable to move on. And I talked about Nannynoo, a bit, too.

All this pain in one small studio: at one point, I thought the walls would explode. But no, we just poured ourselves another glass.

Sometimes I get a strange feeling that life is a computer game. You start the game with several full stores: the serenity store, the strength store, the energy store and the joy store. Along the way, you come across enemies, stand up to attacks, sometimes choose a wrong path, tread on landmines, fall down holes and tackle obstacles. Each time this happens, your stores are depleted, but 'Happiness' bonuses help you fill them again. The 'Marriage' bonus, the 'Birth of a Child' bonus, the 'Promotion' bonus. These bonuses are precious: they determine how well you do in the game, sometimes even how long it goes on. At the end of each level, you have to confront a huge monster. The most terrifying of these include the 'Bereavement' monster, the 'Serious Illness' monster, the 'Unemployment' monster and the 'Break-up' monster. They're tough, it takes time to deal with them. And even if you do, they always use up a good chunk from each store. Eventually, the bonuses just aren't good enough to reinstate your joy, energy and strength.

I'm young, I haven't yet confronted all my monsters. My stores are far from empty. But where will they be in fifty years' time? What if that's why you sometimes meet old people who are defeatist? What if they actually know the truth? What if squaring up to several monsters has seriously drained their stores?

What if I stopped drinking?

Chapter 40

The idea popped up when no one was really looking. It was Elisabeth who voiced it, two days after Marilyn died. Everyone thought it was a good idea so we've gone to considerable lengths to arrange this unusual memorial.

The communal living room is serving as the auditorium. The stage area is edged with tables covered in white paper tablecloths and decorated with cuttings from the grounds arranged by the residents – some more artfully than others. Strings of lights, not all of them working, are hung along the walls. Coloured spotlights point towards a large banner strung all the way across the room. The wording on the banner leaves no room for doubt about the occasion:

Miss and Mr Ocean View Auditions

If Julia Morley saw that, she'd be spitting feathers.

The set-up may be makeshift but it's implemented with steely determination. Everyone has his or her own small part to play, and the retirement home has been transformed into a cheerful hive of activity, an escape route out of the dark tunnel we've all been in.

Marilyn's children are sitting in the front row. The residents who don't want to be considered for election have joined the audience, while my colleagues and I busy around in the wings (normally known as the kitchen), putting together costumes, make-up and last-minute adjustments for the candidates. There is no jury: the winning couple will be determined by the loudest applause. The tension is palpable, with residents rehearsing their performances in quiet corners to maintain the element of surprise. If anyone had ever told me I'd one day attend the selection of a Miss anything, I'd have laughed. If they'd said that I'd also be quivering with impatience, I'd have asked to be committed as a preventative measure.

I come and join the audience after arranging Arlette's hair. I did well, having only very fine hair to hide her hearing-aids and make a bun that doesn't look like a snail. When I finished, she gratified me with a pat on the cheek, which was probably intended to be gentle. I think that means she was pleased. Meanwhile, my ear is buzzing.

Clara has kept a place for me on her left, Greg is already to her right.

'Quick, it's starting,' she says as I sit down.

And it certainly is.

Isabelle has taken on the role of presenter. She's wearing a full-length dress covered in diamante for the occasion. Every time I look at it, I feel as if I'm having an examination at the optometrist.

'Welcome to the Miss and Mr Ocean View Auditions!'

she booms into the mic. 'As you know, this ceremony is intended to honour the memory of our dear Marilyn, who has now joined the stars and is shining in the dark skies among the clouds and the planets.'

I look at Clara. Clara looks at me. Greg looks at Clara. Clara looks at Greg. Greg looks at me. I look at Greg. I think we all agree. Isabelle is out to lunch.

She continues with her introduction, accompanied by theatrical gestures, until Anne-Marie comes to whisper in her ear. Then Isabelle finally announces the first contender and withdraws, but not before giving an elaborate curtsey.

Lucienne is first on stage. She introduces herself in the traditional style of Miss competitions – with one difference: at her age, you're not defined by your profession but by how many descendants you have. Lucienne has a son and a grandson, and that's all, which basically means she's right at the bottom of the Granny scale. Luckily, her clarinet solo is a success and the audience clap loudly. I join them, more to make Lucienne happy than out of genuine enthusiasm. Listening to her, I was transported back twenty years to my own music lessons when we were learning '*Frère Jacques*' on the recorder.

Gustave is next up, sporting the perfect illusionist's costume: tailcoat, top hat, walking frame decorated with gold tinsel and an air of mystery. Exaggerating his every move, he shows us a pack of cards, chooses one, shows it to the audience, puts it back with the others, shuffles the pack, blows on to it and – it's a miracle! 'Before your astonished eyes, the queen of spades is at the top of the pack!' Our astonished eyes are confused: the queen of spades looks incredibly like the nine of hearts. Gustave frowns. 'That's extraordinary, it normally works every time.' Clearly, every time except two, but on the third attempt the queen of spades deigns to appear and Gustave earns a round of applause.

Louise comes on to the stage before Gustave has left. He adjusts the mic to the right height for her then skedaddles while she unfolds a piece of paper. 'My memory needs some help,' she explains. She introduces herself, as well as her four children, ten grandchildren and two great-grandchildren. Then she gives a little cough before closing her eyes and with that half-strong, half-fragile voice peculiar to old ladies, launching into Edith Piaf's 'Non, Je ne Regrette Rien.'

When the song ends, the only sounds are the whistle of the microphone and a few sniffs. The audience is overcome with emotion. I've got shivers from the top of my head to the tips of my toes. For a few suspenseful moments, Louise looks around and seems to realise where she is, and then Gustave gets to his feet and starts clapping wildly, immediately followed by every member of the audience. Memories of Marilyn make the lyrics particularly poignant. Her three children are in tears.

As I sit back down, out of the corner of my eye I see Greg's hand discreetly squeezing Clara's then go back to rest on his own thigh. There are only two possible explanations: either something I don't know about is going on, or Greg is developing a neurological complaint that produces involuntary movements. I need to get to the bottom of this.

Isabelle makes a brief appearance on stage to check that everything is where it should be, and everyone has noticed that she's crying. Her dress looks more and more glittery. I can distinctly hear my retinas bidding me farewell.

Now it's Elisabeth and Pierre's turn: they've chosen to compete as a couple. Wearing evening dress straight out of the fifties, the two lovebirds stand facing each other, looking extremely serious. The old man puts his left hand against his wife's back, draws her gently to him and raises his right hand, which Elisabeth takes. Then she smiles at her husband, and they embark on their first steps as 'The Blue Danube' plays.

There is the occasional mix-up of feet, the odd groan, a few steps in the wrong direction, but the only thing we really see is the love between the two of them. It's all expressed in two or three minutes of dancing. The delicate way he holds her hand. The confidence she shows in him guiding her. The tenderness in her remonstrances when he steps on her foot. The mistakes quickly forgotten. Their eyes glued on each other. The negative overcome by the positive. Their synchronicity, which seems so natural. They make a beautiful couple. Decades ago, they chose each other to take a long walk down an unknown path. Here they are now, almost at the end of the journey, tired, out of breath, tested by wounds along the way, but, as they confided to me: if they could have only one word to describe their life, it would be 'gratitude'. 'Not everyone is lucky enough to find the person who will spend a lifetime with them and still love them as they did on the first day when they reach the last,' Elisabeth told me during one of our sessions. 'For that alone, I regret that life's so short,' Pierre added. 'I'd like to spend more time with her.'

I can feel tears ready to roll down my cheeks, and press my eyelids to stop them. I've cried a lot in the last few days. If it goes on, I'll end up freeze-dried and be put into a sachet for astronauts to eat.

Other contenders come on, one after the other: Mina on the accordion, Arlette making shadow puppets, Mohamed doing charcoal sketches, Jules tap-dancing . . . For a moment, we all forget where we are. We should do this more often.

Isabelle takes the mic one last time, euphoric in her disco-ball gown. If she could, she'd actually be spinning. All the contenders have performed; they now have to come and bow in turn so the applause can be measured and the winners decided.

At the end of the parade, my hands are throbbing from so much clapping. Leon has offered to measure the applause using an app on his tablet. Some saw this as an extraordinary show of generosity on his part, but he quickly quashed them: he loathes cheating and approximation; he's doing this only in the interests of having a reliable result. Well, that's reassuring.

Three contenders now need to be separated in a second clap-off: Louise, Gustave, and Elisabeth and Pierre. In the end, it's the first two who are named Miss and Mr Ocean View, to the warm congratulations of all the other participants. Isabelle is quick to put a sash on each of them as a symbol of their coronation, and can't resist ending with a speech.

'Thank you, all of you, for this wonderful occasion. It was a beautiful memorial to our unforgettable Miss Granny, whose flame will continue to burn in our grieving hearts. That's life, as they say! Congratulations to Louise and Gustave, who certainly deserve to win . . .'

She looks over to them for a few seconds as they stand at the side of the stage, then continues, 'Aren't they sweet together? I mean, really, it's plain as plain can be that something's going on between them, isn't it?'

Louise opens her eyes wide. Gustave blushes all the way down to his walking frame. Embarrassment hovers over the audience.

'It's true, though!' she keeps going. 'Okay, they're different. Louise is on the sophisticated side and Gustave likes whoopee cushions, but they do say opposites attract . . . Go on, give us something to dream about! Give her a kiss! Give her a kiss! Give her a kiss!'

She starts slow-hand-clapping and encourages the audience to join her. In vain. And yet, to everyone's astonishment, Louise gives Gustave a private smile and offers up her lips, where he places a tender kiss which doesn't look like the first. There's a storm of applause: the audience is overjoyed. Clara, Greg and I try to start a Mexican wave. You'd think a golden goal had been scored.

We couldn't have dreamed of a better end to this memorial to Marilyn. If she really has found a comfortable armchair up there, I'm sure she and Helmut are dancing for joy.

Chapter 41

Our plan was perfect. No need to come up with a plan B. It took us a while to fine-tune it, mind you. A whole evening spent dreaming up the best way to restore Clara's ego without actually ruining her ex's wedding. Greg and I had to be quite persuasive; otherwise, the guests might have seen a family of wild boar pitching up at the reception. Or they could have been eating maggots. Or all found they had novelty penises attached to their windscreen wipers. Having the DJ locked up and the bride's dress shredded by specially trained bats were also options considered. There was no stopping Clara.

We eventually agreed on an unusual wedding gift. The strategy was simple: we would manage to get into the hall hired for the occasion, leave the parcel and slip out again. Casual as you please. I was chosen: no one knows me, and I'm ordinary looking – Clara's words; she tried to redeem herself by saying that it was a compliment, it meant I had a universal sort of beauty. Hmm. So I would put the parcel in the room and we'd hide outside one of the many windows, waiting to see Guillaume's reaction when he opened it.

Clara wanted to keep an element of surprise by not

telling us what would be inside. She said it was bound to embarrass him but without spoiling the party or doing the bride any harm. We did check it wasn't a bomb, then agreed to it. It was such a brilliant idea, we opened a third bottle.

It's nearly 9 p.m. It's dark and cold, and we've been staked out by a small, dirty window for hours, standing in the ditch at the back of the hall: the plan doesn't feel so perfect now. Our prying eyes have watched the arrival of the bride and groom, the speeches, the toast, the group photographs, the sit-down meal, two performances, a slide show . . . I'm pretty close to overdosing on this. If someone invited me to a wedding now, I'd make them eat the plastic figures on the cake. But Clara doesn't want to leave. Not until the presents have been opened.

'You never know,' I try to argue. 'They might not open them till tomorrow. Or right at the end. There's still the cutting of the cake, the first dance and probably other things. Are you sure you don't want to go home?'

'Absolutely sure. We didn't do all this for nothing.'

Greg shrugs. No point even trying to get him to help me. He'd walk through Biarritz naked with a seagull's feather up his bum if Clara asked him to. So I blow on my hands to warm them, hoping the opening of the presents will be the next event.

Someone must have taken that as a prayer because, a minute later, all the guests gather around the table where the presents are displayed. The small white box wrapped by Clara is definitely among them, right where I left it, before sneaking back out. The newly-weds are directly in our line of sight, looking radiant. I don't know how Clara can bear to watch. Knowing that the man you love is happy with someone else is one thing, but having their happiness showcased before your very eyes, seeing them kiss, hug, whisper in each other's ears then giggle, wear matching outfits, accept congratulations from their friends and family, cry as they watch a slideshow of their relationship and dry each other's tears with kisses . . . that must be torture. It should have been her. Of course she doesn't want to leave until she's had her satisfaction, I see that now.

The first presents have been opened: sheets embroidered with their names, silver cutlery, matching pyjamas . . . the couple give little squeals of joy. You have to be very happy indeed to go into ecstasies over a set of forks.

It's the bride who picks up the small white box. She shakes it, as if trying to guess what's inside. Let's hope it's not an animal. The groom pulls on the ribbon to undo it. All the cameras are trained on them. Greg puts his arm around Clara's shoulders. She's shaking. So am I. The lid comes off the box. The bride reaches in and takes out a small piece of white lace.

'Knickers?' I hiss. 'Your brilliant present is a pair of knickers?'

'It's the first pair he gave me,' she explains, not taking her eyes off the scene. 'I always wore them for special occasions. He'll recognise them, for sure.'

The bride goes into raptures, flaunting the pretty lacy panties for all to see. Guillaume's face shows no emotion. One of the guests, probably the inevitable Uncle Knobhead, starts clapping and chanting, 'Put them on! Put them on!' Others join in, the bride laughs and, with some difficulty, puts on the scanty briefs under her voluminous dress. When she's finished, everyone cheers, starting with her husband, then she closes the little white box, crushing Clara's ego in the process.

'If I'd known, I wouldn't have washed them,' she quips, to mask her dejection.

'You going to be okay?' asks Greg.

'Yeah,' she says, walking away from the window. 'Right, shall we go? I told you we should have done the joke dicks.'

Yes, the best thing to do is leave. No point prolonging the pain.

We walk along the back of the building to get to the car while the music starts up for the dancing. I should be pleased: I'll soon be nice and warm in my room. But I feel frustrated. I was the one who came up with the idea of Clara getting her revenge, and now she's miserable. If I'd kept quiet the other night, she would probably have spent the whole day thinking about them, she would have imagined, envisaged, pictured and assumed. But she wouldn't have *seen* them. She's hurting, and it's my fault. We can't leave like this. I know I can't avenge her, but I can cheer her up.

I tug at Greg's arm and whisper a few words in his ear.

He nods and laughs. I start running and drag him towards the main entrance.

'Go back to the lookout point, Clara!' I cry. 'And when you see us come back out, run for the car!'

The walls are reverberating to strains of U2's 'One', and the guests are in a circle around the dance floor. No one notices us walk into the hall. My legs are shaking, and I want to turn back, but I can make out Clara's shadow outside the window at the back. I put my brain on pause and my body on autopilot. Arm in arm, we push our way into the circle, right next to the happy couple, who are absorbed in their slow dance.

Greg starts first. To the astonishment of onlookers, he waves his arms, wiggles his hips, zigzags his feet and claps his hands. A skilled combination of 'Cell Block Tango' and 'The Birdie Song'. I join him, doing an approximation of the can-can, just as the bride and groom become aware of us. I've never been so embarrassed in my life. And I've never laughed so much either. With nothing left to lose, I embark on a succession of balletic leaps – or apoplectic leaps, it's hard to tell – while Greg tackles a triple axel. The newly-weds have stopped dancing and the music has died: we have only a few seconds to produce a fitting finale for our crestfallen friend.

'Have you see *Dirty Dancing*?' I call across to Greg.

He bursts out laughing. He can see where I'm going with this.

As Uncle Knobhead starts lumbering towards me,

I launch myself at Greg, who has put one knee on the floor. When I'm about a metre from him, I push off with my feet to take to the air. We're going to do the most perfect lift in history. I'm a bird, I'm a feather, I'm Baby, I'm . . . I'm flat on the floor, flat on my face, flat as a pancake. Instead of landing delicately on Greg's hands, I smack into him. He sways and falls and we crash-land at the feet of the very confused newly-weds.

It's probably time we left.

We run out of the hall, giggling helplessly, closely followed by dozens of furious guests. Clara is waiting for us by the car, holding her stomach and weeping with laughter. We pulled it off. We jump in, and Greg puts his foot down hard on the accelerator. Clara can't stop thanking us. As we pass the bride and groom's car, a small detail catches our attention. In among the flowers and satin bows, two plastic penises dangle from the ends of the windscreen wipers.

Chapter 42

I had a text from my sister this morning: 'I'll drop by this evening. We need to talk.'

I've tried calling her at least ten times and have sent just as many texts to explain that, what a shame, I won't be at Marion's apartment this evening, so we won't see each other.

My sister goes to Paris regularly for conferences. She's a GP, just like in the games we played when we were little, when I was always the patient.

She hasn't got back to me. Just in case, I've asked Marion to play along for me.

'Okay. If she shows up, I'll drag her off to a restaurant!' she said.

'She definitely mustn't go into the apartment, or she'll see I'm not living there any more.'

'Don't worry, babe, I've got this.'

So I don't worry. Right up until I bump into my sister on my way back to my studio after *Plus belle la vie*.

She's stationed herself by the door to the annexe, her eyes glued to the screen of her phone. All my blood rushes to my face. I'm just contemplating running away, or rolling up into a ball – she might think I'm a stone – when she looks up at me.

'What are you doing here?' I ask.

'I could ask you the same thing,' she says, putting her phone away in her coat pocket.

I put my arms around her and hug her hard. Her hair falls softly against my nose; it smells of memories. I'm ten years old. Afterwards, we can make something with Barbie Fashion Designer and eat Tubble Gum while we watch cartoons. Then Mum and Dad will scold us because we mustn't eat between meals.

'Did you really think I wouldn't find out?'

I let go of her, and of childhood. Suck it up.

'Do you want to come up?'

'I'd rather not.'

The site we choose for my explanations is the bench at the bottom of the garden looking out over a grey sky dissolving into the waves. There's a strong wind. It's almost comforting, the aptness of it. The look on Carole's face does not suit fine weather.

'How did you find out?' I ask, not daring to look at her.

'Marc.'

'Marc? How come?'

'He called me at work yesterday,' she explains. 'He didn't like to go behind your back, but he's worried about you. He says you're very depressed, that he couldn't live with himself if he didn't do something to help.'

'Yeah, right. Arsehole.'

'Yup. That's what I thought, too. Are you planning to tell me what you're up to, or not?'

So I tell her. Dad, the loss, the pain, Nannynoo, Marc, the fear, the emptiness, the excesses, the feeling I no longer belonged in Paris and that my life was going on without me. The job offer and my impulsive application. My longing to tell her everything, my need to hold my tongue. My life here. The feeling that I'm getting back on track. She listens without a word, staring straight ahead, and her hands, clamped on her handbag, seem to say, *I could leave at any minute*. When I've finished, we look each other in the eye. I'm searching for a sign, a hint as to how she's feeling. But she's keeping it all locked away. No access to any emotions there.

'How long have you been here?'

'Four months.'

'Four months . . . does Mum have no idea?'

'None at all.'

'And are you planning to keep this from her much longer?'

'I don't know,' I say quietly. 'I've come a long way since I've been here, but I'm not ready yet.'

'But what the hell are you so afraid of?' she blurts suddenly. 'What frightens you so much you won't tell her the truth? You're wasting time, do you realise that? You can't get it back, as we both know!'

I look away.

'I know,' I say slowly. 'I didn't plan any of this. I ran away. I left my unhappiness behind and hoped it wouldn't follow me. When I arrived here, I was completely lost. I didn't know if it was a fucking huge mistake or a lifesaver. For months, I kept all my emotions tied up in a lump which lived in my throat. I woke every morning frightened of facing the day ahead. The only time I felt okay, apart from when I was asleep, was first thing when I woke in the morning, before my brain remembered what was going on in my life. Then I had to face reality. A few weeks ago now, the lump disappeared. I think I made the right decision.'

Her expression has softened, I think. I hope.

'Good for you, Jules. Really, I'm happy you've found a way to feel better. But I'm furious. I'm seriously angry with you. We're a family, for fuck's sake! I thought we were close! I was already angry at you for not being around much after Dad died. Before, never a week went by when you didn't call – you'd come down from Paris at the first opportunity, we knew everything that was going on in your life, and you in ours. I told myself it was your way of coping with it all, and that, even if I did things differently, I had to accept that you needed to withdraw like this. There are so many things I wish we'd shared . . . I felt so alone, having to cope with my grief, and with Mum's. Because, yes, funnily enough: Mum's having a tough time. It wouldn't have been overkill if we'd supported her together, you know. And not being able to help you hurt me, too. You rejected all my attempts. I could see you were struggling. But there it was. Everyone copes in their own way. I told myself what really mattered was that you got through this, with or without us. We'd see each other again, eventually. Like before. And now I find out you've been here for four months. Just down the road . . .'

She heaves a deep sigh.

'I love you, Julia. I love you with all my heart and I'll never stop loving you. But something's broken here. You've let me down, and I don't know whether that can ever be fixed.'

I'm stunned. Lacerated by my sister's words. I don't even have the strength to reply. I feel paralysed, as if in a state of shock. But there's plenty I'd like to say back to her. That she's the selfish one, throwing all this at me when I'm so fragile, that I have every right to protect myself as I see fit, that I'm there for Mum, too, even if it's not as much as she is. I want to argue with her and deviously twist the situation to my advantage, swear that she's wrong (but keeping my fingers crossed behind my back, like when we were ten years old). But I can't do it. Because we're not ten now, and because I realise she's right.

I don't move when she stands up. Nor when she takes a while to straighten the collar of her coat, as if giving me a few extra seconds to redeem myself. Nor when she walks away, leaving me on my own, a forlorn, grey figure looking out at all that greyness. Nor when she throws one last barb before abandoning me:

'I bet you haven't even visited Dad's grave.'

June

'If I had to start my life over again,
I wouldn't want to change a thing:
I'd just open my eyes a little wider'

Jules Renard, *Journal*

Chapter 43

The new resident is called Rosa. She'll be moving into Miss Granny's studio. She has short black hair, at odds with her almost transparent skin. She rolls her Rs when she tells me she's ve*r*y unsu*r*e she wants to live he*r*e. Sitting next to her on the other side of my desk, her daughter fiddles with a hankie, her eyes lowered. This is my first admissions interview, but I already know I don't like it.

'She had a bad fall,' the daughter explains. 'She broke her hip. She spent two weeks in hospital and a month recuperating in a convalescent home, but walking is still difficult for her. In her house, everything is up and down stairs; she can't stay there . . . I live in Toulouse; I'd happily have her with me, but she doesn't want to leave the Basque country—'

'I am here!' interrupts the old lady. 'You don't have to talk about me in the third person!'

'Rosa,' I say. 'No one's going to force you to live here if it's not what you want. It's not a prison. Our residents' happiness is our primary concern. I'm going to be honest: it might take a while to adapt, but we'll do everything we can to make you feel at home.'

'It isn't my home and it never will be. But I suppose

I don't have a choice, given that my daughter's chosen to live on the far side of the world—'

'Mum, don't exaggerate! Toulouse is barely two hours away.'

'The director said I could have a trial period,' she goes on, as if the interruption never happened. 'I'll live here till the end of the month, and then we'll see.'

'That's a good idea,' I say. 'Will you be moving in today?'

'Yes, we have her things in the car,' replies the daughter. 'The director would prefer her to move straight into the free studio, but she explained that there are studios in the smaller building and relatives can spend a few days there so she doesn't feel so lonely.'

'Ah, are you going to stay here? That's a very good idea!'

'No, not me . . . I have to get back to Toulouse for work. But my son should be here soon. He's going to stay with his grandmother for a week. They adore each other. He lives in London, but he comes over whenever he can to see her. I'll be back this weekend and I'll call every day.'

Rosa clicks her tongue.

'You're talking about me as if I wasn't here again!'

I see them back out to the car park before going to Leon for his weekly session. Anne-Marie and Greg are waiting to help them unload the car. I tell them they can call on me at any time if they need me, and I'm just about to leave them when a taxi draws up to the front door. A man climbs out and Rosa totters over to him with her walking stick.

'My big boy, there you are! Did you have a good trip?'

He hugs his grandmother, kisses his mother – who nags him for being late – and then comes over to us with a broad smile.

'Hello, I'm Madame Goncalves's grandson.'

'Hello, I'm Anne-Marie, director of Ocean View,' she replies, proffering her hand. 'So is it you who's planning to stay here?'

'That's right. You said on the phone I could stay in a studio. I'm planning to be here a week.'

'Perfect! Follow me. I'll introduce you to Isabelle. She'll show you around.'

Anne-Marie goes inside, followed by the newcomer, with his grandmother clinging to his left arm and his mother on his right.

Greg looks at me.

'What's the matter with you?' he asks.

'Nothing, why?'

'Because you're smiling.'

Oh, yes. I'm smiling.

'Hmm, I think this is going to be an interesting week!' he says, walking towards the door.

Leaving me alone, with this idiotic look on my face.

Chapter 44

Leon is not alone in his studio: his son is sitting by the window. I've met him several times. He's a polite, smiley man, the exact opposite of his father. Except for one thing: they clearly have the same plastic surgeon. His face is as smooth as a bidet. I'm sure his toes move when he blinks.

I suggest postponing Leon's session so he can make the most of his son's visit. He shakes his head.

'I'd rather my son were here.'

'Great!' I say, sitting on the wooden chair. 'So, how are you today?'

'Oh, I manage,' he replies, in a feeble voice I don't recognise.

'You don't seem to be on top of the world – is there something you'd like to talk about?'

'I don't know if that's a good idea,' he says, looking away.

'Do you want me to leave?' asks his son.

'No, no, it's good you're here. It's just that . . . I don't want this all coming back to bite me.'

'We'll hear whatever you have to say,' I encourage him, intrigued.

I've never seen Leon so fragile. He looks as if he might dissolve into tears at any minute.

'All right . . . I'm not happy here,' he whispers eventually. 'I try very hard to fit in, but it never seems to be enough. They all reject me. No one's nice to me. I feel lonely. Very lonely . . .'

Wow. Coming from the great Leon. I almost believe him; I'd quite like to clap. His son looks horrified; his eyes are popping out of his head. More than usual, I mean.

I decide to let Leon play out his little sketch without joining in the performance.

'I'm friendly enough. I don't think I deserve this treatment. I suppose every community needs its whipping boy, I just drew the short straw. Never mind, I haven't got long to put up with it, anyway.'

He gives a weak cough. Hamlet is in the building.

'But you've never talked to me about this!' his son says, amazed.

'I didn't want to worry you, my boy. I know you have enough on your mind, you don't need to be burdened with your old father's problems. But it's really weighing on me, I couldn't go on keeping it to myself.'

'You're right,' I say. 'What can it possibly be but jealousy? You're such a sweetheart, Leelee . . .'

Leon looks up at me, his eyes shining with fury. He knows I'm taking the piss. This is war.

'I don't know, I mean, I don't have anything for anyone to be jealous of. It's very hard. I wish I could spend my last months surrounded by people who love me. Instead, I'm alone against all of them. The other day, someone hid my dentures. And it made everyone laugh, even the staff.'

His son is now ashen.

'The staff?!' he exclaims. 'Are you saying the staff make fun of residents?'

Leon's back is stooped, his head held low. He's got a good handle on the role of victim. I almost feel sorry for him.

'Not of the "residents" plural, but of me.'

Almost.

'If you only knew,' he continues. 'I'm never included in activities, even though there are things going on every day.'

I want to jump to my feet, shout at him, tell his son he's lying and he's the one who refuses to join in. I feel like taking him apart like a piece of Ikea furniture. But that's exactly what he wants. So I play it cool.

'I'm so sorry, I wasn't aware of all this. We're going to remedy this situation. From now on, nothing will happen in this place without you. You will automatically be signed up for all activities and a member of staff will come to collect you to make sure you come along.'

'That seems like a good idea, although it should have been done much sooner!' says the son.

'This is entirely my fault. I didn't appreciate how unhappy your father was. Something else I'd like to offer,

Leon, is to help you integrate with the others by setting up small conversation groups. It will give you an opportunity to chat, and they'll have a chance to get to know you and all the good things about you. Would you like that?'

He doesn't move; he's still stooped, as if in mourning for his entire family. Can't someone tell him he's laying it on a bit thick?

'Would you like that, Dad?' his son repeats my question.

'Yes, yes,' he whimpers. 'But I know it won't actually happen, anyway.'

'What do you mean?' his son asks.

Leon shakes his head.

'I can't . . .'

'You can talk, Leon. You have nothing to be afraid of.'

He looks up at me and takes a deep breath before embarking on his speech, with a quavering voice but glinting eyes.

'I'm not sure I can trust a psychologist who plays on her phone during my sessions rather than listening to me.'

I'm struck dumb by the shock. So is his son. His whole face is quivering. His chin's going to fall off.

I should argue, explain, tell his son what really happened, say how intolerable Leon is and how keeping himself to himself is his own choice. But I'm tired of Leon's little games and I've stopped thinking that, under his grumpy exterior, he's meek as a lamb. Yet more proof that the elderly aren't a different species: like with everyone else, there are weak links. So I stand up, gather my things and leave the room without saying goodbye. Leon will have to cope without my consultations from now on.

And I'll cope without his stupid face.

Chapter 45

Like every Friday, it's fish and rice for lunch today. The advantage of the catering here is that there are no surprises: every day, the food is as unimaginative as the day before. No salt, no fat, no taste. It's so bland today that my teeth want to up sticks and leave.

'The grandson's not bad, is he?' Clara says.

'Julia's already on the case,' Greg mutters.

'Excuse me?!' I cry in my defence. 'He's a resident's grandson, he's off limits . . . even if he does have the sort of eyes that make bra straps snap.'

Clara almost chokes on her rice. Greg sighs.

'You complain about men . . . but you lot are worse!'

'Jealous!' says Clara.

'Pfff! Nothing to be jealous of. *My* eyes make knicker elastic snap.'

The three of us laugh out loud. Isabelle looks up from the other end of the table.

'Are you talking about Raphael?'

All the staff turn to watch us. Isabelle waits for her answer, eyebrows arched. She's nice, but she has the IQ of a toilet brush.

'Raphael?' I ask.

'Yes, the new resident's grandson,' she replies, tilting her chin towards the next table.

Raphael is sitting beside his grandmother, surrounded by Louise, Elisabeth, Gustave, Leon and Pierre. Judging by the laughter resounding on their table since the beginning of the meal, he's won unanimous approval. Raphael. Lovely name.

'No, no,' Clara replies. 'So, do you do that a lot, then? Listen to other people's conversations?'

'Of course not, I didn't mean to . . .' Isabelle stammers. 'It's just I wanted to ask Julia something.'

'Oh?'

'Yes. I wondered whether you've found a job to go on to afterwards.'

'Not yet. I'm only halfway through my contract. I've still got four months to look for something, I should be fine.'

'Yeees . . . I wouldn't be so sure, if I were you,' she says, biting into a piece of bread. 'It's not easy finding work around here – there are a lot of people looking. If it were me, I wouldn't be hanging about . . .'

'Didn't Anne-Marie say she'd give Julia your job?' Clara pipes up.

'No, she did not,' she says, shrugging her shoulders.

Anne-Marie, who's sitting next to her, looks up from her plate.

'It's true. I was planning to talk to you about exactly that. I think Julia would make a wonderful meet-and-greeter.'

Isabelle stops chewing on her chunk of bread. Judging by how white she's gone, it's likely she's also stopped breathing. The director, who's not keen to have a death on her conscience, reassures her.

'We're joking, Isabelle. Just joking!'

Isabelle's cheeks come back to life. And her eyes, apparently, have too, because they look glossy now.

'Don't scare me like that – I'm sensitive, you know!' she says shakily. 'Phew! I thought I was going to have an *embogasm.*'

No one picks up on the mispronunciation; she's had enough for one week. And anyway, we're distracted by suddenly raised voices from another table. The usually inseparable Lucienne and Mina are laying into each other. Moussa and Sarah, who are on duty for today's lunch, are trying unsuccessfully to calm them. The two old girls are going at each other hammer and tongs.

'I knew I couldn't trust you, you old floozy!' Lucienne roars. 'You nicked my Babybel!'

'*Floozy?* What a cheek! What you don't have in looks, you should make up for in manners, you know!'

'You should be grateful you have osteoporosis,' Lucienne retorts, 'or I'd have rearranged your face for you!'

'And you'd better make sure you don't get in my way, or I'll take pleasure in driving right over you!' snaps Mina, before trundling off in her wheelchair.

The dining room has never been so quiet. Everyone, staff and residents alike, has paused to enjoy today's show. When Mina leaves, we all press Play again. Rosa whispers something in her grandson's ear. Probably 'Get me out of this madhouse.' He kisses her cheek, gets up and heads for the door, treating my eyes to the mood-enhancing sway of the back pockets of his jeans.

Chapter 46

Raphael is sitting on a bench in the garden with a cigarette in his hand when Clara and I come outside to smoke ours.

'You should go and talk to him,' she says, snapping her lighter.

'What do you want me to go and talk to him for?'

'Erm, because it's your job? He doesn't look very happy, I think he could do with opening up to someone . . .'

I watch him. He's sitting on the backrest of the bench with his feet on the seat and his elbows resting on his thighs. He's looking off into the distance, probably lost in thought. Clara's right: it must be traumatic bringing someone you love to their final home. I'm not used to working out of doors and with a cigarette in my hand, but I can bend the rules.

'You're right. I'll go and see,' I say, lighting my cigarette from her lighter.

She gives a peal of laughter.

'Oh my! It doesn't take much to persuade you! Greg was right.'

'What? Greg was right about what?'

'You're seriously into him.'

She looks at me with a broad smile. She's so pleased with herself!

'You're crazy, the pair of you . . . Don't you have anything better to do when you're alone together than talk about me? Should I give you an illustrated instruction manual?'

She sniggers.

'Come on, be honest. Do you like him?'

'I have no idea! I've barely seen him for more than three minutes!'

'You get a smile like Mickey Mouse on ecstasy every time you see him or someone mentions him. We do have our eyes open, you know!'

'Well, you may have your eyes open . . . but, but you're having major hallucinations. Yes, he's quite nice-looking, but that's all there is to it. I'm not some hysterical teenager who can't control herself and falls hopelessly for just anybody. And, as I already said, he's a client. I can't see him any other way. And now, solely in my professional capacity, I shall step forthwith in his direction and lend him the listening ear that he needs.'

Head held high, I make my way over to the bench. I can just imagine the look on Clara's face, and I make a conscious effort not to laugh. They've clearly decided to pair me off with the first available candidate – head cases, the pair of them. Well, they'll be disappointed: that's absolutely not part of my plan.

Before coming to Ocean View, I'd never really been on my own. There was Olivier, my first boyfriend from school, then two relationships in two years, then Marc. After him, I had a succession of one-night stands: I've forgotten most of them, but they gave me the illusion of not being alone. And yet I've never been lonelier than I was then.

I came here on a whim. It was an emergency. I had to get out – I mean, get out of the hole I'd dug myself into and, literally, get out of Paris. One of the unexpected up-sides is that, isolated from other people, I've grown closer to myself.

In the early days, I thought being alone would be the hardest part. I gradually got used to it, though. Of course, there are times when I'd like to have someone . . . but it's just a wish, no longer a need. Maybe the last months with Marc helped me understand that, even in a couple, you're on your own. Maybe those one-off nights with strangers, trying to find some kind of fleeting affection, nudged me into realising that other people can't fill the void inside. Since I've been here, I've been alone. But I don't think of myself as lonely.

My journey isn't over. I'm going through the reconstruction process. I still have some bumps to come, but I intend to deal with them on my own. When I'm finished, I hope I'll be strong enough to hit the road again without being afraid of what lies ahead.

I reach Raphael just as he's lighting another cigarette. He turns to face me and smiles.

Sometimes, it must be nice to be a cigarette.

Chapter 47

'Hello,' I say, reaching out my hand. 'I'm Julia Rimini. I'm the resident psychologist.'

'Raphael, Madame Goncalves' grandson,' he replies.

'Yes, I saw you arrive earlier. Do you mind if I have a cigarette with you?'

'Not at all, quite the opposite. Actually, you may be able to answer my question: do you organise granny fights every lunchtime, or was today an exception?'

His face is unreadable. I don't know whether he's joking so I opt to play it safe by taking this at face value.

'Don't worry, it's usually much quieter. Sometimes, they bicker a bit, but it never amounts to much.'

He nods.

'Okay. So I don't need to teach my grandmother how to do an armlock.'

He still looks serious, but now the irony is clear to see.

'No, armlocks won't be necessary,' I reply in a professional voice. 'But I hope she knows a bit of chemistry.'

'Chemistry? Why?'

'For our Sunday workshops.'

He looks at me, eyebrows raised.

'What do you do on Sunday?' he asks.

'We make drugs, of course.'

Creases appear in the corners of his eyes and he gives me the beginnings of a knowing smile.

'I thought there was something strange about the place.'

I nod in agreement.

'And you haven't seen the half of it. On Saturday evenings, the residents put on a show for us that's halfway between the Moulin Rouge and the Chippendales. Tickets change hands for a fortune, and they finance the arms for the bank raids.'

Now he's laughing out loud.

'I'm delighted to see we've made the right choice! My grandmother will feel right at home here.'

He gazes off into the distance again. A silence loaded with unspoken words settles around us.

'If you need to talk about it, please don't hold back. It may not be obvious here, right now, but it's my job.'

'Thank you. Unfortunately, talking won't change anything. And that's the only thing that would make me feel better.'

He sighs.

'I come over to see her as much as possible, but my work's taken up so much of my time recently. It's six months since I've last been. Six months is nothing in a lifetime, but it's a lot when there's only a little bit of life left. I was shocked when I saw her yesterday. She seems to have got smaller. As if she's gradually fading away.'

'You mustn't feel guilty. You're here now, and you're going to spend a week with her. That's wonderful!'

'I don't feel guilty, it's just painful. Especially for her, because leaving her home is such an ordeal. She was born there, she's always lived there, all her memories are there. She doesn't give much away, that's what we're like in my family . . . But it must be hard landing up some-where new exactly when she most needs familiarity.'

'It's difficult, yes. I won't say it isn't, that would be lying. But I can promise you that the team at Ocean View is fantastic, and we'll do everything possible to make her feel at home.'

'Yeah,' he says, with little conviction, getting up and stubbing out his cigarette against the bench. 'That's what you would say, though, isn't it? So she'll live happily ever after and have lots of children. Yay.'

And he marches away with the determined step of someone trying to disguise a limp.

Chapter 48

'We have to talk about Leon.'

Anne-Marie's tone of voice does not bode well.

As it does every second Tuesday of the month, the staff meeting is taking place in the dining room. The whole team is sitting around a table stocked with pastries and photocopied notes, going over the previous month and planning the next. Top of the agenda: Leon.

'I had a meeting with his son yesterday – a charming man, incidentally. His father is being frozen out by the other residents – deliberately, according to him.'

Weary sighs from around the table.

'That's not all. He's accusing the staff of not doing anything to alleviate his suffering and, worse than that, of stoking the other residents' ribbing.'

'Oh, come on, we all know Leon!' Clara exclaims. 'He's run out of ideas to piss us off!'

'It's true,' chips in Laura, the physio. 'He's the only one who's unpleasant. He freezes himself out.'

Anne-Marie turns to me.

'Apparently, you discussed this with him, Julia.'

'I did. I'm not allowed to divulge the contents of our

sessions but, basically, he complained – in his son's presence – of being abused by the residents and the staff. I realised this was one of Leon's little games, so I tried to call his bluff by suggesting he should automatically be involved in all the activities.'

'Good idea!' says Greg. 'We could start with bungee-jumping!'

'Or archery,' Sarah adds. 'He can hold the target.'

'His son mentioned this to me,' Anne-Marie continues, still facing me. 'He also told me you brought the conversation to an end by storming out of the studio.'

I snigger.

'Like father, like son . . .'

'I'm glad you find it amusing. Accusations like that can damage our reputation. This is very serious. We need to sort it out. I'm going to ask you all to make a particular effort to get Leon involved.'

'We can make as much effort as we like,' Greg retorts, 'but Leon will keep playing the victim. If we play along with him, it'll be worse. We'll be his puppets.'

Lots of nodding around the table. Everyone agrees: that's not how to bring an end to Leon's latest hobby.

'What do you suggest?' asks Anne-Marie.

Isabelle puts up her hand.

'I have an idea!' she whispers, as if the room is bugged. 'We just need to get rid of him. My cousin's a pharmacist; he could give me some barbiturates. Afterwards, we chop up his body – I've got a friend who's a butcher – and we chuck him in the sea. No one would ever know. We could just tell his son that he went off for a walk and never came back.'

No one is commenting now. Everyone stares at Isabelle, not sure whether to be shocked or perplexed. She must have been away the day the brain cells were handed out. There's no other explanation.

'Oh my god, I'm *joking*!' she cries. 'Did you really think I'd gone mad? Anyway, there aren't any sharks round here, so the bits of him would get washed back up on the beach.'

'Does anyone have a less radical suggestion?' Anne-Marie asks, with a sigh that says, *What the hell am I doing here?*

'Can't we get him to leave?' asks the doctor.

'Stop! We really can't chuck him out!' says Moussa, the nurse. 'Yes, he's a pain, but he's an old man, he doesn't deserve that.'

'Easy for you to say. He doesn't call you twice a week to claim he's suffering from conditions he's found on the internet . . .'

'Don't let's get heated.' Anne-Marie shushes them. 'It's not that easy to get rid of a resident and, even if it were, we wouldn't do it with so little justification. But we need to find some way of stopping his accusations. Julia, seeing as you're directly in the firing line, perhaps you have an idea?'

I shake my head. I have no idea what we can do to reinstate the truth and persuade Leon to stop his ranting. But I certainly intend to come up with something.

Chapter 49

It's close to midnight when a howling sound makes me jump out of my skin.

I'm toasty under my duvet, numbed by tiredness and fighting gravity with my eyelids to finish the whodunnit that has me on tenterhooks. I'm well set for a good night's sleep after the evening of pampering I've treated myself to: scented candles, soft music, hot chocolate, flannelette pyjamas and a good book. Just one thing disturbed the mood: the creak of Clara's door immediately followed by stifled laughter and the slam of Greg's door. If I'd had a band and some pompoms, I'd have gone and done a celebratory cheer routine. Two days before Greg's due to move out, it's practically a romcom.

Then the cry rang out.

It's coming from the grounds, same as before. Now the nights are milder, the voices and noises that terrified me the first evening are becoming more frequent. I don't know whether it's sheer exhaustion or the fact I'm reading a thriller that emboldens me, but I extricate myself from my duvet, determined to get to the bottom of the mystery: who hangs about in the grounds of a retirement home in the middle of the night?

I pull on a jacket over my pyjamas, slip my feet into a pair of boots and grab the only thing close to a weapon in my studio: a round-bladed knife. People often under-estimate how useful a round-bladed knife can be when confronted with a serial killer. If I find myself cornered, I could spread jam all over him.

By the time I'm in the middle of the garden – and completely awake – I can no longer think of anything I have in common with the hero of my book. The moon is hidden by clouds and gives off just enough light to cast menacing shadows on the ground, and there are disturb-ing noises all around me. I'm shivering, partly with the cold, mostly with fear, and there's only one thing I want: to get back to my bed safe and sound. Brandishing my knife like a sword, I manage a feeble 'Hello-o . . . Any-body there?' which comes out remarkably like a whisper, then I embark on a strategic retreat.

I've hardly taken two steps before a man's voice roars, 'Who's there?' and a towering silhouette looms out of the darkness, coming towards me. Taking instructions from my courage alone, I start running so quickly my shadow gets left behind.

I feel like I'm flying. I hurdle tree roots and dodge holes, my speed increased tenfold by my terror. The wind almost deafens me, so I don't know whether my assailant is follow-ing me, but I can clearly hear the little, frightened-animal bleats coming from my own mouth. Let's hope he's not into field sports.

The building's getting closer, and hope gives me a final

surge of strength. I leap to the door, pull the keys from my pocket and slip the key into the lock on the first attempt. I'm almost heaving my first sigh of relief when a hand comes down on to my shoulder.

Farewell, this life. It was good, in spite of everything.

Chapter 50

I haven't died. Well, I have, but just of shame.

Raphael is crying with laughter. Apparently, I looked like, and I quote, 'a wild animal being electrocuted'.

'But what were you doing in the garden in the middle of the night?' I ask him through chattering teeth. 'You're a psychopath!'

'I heard a cry and came to see what it was,' he says, starting to get himself under control. 'Was it you?'

'Yes, of course it was. I come into the middle of the garden every night and howl. They say it makes your hair grow faster.'

He looks at me as if I have a colander on my head.

'Of course it wasn't me!' I say. 'I'm normally asleep at this time of night, funnily enough. But it's not the first time – I've often heard voices ...'

'So you made sure you were heavily armed, and you came out,' he says, noticing my knife.

I eye him for a moment, not sure how to reply, then I look down at his hands.

'And what exactly did you think you were going to achieve with a four-colour pen?'

He smiles and puts up his hands.

'All right, all right, I'm not the bravest man on the planet. But I did bring extra ammunition as back-up,' he reassures me, producing two more pens from his pocket.

I burst out laughing, half at him, half out of relief. I can think of worse types of assault. I open the door to return to my room, and he takes hold of my arm and holds me back.

'This may not be the right time, but I wanted to see you. Shall we have a cigarette?'

I agree to this. He hands me an open packet, I take one out and put it to my lips and he flicks on his lighter. The wind makes the flame writhe around the end of my cigarette without lighting it. So Raphael forms a double shield: the first with his hand and the second with his body, which he moves right next to mine so there's no space between us. This scene could have great erotic potential, if I weren't wearing pyjamas dotted with little multicoloured ponies.

'I wanted to apologise for yesterday,' he says, when both our cigarettes are alight. 'I shouldn't have got angry.'

'It's fine. Don't worry about it. I understand – it's a sensitive subject.'

'Yup. It's tough. I've been trying to prepare myself for this for a while, but I can't get used to it. My grandmother pretty much brought me up. My mother was very busy with work so Rosa sort of took her place . . . Well, I'm not going to tell you my life story, but I wanted to say I'm sorry. I don't speak to people like that, usually.'

'There's nothing to apologise for. I didn't take it

personally. And anyway, I'm used to it: psychologists are like customer services for the mind. We never get to see the easy cases.'

In the light coming from the doorway, I can see he's looking at me and smiling.

'Right,' I say to disguise my embarrassment, 'it's getting late. I'm going to bed. Forget about the mystery in the garden. I have to face the facts: I'm definitely not an adventurer.'

'I think that's a wise approach. But you definitely shouldn't regret your moment of courage. If it wasn't for that, I wouldn't have made a major discovery.'

'Really? What's that?'

'I've found out that you have great taste in pyjamas.'

I'm about to come up with justifications when we hear a howl. With just a glance, we reach an agreement: enough of playing heroes, we're both going quietly back to our rooms. Ten seconds later, I'm in my studio, out of breath and laughing to myself as I enjoy the mental picture of Raphael scuttling back to his room like a wild animal being electrocuted.

Chapter 51

Pierre has always struck me as the most resilient of the residents. Tall and sturdy, he still has thick, dark hair, which makes him look younger than he is, even though he sometimes complains that his body's failing. But today he looks ten years older. He sits on his sofa, which is covered with books and magazines, and sighs.

'I read to make the time pass more quickly, but it doesn't work. In fact, every second I'm away from her seems to draw itself out into slow torture.'

'Have they said how long it will take?'

'They're saying several weeks, what with hospital, then recuperation . . . that's all I know – it all depends on how things go. How am I going to cope with several weeks without my wife, can you tell me that?'

No, I can't tell him, because I don't have the answer. Elisabeth is in hospital. Yesterday, on her way to meet Louise for their daily get-together, she missed one of the steps down from the front door. She's fractured the neck of her femur. When Clara, Greg and I visited her in her little white room, we wondered how she would be coping with the pain and the disorientation of being away from familiar surroundings, given how anxious she can get.

We were surprised to find her very serene: everything would be fine, and could we ask the stripy cat to make less noise chomping on those nails, thank you kindly. Clearly, the morphine is doing the trick.

Elisabeth has the injury, but it's Pierre who's taken a blow.

'I've never slept without her since we married, you know. Not once!'

'Do you feel lonely?'

He looks out of the window and thinks for a long time.

'I don't feel lonely, I feel incomplete. After so many years together, we've become one person. Elisabeth and Pierre, Pierre and Elisabeth. But Pierre on his own, I don't know who that is any more. I've spent three times as many years living with my wife than without her. By myself, I'm just half of me, and not the half that has my heart.'

'What a beautiful thing to say . . .'

'I don't know if it's beautiful, but it's definitely true. I love my wife even more than when I first saw her. When I see young people today, separating when they come to their first hurdle, I think we were lucky to have lived in those days. Otherwise, we would probably be strangers now and I wouldn't even know the happiness I'd missed out on. I'm not saying it's always easy, though! Oh no, it's easier to stop loving than to make the effort to carry on. Every evening when I go to bed I . . .'

He breaks off.

'You what?' I ask.

'No, nothing. You'll laugh at me.'

'Of course I will, that's just like me . . .' I say drily. 'Go on, what do you do every night when you go to bed, Pierre?'

'Every night when I go to bed I carry out the same ritual I've been doing for sixty years: I take my wife in my arms and hug her, and I thank heaven for making our paths cross. We wish each other a good night, she snuggles up to me, I breathe in her scent and my heart starts beating just like on the first day. You never get used to loving. I've counted now: we've done that twenty-one thousand eight hundred and seventy-five times. That's quite something . . . Yesterday evening, my arms were empty, and my heart was even more so.'

I close my eyes hard to stop the tears getting out. I can't think of anything more touching than people so vulnerable they let down their guard. Their words aren't filtered by the brain, they come straight from the gut.

'You'll have to find a way of cheering yourself up while you're waiting for her to come back. Have you thought about that?'

'Well, I'm planning to visit her every day. Anne-Marie has offered to drop me there after lunch and pick me up a few hours later. And the rest of the day, well, I'll just count the seconds . . . I was planning to have a surprise party for our sixtieth anniversary, but that's had it now.'

'When is it?'

'Seventh of July, less than a month. She won't be back, that's for sure. I'll just sit here on this sofa and wait for her to come back.'

228

I think for a few minutes while Pierre lists all the things he normally does with Elisabeth and that he will miss. Then I have an idea.

'Pierre, I've got a suggestion for you.'

He screws up his eyes and peers at me intently.

'I can help you organise something for your anniversary. It probably won't be the sort of big party you had in mind, but we could still do something nice. There's no way we're not going to mark the day, and I'm quite good at organising surprises. Especially if I'm not given an opportunity to open my big mouth in front of the person the surprise is for . . .'

His face has suddenly come back to life.

'Would you do that?' he asks enthusiastically.

'Yes, and I'm going to.'

'But I don't have enough money to pay you, I can't have you spending hours arranging a party for us without paying you.'

I shake my head.

'Don't worry about that, it's my pleasure, I don't need any remuneration. Unless . . .'

'Unless what?'

'You're closer to Leon than anyone else, wouldn't you say?'

Chapter 52

Greg is leaving. I knew it was happening and I've watched the date draw near, but that doesn't alter the fact that I already miss having him as a neighbour. I've always been like that. I start regretting things before they're actually over. I obviously have a problem with endings, whether it's a bar of chocolate, a phase of my life or a relationship. So my mind subconsciously tries to prepare me by sending out warnings: 'Watch out, it's nearly over'; 'Make the most of it, this may be the last time'. Which means I never manage to enjoy the moment, because there's always a part of me being a killjoy. I'm nostalgic for the present. And it's even worse with the past.

The van Greg has hired to move his things is outside the annexe. Clara and I are carrying down bin bags full of his clothes; he left it too late to get cardboard boxes. He thinks we're doing it to help him but, really, we're just trying to keep him here a bit longer. To be honest, if we go any slower, we'll be going backwards.

'Come on, girls, nearly finished,' he says brightly, when I grant myself a much needed rest after carrying down a bag of cushions.

Clara glances over at me. If Droopy and Eeyore had

a daughter, she'd look like her. I join her in the back of the van.

'You going to be okay?'

'Yeah . . . it's mostly just strange. Basically, I didn't think I'd feel like this about it. I've wanted to cry ever since I got up this morning.'

'I understand . . . I keep thinking it's the end of our socials, we won't have any more of those evenings together, chatting and laughing, so I can't even imagine what it's like for you.'

She frowns.

'Well, it's the same for me. No more or less.'

'Of course it is,' I say with a knowing smile. 'No more or less.'

'Stop it!' she giggles. 'Fuck's sake, I don't know what you're implying . . .'

'You're right, neither do I. Especially considering I definitely didn't hear you together the other evening.'

'So long as you haven't heard me call him Rocky . . .' she trills, heading back into the annexe.

Raphael comes out at that exact moment. With all her characteristic discretion, Clara turns round and gives me an exaggerated wink. He smiles at us and comes towards me with his hands in his pockets.

'Are you over the traumas of last night, then, Julia?'

He must notice me hesitating because he adds, 'I hope you don't me calling you Julia? It feels a bit formal saying "Miss Rimini" . . .'

'No, of course, I'd prefer it. I managed to get to sleep

okay, but I'd like to get to the bottom of this mystery . . . How about you? Did you sleep with your pens under your pillow?'

He smiles and looks at the van.

'Is someone moving out?'

'Yes, Greg, the activities coordinator. The renovations in his apartment are finished so he's leaving us.'

Greg comes out of the building with his TV in his arms.

'Do you need any help?' Raphael asks.

'No, but that's very kind,' I say. 'Your grandmother must be waiting to see you.'

'I wish! Her Ladyship is spending her Saturday afternoon at an embroidery workshop. She's made friends with another resident, someone called Louise, and doesn't need me. And I was planning to spend the whole evening with her. It's my last night. I'm off tomorrow.'

'In which case, I'd be very grateful for your help!' Greg calls from the van. 'Because if I keep on with just these two girls, I'll still be here next year.'

Greg's apartment has undergone a metamorphosis since our last visit. He was right: it's amazing. The grey floor tiles and white furniture give the living room a cosy Scandi feel, which is enhanced by the light streaming in through the large picture windows. The kitchen floor has small, red-and-blue patterned tiles that contrast with the modern appliances. The bedroom has been partly cleared and now looks like a real haven of peace. If his personal style left any room for doubt, we now have confirmation: Greg has great taste.

'Wow!' I exclaim for the tenth time. 'Even the toilet's a knockout. Your place is like a show home!'

'Come and look at this, Julia, you're going to die!' Clara calls from the bathroom.

I join her and find her lying in a large corner bath with her arms and legs spread wide. A blonde starfish.

'You could get twelve people in here! Did you rob a bank or something, Greg?' she cries.

'No,' he replies from the living room, where he's putting books on to the shelves. 'Jean-Luc left me his fortune. You remember Jean-Luc, my ex?'

Clara throws her head back and laughs.

'Actually, I've been saving all my acting fees. TV doesn't pay well, but advertising's the jackpot!'

'Have you done some ads?' Raphael asks, coming into the apartment with a couple of bin bags.

'Just one, a long time ago.'

'Ah, maybe that's why I thought I'd seen you before. What was it advertising?'

'Oh, you wouldn't have seen it . . .' he mumbles. 'You're more likely to have seen me in a TV series. I've had some quite good parts.'

Why the hell doesn't he want to tell us what the ad was for? It can't be that awful! Before he has time to stop me, I open the door to his bedroom and rush inside, determined to find the corkboard with the pictures of his performances that I saw last time. It's no longer propped against the bedhead, but it can't be far away. I look all around the room as Greg's footsteps draw closer and closer. Aha, there it is! I can see the frame sticking out from the lower shelf of the bedside table. I grab it and run for the try line – I mean, the door – trying to dodge Greg, who launches himself at me. He tackles me, slamming me down on to the bed, and at the last moment I offload the frame to Raphael, who's just come on to the pitch. He catches it and races off, with Clara cheering hysterically. Converted try.

'Okay, well, you'll never see me in the same way again,' Greg says with an exaggerated sigh. 'You're a pain in the arse . . .'

'Look who's talking!' Raphael calls from the living room before bursting out laughing.

Clara's giggling. Greg watches me, waiting for me to catch on. It takes me a few seconds to put all the clues together. I've always been rubbish at Cluedo. And then I get it; it comes back to me. The beach, the coconut, the handsome guy, the old saying. The ad was all over the TV for months; you couldn't miss it. Without a word, I get up, take my phone from my handbag and do a search. The video starts.

A paradise island at dusk. Greg, looking tanned and gorgeous, leans nonchalantly against a palm tree with a coconut in his hand. Looking straight to camera with a big smile, he proclaims: 'According to a local proverb, "he who swallows a coconut, trusts his anus". I prefer trusting to Calmicoid.' Two dancers in colourful sarongs join him, singing the slogan to a tinny, synthesised tune: 'For haemorrhoids, remember Calmicoid!'

I look up from the screen: three pairs of eyes are trained on to it. I can't contain myself any longer: my whole body goes into spasm. Clara's face is deformed, she's going to such efforts not to explode. Raphael is managing better, but the quiver in his lips isn't a good sign. In the end, Greg releases us by cracking first. For a few minutes that seem to go on for ever, the four of us laugh with complete abandon, wiping our tears and holding our stomachs, and when we start to calm down, we set off all over again at the sight of each other's faces.

'Seriously,' I say, trying to catch my breath. 'Quite apart from the product, it looks like something from the eighties!'

'That's exactly what the agency were going for,' Greg explains. 'But, given how many letters the brand received and the stuff people said to me whenever they recognised me in the street, it seems the days of taking things at face value aren't anything like over yet. Still, their turnover went through the roof, so they were happy. In celebration, they air it again from time to time . . .'

'That must be a bummer for you . . .' says Clara playfully, unleashing another gale of laughter.

When we've all regained our composure, we get back to work. Raphael needs to go back to see his grandmother, and Greg has to return the van. While Clara and I make piles of Greg's clothes, the boys try to move a cupboard from the bedroom to the living room. We can hear them grunting, groaning and heaving; it's a heavy piece of furniture and it's tough work. Ten minutes later, a dig in the ribs from Clara makes me turn to look at them. The vision before us leaves us speechless: both men have taken off their T-shirts. Clara mimes fanning her face with her hand, clearly having a hot flush. I wish I could say I don't feel the same at all, that broad shoulders have never done anything for me, that the scene definitely doesn't make me want to slip into Raphael's muscly-but-not-too-muscly arms. I'd like to say that. But the truth is this man has more effect on me than ten All Blacks calendars, two performances of the Chippendales and four Brad Pitt films all rolled together. Luckily, I've learned to be wary of my own urges. The last one saw me back in bed with my ex.

'If we put the heating on, do you think they'd take the bottoms off, too?' Clara whispers, swooning.

I smile, and try to refocus as best I can on folding clothes. A T-shirt, a pair of trousers . . . his eyes alone could light a barbecue . . . a pair of jeans, a T-shirt . . . good sense of humour, too . . . socks, more socks . . . he's sensitive . . . a jumper, a sweatshirt . . . he's got a great body . . . a pair of Bermuda shorts, a shirt . . . he's great chat . . . I may not be in the right headspace for this, and I may not want to fall under the spell of a patient's grandson, but if this guy doesn't produce a flaw pretty damn quick, my resolve is likely to go on strike.

Two hours later, the abs are covered and everything is

in its place. Greg is, too. He looks at the finished result of his new home like a child finding a haul of presents underneath the Christmas tree. He knows it's all for him, but he still needs to claim ownership of it.

'I'm just going to have a last look round, then I'll drive you back,' he says, heading off to the far end of the apartment.

'We'll wait for you downstairs,' I call out, thinking he should be alone to savour this moment.

I leave the door open so the other two can follow me, and I set off down the stairs. I've climbed down two flights when I realise Raphael is behind me. I mean, *only* Raphael is behind me.

'Where's Clara?'

'She stayed upstairs. I saw her shut the door behind us,' he says, raising a conspiratorial eyebrow.

I snigger to myself. She clearly hasn't given up on her idea of throwing me into Raphael's arms. If there were a lift, I can't say what might have happened, but stairwells don't exactly fuel my fantasies. I climb back up silently, determined to catch them out as they plan my wedding. Raphael follows me, visibly amused. Just as I open the door, it occurs to me it could be their own they're planning.

Too late.

In the middle of the living room, right by the heavy cupboard, Clara and Greg are very much into an in-depth exploration of each other's mouths.

Chapter 53

It was nearly ten in the morning when Clara came knocking at my door.

'I need a change of scene,' she admitted. 'Are you free today?'

I'd been planning to make the most of this sunny Saturday to go for a wander in San Sebastián, over the Spanish border. We often used to go there as a family: my parents, my sister and I. My conversation with Carole has shaken me up. I can't stop thinking about it, I'm not sleeping well, I can't concentrate, I've even found myself crying more than once, for no particular reason. Immersing myself in a place loaded with memories seemed like a good way to get things straight in my mind. But if I'd abandoned Clara and her pale little face, I'd have been guilty of ignoring a friend in need.

We thought about what we could do. Something comforting that takes no effort at all. We quickly agreed on just the thing.

As we reached the car, our bags under our arms, we came across Louise sitting on her bench. There's no I in Team Granny. She asked us where we were going and, when we told her, her face lit up. We didn't have the heart to leave her behind.

And that's how Clara, Louise and I have ended up in swimming costumes and caps, soaking ourselves in the 'lagoon' at Anglet's spa: a huge pool of warm, bubbling seawater with jets and currents.

'It can be our secret,' Louise said on the way there.

'It had better be, otherwise they'll all accuse us of favouritism,' Clara replied.

'I told Anne-Marie I was going to see my daughter, and I was terribly sorry I hadn't told her earlier, it had completely slipped my mind. She believed me!' Louise announced with a mischievous smile.

'Ooh, you rebel!' I teased, winking at her in the rear-view mirror.

She looked flattered.

The bubbles of the jacuzzi run up my legs and over my back. My muscles loosen one by one. It takes only a few minutes for my body to be completely relaxed. I give an involuntary groan of pleasure, then squint one eye open: my two accomplices are in the same state.

'I want to live in a jacuzzi,' Louise says, her eyes half closed.

'Me, too! A big jacuzzi I could share with Gr–' Clara starts to reply, before realising she might be relaxing a little too much.

'And Louise can share hers with Gustave!' I add

with a giggle, just as a squirt of saltwater lands in my right eye.

They both laugh, then Louise looks more serious.

'Do you know,' she says, 'the first time I saw Gustave, I thought he was awful. I'd just lost forty years of memories and had landed up in a retirement home, surrounded by strangers, one of whom trotted out puns and practical jokes from dawn till dusk . . . I don't like hurting people so I didn't say anything, but that didn't stop me thinking it. One morning – I must have been here about a month – I noticed he wasn't at breakfast. He didn't come to lunch either. He didn't set foot out of his studio for a week. Flu . . .'

'I remember that!' says Clara. 'It was almost too quiet . . .'

'Well, would you believe, I missed him,' Louise continues. 'His attentiveness to others, having him around, even his jokes! When you like someone's little quirks, it's a good sign, isn't it?'

'But are you actually together?' I ask. 'You can't get away with just that – I want all the gory details!'

'That's right, gory details,' Clara agrees.

Louise smiles. Under her old-lady costume, there's a girl with shining eyes.

'I started getting anonymous letters at the beginning of the year. Someone was slipping them under my door. The first time, I wasn't sure who could be writing me such nice things, although I had my suspicions, because of the little heart dotting the *i* of my name. Not many adults would do that . . . The second time, I heard the walking frame hurrying away.'

The three of us laugh as we picture Gustave legging it with his walking frame in the hope he wouldn't be caught. Like a child playing knock down ginger.

'What did the letters say?'

'They said he loved me. He told me what he felt, what he liked about me – he was courting me by letter. They were simple, sometimes awkward, but that's just it, those straightforward words with no pretentions go straight to the heart.'

'So you're trying to make us believe you've only exchanged letters!' laughs Clara. 'At the evening for the Miss and Mr Ocean View competition, it was obvious that wasn't your first attempt . . .'

'You're right. We'd had a lot of practice,' Louise agrees, misty-eyed. 'I gradually started seeing Gustave in a different light. I found him touching, brave, generous. You really need to be generous to spend your whole time trying to make other people laugh. I loved receiving those beautiful letters, but I thought it would be even better to get all that attention in person. So one evening, I went to find him. It was after a particularly moving episode of *Plus belle la vie* . . .'

I realise Clara and I are hanging on her every word, as if she were calling the numbers for the national lottery. Louise straightens her swimming cap to spin out the tension.

'I just told him I knew it was him!' she blurts out, chuckling.

'And?' we chorus.

'He acted as if he didn't know what I was talking about. "What do you know is me?" he asked, looking as innocent as a puppy that's destroyed a pair of slippers. So I pushed aside his walking frame, planted a kiss on his lips and went back to my studio. I might as well tell you, the next day, the letter was signed . . .'

'Oh, I see!' I say, pretending to look shocked. 'You're quite the seductress!'

She laughs out loud.

'I suppose so, my dear,' she says. 'At our age, we don't have time for the preliminaries!'

All three of us laugh again.

'But is it serious between you?' Clara asks.

'Oh, you know, it's not serious when you're eighty! We're happy to see each other each morning, we like chatting and he makes me laugh. It's amazing! Sometimes we make secret assignations and I feel like I'm twenty all over again and having a forbidden love affair . . . We don't think about the future – our plans are behind us, anyway – but this relationship's doing us good.'

'Do you love him?' Clara presses her.

She hesitates for a moment.

'I don't know if you can call it love . . . But I feel happier with him than without him, that's for sure!'

The three of us sit, thinking, for several minutes, then we reach the difficult decision to move from the bubbles to the massaging water jets. Life is full of impossible choices.

*

The jet probes through the hot water and hits my back right between the shoulder blades, soft yet powerful, washing away the last traces of tension. I wonder why I haven't thought of coming here before. Even under general anaesthetic I'm not this relaxed; it's as if all my anxieties and aches and pains are being carried away on a tide of hot water. Clara is moaning with pleasure as the water massages her lower spine, while Louise, who's gone for a gentler flow on to her calves, has a beatific smile permanently on her lips. I could stay here for hours. I could . . . if Clara hadn't decided to burst my warm-seawater bubble.

'So, what about you, then? Not too sad the handsome Raphael has left?'

'Not at all. I can't see why I'd be sad.'

Louise opens half an eye and casts it over us.

'What's going on with young Raphael, Julia?'

'Nothing. Clara sees pink and red hearts everywhere since she's been love-birding with Greg.'

'Clara and Greg?' exclaims the old lady, opening both eyes wide. 'I'd never have guessed . . .'

We obviously weren't the only ones to have had doubts about Greg's sexual orientation. This turn in the conversation suits me. I'm delighted to have diverted their attention. To be absolutely sure I'll be left alone, I lay it on a bit:

'Well, you should have seen them last night: their kiss was almost as torrid as yours with Gustave!'

They both shrug their shoulders, trying to look embarrassed, when they're clearly not.

*

Almost four hours have trickled past by the time we get back to Ocean View, batteries completely recharged, tummies fed, and well set up for a siesta. I drop Louise by the gate to avoid arousing suspicion. Clara and I are going to take a little drive around Biarritz, and we'll be back later. I help Louise out of the car and sit back in my seat as she heads off down the drive. When she's walked a few paces she turns and comes back, to lean in through my car window.

'Thank you for a wonderful time, girls. I was with two friends – our ages didn't matter at all. You can't imagine how nice it was not to be old for a few hours.'

She's already started walking away when I murmur my reply, 'It was nice for me, too.'

Chapter 54

I'm going to need a bit of time to chew over and digest my sister's words. She drove her hand deep into my heart, went straight for all the feelings I've chosen to anaesthetise and woken them up with a jolt. I've been consumed by guilt ever since.

I don't regret dropping everything. I take responsibility for my decision not to tell my family that I was here, and I'm not ready to tell them the truth. Not yet. But even though I try to think of good excuses, I'm having trouble forgiving myself for being so selfish. I only thought about little old me, about how I could clamber out of the abyss without leaving too much of myself behind. I noticed every tiny manifestation of my own grief, but paid no attention to anyone else's. I should have called them every day, even if there was nothing to say. I should have gone to see them. Even on New Year's Eve, I chose to sit down to eat with complete strangers rather than my family. I've thought about them, a lot. I imagined their pain, but kept it at arm's length. I sent texts, lots of them, and called, sometimes. Always hoping I'd get voicemail. I applied what I'd learned at university: you can't help others if you're in a bad place yourself. But I lumped

245

helping and just being there into the same bag. Then I tied it up tight and put it on the shelf of things to be dealt with later.

I called my mother a few days ago. This time I wasn't hoping to get her voicemail.

'Hello?'

'Mum, it's me . . .'

'Sweetheart! How are you?'

'I wanted to ask . . . could I come to stay for the weekend?'

Silence on the other end.

'Are you there, Mum?'

'I'll make your bed, my love. Do you still like hot chocolate for breakfast?'

She insisted on coming to pick me up from the airport. I insisted she waited in the car park. I didn't exactly relish the idea of travelling from Biarritz to Paris and Paris to Biarritz, just to cover my lies.

She found a compromise between my request and her impatience: she'd stand by the main doors. I've looked at flight times and have snuck in among passengers arriving from Paris. Let's hope it's this easy on the way back.

I spot her before she sees me. She's checking her watch, her short hair buffeted by the wind. Mum. I start walking faster, as if to claw back a few seconds of lost time. Protecting myself is suddenly the last thing I want. For two days, she's going to be my mother, I'll be her daughter, we'll be a family. Different, with a vital part missing, but a family all the same.

She sees me. She smiles at me. She's relieved; she can't quite believe it. The doors open. So do her arms. I melt into them. I'm just a little girl. And she's my mum.

We stay like this a long time. An oasis of comfort before setting off again.

She talks all the way home. The water leak, and how it had to be repaired, her friend Anna who's bought a new car, and how are things at the clinic, have you still not found an apartment, is it working out with Marion? I answer her questions, careful not to make mistakes. I could tell her everything, but I'm not ready. This lie is my last escape route.

She parks in front of the house. This is the moment I dread most. As if sensing this, she interrupts the swirl of small talk to ask if I'm okay.

'I will be, thanks. It's been a long time, that's all . . .'

'I know. Last time was to say goodbye to him. I've moved the furniture around. You'll see how much more light gets in.'

'Did you tell Carole I was coming?'

'Of course I did! She would have liked to see you, but she's not around this weekend. A conference in Madrid, I think.'

'Shame. Next time. On you go, Mum. I'll be with you in a bit.'

I stay in the car for several minutes. Preparing myself.

The hedge hasn't been cut; I've never seen it so tall. At the end of the road, I can see the white metal gate I've walked through so many times. Nannynoo's gate. I get out of the car and take a deep breath. Welcome home.

Mum's right: there is more light. A new sofa and coffee table have found a space for themselves alongside my father's green armchair. The smell has changed, too. Imperceptibly. Even blindfolded, I'd recognise this smell – the smell of home. A combination of old stone and wood, of washing powder, cooking and caramelised tobacco, a smell that instantly spreads through my body and deactivates the alarm bells. I'm safe here. Nothing can happen to me.

My father smoked his pipe every Friday evening. He would go up to his room, open the window that looks out over the garden, with its lawns and the plum trees we'd spent so many hours climbing, fill his pipe with tobacco and savour the taste of it while his thoughts wandered freely. I liked the slightly sweet smell of its smoke, which eventually impregnated the walls, despite his precautions. I liked the ritual which signalled the end of the week and the start of freedom over the weekend. I liked his face when he came back down, having let his work-related concerns go up in smoke. Today, I can smell the old stone, the wood, the washing power and the cooking. But the caramelised tobacco has almost disappeared.

'Come on up. I've made your bed,' my mother says, leading me towards the stairs.

My old bedroom has been turned into a guest room. I put my bag down on the rug and glance out of the window. The garden hasn't changed.

'I'm so happy you're here, my love.'

'Me, too, Mum. I'm really sorry I haven't come sooner.'

She shakes her head and tuts quietly.

'I know you've got a lot of work on, and time must fly by with Marion. She's great fun, that girl. I've always liked her.'

I feel like telling her. That it's nothing to do with work. That I haven't come sooner because it turns my stomach upside down, just thinking about it. That coming home when I know two people I love won't be here is torture. That seeing her here, all on her own, when, just a year ago, she still had her husband and her mother, does my head in. That I can't bear to think of her crying. So seeing her . . . I want to tell her all this, and for us to talk, properly, for us to sit down at a table and pour our hearts out. But what she wants is to talk about the leak, the light in the house and her friend Anna. Or about Dad and Nanny-noo, but as if she were talking about the leak, the light in the house or her friend Anna. I owe her that, at least.

The first evening, it feels as if I've never been away. I switch off my phone so it's just us, and we cook together. We chat about people we know over supper, then collapse on the new sofa to watch a DVD. When I kiss her goodnight she seems reassured that some things have stayed the same.

As she turns off the TV, she says, 'I'm going to see Dad and Nannynoo tomorrow morning. I go every Sunday. Would you like to come?'

I shake my head. I'm not ready.

'No, Mum. I'm really sorry, I can't . . .'

'I understand, my love. Take your time . . . When you're ready.'

I head for the stairs, aware of her watching me. Grit my teeth. Hard. Wait till I'm in my room to cry. They say mothers suffer more for their children than for themselves. I'm not here to pass on my burden of pain to her.

'Julia?'

I turn around. Grit my teeth again.

'You know, my love, I think about this a lot. With Dad, there's no silver lining. He was young, he was healthy, it's unfair and it's incomprehensible. But with Nannynoo . . . it's sad, but I think she's better off where she is. She was tired, you know . . . Go on, you go to bed, you need to rest. In the morning, remind me to tell you what happened to Madame Poulain, you know, from number seventeen. You're going to laugh, I'm sure you are. Goodnight, sweetheart.'

Grit my teeth. Grit my teeth. Grit my teeth.

Chapter 55

There's no name on the letter box now. It's not her house any more. It's no one's house.

I place my hand on the white metal and push the gate open. I hear the creak almost before it happens. I hold the gate behind me so it doesn't slam. Like I used to.

The cherry tree is the first thing I see. Like it used to be. I imagine the fruit, bursting with sugar, that recently weighed down the branches. Those cherries used to promise streams of red juice down our chins, clafoutis pudding straight from the oven, improvised earrings and endless strategies to outwit greedy blackbirds. This year, the red juices will have been on the blackbirds' beaks.

The daisies are dancing in the wind. I close my eyes to remember. Picking those little white flowers. Piercing the heads with a fingernail. Driving a stem through the yellow centres until it was covered with flowerheads. Here, Nannynoo, a crown of daisies for you.

There are clover leaves, too. I used to spend hours scouring them in the hopes of finding one with that extra leaf to bring me good luck. Maybe if I'd found one, she'd still be here. I used to scratch at the window; it was our code. I'd open the door, she'd come towards me with that smile that wiped away all my troubles and then, in that soft voice which was never raised, she'd say, 'Come in, my darling, how lovely to see you.' We'd do something, anything, play Scrabble, bake a cake, have a cuddle, have a snack, read poems, chat. Any excuse to spend time together. I'd catch her watching me, her eyes filled with that mixture of love and concern that we have for those who really matter to us. She'd catch me watching her, too. Hiding behind an affectionate kiss, a lingering smile or a casual compliment, there were things we didn't say because there are only three words to say them, and they're not words you just come out with, for no particular reason.

The swing seat hasn't been covered. The fabric has faded, it's stained, and the metal has rusted. The garage door is dirty. There's dried mud on the concrete flagstones. Winter has done its work here. The shrubs are bowing their heads, the grass is long, the maple tree is casting its shadow over the irises and they're sulking. Nannynoo's not here any more. Nor are my memories.

I turn and walk back, one last time. I say a silent goodbye to this place, which has witnessed me crawling, gurgling, stumbling, laughing, crying, sleeping, playing and loving. Growing up.

I put my hand on the white metal and pull the gate shut. I hear the creak almost before it happens. I hold the gate behind me so it doesn't slam. Like I used to. But there's something extra today: I now know you mustn't wait for a special reason to say those three words to the people who matter.

Chapter 56

I insisted she dropped me at the airport car park. She insisted on accompanying me inside. We found a compromise between her longing to keep her daughter a few minutes longer and my need to hide my lie: we said our goodbyes at the door. I wasn't going far, but when she hugged me and I could feel the sobs she was trying to hold back, it was as painful as if I was heading for the other side of the world, for ever.

I get back to my studio with my bag full of cake and my heart bursting with contradictory emotions.

It was a good weekend. It was soft and comfortable, like a pile of cushions you can flop on to without worrying you'll hurt yourself. It was full of reserve and unspoken words, too. But it was mostly full of the unconditional love that exists between a mother and her child from the moment they set eyes on each other. In our house, we don't bandy it about, this special kind of love. The first time I said, 'I love you,' to my mother was on the phone, after Miss Granny 2004 died. When we hung up, she called Marion to tell her to keep an eye on me: I must have been contemplating suicide. In our house, love hides in the little things. In a blanket pulled up over someone sleeping, in a film you want to watch but would rather wait till you can see it together, in a smile when you're on the verge of tears, in the last slice of chocolate cake left for someone else, in a head laid on a shoulder, in a laugh when the joke wasn't funny, in the wrapping paper kept because it has 'To my darling girl' written on it.

I hope she'll forgive me.

Clara isn't here. She texted me a heads-up: 'I'm spending the night at Greg's. If you need me, let me know, I'll come back.' I think her company would have helped me snap out of these particularly intense Sunday-evening blues, but I would feel bad disturbing her while she and Greg are doing what consenting adults do in private. I make myself a hot chocolate, unpack my bag, put my things away, put my pyjamas on and switch on my laptop.

His name pops up among the special offers for shops I've never heard of, the newsletters and the messages sent by generous people reaching the end of their lives who would like to give me millions without any conditions . . . except furnish them with my bank details.

From: Raphael Marin-Goncalves
Subject: News

It's fortunate that no one can see me. There's a strong chance I look like the village idiot as I open this email.

254

Hi Julia,

I hope you're well.

I hope you won't mind my emailing, I found your address on the Ocean View website. I got back to London okay and life has picked up again at its hectic pace, but I think about my grandmother a lot. I call her frequently and she tells me everything's fine, but she'd say that if it wasn't, so that doesn't put my mind at rest.

Would you mind if I asked you for news every now and then? I don't know you very well, but I feel I can trust you.

I hope I'll hear back from you. I'll be over for a few days as soon as possible.

Best regards
Raph

The email was sent three days ago. He must think I didn't like him contacting me. I click on reply.

Hi Raphael,

I'm fine, thanks. I hope you are, too.

You were absolutely right to email me. I'd be very happy to give you news of your grandmother. Last week, I had an opportunity to spend some time with her, and she's settling in gradually. You probably know she's decided to stay here permanently. I won't say she's over the moon, but she's already made friends with several other residents and she enjoys joining in the activities. She even admitted she wasn't expecting to like it.

Of course, she also says she misses her house and is finding it hard to get used to the loss of independence, but that's to be expected, and the fact she sees the positives is very encouraging.

It's a good idea to come and see her soon. I'm sure she'll be happy to see you.

Don't hesitate to ask me for updates whenever you like. You could also call me, if that's easier for you: 06 56 44 85.

Have a good evening
Julia

Send.
Shut down my laptop.
Stop smiling idiotically.
Ask myself how many sleeps 'as soon as possible' is.

July

'Life isn't about waiting for the storm to pass.
It's about learning to dance in the rain'

– Seneca

Chapter 57

The minibus finds a space in the car park while Anne-Marie gives a few final recommendations to the residents gathered on the front steps.

'This went very well last year, which is why we're doing it again. It's not the same youngsters, but they're here for the same thing: to get off their estates and see the sea. For many of them, it'll be the first time. Be tolerant: some of them may be quite abrasive, but they don't have easy lives and their teachers are here to supervise them. Thanks for agreeing to take part in this and let's make the most of it!'

The teenagers step down from the minibus and head towards us as we walk towards them. It's like something from *West Side Story*.

A tall, dark-haired boy in white sweat pants gives a bow.

'Good day to you, my lieges and my ladies, how go you this fine day?'

His friends explode with laughter.

'What you doing, Moundir? Why you talking like a court jester?'

'You what?' he says defensively. ''S how they talked in like medieval times! I know how to adapt, I do, my lord!'

The whole group starts talking at once. A teacher raises her voice and asks them to quieten down. After several repeated interventions, they fall silent. Just as Anne-Marie is about to make her introductions, a bleating little voice comes from the group of residents.

'Chill, boyz, did ya think we was past it?'

Eyes are popping out of heads in the other camp. I'm glad Greg is filming this: I can watch it on a loop on bad days.

All the residents turn to look at Rosa. She gives a shrug.

'What? I used to watch Ali G with my grandson . . .'

The teenagers burst out laughing again, and the residents join in. This is going to be a memorable day.

The introductions are done in the main living room, starting with the residents: name, age and what they hope to get from today. Then it's the turn of the young visitors: name, age and what they hope to get from today. The former are mostly hoping for some sort of exchange, dialogue, a shared experience. The latter are hoping to see the sea. The former have to be stopped from telling their whole life story. The latter have to be prompted to say a bit more about themselves, between embarrassed giggling.

Anne-Marie explains how we'll be spending the next few hours: set off in the minibuses as soon as everyone is ready, go to the beach, swimming and games, picnic, swimming and games, return to Ocean View for four o'clock.

'Does anyone have any questions?'

No one has any questions.

Linda, the teacher, then takes over, reminding her charges of the rules. Stay in groups. Always be with a member of staff. Go into the water one step at a time. Don't go out of your depth. Be careful not to run into people. Not too much screaming and shouting. No putting sand in your friends' mouths. Please avoid dunking people's heads underwater for more than ten minutes. When they start going blue, it means they're not feeling so good. Make the most of this, have fun and come back with lots of good memories.

'Do you have any questions?'

'Yeah!' says Marie, one of the students, putting her hand up. 'Can we scream if we see a shark?'

The *Grande Plage* is heaving with people. Holidaymakers started arriving as soon as we were into July, and the sun is here to stay. We identify a little patch of sand, plant a parasol in it and put down the cool box. Now we just need to lay out our towels.

'We could form a circle,' suggests Louise. 'Then we could all talk to each other more easily.'

The residents nod: it's a good idea. The students exchange looks, as if we've just suggested they swallow arsenic. Their only reply is to sling their bags on the ground, tear off their clothes and cluster round their teachers.

'C'mon, miss, sir. We want to go in!'

'We'll wait till everyone's ready,' replies Younes, a member of staff.

'That's well tight, they'll be hours!' complains one of the teenagers.

It doesn't take hours, but it does take a good ten minutes. Disappointment at the youngsters' attitude is clear to see on the residents' faces. I suspect they're deliberately drawing out their preparations. They're undressing in slow motion, folding their clothes, stowing them in bags, adjusting their swimming things, rubbing themselves with sun cream, putting on hats and checking they haven't forgotten anything.

'Last year's group were more polite,' grumbles Lucienne. 'If I'd known, I'd have stayed indoors, out of this heat.'

When this extended performance is over, the kids cheer and start running towards the supervised swimming area, obviously not aware that other people's towels aren't meant to be treated like carpets.

Once they reach the water, though, there's a volley of shrieks.

'Whoa, that's Baltic!'

'Oh, don't be such a pussy!'

'We'll end up like that man in *Titanic*!'

'Wet the back of your neck before you go under!'

'You're the *Titanic*!'

'Mate, it's so cold my snail's going back in its shell!'

'No way I'm going in. This beach is for polar bears!'

They're in up to their knees, laughing almost as much

262

as they're complaining. Moundir is more intrepid than the others and edges further in on tiptoe, as if that could delay the effects of going deeper. When the water is up to his chest, he turns to face his friends, as proud as if he's swum across the Atlantic.

'So, losers, who's the boss now?'

The losers are careful not to tell the boss that a big wave is coming up behind him. It crashes over him, washing away his smile, and then all of him, churning him in a great roll of foam from which the occasional arm, foot or tuft of hair appears. The others laugh helplessly, and so do the residents, and Moundir emerges from the swirling water, straightening his trunks and his hair, while the whole group cheers.

Louise steps closer to Sonia, one of the girls.

'The secret is to tell yourself it's hot. If you concentrate on thinking it is, you'll feel as if it really is.'

Sonia tries this out, while Pierre approaches Rayane.

'The first time I swam here,' he says, 'I thought I'd lose all my limbs. But once you're in, it's lovely. It's worth persevering.'

Very gradually, the two age groups mix. The old help the newcomers; the teenagers communicate their youthful exuberance to the old. I must be far too sensitive at the moment, because I'm finding this moving. The circle of life. Yesterday's youngsters and the pensioners of tomorrow. The past and the future in the present. We're all in up to our waists when there's a loud scream.

A shark?

A corpse?
A tsunami?
Nope.
Just Isabelle, who caught Greg and Clara holding hands underwater.

Chapter 58

This morning, two minibuses dropped us at the beach. One for the students and one for the residents.

This afternoon, two minibuses drop us back at Ocean View's car park. One with the teenagers and residents together, and one with residents and the teenagers together.

Lucienne comes over to me.

'I've changed my mind. I actually prefer these ones to last year's lot.'

As we gathered around the blue-and-white parasols, cool boxes and towels arranged in a circle today, we were all the same age.

At first, wariness met arrogance, and there were frowns of mistrust as well as strongly held preconceptions. The unknown. And then, as the minutes and hours passed, connections were made, across the generations.

We ran to escape the spray, we jumped into waves – or the more agile did – we let the wet sand bury our feet, we built sandcastles that looked as if they'd been bombed, we ate doughnuts, we spoke street slang and good old-fashioned French, we compared euros and old francs, we wondered whether anyone was having the same sort of experience on the other side of the Atlantic, we collected seashells and watched the endlessly changing choreography of seagulls overhead.

We have tea and biscuits in the living room, all of us around one table. In an hour, the teenagers will be gone.

'Do you know,' Rosa says, 'I haven't been here very long. I almost didn't come today, I thought my hip would stop me enjoying the outing. But I thought I ought to join in, if only to do something for disadvantaged youngsters. I was right about one thing: it's not easy jumping waves with a plastic hip. Luckily, Greg was there to hold me up. On the other hand, I was pretty presumptuous about everything else . . . it wasn't me who gave you something, but the exact opposite.'

'Seriously?' asks Sonia. 'What did we give you?'

'Seriously. All day, I watched the amazement on your faces when you saw the sea, the wet sand, the seagulls . . . I've known those things all my life – they've become second nature, I don't notice them. It's my indifference, that's what you've changed, that's what's at issue.'

Rayane lunges towards her.

'Here, I've got a bit of old kitchen roll.'

'Whatever for?' Rosa asks, recoiling slightly.

'Well, like, you suddenly stopped talking and said "a tissue". I thought you was going to sneeze, or had a nosebleed or something.'

It takes a moment for everyone to catch on, and a ripple of laughter goes around the room.

'You're so dumb, Rayane!' Brice pitches in. ' "At issue" is a posh way of saying, "that's what I'm talking about".'

'Well, anyway,' Rosa resumes. 'I wanted to thank you. Thanks to you, I've realised how lucky I am to have lived with these treasures. I don't feel like complaining any more.'

A lot of head-nodding supports Rosa's view. My own head included. Today, I experienced everything through the filter of a first-time experience. Hearing shrieks of joy and howls of laughter made it all the more enjoyable.

'Why did you talk about yourself in the past tense?' Sonia asks. 'It's like you're dead . . .'

'We're not dead,' Pierre explains, 'but our lives are behind us.'

'Nah, man!' exclaims Moundir. 'My great-grandpa's a hundred and two, and my baby brother died when he was three. There's no way of knowing how long it'll last. Life is right here, right now, it's not yesterday and it's not tomorrow . . .'

'Well I never!' a voice comes from the doorway. 'Your little knees-up sounds very cheerful . . . I'm almost sorry I didn't join in.'

Leon is watching us from the doorway with his usual rictus expression.

'Yup,' says Louise with a shrug. 'Old people can be really dumb, too!'

We wave wildly at the minibus as it drives away. The teenagers have congregated in the rear window to say goodbye. Before getting in, they thanked us and promised to come back. We all know they won't, but we agreed to it. There was a palpable urge to clasp them in our arms, but it was our hands that did the clasping. Probably more out of respect than wariness this time.

When the minibus is out of sight, we all turn on our heel, ready to go back to our day-to-day existence.

'Wait a sec!' Greg stops us. 'Linda, the supervisor, gave me this. She told me they felt more comfortable putting it in writing.'

He opens out a sheet of white paper and holds it up for all of us to see. Written in black felt-tip surrounded by hearts are the words:

'Thank you for everything. You guys are sick!'

It is signed with all their names.

No one reacts except for Greg, Clara, Rosa and I, who burst out laughing.

'I don't understand. We're old, not ill,' says Pierre.

Clara catches her breath and replies:

'It means you're great!'

Chapter 59

Elisabeth doesn't suspect a thing. Pierre has warned her that he can't come to visit today because he has to have some medical tests. He was terribly sorry, he hadn't noticed the date, but he would definitely call her to wish her a happy anniversary. Sixty years is not to be sniffed at. Elisabeth was so blinded by disappointment, it didn't even occur to her he might be up to something.

'Even if you call a thousand times, I won't pick up,' she announced.

He chuckled as he reported this reaction, but now, just before curtain up, he's looking much less sure of himself.

As promised, I've taken responsibility for the bulk of the arrangements. With help from Clara and Greg, who went about it so wholeheartedly you could be forgiven for thinking they're projecting into their own future. I've organised a surprise that should leave Elisabeth speechless.

I knock on her door at the convalescent home, and she invites me in with a muted little voice.

'Hello, Elisabeth, how are you?'

The grim set of her face is all the answer I need: not fantastic. Sitting on her bed, staring at the TV, she's listlessly channel-hopping.

'It's our wedding anniversary today,' she says, when I sit down on a chair. 'And can you believe, my husband decided he'd rather have his insides filmed than come and celebrate it with me.'

'I heard about that. He didn't have any choice – the next appointment was in six months.'

I seriously contemplate adding a new skill to my CV: expert liar.

Elisabeth shakes her head.

'I should have divorced him when I had the chance, and there's an end to it.'

I'm not sure my hearing's quite right.

'Pardon?'

'Yes, I nearly left Pierre ten years ago.'

'No! If you start, too, how do you expect the rest of us to go on believing in love? You're the perfect couple!'

'It's precisely that striving for perfection that nearly tore us apart. Ten years ago, I couldn't bear anything about Pierre any more. Everything I once loved about him or hadn't previously noticed drove me up the wall. The way he walked, the noise he made when he ate, the way he asked for a kiss when I was just going shopping, the way he made everything about himself, his smile . . . no two ways about it: I was no longer seeing him through rose-tinted spectacles. I really envied my sister, who never complained about her husband and thought he was wonderful. I ended up thinking this couldn't be right and that I didn't love Pierre any more. I could only see the negatives. It almost made me nasty, constantly picking on him. Poor man, he didn't understand what was going on, *he* hadn't changed . . . I arranged to meet a lawyer who specialised in divorce cases, to get some information. My sister came with me, even though she didn't agree with what I was doing.'

I'm stunned by her confession. She and Pierre had often told me it wasn't always easy, but I hadn't realised just how bad it could be.

'What made you change your mind?' I ask.

'The truth. From our childhood, we're bombarded with talk of perfect love, which never has any ups and downs and stands up to everything. Your heart beating like a drum, butterflies in your stomach, shivers down your spine, passion . . . the lawyer was running late. I chatted to my sister in the waiting room. "What do you think?" she asked. "Do you think I get butterflies every time Jean comes near me? Do you honestly think there aren't times when I want to shout at him, pack my bags and never see him again? Do you think love is a Mills & Boon romance?" There were two other people in the waiting room: a man and a woman. It ended up as group therapy! The woman was younger than us and was leaving her husband, who'd cheated on her with everyone in town. The man had just been left by his wife and was devastated. I pictured Pierre, and my heart constricted. He didn't deserve this. And neither did I. I'd have missed him too much! The love was still there, well hidden under the irritations. When you live with someone the whole time, you end up only seeing the bad things. It's like when you buy new clothes: at first you love them, then you think they're boring and, eventually, you can't stand the sight of them. It takes quite an effort not letting yourself be polluted by the little negative details. They wear you out, over a lifetime. But, definitely, the most important thing is not thinking love is supposed to be perfect. It's quite something to share your everyday existence and even your thoughts with someone. And if there weren't the lows, you wouldn't appreciate the highs.'

'Well, I would never have thought . . .'

'Louise, who loves knitting, came up with a wonderful metaphor the other day. Love is like a piece of knitting: you work your way steadily through the rows, you incorporate pretty patterns that you're proud of, and every now and then you focus on a dropped stitch. But what you're left with at the end of the day is a warm, comforting jumper.'

I'm so lost in what she's saying, I've almost forgotten why I'm here.

'Come on, I'm going to take you out for a little wander! It's a gorgeous day, we should make the most of it.'

'I don't feel like it. And I can't walk far, anyway.'

'Yes, you can! Come on, it'll cheer you up.'

'No, really, I'd rather watch TV. You're very sweet to come and see me regularly, but you've caught me on a bad day.'

I hadn't anticipated this eventuality. I absolutely have to

get her to move. I hope I don't have to resort to drugging her. I stand up and move her wheelchair up to the bed.

'Come along, up you get! Nip into the bathroom to sort your hair out a bit and then we're going outside. I warn you, I'm more stubborn than you are.'

Twenty minutes later, I push her wheelchair out through the main entrance. Elisabeth sits in stony silence. At the corner of the building, where the path turns towards the gardens, she gives a little cry.

They're all standing waiting for us. Pierre is at the front, holding a bouquet of flowers. Then their children, grandchildren and great-grandchildren, and the residents and staff of Ocean View. In all, there are nearly fifty people who have come to celebrate their sixty years of love. Elisabeth turns towards me, her eyes full of tears.

'I should have guessed he'd find an excuse not to have that colonoscopy.'

Iced drinks and cakes, which we made in yesterday's cookery workshop, are laid out on prettily decorated tables. Bunting hangs from the trees. Several patients from the convalescent home have joined the party. Pierre comes over to me while I'm helping myself to my third bowl of tiramisu.

'Thank you so much, Julia, this is better than perfect!'

'It was honestly a pleasure getting it all ready for you, and I had a lot of help from Clara and Greg. If I don't find a job after Ocean View, I could always reinvent myself as a party planner. But I'll have to stay away from tiramisu . . .'

'Just listen a moment, Julia,' he continues, more seriously. 'I don't really know how to say this sort of thing, but I want to say it. You can't imagine how happy you've made us. If it weren't for you, we would probably have blown out a single candle while watching a foreign soap opera. But we'll never forget this day. At our age, we can get a bit blasé: we've had huge happy occasions, our wedding, the births of our children, and then their children . . . It's difficult to top that. But I have very strong feelings today. And I can tell from the look in my wife's eyes that she feels the same. Look at her. Can you see it, too?'

I look over at Elisabeth. She's standing, with support from one of her daughters on one side and a little boy holding her hand on the other. If fulfilment had a face, it would be Elisabeth's right now.

'I know this was your side of a bargain,' he goes on. 'And meanwhile, I haven't yet found anything on Leon, but I'm still looking. You could easily have arranged something simple, but you put your heart into this. It must have taken up a lot of your time.'

'Dad! Come on, we're doing a family photo!' Pierre's son calls.

He excuses himself with a smile and heads off towards the group. After a few steps, he turns back.

'You're a wonderful person, Julia. You deserve to find a

love like ours, because it's the only thing that makes any-one truly happy. I hope with all my heart that you do.'

He joins his family for the photo, which will have pride of place in every one of their homes.

I'm off for more tiramisu.

Chapter 60

From: Raphael Marin-Goncalves
Subject: News

Hi Julia,

It's been a while since I've asked for news of my grandmother and even though I talk to her a lot on the phone I'd still like your professional opinion.

I almost called but realised it's gone midnight . . . I'm only just home from work. It's like that every evening at the moment. I work hard for the money, as the great social philosopher Donna Summer said.

I'm relying on you to tell me whether Rosa's really settling into her new life. She told me about a day with some teenagers, which she loved! She also said you drop by to chat to her a lot, and she really appreciates that. So do I.

I hope everything's going well for you, that you're not missing Greg too much and that your pyjamas have recovered from their terrible shock.

Nearly forgot! I'm coming over next weekend. Don't say a word to Rosa: it's a surprise ;)
Best
Raph

It's one o'clock in the morning when I find this email. I now check my work account every evening before going to bed. Clara has just left, after a night spent bingeing on old episodes of *Friends* and eating cheese and chocolate. Oh, and we drank some wine, too. Just a bit.

From: Julia Rimini
Subject: Re: News

Hi Raphael,

This is Snuggles talking, Julia's pyjamas. I'm glad someone's finally taking an interest in how I feel! I'm more accustomed to being used when I'm needed and then thrown into a basket and washed with powder that's not even right for me. Now I've been dumped unceremoniously on a shelf between a woolly hat and a coat, waiting for next winter. I'm seriously contemplating contacting the LFDP (Liberation Front for Distressed Pyjamas).

Rosa's fine; I've heard Julia talk about her. She joins in enthusiastically with all the activities and gets on well with the other residents. She'll be very happy to see you again – what a lovely surprise!

I'll say goodbye, or should I say adieu, as there's little chance I'll ever see you again. Do something for me: look after your pyjamas. They're sensitive creatures.

Snuggles

Okay, so maybe I drank more than a bit.

Chapter 61

If this isn't an ambush, it still looks very like one.

This afternoon, Greg asked if I'd like to have a picnic this evening on Sables d'Or beach in Anglet with him and Clara. I was happy to accept the invitation; it would remind me of evenings in my youth, when we gathered around guitars and djembe drums through until dawn. After the age of thirty, nights under the stars happen indoors with phosphorescent stickers on the ceiling. What I hadn't grasped was that Raphael, who's here for the weekend, would be part of the deal. I would have reached the same decision, but I probably wouldn't have such a strong feeling that my friends had set the whole thing up.

'Should we light a fire?' Greg asks.

'That's not allowed!' I tell him. 'Apparently, there are masses of unexploded bombs from the Second World War under the sand and a fire could detonate them.'

'You really are a killjoy . . .' he says.

'Yes, but she's got lots going for her, too,' Clara chips in. 'She's generous and funny, she's intelligent and, when she dresses up, she looks gorgeous!'

I'm just waiting for her to say, *The whole package for the modest sum of 99 euros. It's a bargain, sir, and if you take her, we'll give you a ten-year guarantee!* But no, she just smiles. She's proud of herself. Thank goodness Raphael doesn't seem to have noticed their antics; he's lost in contemplation as the sun dives towards the ocean. I get up, grab a sandwich from the bag and sit down right next to him. That pair of schemers are almost having heart attacks.

'Happy you've seen your grandmother?' I ask.

'Yes, it's great to see her. Even though the first thing she did was comment on my new grey hairs!' he replies, laughing.

'You can't see them at all,' says Clara. 'Can you, Julia?'

I glare at her furiously, which makes her chuckle. I'm going to drown her.

'Anyway,' Raphael continues, as if nothing has happened, 'it's good to see her so settled. I was dead against my mother's decision to move her here. I was convinced she'd just let herself waste away. But she's doing the exact opposite and starting to make new plans. She's even asked me to set up a computer for her since I told her everything you could do with them.'

Clara sits between Greg's legs and he puts his arms around her. All four of us admire the sunset: technical skill – 10; artistic impression – 10. Raphael leans close to my ear.

'How's Snuggles?'

Shit. I'd hoped that – best-case scenario – that email had got lost in transit or – worst-case scenario – he'd seen it but forgotten. But here we are with worse than worst. No point trying to remedy the situation now.

'He's in bad shape, I'm afraid. I'd ca-te-gorically for-bidden him to touch my computer, but I was pretty sure I couldn't trust him. I've punished him, scrunched him up in a ball next to his worst enemy – my pyjamas with the sparkly hearts.'

'Ouch, that's gotta hurt!' he says with a grimace.

'Yup, I know. Tough love. Do you want some crisps?'

This embarrassing business with the pyjamas has at least given us a chance to start a conversation. Greg and Clara are busy inspecting each other's tonsils (they must think that, like yawning, watching people kiss makes you want to do the same), so we have plenty of time to find out a bit more about each other. Every now and then, Clara or Greg interrupts their caving expedition to mention things Raphael and I have in common. The best I can say is they're clutching at straws.

Raphael is thirty-four, I'm thirty-two: 'That's amazing, you're from the same decade!'

Raphael is a graphic designer in London for a start-up computer-games company: 'Julia's really good at drawing the *Super Mario* mushroom!'

Raphael hates vinegar on his chips: 'Julia never puts dressing on her salad!'

Raphael shares a flat with a French friend: 'That's amazing, Julia and Clara are basically flatmates!'

Raphael loves London, but he misses the sea: 'What a coincidence! Julia's crazy about the sea, too!'

I've tried discreetly stopping them, I might even have

broken Clara's tibia with one of my kicks, but there's nothing for it; they think they're being subtle. Raphael must have noticed my exasperation because he winks at me before coming out with:

'Apart from that, I can rotate my dick like helicopter blades, and I bet you've been for a helicopter ride, haven't you, Julia?'

I try to keep a straight face, but Greg and Clara's shocked expressions get the better of me. Raphael doesn't appear to get the full extent of what he's said, which makes me laugh even harder. But this is exactly what Bonnie and Clyde over there needed to deliver the crowning moment of their ridiculous plan. They both stand up at the same time.

'We're off to get ice-creams. We'll be back soon,' says Greg.

'Be good!' simpers Clara.

And off they go, before we've had time to react.

'Soon' clearly doesn't mean the same thing to everyone. An hour later, it's completely dark, groups of people have gathered here and there on the floodlit beach, and we've finished the crisps and exhausted every possible topic of light conversation: work, a bit about university, the odd amusing anecdote, some superficial plans. The next layer down is family, love life, heartache and hopes for the future. We get along well, he makes me laugh as I think I do him, we have more obvious things in common than Clara and Greg think, I'm tempted to confide in him about a few things, but perhaps because he's a patient's grandson and therefore to some extent a client, perhaps out of wariness, perhaps because I sense it could be dangerous, I don't feel like saying more. And that's something else we have in common, because he cuts short the increasing awkwardness by jumping to his feet.

'Come on, let's go for a swim!' he says.

I frown at him in amazement.

'Have you had a blow to the head? Look,' I say, lifting my hand. 'How many fingers?'

'Stop it, I'm being serious! There are loads of people in the water – doesn't that make you want to go in?'

'Honestly? No.'

'Are you scared?'

'Not at all!' I cry, a little too loudly.

'Well, come on, then! It's gonna be great. You'll love it.'

Oh, well, if I'm going to love it . . . I get up with forced enthusiasm, take off my dress, checking my breasts don't pop out of their cups, straighten up my swimming costume, suck in my stomach and follow him towards the water's edge.

The truth is, I'm really frightened. I could have admitted it, but neither the size of the waves (small) or the temperature of the water (warm) would have justified a refusal. I really can't tell him I'm scared of sharks. He'd laugh, and he'd be right: no one's ever seen a man-eating shark on the Pays Basque coast. But ever since I watched *Jaws* as a child, I'm filled with irrational terror as soon as I'm out of my depth, even in a swimming pool . . . Not knowing what's beneath my feet makes me hysterical. So swimming in the ocean in the dead of night . . .

'You see, it's really warm!' Raphael says, jumping into the foam.

'Wonderful. Shall we go back now?'

He laughs. I'm in up to my waist and I'm starting to feel okay about this. We're not the only people in the water, and some are a long way out, and sharks seem like a lazy bunch, so they probably attack the people nearest them first. That'll give me time to get out with all my limbs intact. I jump every time a wave rolls past me, but the water has a soothing effect: I'm almost completely relaxed. Raphael tilts his chin towards an approaching wave that's bigger than the others.

'Shall we catch it?'

It's a rhetorical question: he doesn't give me any choice. He grabs my hand, we turn to face the beach and push ourselves off when the wave reaches us. We glide over the water, we're flying, the foam billows around us, I get whirled round and round as if on a spin cycle, and end up floundering in ten centimetres of water with my head in the sand, laughing and very probably looking like a beached whale. Raphael is in the same state himself.

'Shall we do it again?' I ask, jumping to my feet.

He follows me, laughing. I'm not frightened at all now, just full of the thrill of it. I'd forgotten how much fun it is, playing in the waves. We get into position to catch the next one. Raphael's holding my hand and I think I can feel him stroking it with his thumb. I look at him, he looks at me, I smile, he smiles, I see something move a little way behind him, he smiles, I freeze, he smiles, I scream:

'A FIIIIIIIIINNN!'

And I run for the shore, tugged into slow motion by the water, which is suddenly my enemy.

I discover later that it was the head of a young man swimming further out to sea. What was he thinking, having a pointy head! Greg and Clara chose that exact moment to come back, with no ice-creams but with plenty of sand in their underwear. So they got to see the end of the scene and Raphael told them how it started: the three of them laughed till they cried and called me Bolt for the rest of the evening in reference to my slo-mo sprint.

Clara gives me a big hug when she says goodnight. She pats my back, throws me an apologetic little look and hurries off to her room. Poor girl, it's a hard knock. It will take her a while to understand that, despite their best efforts, they'll never succeed in finding someone sufficiently mad to take an interest in me.

Chapter 62

'How are you feeling today?'

'Oh, with my fingers. How about you?'

Gustave has tidied his studio. More or less. The posters have come down from the walls, the ashtray is almost empty, the acrid mentholated smell that usually hangs in the air is slightly less pronounced, the comics are in a pile and there are no clothes strewn over the floor: they're in a compact heap at the end of the bed. You can see more clearly. So much so that I notice a detail which makes me smile.

'I see you've added a pillow!'

I didn't know he was capable of blushing.

'It's for my cricked neck. I sleep better with two pillows.'

'Of course!' I say, going over to the bed. 'And are these pills for your cricked neck, too?'

This time he doesn't so much blush as go purple.

'The doctor prescribed them for me . . .'

'I hope you didn't buy them from a dealer on the corner of the street!' I say with a laugh. 'You shouldn't be ashamed, Gustave, it's called love.'

He sighs.

'I know, I know, but Louise would rather it didn't get about. I get the impression she wants to take things slowly . . . whereas I want to spend every moment that's left to me with her.'

I've never seen him so serious. Maybe life doesn't feel like a joke to him any more.

'Julia, we don't have the time to take our time. Would you mind helping me?'

'Helping you?'

'Yes. You did a very good job of organising Elisabeth and Pierre's wedding-anniversary party. He can't stop talking about it – they're so grateful to you. It was a wonderful party.'

I've no idea where he's going with this, but his eyes are glittering with excitement. Under his wrinkles, I can almost see the eight-year-old boy.

'I'd like you to help me arrange an unforgettable proposal.'

'A marriage proposal? The full works?!' I squeal, having to stop myself from throwing my arms around his neck because the idea makes me so happy.

'Yes. I'd like Louise to be my wife. I want us to live together, I want us to stop hiding. But most of all, I want to fill her life with love and see the sparkle in her eyes.'

What a wonderful idea! Getting married at their age, when they've nothing left to prove, nothing to build together but a few memories, for the sheer pleasure of being together and being part of the same family – how fantastic. I'm incredibly flattered to have a part to play in his plan.

I've just started thinking about the best way to organise a proposal worthy of their love when a crucial question occurs to me.

'Do you think she'll accept?'

'I don't know. But I'll only get an answer if I ask the question. You are a twit sometimes!'

Aha, so Gustave hasn't completely changed.

'What about your daughter? Will she be okay with this?'

He sits down in the chair opposite me.

'I don't know. I have to admit, that's what I'm most worried about.'

Chapter 63

From: Raphael Marin-Goncalves
Subject: For Bolt

Hi Julia,

How are you?

I know I only left three days ago, but I'm worried about my grandmother. I got the feeling she was sad to see me go – she didn't really say goodbye and wouldn't look me in the eye.

I feel like she's not unhappy and her days are busy, but I want to be sure she doesn't miss me too much. I think about her a lot.

I hope everything's good for you. I had a great evening with the three of you on Saturday!

See you soon

Raphael

PS Look out, there's a shark behind you.

I click reply and start typing my reply but then stop to reread his email. Once. Twice. Three times.

I'm not at all sure about this, but there's enough of a suspicion for me to go and ask Clara her opinion.

August

'The present time has one advantage
over every other – it is our own'

– Charles Caleb Colton

Chapter 64

'So who's this Pomponnette you're talking about?' Clara groans, with sleepy eyes and bird's-nest hair. I think I've woken her up.

She splashes her face with water and sits down on her bed.

'Explain the whole thing.'

So I explain. Raphael's email, which was different to the previous ones, the feeling that it can be interpreted in two ways, the Pomponnette factor.

'Who the hell *is* this Pomponnette, for God's sake?'

'Haven't you ever seen *The Baker's Wife*?'

'What, at the Golden Brioche? Is his wife's name Pomponnette?'

I laugh out loud. God, I love her!

'No! *The Baker's Wife* is a classic film by Marcel Pagnol. In a nutshell, it's about a baker whose wife leaves him for another man, and the baker's miserable. The last scene is the really telling one. His wife comes back and he forgives her, but when the cat, who's called Pomponnette, comes in to drink its milk, he starts ranting at it: "Bitch, slut, scum! Did you think about poor Pompon while you were out with that alley cat?" I know my Marseille accent is a bit dodgy, but you get the picture. When he has a go at the cat, he's really talking to his wife.'

Clara looks at me as if I'm transforming into an alien.

'I have absolutely no idea what you're talking about. Have you been drinking?'

I hand her a print-out of the email. She reads it.

'Yes, and?'

'Well, I wonder whether he's really talking about his grandmother.'

'Or maybe you've taken drugs . . .'

'Of course I haven't! Look!' I say, pointing at his words. 'There, can you see, when he wonders whether she misses him, perhaps he's asking whether *I* miss him.'

For several seconds, Clara doesn't react at all. Is she even still alive? Then I see the beginnings of a smile.

'You could be right . . . "she was sad to see me go"; "her days are busy"; "I think about her a lot" . . .'

She jumps to her feet, now fully awake.

'Omg, that's exactly what it is! It's Pompom thingy!'

I go back to my studio armed with Clara's advice: call him straight away and tell him I'm madly in love with him. She's suffering from lack of sleep; no two ways about it.

I don't know if I'm right. I don't know if he wants me to read something between the lines. I can't help acknowledging that I may *think* he is simply because it's what I'd like. But at the same time, all those safety locks I've deliberately put in other people's way have ended up confusing my emotions. I don't know what I want, I don't even know what I don't want, and I don't know when I will know. So let's play it safe.

> *Hi Raphael,*
>
> *I'm fine, thanks. How are you?*
>
> *I don't think your grandmother was more upset when you left than last time, but if that's the feeling you got, I'll look into it tomorrow. It's true she misses you a lot but, like you said, we're doing our best to keep her busy and make sure she has a nice time. If I think she's feeling a bit low, I'll let you know, I promise.*
>
> *Yes, it was a really good night. Greg and Clara had a great time, too. Let's do it again ;-)*
>
> *Have a good evening and see you soon*
>
> *Bolt*
>
> *PS Look out, there's a helicopter in your boxers.*

Chapter 65

Elisabeth and Pierre are sitting on the sofa, so close together they look like conjoined twins.

'I'm so happy to be back!' she keeps saying. 'To give you an idea how much, I even missed the food.'

Pierre squeezes her hand.

'I've come back to life,' he says. 'We all use the expression "sharing your life with someone", but you don't appreciate what it means till you're suddenly on your own. Sixty years of living together: all my habits involve having my wife there. Waking up, brushing my teeth, watching television, eating, admiring a view . . . I don't know how to do anything on my own any more.'

I feel almost superfluous with them so happy to be together again. I'm not used to it. My parents were discreet in their affections; I don't remember ever seeing them kiss, except in their wedding photos or a little peck on the lips for good morning and goodnight. They didn't love each other any less; they just showed it in different ways. I was also embarrassed by Clara and Greg cuddling on the beach the other day. As if love is an assault on my senses. I need to get over that.

For now, I get up and suggest I should leave them to enjoy being back together.

'You've only just got back, and we'll have plenty of time to chat later. If you need me, you know where to find me.'

I gesture at Elisabeth not to get up – the neck of her femur is still fragile – but Pierre stands and hurries to the cupboard by the door.

'Wait, with all the goings-on, I almost forgot!' he says, handing me an old digital camera. 'I think you'll find everything you need on here.'

Almost before I've closed the door, I start scrolling through the images on the clouded little screen. It's not very clear – I'll be able to see better on my laptop – but what I can make out makes me gasp with surprise.

'It can't be!'

Then I smile.

Game on, Leon.

Chapter 66

A year.

A year ago today, 'before' ended and 'after' began. The after-Dad's-death years. Life as one of those who know.

I've been crying since I woke up this morning. Luckily, it's Sunday. My mother has tried to get hold of me three times, but I didn't have the strength to pick up. I wouldn't be able to grit my teeth hard enough today. I'll call her this evening. Clara knocked at my door more gently than usual, almost tenderly. I didn't open it. A few minutes later she slipped a little note under the door: a big heart and the words 'I'm here'. I cried even more.

Marion called me the other day and told me I was strong for getting over all this. Dad, Nannynoo, Marc. I'm not strong. If I had a choice, I'd slip out of my body and let it get on with living through it all. If I had a choice, I'd close my eyes and go to sleep until it stops hurting. The sun still rises every morning, the waves still roll on to the beach and my body still works. I have to go along with it. You can't put it on pause.

I've taken out my old photos. I often make a point of thinking about other things so I'm not overwhelmed by grief. But I feel like spending the day with him today. It's as if I'm no longer frightened of my pain. I think I may be growing up here.

I live with people three times my age. They've seen plenty of heartache. Like me, they thought they'd never get over it, they thought they wouldn't be strong enough. They may be broken into a thousand pieces on the inside, they may have wounds so deep they'll never quite heal, but they smile and laugh and get on with life. Worse than that, they're happy. They've had painful experiences and drawn a particular strength from them: seeing what really matters.

With them around me, I'm learning resilience.

I never used to appreciate the little things as much as I do now that I *know* it will all come to an end. I now know their value. I'm more and more convinced that happiness is made up of small odds and ends picked up along the way.

I haven't yet managed to see any positive aspects to these events. I'm not sure I want to. But I can see how lucky I am to understand the value of life itself.

That's something Ocean View has given me.

I open the album's heavy leather cover. The inner pages are protected by plastic film and stick together as I turn them. This is my album. From the moment I was born, my parents compiled photos of me, then they gave me the album on my eighteenth birthday. My sister has one of her own. I cry at the sight of my father looking so young, proud to be posing with his baby in his arms. I laugh at a picture of him with a moustache. I cry seeing him so happy with my mother, and laugh when I'm reminded of my face as a schoolgirl with braces on my teeth, glasses on my nose and a monobrow. I cry over the picture of Nannynoo teaching me to knit, and laugh when I remember the time I put make-up on my father. I stroke the photo, wishing it was his skin. It was always slightly prickly and I whinged about it when he kissed me. I don't ever want to forget that.

I'm tugging the umpteenth tissue from the box when Clara knocks again at the door. I don't answer; I'm not ready. This evening, after I've called Mum, I'll go and thank her for being there. If she likes, we can watch *Friends* and have cheese, chocolate and wine. But not now. For now, I'm with Dad. She knocks again. I sigh. She's kind, but it would be good if she could understand. She knocks a little harder. Then harder. Then I hear a voice.

'Open up, Julia. It's me!'

It's not Clara. I open the door, and my sister tries to smile at me through her tears. She's clutching something to her chest and I recognise it straightaway. It's her album.

Grief unites those who share it. Which is a good thing, because it's a lighter load if you carry it together.

We've pored over every page of both albums. We've cried (a lot) and laughed (also a lot). The memories themselves aren't painful; it's knowing they belong in the past that hurts. We've talked about Dad, we've chatted about Nannynoo, we've lambasted Marc, we've emptied three boxes of tissues and about the same of chocolates. We called Mum, at intervals, so she didn't suspect anything.

It's dark when Carole leaves. She hugs me tight and whispers that she doesn't resent what I'm doing. Then she goes down the stairs and I see her as she was, aged seven, with her ponytail swinging and her toothy grin. My little sister.

My father died on 8 August. The eighth of the eighth. Double infinity. I think from where he is, he must be proud of his two infinities.

Chapter 67

Leon's got his grumpy face on. His normal face, then. Mouth pinched, eyebrows knitted, he stares at the floor while Anne-Marie asks him whether his son's allegations are true.

'Come on, Dad,' his son pleads with him. 'You needn't be frightened. Tell them what you told me.'

He shakes his head and glowers at me. It wouldn't take much for him to start breathing fire.

'I invented all of it,' he eventually admits.

'What?' his son squeaks. 'Someone's threatened you, is that it?'

Leon looks inconsolable.

'You really did inherit all the worst characteristics . . . Do you think we're talking about the Mafia here?'

His son is losing the plot, shaking his head furiously. He looks like one of those little dogs on the parcel shelf of a car. If he keeps this up, his nips and tucks will break open.

'But why did you do that?' asks Anne-Marie.

'Why, why? Does there always have to be a reason for everything? I was bored, that's all. Can I go back to my studio now?'

'You may,' the director replies firmly. 'I hope you'll find other things to keep you entertained. We won't tolerate accusations of this nature in future.'

Leon leaves her office, his face unreadable. I chuckle to myself, remembering his very readable expression when he realised I knew everything. That was three days ago.

When I knocked at his door, he greeted me with his perennial friendliness:

'What are you doing here? I thought you'd grasped the fact I don't want any more of your snivelling sessions.'

I gave him a sardonic look.

'Perhaps *you* don't, but Matteo might need to open up to someone . . .'

In that moment, his face was worth more than any confession. He went so red I thought steam might start coming out of his ears. It didn't last: he quickly resumed his usual rictus of contempt.

'I don't know anyone called Matteo. Leave me alone,' he spat as he closed the door.

I stuck my foot in front of it and pushed my way into his studio. Oddly, he didn't really put up any opposition and let me sit down. I felt uncomfortable. I've never much liked playing bad cop. I take no pleasure in upsetting people, however unpleasant they may be, and the prospect of confronting Leon about his strange escapades didn't exactly thrill me. But I had no choice: if I wanted him to stop blackmailing Ocean View, I had to play him at his own game.

Pierre had been an expert detective. When I'd asked him to try to find something sensitive on Leon, he remembered a time when the cantankerous old man had appeared embarrassed when he, Pierre, had caught him typing away on his tablet. Pierre knew nothing about technology, but he was pretty sure that, if there was anything suspect, he would find it on this contraption. So he'd made the most of one of Leon's appointments with the chiropodist – the only time he consented not to take his devices – and sneaked into his studio (for safety reasons, the doors are never locked). He switched on the tablet, clicked on icons at random and photographed what popped up. And what popped up went way beyond my hopes.

'I'm not your enemy, Leon. I wish it hadn't come to this, but you've left me no choice. I don't want to wrong you in any way, just find a solution. You know I know all about Matteo. I won't mention it to anyone, I promise you that, if you stop your false accusations. We'll never discuss it again. Do you agree?'

He stared at me, his expression inscrutable, then sat down in his massage chair and spent a while opening a program before replying.

'Don't you go thinking you've won, you little schemer. If I choose not to speak further about the abuses I've suffered, it's simply because I don't have the time to waste on that. Your attempted blackmailing has no purchase whatsoever. I have nothing to be ashamed of.'

Leon, true to himself.

'You might *think* you're not doing anything illegal,' I agreed. 'But I'm sure you wouldn't want everyone to know what you're up to. It's called identity theft, you know.'

He gave a haughty grimace and sniggered.

'You wouldn't understand. I've spent my whole life in the shadow of celebrities . . . I rubbed shoulders with actors, socialised with directors, but no one ever saw me. I now have fifty-six thousand fans on Facebook, eighty thousand followers on Instagram and the same amount again on Twitter. The first thing I do every morning is check my tablet to see how many likes I've had. It's the barometer for my mood. I post photos, take my followers on trips to the Bahamas, show them the latest thing I've bought, put up pictures of my cat doing interesting things, introduce them to my younger brother, show off my abs, give them selfies – I fuel their dreams. They tell me I'm gorgeous, they love my cat, I have a dream life and they want to be me. Some people are envious and hate me. I don't reply to them – my fans take care of them for me. Sometimes I look at their photos, to see who they are. I pity them – they're ugly, or fat, or old, or poor. Some are all four. I can see why they'd rather follow my life than their own.'

'But it's not your life!' I squawked. 'You're stealing someone else's!'

He looked at me witheringly, as if I were too stupid to understand.

'I'm not stealing anyone's life, I'm copying photos that he publishes on his Instagram account of his own free will. Apart from that, I came up with his name – Matteo – his age, where he lives, his cat's name . . .'

'Aren't you worried someone will eventually find out?'

'As you can imagine, I didn't choose him just like that. As well as having the perfect body, this boy has the good taste to live in Bulgaria, where he's a complete unknown. His eighty-three little followers aren't going to recognise him . . .'

I hovered between compassion and disgust. There was something touching about this old man who hated his own life so much he'd invented another one, but he was deceiving thousands of people and deliberately lying and had absolutely no qualms about it. The last thing he said made up my mind for me:

'Perhaps you'll respect me now. I do have fifty-six thousand fans on Facebook.'

Chapter 68

From: Raphael Marin-Goncalves
Subject: Dada Dada Dadadadada*

Hi Julia,

It's almost midnight and I've just got home. My days are getting longer and longer, and things are very tense – we've just had another big contract taken from under our noses by a competitor – I need some space to breathe . . . Net result: I've booked my tickets, I'll be there next weekend!

How's my grandmother? I think about her a lot, picturing her in her little studio, all alone, and it breaks my heart. I hope I'll be able to come and see her much more in future. She likes seeing me and it does me so much good you wouldn't believe.

How about you? How are you doing? Do you have a holiday planned this summer?

See you soon
Raph

* I hope you recognised the music from Jaws.

Is that Pomponnette, or not?

I'm not so sure as last time. If there *is* a double meaning to his email, it's very well disguised. But if there isn't, the very fact he's sending me emails to tell me about his feelings for his grandmother raises questions of its own. Either that, or he thinks I'm his counsellor, too.

There's only one way to find out.

Hi Raphael,

I'm so sorry to hear how exhausted you are, and that you lost a client. I hope it doesn't mean your company's in difficulties but, if it is, you needn't worry: I think you're ready for a career as a film-score imitator.

That's great that you're coming over! Your grandmother will be happy to see you. She talks about you a lot, she misses you, but she's so proud to have a grandson who lives in London! The other day she said she was worried you're losing weight and she wonders whether you're getting enough to eat . . .

Don't worry, she's not unhappy. She doesn't seem to object to being on her own. Mind you, sometimes I catch her daydreaming: she's probably thinking about you – the two of you have a wonderful relationship. But I can reassure you that she's not showing any signs of depression, so don't lose any sleep about that.

I don't have any holiday time; my contract's finishing soon. Still, living in Biarritz feels like being on holiday all year!

See you soon!

Julia

I hardly have time for a quick browse on Google to check that the red spot that's appeared on my chin doesn't mean I have cancer, when he replies.

Me again.
   I didn't know your contract was coming to an end, that's a shame . . . My grandmother's got used to you: you'll be missed.
   But please reassure her I'm eating fine and not losing too much weight. Proof attached ;)
   Raph x

I open the attachments, slightly flustered by the 'x' at the end of the email. The first is a picture of him eating a huge hamburger; the second shows him bare chested, stomach sucked in and arms braced like a bodybuilder in full competition stance.

I burst out laughing. It's very funny, but it no longer leaves any room for doubt. Raphael is definitely coming on to me.

Chapter 69

Rosa comes to find me in my office just as I'm getting ready to leave.

'I wanted to ask you a favour, Julia, but you have to promise to keep it secret,' she whispers. 'It's a big, big secret.'

Right, okay. So she's going to tell me she's keeping the bodies of every lover she's ever had under her bed. This should be fun.

'I'm all ears, Rosa. What can I do for you?'

She looks around, checking for possible spies who might hear her confidences.

'Meet me in my studio,' she says, under her breath. 'Knock seven times on the door, I'll know it's you. See you in a bit.'

And she toddles off, her walking stick clicking down the corridor.

One minute later, I rap seven times on her blue door.

Two minutes later, I rap another seven times on her blue door.

Four minutes later, I rap fifteen times on the blue door and sigh.

Five minutes later, Rosa appears at the end of the corridor.

'How on earth did you get here before me?' she asks breathlessly. 'Did you run?'

'No, I walked.'

She casts an eye around her, opens the door and tugs me inside.

'Are you sure no one followed you?'

'I don't think so, Miss Marple.'

A pedestal table has appeared in one corner of her studio. Hand towels have been used to cover something bulky on top of it. Rosa is about to pull them off to bring an end to all the mystery. First, she looks up at me solemnly.

'I'll ask you one last time. Are you sure you can keep this secret?'

Okay: now, I'm frightened. I can't make out what's hiding under the towels and, confronted with Rosa's strange behaviour, I'm expecting the worst. A kilo of cocaine, a bomb, a stuffed coypu, a human head . . . Let's get it over with.

'I'm sure. Go on, or you'll have to resuscitate me.'

With her long, veiny hands, she gently slides off the covering. Underneath, a large cardboard box keeps up the suspense a little longer. A last glance at me convinces her I'm ready to see this. So she lifts up the box. And I laugh with relief.

'Why all this fuss about a computer?'

I've been trying to think where we could bury a body.

'Shush! Don't talk so loudly, for goodness' sake! The walls have ears, you know.'

'Are you going to explain this to me or not?' I ask more quietly.

Rosa wrings her hands.

'My grandson Raphael gave me this thingamabob. He told me I could visit other countries, send letters and listen to music with it.'

'But do you know how to use it?'

'He told me how. I wrote it all down,' she says, reaching for a sheet of paper covered in notes. 'Right, you have to switch it on by pressing the green button, then you click on the planet thingy and you type into the goggle. Then you can go surfing on the ant's nest – no, the spider's web.'

I can't decide whether to laugh or jump out of the window. We've got quite a way to go here.

'What exactly would you like me to do?'

'Well . . . the other day, I was watching that chat show – you know, the one that's on just after lunchtime. I really like the host – you get the feeling she's really listening to her guests, not like those presenters who keep butting in. Did you know she's from Bordeaux? That doesn't surprise me, they know how to live properly in that part of the world. I know quite a few people from round there . . .'

'Rosa, can we get to the point?'

'Yes, yes, sorry! Where was I? Oh yes! So, on the show, they were talking about lonely-hearts ads. They said you could put them on your computer and people all over the world would see them. Given how many men there are on the planet, that gives me a chance to find one, don't you think?'

'Would you like me to sign you up to a dating site?'

She smiles shyly.

'Yes, that's it. I didn't know who to ask, and you're so kind to me. And because of your work, you have to respect client confidentiality. I know it'll stay between you and me. Would you do that for me?'

She looks like a little girl asking for a sweetie after a meal. How can I refuse?

I sit next to her at the computer and introduce Rosa to the workings of a dating site. I did a bit of this myself when I was younger, and my memories of the experience are the sort that belong on the 'to be forgotten as soon as possible' pile, but there's a chance that older men aren't such freaks as the young. Maybe, when they get past a certain age, men think about exchanging a few words with a woman before asking for a photo of her breasts.

'You have to choose a username,' I say, biting into the biscuit she's given me.

'What do you mean, "use a name"?'

'It's the name you'll go by, like a nickname,' I explain, spitting the biscuit into my hand. 'This biscuit tastes very strange. Did you check the sell-by date?'

'I made it in the cooking classes last month.'

'Right. So we won't tick "cooking" in our list of talents. Do you have an idea for a username?'

'Not really . . . would Roro work?'

'Hmm . . . let's have a look at other women's usernames: SoftCentre78, PrettyRedhead77, BookLover54 . . . You need something more original, something that captures who you are and makes people want to get to know you, and you can include a number that's important to you.'

She thinks in silence for several minutes, then her face lights up just as I take a gulp from my cup of tea.

'I've got it! LovesToEat69, it's perfect!'

I almost choke, and spray my mouthful of scalding tea on to the screen.

'Are you serious? Do you want to attract perverts or something?'

'Whatever makes you say that?' she asks, in a surprised little voice. 'You told me to pick something that captures me, and I love eating. And I was born on 6 September. I can't see what's wrong with that!'

Having eventually opted for Epicurean64, put in her age (81), her interests (reading, walking, classical music, crosswords, *Catchphrase*), eye colour (dark brown), hair colour (L'Oréal's Brasilia) and profession (retired), all that remains is to write the paragraph that will make men want to meet Rosa.

With the proud smile of someone who's done a good piece of work, she picks up a small locked box, opens it and takes out a sheet of paper, which she unfolds and puts in front of me.

I love sunsets. I love reading and I always start with the last few pages in case I don't have time to read the end. I love good

food. I love how beautiful the world is. I love playing Scrabble.
I love cats. I love spending time with my family and friends.
I love roses when the buds just start to open. I love the smell of
the sea when the waves pound the beach. I love looking after
myself. I love being bored. I love to think that, one day, you'll
write to me and say a few words which will end up with us
conjugating the verb 'to love' in the first person plural.

It takes my breath away. Her words are perfect: there's nothing to edit out. No need to ask where Raphael gets it from.

'I've been thinking it over for a while,' she admits, staring at the screen. 'I hope I'll have plenty of suitors courting me! Oh, look, Julia! The Internet says ILove-Life45 wants to get in touch with me!'

I briefly explain how the site works and then leave her to it: she's asking her first suitor if he can send her a recent photo.

Chapter 70

Anne-Marie gestures for me to sit down. She pulls the pencil from her curls and scratches the back of her head. She seems to be struggling to put something into words.

'I've had a call from Lea,' she begins, 'the psychologist you've replaced while she's on maternity leave. As you know, she had a little boy a few weeks ago. Everything's okay, but she has postnatal depression and she thinks being a stay-at-home mum isn't for her. She's asked whether she can come back to work early.'

I feel like one of those people who walk along the pavement with their heads in the air, admiring the world around them, then walk smack into a lamppost. I'm stunned.

I know my contract ends soon. I should be glad: this was only meant to be a transition, after all; it's something of a miracle it's lasted this long. When I came here, I was sort of backing blindly into a corner, sure I'd made a mistake and would very soon regret it. But then there was Clara, and Greg, and Louise, Gustave, Miss Granny 2004, Elisabeth and Pierre, Lucienne, Isabelle . . . I'm trying to prepare myself for leaving, but the thought of being asked to go before the agreed date just makes me want to cry.

It obviously shows, because Anne-Marie adds, 'I've agreed that she can come back earlier, but I warned her that I can't cut short your contract.'

Couldn't she have started by saying that, the sadist?

'I'm not allowed to,' she explains, 'and I wouldn't want to. I really hesitated before taking you on, you know. You had no experience with the elderly, apart from that one work placement, and I have to admit, I wouldn't have chosen you if I'd had another applicant. But it was urgent, you were the only one, I didn't have a choice. My first impression of you wasn't very reassuring: you were late and you looked as if you'd stepped out of a zombie film.'

I hope she's got something nice to say after this; otherwise, I'll be asking her to excuse me for a few minutes while I go to hang myself with the curtains.

'You're good at what you do, Julia. You're committed, you don't try to get out of the activities, you don't clock-watch. But, above and beyond that, you're generous. You do whatever you can to make people feel good, you're nice to have around, you've really done a lot for Ocean View. And I don't want you to think I'm prying into your personal life, but I get the feeling Ocean View has done a lot for you, too.'

I nod my head.

'You have no idea how much.'

'It shows. I'm going to tell you something: when Lea called, I was hoping she'd say she didn't want to come back. I'd really like to keep you here with us. Sadly, our budget won't run to having two psychologists, and Lea

315

was here first. She refused my offer to come back and work alongside you for a while; she's keen to be single-handedly responsible for her patients. So she'll be back on the agreed date, which gives us another two months together. Have you started looking for another job to move on to?'

'Not yet. I'd better get on with it.'

'If I hear of anything, I'll let you know. Please don't hesitate if you need a reference. I'd be delighted to give you one.'

'Thank you. That means a lot to me.'

She drives the pencil back into her hair and smiles at me.

'No, I'd like to thank *you*, Julia. I think a lot of people here are going to miss you.'

I'm reeling slightly when I leave the room. In two months' time, Ocean View will be just a memory.

Chapter 71

'Do you think they'll be eaten by a shark?'

'Stop it. You're making me laugh too much, my stomach hurts.'

Raphael takes a drag on his cigarette. We're sitting side by side on the back of the bench at the far end of the grounds. Down below the cliff, dozens of surfers are sitting astride their boards, waiting for a good wave.

I was on my way back from the beach when I bumped into him. He was coming out of the annexe as I went in. He asked if I'd like to come and have a cigarette with him. I'd just stubbed one out, I had sand in places I didn't even know I had, my skin was itching terribly from the saltwater, I must have looked like one of those dolls you find after years in the attic, but I said yes.

'So is this break doing you good?' I ask.

'Seriously. I absolutely love London and I absolutely love my job, but it's really tough at the moment. I was counting down the days.'

'That tough?'

'Yup. I'd rather not think about it too much, if you don't mind.'

'No problem. When are you here till?'

317

'Tomorrow evening . . . So, anyway, you're leaving soon, are you?'

'Yup . . . in just under two months.'

He nods.

'Two months . . . Do you know what you're doing after that?'

'No idea. I didn't notice the time passing. I need to do something about it. And find a flat, too.'

'Have you been single for long?'

He asks this so suddenly, as if on a reflex, between two nicotine rushes. A jab of a drill through my protective shell.

'A few months,' I say, getting up. 'I really have to go and shower. Are you around later?'

'I'll follow you in – my grandmother wants me to teach her how to do smileys,' he says, getting to his feet. 'I think it's going to be fun . . .'

We walk across the grounds in silence. His question has put a chill in the air, and I'd like to say something to ease the tension, but I can't think of any small talk. He's thrown me. You can't ask that question like that, so innocently. Well, not unless you're seven. When you grow up, you get taller, you get hairs or breasts on your chest, maybe some spots, but you definitely get filters, too. You stop picking your nose in public, you stop telling people they're ugly, especially if they are, you don't show your knickers when you're queuing in the post office, and you don't ask people you hardly know whether they're single. Unless you have ulterior motives.

I should be flattered. The more I get to know him, the more boxes Raphael ticks in the description of my perfect man. That's exactly the problem. I know I'm doing it: waiting to get his emails, looking forward to him being here, hoping to make him smile. But this can't be happening now. His timing's all wrong. It's like the postman ringing the doorbell just when you've stepped into the bath. It's like needing to do a wee as you finish putting on your nail varnish. It's the piece of lettuce between your teeth during a job interview. It's too soon. I'm still too vulnerable: if anyone hurts me, I'll fall apart. And he scares me. If only I were immune to him . . .

'Would you like a tomato?'

That's all I can think of to defuse the awkwardness. I despair, I really do. He obligingly follows me to the vegetable plot, where we pick a few tomatoes, clinging to them like buoys in rough seas. I turn to head back to my studio.

'Who looks after this kitchen garden?' he asks.

'Gustave does. Apparently, he asked if he could have a little plot when he first arrived. They use his fruit and vegetables in the canteen. I've never had such good strawberries!'

Raphael gives me a weird smile.

'Is Gustave the old boy with the walking frame, the one who's always making jokes?'

'That's the one. Why?'

'Because I think I know whose voices we hear in the night.'

Chapter 72

It's nearly midnight when a noise comes from the grounds. Raphael signals to me: this is it.

Before going to see his grandmother earlier, he asked me whether the voices in the night came at random or on particular days. On reflection, I thought I heard them sporadically, but often on Saturday evenings. So he suggested we should try to catch them out tonight. I was up for that. He said we should meet up towards the end of the evening to put the finishing touches to our plan and be sure we didn't miss them. I was up for that, too. He added that we could meet in my studio. I was up for that and I felt something weird going on in my stomach.

We go downstairs in the dark, lit only by the screen of Raphael's phone. We mustn't be seen or heard. I don't know about him, but I'm as excited as the first time I sneaked out without my parents' permission to meet friends on the beach. The last time, too, actually, because my father was waiting for me in the garden. The fact that I had gone to bed in a dress clearly put him on to me. My heart's hammering in my chest, my body is electric, I'm stifling nervous laughter. Raphael quietly closes the annexe door behind us.

'Let's run across,' he whispers in my ear.

He takes my hand, and I shiver.

Hand in hand, we run over to the main building. I realise halfway that I'm running on tiptoe. My brain and I are having a trial separation at the moment.

'Now we can hug the wall round to the back of the building,' he whispers, even more quietly, even closer.

It's because no one must hear us.

We make our way stealthily around the building. We're almost there when we hear a laugh. We freeze, our backs against the wall. My heart's beating in my throat, in my ears. What if Raphael was wrong? What if the voices came from a group of murderers escaped from prison?

'I'm scared,' I breathe.

He reaches blindly for my hand, takes it in his again and strokes it with his thumb. If that's meant to calm me down, it's not working very well.

'Come on, we're nearly there,' he says, under his breath. 'Do you still want to go?'

His face is only centimetres from mine, and I'm looking into his eyes. The darkness, his whispering voice, his thumb stroking my hand, his breath on my cheek . . . for a few moments, time goes on pause. His breathing gets faster. I have to make a conscious effort to keep mine under control. He links his fingers into mine. I close my eyes. My brain starts playing an erotic film. My whole body is urging me to surrender. But my mind is still standing guard.

'I'm sure,' I say croakily. 'Shall we go?'

'Let's go,' he whispers.

The voices get louder as we approach the kitchen garden. I recognise one of them. Then another. Raphael
was right. A glow of light appears from behind the wall.
We walk around the wall very quietly then jump out and
confront the people who've been haunting my nights for
months.

Gustave is sitting on a garden chair, calmly rolling a
joint.

Chapter 73

He jumps when he sees us and drops everything on the ground.

Sitting around the table with him are Pierre, Elisabeth and Louise – all paralysed with shock.

'Aha!' I say triumphantly. 'We've caught you at it, you reprobates!'

It seems that I'm not very credible and that Gustave's crop is a particularly good one, because he bursts out laughing, soon joined by his joint-smoking friends. And by Raphael.

'And all you can do is laugh?' I ask, trying to keep a straight face as I contemplate this improbable scene.

'Well, you wouldn't want us to cry, would you!' squeaks Elisabeth, wiping her eyes before roaring with laughter again.

'She's going to tell us it's bad for our health,' guffaws Pierre.

Confronted with all this merriment, I give in and start laughing with them.

Louise looks at me with twinkling eyes.

'Would you like us to roll a three-skinner?'

Half an hour later, I've said, 'No, thank you' a hundred

times, and I'm not into it and it would be completely unprofessional. I haven't said that I'm too much of a good girl, and that the only joint I've ever smoked made me feel really nervous and panicky. Meanwhile, Raphael is nonchalantly taking long tokes on the joint while the fantastic four have started making confessions. The weed has loosened their tongues.

Gustave has been growing cannabis since he first arrived.

'I smoked my first joint in 1968, when I was about thirty. My wife and I had just bought a house in Anglet. Our new neighbours lived as a commune. They were very open and we quickly became friends. Our life was much more conventional than theirs, but we hung on to this habit our whole lives. When she was ill, I'd get her to smoke in her hospital bed. It eased the pain a bit . . . When I came here, I asked if I could have a vegetable plot.'

Ever since, he's been growing cannabis plants in among the tomatoes and strawberries. He dries out the flower heads in a hidden space under his sofa.

'So is that the smell in your studio?'

It's all making sense. Even the howling the other night.

'Leon heard us talking one time,' Pierre explains. 'We were worried he'd report us, so we invited him to join us. There was a full moon that night, and he thought he was a werewolf for a good hour. He's never mentioned it again.'

'I wonder why!' Elisabeth giggles. 'Gustave convinced

him he'd filmed him, just when he thought he was growing claws. He must be worried it'll get out . . .'

Raphael laughs.

In the early days, Gustave smoked alone. Then, one evening, when he was walking past Miss Granny 2004's room, he heard her crying. She'd just had a letter telling her an old friend had died; she didn't reveal any more than that but seemed really devastated. Probably Helmut . . . I think. Gustave asked whether she'd like to join him. Later, Pierre and Elisabeth joined in, then Louise, the third member of Team Granny. They meet up at least once a week.

'Preferably Saturday,' Louise says, 'because Sarah's on duty on Saturday nights and we know she sleeps like a log.'

Raphael laughs again. He's off his face.

'But how come no one's ever seen you? Or heard you?' I ask.

'No one shows any interest in the kitchen garden,' Gustave says, 'and we're careful not to make too much noise, although that's not always easy. Anyway, all the studios that overlook this part of the grounds either belong to us or to people whose hearing isn't what it used to be. That's also why we come out so late. But how did you find out?'

'It was me,' Raphael chips in, taking another drag on the joint. 'I haven't smoked for a long time, but I immediately recognised the plants in the vegetable plot. Well done, brother, this is good dope!'

Delirious laughter all round.

'I've heard you several times,' I say. 'I've even tried to find out where the voices were coming from.'

'Oh, we know that!' says Gustave. 'We saw you prowling once – you scared the life out of us! You won't say anything, will you?'

All eyes turn to me while they wait for my answer. I don't take long to think about it.

'I promise I won't say a thing. And who'd believe me, anyway?'

I head back to the annexe, my mind at rest. Now if I ever hear voices in the grounds after dark, I'll know that a cabal of grannies and grandpas are treating themselves to a guilty pleasure. Raphael is walking back with me.

'What if,' he says, 'the spat between the two old dears in the canteen was about their cocaine-dealing . . .'

'Yeah, right. And Arlette is deaf because she's hiding her LSD in her ears!'

He almost chokes with laughter. I open the door and we step into the dark corridor. Neither of us switches on the light. I put one foot on the first stair.

'Goodnight,' I say in a whisper, although I'm not sure why, because we're the only two here; Clara is spending the night at Greg's place.

Then it all happens very quickly. He strides across the gap between us, plants a brief but insistent kiss on my lips, puts his key into the lock of his studio door and disappears, leaving me all alone with my palpitations.

Chapter 74

I take on Louise, Gustave and Elisabeth at Scrabble. At Ocean View, the rules are adapted to the residents' age. No egg-timer here: each player takes however long he or she wants to find a word. We've just started the game and I'm already at the end of my tether.

'It's your turn, Louise.' It has been for sixteen minutes.

She moves her letters around, forms a word, then another, heaves a sigh; nothing seems right, aha, what if she tried . . .

'Can I change my letters?' she asks eventually.

'Yes, you can, but you have to miss your turn,' Elisabeth replies.

'Even if I only change two?'

I should have gone to the macramé workshop instead.

Ten days later, she finally puts down the word NOTE, using the E of Gustave's BRIDE. Four points: not much of a return per minute.

It's my turn. With Louise's O, I make the word COUPLING. Scrabble.

'Beginner's luck,' Louise almost snaps, unsportsmanlike.

'Either that or she's got something on her mind!'

sniggers Gustave. 'I mean, things seem to be going well with Rosa's grandson . . .'

The two women nod knowingly.

'Oh yes!' Elisabeth agrees. 'Their eyes were shining the other night . . .'

'Nonsense!' I exclaim. 'You need to stop smoking that stuff, it's making you hallucinate . . . Come on, Elisabeth, it's your turn. If we carry on at this rate, they'll find us dehydrated on to our chairs.'

The old man smiles at me conspiratorially, as if he knows that I know what he knows. Elisabeth puts down her word.

'R – I – N – G – S. Rings. Double word score.'

Gustave takes time to think – approximately as long as it would take to roast a chicken – then uses Elisabeth's R to write his word.

'MARRY, with double letter score for one of the Rs: nine points.'

Louise follows that swiftly with a well-placed KEY that puts her back in contention. Then I put down my PROPOSE and Elisabeth her FIANCEE.

Gustave shoots one hand under the table. The time has come. Elisabeth smiles at me excitedly while Louise shuffles her tiles, trying to make a good word. Gustave puts down the first letter. Then the second. Then the ninth.

'You've used far too many letters!' Louise complains, before grasping what's happened.

There on the board, straddling his previous word in black letters on cream-coloured tiles, is his proposal:

WILL YOU MARRY ME

She stands up and brings her hands to her face. Her eyes are popping out of her head. Despite the clues all over the board, she wasn't expecting this at all. Gustave leans on his walking frame to put one knee to the floor. At this exact moment, Pierre, who's been hiding in the corridor from the start, launches into the Wedding March and comes into the room scattering rose petals, followed by almost all the residents and staff of Ocean View.

Louise hasn't moved. She's turned to stone. Gustave has tears in his eyes. So do I. Everyone forms a circle around the couple.

'Dear Louise,' Gustave begins, 'I won't make a long speech – we don't have time for all that at our age. I want to live every second that I have left by your side. I can't cope without your laughter any more. I want to make you happy the way you make me happy, until my dying breath. My darling, would you like to be my wife?'

Louise is laughing and crying at the same time. She lowers herself so she's on a level with Gustave, who is struggling to get back to his feet. Silence hangs in the air. She puts her wrinkled hand on his cheek.

'Nothing would make me happier.'

Everyone claps, and I wipe my tears. I'm going to miss all these people so much.

Chapter 75

From: Raphael Marin-Goncalves
Subject: None

Hi Julia,

How are you?

So sorry I didn't say goodbye on Sunday. I came and knocked on your door, but I don't think you were there. I wanted to let you know I had a wonderful weekend.

My grandmother tells me there's been a marriage proposal, I wish I'd seen it!

On the subject of my grandmother, how do you think she is at the moment? I think she's a bit up and down, bright one minute and clamming up the next. Do you know if anything's happened? I hope she doesn't find me too intrusive . . .

See you soon

Raph x

I was in my studio when he knocked on Sunday. I sat motionless until his footsteps receded down the stairs. Saturday evening shook me up. That kiss got to me. My feelings got stirred up. I need to protect myself.

Hi Raphael,

I'm fine, thanks, I hope you are, too.

Don't worry about Sunday; it doesn't matter. I'd gone out for a walk.

You're right, Gustave proposed to Louise, and it was magical. Greg filmed the whole thing so he could show it to you.

I don't get that feeling about your grandmother. In fact, I think she's perfectly relaxed and has more and more confidence. Maybe you take things too much to heart.

Have a good evening

See you

Julia

I've written friendlier letters to the Inland Revenue. It's difficult for me to be so cold, and I click Send unwillingly. I don't want to hurt Raphael. I just want to avoid being hurt myself.

My phone rings as I shut down my laptop. It's Marion.

'Hey, babe! So have you forgotten your best friend?' she chides.

'And this from the girl who's been meant to come to see me for six months! How are you?'

'Really good, and I have loads of stuff to tell you, but it can wait till 7 September.'

'Why 7 September?' I ask, dropping down on to my sofa.

'Because you're coming to Parisssss! I warn you, you're gonna love me. Can you believe it, the other evening I was at Peter's birthday – you know Peter, Charlotte Cartel's boyfriend? Anyway, it was very swanky, and I met Jacques Martin—'

'But he's dead, isn't he?' I interrupt.

'That was Jacques Martin the TV host, this was Jacques Martin who runs the Hair Clinic in the 15th Arrondissement. Do you know it?'

'No, but the name doesn't leave much to the imagination.'

'Exactly. And do you know what? People who lose their hair can't always come to terms with it. I'll cut to the chase: they're looking for a therapist. I told him you were the best, and you're seeing them at eleven o'clock on the 7th. So who's the best friend in the world?'

The best friend in the world is me. Because, so as not to crush Marion's excitement, I go into ecstasies and thank her, when all I want to do is hang up and bury my head under my pillow.

September

'In all cases, hope takes us further than fear'

– Ernst Jünger, *An der Zeitmauer*

Chapter 76

I know the theme tune of *Plus belle la vie* by heart. Every evening when it starts up, I have to restrain myself from singing along. The Julia from the beginning of the year would have a good laugh if she could see me now.

This evening's episode is compulsory viewing: we're finally going to see the face of the priest who's been setting Melanie's heart on fire for months. The tension is unbearable, the residents' eyes are glued to the screen, their hands clutching the arms of their chairs. Like every other evening, Greg and I are sitting in the last row of armchairs. Unusually, though, Clara is here, too: Greg has promised her a surprise if she joins us.

On screen, Melanie is walking along a station platform, and taking her time about it. They have to spin out the suspense – viewers have only been waiting six months. She asks a guard whether this is the right platform for the train from Paris.

'What did she say?' asks Arlette.

'Shush!' grumbles Leon, who's taken to sitting in the front row, in order to be as far away as possible from me, ever since I had the nerve to thwart his plans. Any further forward and he'd be inside the TV.

The train draws into the station. Melanie takes out a hankie. So does Louise.

Change of scene. Samia's crying because her husband, Boher, doesn't believe her when she tells him his ex is completely crazy and has threatened to take their baby.

'If I were her, I'd divorce him straight away,' Elisabeth announces.

'If I were her,' I say, 'I'd pull his teeth out one by one and feed them to him.'

Several residents turn around and give me odd looks. Maybe I take things too seriously.

Back to the station platform. Melanie looks at her phone to check the number of the carriage Luke is travelling in. 'Father Luke' to his close friends. The doors open, a foot steps out, close-up of a black shoe, change of scene. Greg can't sit still.

'You okay?' I ask.

'I'm fine. I just want to see what he looks like.'

On the TV, Barbara's wondering whether she should tell Ahmed she cheated on him. Pierre shakes his head.

'You should never admit that sort of thing. All it does is ease your own conscience and hurt everyone else.'

Elisabeth looks horrified. She's just opening her mouth to respond when Melanie reappears on the screen. The time has come. We're finally going to see Luke's face. The black shoe steps down on to the platform, the camera pans up his legs, his torso, his neck. So what does this priest look like?

'He looks so like Greg!' exclaims Louise when his face is revealed.

I look at Greg, then at the screen, then at Greg, then at the screen. I can't believe my eyes. Neither can Clara, judging by how far her jaw has dropped. All the residents have turned to stare at Greg. He, meanwhile, is smiling.

'Is it you?' Clara manages to ask.

'Yup, it's me!' he says proudly.

'But when? How? Explain!' I cry.

The images keep telling their story on screen, but the story we're all interested in now is the one about the retirement-home activities coordinator who shows up in *Plus belle la vie*.

'You remember when I had a week's holiday? Well, I was in Marseille. I went to a casting session at the beginning of this year – that's why I took a couple of days off – and they gave me the part of the priest.'

'Will you have to be away a lot?' Clara asks anxiously.

He laughs.

'I'm only in two episodes at the moment . . . sorry to ruin the suspense, but Luke's only come to tell Melanie to her face that nothing's going to happen between them.'

Elisabeth starts to cry.

'Why's she crying?' Leon grouches. 'Would she rather the priest lived in sin?'

'That's not it at all,' Elisabeth sniffles. 'I'm sad because Greg will have to leave us now that he's a star . . .'

Pierre takes his wife in his arms and comforts her. Lucienne glowers at Greg. Everyone's waiting for his answer. He clearly wasn't expecting this reaction.

'Actually, I didn't want to tell you,' he says, looking away, 'but I had a call from Tarantino this morning . . . He wants me to play the lead in his next film. He's given me some time to think about it but, obviously, I don't need to. You don't need to think about a decision like that.'

'What did he say?' asks Arlette.

Louise puts her hand to her mouth. Clara looks as amazed as I am that they can be so gullible. You could tell them a dinosaur was coming to supper and they'd wonder what to cook for it.

'So I told him it was very sweet of him, but I'd rather carry on looking after my lovely residents.'

Their faces light up.

'You're a good man, Gregory!' Pierre declares.

'And a star, too!' Lucienne adds.

Greg preens.

'Don't you want to name Ocean View after him, while you're at it?' Clara asks, laughing.

'Why not?' Gustave replies. 'The Gregory Retirement Home has a nice ring to it.'

'Either way, we're very proud of you, darling boy,' Louise says. 'You've had quite an adventure and we've sort of shared in it.'

'I'm glad some people are proud of me . . .' Greg says, smiling at Clara.

Her only reply is to take his face in her hands and kiss him on the lips. The residents are stunned: it's the first time the couple have gone public. While Clara relaxes her grip, Rosa turns to me.

'I didn't quite follow that,' she says quietly. 'Is she an actress, too?'

Chapter 77

Marion has made up the sofa for me with my favourite sheets: the white, embroidered ones.

It feels so strange to be back in the Paris apartment where I spent several months. Those days seem to belong to another life but, at the same time, it all comes back to me automatically, as if I've never been away. I'm sitting on the left-hand side of the sofa, as I used to.

'So have you missed Paris?' Marion asks, putting a coffee capsule in the machine.

'Honestly? Not for a minute. The only thing I miss is Starbucks, but that's not much of a drawback when you're looking out over the Atlantic.'

She closes her eyes and tilts her head back.

'Oh, the sea . . . I really must come to see you. But you won't be too sad to come back, will you?'

Her question feels like a slap in the face.

'Nothing's definite yet, I haven't even had the interview!'

'No, but I bigged you up! I'm sure you'll get it.'

I've thought about this opportunity a lot since Marion mentioned it to me. I've picked up my phone several times to ask her to cancel the interview. But I've always hung up before the first ring. I don't want to come back and work in Paris. But if I were offered the chance, I wouldn't want to go and work in Rome, Bordeaux or Biarritz. What I want is to carry on working at Ocean View. But Anne-Marie was clear on this: in a month's time, my contract comes to an end. I have no choice, and the job in question doesn't sound that bad.

'Try to curb your enthusiasm,' Marion says sarcastically, handing me a steaming cup.

'No, no, I'm really keen, I promise! The only thing that bothers me slightly is having to move away from my family again . . .'

'Have you done it, then? Have you told your mother everything?'

'Not yet, but I feel like I'm really nearly there. Just a few more barriers to break down and I'll be ready. Which means it'll be like, "Hi, Mum, I've spent eight months within walking distance of you without letting you know, and now that you do know, I'm off again. Bye!"'

'She'll understand – I'm sure she will.'

'I hope so . . .'

Marion smiles at me fondly.

'What about the real reason you went back to Biarritz? Do you want to talk about that?' she asks softly.

I shrug in silence. She knows I'll say no, so she moves on seamlessly with, 'I've met someone.'

'You never! Tell me!'

Marion chuckles and tells me how she fell head over heels for Issa.

'I broke a tooth biting into a sandwich. Not a back tooth, or it wouldn't make a good story, oh no, a front tooth. You should have seen me, I looked like the love child of Lara Stone – I wish! – and SpongeBob SquarePants. It was not good: I could have made a dildo lose its erection. My dentist was away, and his stand-in saved my life. His name's Issa. He knew the inside of my mouth before he knew me – he'll never leave me!'

She laughs, and I'm struck by the realisation that I haven't missed her. As if she'd always been there on the side-lines. As if knowing I could call her any time day or night, that she was there, was as good as actually calling her.

Marion took me in one evening with bags in my hands and more bags under my eyes. She didn't ask any questions, put the white sheets on the sofa and cooked up the most disgusting pasta I've had in my life. She never asked how long I'd be staying or made me feel as if I was in her way. She didn't judge me when I got back at dawn smelling of drink and that particular night's man. She slipped condoms into my handbag. She told my mother I was fine when Mum was worried because she hadn't heard from me. She encouraged me to go down to Biarritz, even though she was going to miss me. I've seen friends come and go. Some mattered, a lot. My gang at school, friends from uni, others from evenings spent together. There have been house moves, rows, characters changing, and opinions, too, phone calls fizzling out and memories fading. But with Marion, there are no doubts:

we'll be discreetly straightening each other's wigs in our eighties.

'How about you? Still determined to stay single till the end of your days?'

I take too long to reply, and that's a mistake.

'Omg, you've met someone!' she squeals.

I shake my head, shrug my shoulders and say no, twice. That's a mistake, too. Marion comes and sits next to me and looks me in the eye with a little smile playing on her lips. She knows me too well. I burst out laughing.

'I want to know everything,' she says.

'There's not much to tell. The grandson of a new resident has been flirting with me and, in different circumstances, I wouldn't be against it.'

'What circumstances?' she asks, frowning.

'All the circumstances. I'm just building myself up again – I can't risk being hurt now. Anyway, after Marc, I don't think I'll trust anyone again. Plus, he's the grandson of a patient. And I went back to Biarritz to remind myself who I am. I mustn't let myself be distracted. And also . . .'

'Is there much more of this? Listen, Julia, you know I adore you. But I've never heard such rubbish reasons for rejecting someone. What else is there? Are your star signs incompatible?'

I shrug again, upset.

'I don't have any reason to lie. I can't think why I'd make up excuses.'

She bashes me gently with her shoulder.

'You're the therapist, sweetheart. But it looks like you think nothing good will ever happen to you again. Life isn't just made up of the bad stuff, you know.'

I sit in silence for a while. What she's just said has really shaken me.

She's right. Without realising it, I've convinced myself that I've exhausted my quota of happiness and that my father's death opened the way for all the ordeals I now have to confront. And the worst of it is, I'm at my most anxious when things are going well. As if I know I'll have to pay for it later. It's no coincidence that I've had an old saying of my mother's going round in my head a lot recently: 'Some people think life's a bowl of cherries, but I feel like I just get the stones.'

I fall asleep a few hours later, to the almost forgotten sounds of Paris by night, happy to be back with my friend, nervous about the interview in the morning and feeling like someone who's just put on glasses when they haven't been seeing things clearly at all.

Chapter 78

Jacques Martin watches me closely while I do as he has asked: I introduce myself in a few sentences. I feel like a box of washing-powder that has to convince customers it washes better than its competitors. There were two other people sitting in the waiting room to see the Hair Clinic's director. I lost marks the moment I stepped into his office: I'm pretty sure I did a double-take when I saw that he was bald.

'Why do you want to work at the Hair Clinic?'

Because I've been passionate about hair since I was a little girl. I've even had a lock of it grafted on to my heart. Next question.

'Being with people when they're suffering is my speciality, and I think people can really suffer because of hair loss. You help them physically, with transplants, and I would help them psychologically, giving them the support and understanding they need.'

He smiles and crosses his arms.

'What are your three best qualities?'

I can defend myself with a round-bladed knife, I can crick my back doing geriatric-friendly gym and my chosen specialised subject is Plus belle la vie.

'I'm a very good listener, I'm patient and I'm organised.'

He makes a note of my answer on the back of my CV, then moves on to the next question.

'Our clients are often busy people with very full lives. They can't fit in appointments at the same sort of times as your average man or woman on the street. Would you be happy to work unusual hours?'

'Unusual?'

'Sometimes early in the morning, sometimes late in the evening, sometimes at weekends. We don't often get much warning. Our motto at the Hair Clinic is "We adapt". Would you be prepared not to count the hours you put in and to be flexible?'

Would you be prepared to add a few digits to my salary and pay me whenever I want?

'I can be flexible when I'm passionate about something.'

He smiles. He's started to like this box of washing-powder.

The interview continues, punctuated by all the standard questions – What is your greatest professional achievement: (*I beat Lucienne at Scrabble*); Do you plan to have children in the next ten years? (*Fifteen of them, all in one go if possible*); What are your interests? (*Sleeping, making smoke rings, and watching documentaries about marmots*), I'm wondering what the hell I'm doing here. Exactly like the day I first arrived at Ocean View. Maybe it's a sign.

Jacques Martin clicks in the nib of his biro and sits back into his chair. The interview seems to be coming to an end.

'One last question, Julia. You said your contract was about to end. I see that you previously worked at the cosmetic-surgery clinic in Les Buttes. Why did you leave?'

Because my father died, my boyfriend preferred cuddling up to his computer than to his miserable girlfriend, I lost my grandmother after she had a stroke, and I just had to get out of Paris before I banged every man in the place, along with the Eiffel Tower.

I'm trying to think how best to reply when he pushes back his chair and stands up.

'Thank you for taking the time to come and see me,' he says, proffering his hand. 'I'll be in touch as soon as I've made a decision.'

I shake his hand and head for the door while my blood freezes in my veins.

Fuck. I just said that last bit out loud, didn't I?

Chapter 79

From: Raphael Marin-Goncalves
Subject: By the way

Hi Julia,
   A slightly different message this time. It's three in the morning, I'm exhausted and I just wanted to tell you that my trips to Ocean View really won't be the same when you're no longer there.
   I hope I won't regret writing this in the morning . . .
   Raph xx

I quickly delete the email. As if to short-circuit my mind before it registers the pleasure.

Shame there's no delete function in the brain.

Chapter 80

Gustave's daughter, Martine, has found the time to pay us a little visit. We've almost finished our monthly staff meeting when she strides into the refectory without knocking and waves a piece of card.

'The two old women on the bench said I'd find you here. What sort of a joke do you call this?' she asks, slapping the card down on the table.

It's too far away for me to see, but I know what's written on it because I went to have them printed.

What are you doing on 11 October?
  What Louise and Gustave are doing is getting married!
  You are warmly invited to share in their happiness at the ceremony, which will take place at 1 p.m. at Biarritz Town Hall.

Martine is standing with her arms crossed, waiting for an answer.

'Who's she?' Clara asks.

'I'm Martine Luret, Gustave Champagne's daughter.'

Anne-Marie gestures towards a chair for her.

'Do sit down, please.'

'I don't want to sit down. Can anyone explain?'

'Your father can probably explain better than us,' I say, trying not to curl my lips.

'My father is an elderly man who no longer has all his faculties, if – that is – he ever had them. I thought when I brought him here I would have some peace of mind. How could you let this happen?'

'Your father knows what he's doing,' Greg pipes up. 'You really should talk to him about it. They're wonderful together . . .'

'I have absolutely no desire to watch my father behaving like a teenager, thank you very much. That woman knows what she's doing, she didn't set her heart on just anyone . . . I warn you, I'll ask for guardianship and send him somewhere else.'

'I've had about enough of this circus act,' Clara says, getting to her feet.

Greg puts a hand on her arm, Anne-Marie opens her eyes wide and Gustave's daughter flushes scarlet.

'Pardon? Are you talking to me?'

'No, your mum! Do you realise what you're doing? Your father's a sweetheart. Why the hell would you want to ruin his happiness?'

'Clara, please hold your tongue,' Anne-Marie intervenes.

'Can I hit her, then?'

There's tittering around the table. I have to restrain myself to avoid laughing out loud.

'Clara, please sit back down,' Anne-Marie insists, then turns to Gustave's daughter and says, 'We can't help you with this, Madame Luret. This is something you need to discuss with your father himself – we have no power over his decisions. If you'd like to discuss this further, I'd be grateful if you arranged an appointment. For now, we have a meeting to finish.'

Martine leaves the room without a word. The door slams, and there's a general burst of laughter. Our reactions are unanimous:

What a number!

Poor Gustave, he's so lovely . . .

Is it safe now?

The meeting ends a few minutes later. I go out for a cigarette with Clara, who's still wound up like a spring. Gustave is out in the car park, standing next to a car. His daughter is inside, with the door ajar, and she's talking to him. Louise, who's sitting on her usual bench, is watching the scene. We go over to join her.

'Have you met your future stepdaughter?' I ask playfully.

'She wouldn't say hello to me,' Louise replies sadly. 'Gustave has told me so much about his daughter and I was really looking forward to meeting her. He says she was different before . . .'

'Maybe if you press really hard, she'll revert?' Clara suggests.

Gustave is still talking when the car drives away. He stays there alone for a moment, leaning on his walking frame, watching the car drive off, then he turns around and comes towards us. He has almost reached us when the car reappears, reversing. His daughter opens her window.

'I warn you, Dad,' she snarls, 'if you go ahead with this, you can say goodbye to me.'

'My darling, I said goodbye to you a long time ago. I love you, and I'll love you till my dying breath, because I remember the cuddly, giggly little girl you once were. You laughed the whole time. That little girl vanished long ago. I know you're angry with me, my darling, I'll always regret how much I hurt you. I've apologised dozens of times, but I can't *make* you forgive me. I hope you can be happy. That's what I want more than anything in the world, even if I don't get to see it. I have a right to be happy, too, and I won't let you ruin this. I'm going to marry Louise, whether you like it or not, and I'm going to spend what's left of my life with her. If you choose not to be a part of it, I accept that. I've been missing my daughter for years, as it is.'

He stops talking. You can see the hope in the way he holds himself; his hands shake on his walking frame. His daughter keeps her eyes pinned on him, inscrutable. Slowly, the window glides up until it closes completely. Then we hear a gear engaging and the car pulls away.

He shrugs and turns around with affected indifference.

'Well, that's one less guest to pay for!'

Chapter 81

'How are you?'

Louise is bending over her table, knitting small pouches to hold sugared almonds for her wedding guests. I blow on to the hot chocolate she's given me. I'll miss this weekly ritual.

'Wonderfully well! I so clearly remember the preparations for my first marriage. I was the happiest girl in the world. I never thought I'd experience it again – how lucky I am! And how are you?'

My sessions with Louise are more like conversations with someone close to me than consultations. She always takes an interest in me, asks me questions, wants to hear my news. She's the only patient with whom I occasionally allow myself to let slip confidences. A secondary effect of the hot chocolate, perhaps.

'Everything's fine. Do you know whether Gustave has heard from his daughter since the other day?'

'He hasn't mentioned it to me, so I suppose not. How about you? Have you heard from Raphael?'

'From Raphael?' I ask, surprised.

'Oh, don't act all innocent, Julia. When you left us the

353

other evening, in the vegetable garden, we took bets on when you'd first kiss.'

I have no idea what to say. It seems the whole world knows something about me that I don't know myself.

'I can tell you there's absolutely nothing going on between Raphael and me. To be honest, I'm a bit bored of people talking to me about him. Isn't it okay to spend time with someone without having ulterior motives?'

She sighs.

'Julia,' she says, 'when you ask me questions, I try to answer as honestly as I can. Otherwise, what's the point? Will you do the same?'

I nod.

'There *is* something going on with Raphael, isn't there?'

I've never put the question to myself so directly. It takes me a few seconds to work out how to reply.

'I don't know . . . I think so. I like him. A lot. Too much. I'm scared, so I'd rather keep my distance.'

She puts down her knitting and takes my hand.

'You're the same age as my grandchildren, so I'll talk to you as if you were my granddaughter. Is that all right?'

'Yes,' I say, my throat tight.

'If you were my granddaughter, I'd tell you that fear's a necessary emotion and it can save you from certain dangers. But it can paralyse people who give it too much space. I don't know what happened to you, Julia, but you leave a trail of little pebbles of fear everywhere you go. If you were my granddaughter, I'd tell you to use that fear.

It should be fuel for you, not a braking system. What are you most afraid of?'

Her words are disconcerting. It feels as if she's taken a stroll around inside my head: she's nailed me with impressive accuracy.

'I don't know. I'm afraid of being hurt, I think. I feel I'm constantly on high alert, as if expecting something disastrous to happen to me. It hurts so much when everything falls apart, just like that, with no warning. It's like my subconscious is trying to prepare itself for the danger by looking out for it.'

'Because you have no faith in yourself. Your biggest fear is yourself. If you were my granddaughter, I'd tell you that, if you could just shake off this fear, then you wouldn't be afraid of anyone. No one can ever hurt you if you believe in yourself.'

Each of her words feels like a plaster being ripped off. It hurts, but the wound underneath is starting to heal. Louise understands my operating manual better than I do.

'I've forgotten forty years of my life,' she goes on. 'And that taught me something fundamental, probably the secret of happiness: life is the present. It's here and now. You must keep only what's positive from yesterday. And expect nothing of tomorrow. You can't change the past or see the future. Sadly, we learned that with Marilyn. Fear trickles out of the past and ruins the future. Stop carrying all that baggage, Julia. A lot of people don't understand the value of the present until the end of their lives. You're lucky to be surrounded by people who have their eyes open. Make the most of it.'

She strokes my hand. I'm crying. It's becoming a habit. I feel as if I spend more time crying than not in this place. You never know, I might be the solution to the global water shortage.

I come away from the session completely dazed. Luckily, it was the last of the day. I get back to my studio – I have something important to do before supper.

I turn on my laptop, put it on my knee and type into Google: 'How to get rid of fear'.

Chapter 82

Raphael is sitting at the same table as his grandmother. I chomp on my grated carrot and try not to look at him too much. He hardly even nodded hello to me. Any colder, and he'd be a snowman.

I didn't know he was coming this weekend. He hasn't sent me any more emails since the one I didn't answer. I felt weird things in my stomach when I saw him earlier. Not butterflies. More like bats.

He goes out before dessert arrives, his packet of cigarettes in his hand. I wait a few minutes and then join him. He's on the bench at the far end of the garden.

'Hi!' I say brightly. 'I didn't know you were coming. How long are you here?'

He stares straight ahead. He's upset. I would be, too, if I were him. I don't know what to say to make things better. Conversations with Marion and Louise haven't dissolved my fears, but they've made me determined to give them a good kick up the backside. If I don't take any risks, then the real danger will be stagnating in this torpor I've been in for months. The first risk I want to take is to open up to Raphael. Not necessarily open the door wide, but maybe a window. A little skylight. An arrow slit. How could he hurt me through a really small window?

'Are things any better at work?' I ask.

'It's okay.'

The weekend is covered. Work is covered. I'm not going to stoop so low as the weather.

'And it's a gorgeous day. You're lucky – it's been raining all week!'

'I'm going back in to see my grandmother.'

He crushes his half-smoked cigarette, gets up and walks away without looking at me.

I've just had the window slammed in my face. It hurts.

Chapter 83

I have a Saturday evening under the duvet lined up but someone comes hammering at my door. I open the door and find a frantic-looking Elisabeth on the landing.

'Come quickly, Julia! We need your help!'

I don't ask any questions. The fact she's climbed the stairs is enough to persuade me this is serious. I pull a jacket over my pyjamas with the pink rabbits on and follow her downstairs. She doesn't say a word, but I have my arm linked through hers and I can feel her shaking. Either that, or it's me.

There isn't a sound in the main building. It's been dark for some time and we all went back to our own studios after supper. I follow her along various corridors, fear brewing in my stomach. What am I going to see? If she came to fetch me rather than whoever's on duty, it must be important. I feel it could be something to do with their secret get-togethers. I hope nothing's happened to Pierre, Louise or Gustave.

We come to the double doors to the refectory and she stops.

'My dear Julia, you must on no account tell anyone

what you're about to see. We absolutely must keep this a secret to the very end.'

'Okay,' I say, feeling my heart thudding through my whole body.

'I'll have to blindfold you.'

'What?' I cry. 'Why do you want to blindfold me?'

'Shush! Don't talk so loudly, for goodness' sake! I have to take every precaution. Please, Julia, don't ask any questions.'

Her eyes are pleading. This doesn't make any sense but, although I couldn't say why, I let her tie a scarf around my eyes – it reeks of eau de cologne.

'How many fingers am I showing?' she asks.

'No idea, but you won't have any soon, if you leave me like this.'

I hear the door open, then whispering, several people taking a sharp breath. I can also hear a regular beating on the ground, like a walking frame. I feel for the floor in front of me with every footstep. Elisabeth's hand leads me towards the unknown. Now she puts gentle pressure on my shoulders and tells me to sit down. Then there are other sounds, smells, footsteps. I've rarely felt so anxious, my brain's in a complete whirl and I have no clue as to what's going on.

'One, two, three!' says a man's voice.

Someone unties the scarf, and I can see again. It takes my eyes a moment to adjust to the light, even though it's not bright. It takes even longer for my brain to decipher the scene before me.

I'm sitting at a table covered in balls of cotton wool, with two birthday-cake candles standing in hunks of bread. Forming a circle around me and looking very smug are Elisabeth, Pierre, Louise, Gustave and Rosa. Sitting facing me and looking as stunned as I am is Raphael.

'We didn't have any rose petals or candlesticks,' Elisabeth says. 'We improvised with what we had to hand.'

'What's all this about?' Raphael asks.

'Good question. What do you want us to do?'

'Nothing at all!' says Gustave, coming over all innocent, but he's not convincing anyone. 'We just wanted to thank you for being so kind by making you a nice dinner.'

'But we've already eaten!' I protest.

'Tut tut,' says Rosa. 'There's always room for something nice. We'll leave you alone to enjoy the evening. We'll be in the kitchen if you need us.'

They walk away, tittering among themselves. I can't help being touched by these dear old people who've taken on the disguise of teenagers this evening. But then my eyes come to rest on Raphael's grim face. At least I've found something wrong with him: he's a grudge-bearer.

'Are you okay?' I ask him.

'I'm okay.'

'Did they dig you out of a nice quiet evening, too?'

'Yup.'

I don't persist any more. I wouldn't want to disturb him while he craps out his cactus.

*

The first course – 'Golden island and white sand' – is served by Pierre and Rosa.

'Tabbouleh and bread,' I say, smiling at Raphael. *'Bon appétit.'*

'You, too.'

He doesn't touch his plate. I'm upset for the sake of our 'hosts', who drift past the half-open door with varying degrees of discretion. We can't go through the whole evening like this.

'Can I ask you a question?' I ask.

'Go on, then.'

'Do you think it's normal behaviour to sulk because I didn't reply to your email? What does that mean? That if someone doesn't do exactly what you want them to, they're punished. Have you heard of free will?'

He looks up, apparently shocked.

'I'm not sulking.'

'Well, congratulations, it's a hell of an impression!'

He smiles.

'As for that email, I'm more annoyed with myself. I sent it in the middle of the night, I was knackered, I was ashamed when I read it back in the morning. No, there's something else eating me up. I'm really sorry if you thought I was having a go at you. Just before I got on my flight, I heard that my company's calling in the receivers. I don't have a job: either I find one really quickly, or I'll have to leave my flat in London. I'm a bit dazed, to be honest.'

Now, I'm the one who's ashamed. Luckily, Elisabeth

and Louise come to clear away our plates and serve the next course.

'Rippled leaves of game with gilded foam,' Louise announces.

In other words, slices of ham with mashed potato.

'Everything going well?' Louise coos.

'Very well, thank you!' I say. 'Could we see the wine list?'

The two old girls exchange a look and return to the kitchen without a word. Gustave appears a few minutes later and puts a bottle of rum on the table.

'I found this in the pastry cupboard. Hope you like it!'

There were just some dregs left, enough to relax us a bit. By the dessert ('Caribbean Milky Way', for which, read: vanilla-flavoured yoghurt), Raphael isn't actually laughing about his situation, but he's a bit less gloomy.

'I haven't said anything to my grandmother. Not a word, okay?'

'I promise. Are you hoping to stay in London?'

'I think so. I love the place and the English, but I'm not sure I want to spend my life there. Maybe now's the time to make a decision. How about you? Where have you got to?'

I tell him about my job interview, and he bursts out laughing when I tell him what I said.

'Okay, so I don't really believe it'll happen but, you never know, he might like my honesty and give me the job.'

Louise, Gustave, Elisabeth, Pierre and Rosa come out to join us.

'Sir, madam, the restaurant will be closing soon. Could we clear the table?'

'Already?' Raphael asks, amazed.

'I'm afraid so,' Gustave replies with a mischievous smile. 'It's past midnight, and the staff need their weekly meeting in the garden.'

I nod. Raphael opens his eyes wide.

'Granny,' he says, looking at Rosa. 'Are you going to the meeting, too?'

'Yes. I haven't missed a single one for three weeks!'

He shakes his head and gives a nervous laugh.

'I'm way out of my depth. I think I need to go to bed.'

Louise sees us to the door, catches hold of my arm and whispers in my ear: 'Don't forget, Julia – here and now.'

Chapter 84

We're having a cigarette by the door to the annexe. It's cold, and there's no moon. We haven't turned the light on, but we can hear occasional bursts of laughter coming from the gardens.

Tonight, I must have eaten the most repulsive meal it's possible for a human to ingest. I've spent the evening with someone who's preoccupied, closing me out a bit. I've been by turns embarrassed, irritated and tired. And yet I don't want it to come to an end. To spin it out a little longer, I light another cigarette.

We're not talking. I can make out his outline a couple of paces away. He also takes another cigarette from his packet. I flick on my lighter. He steps forward and inhales as he leans his cigarette into the flame. His eyes look directly into mine. His cigarette lights and I release the pressure on my lighter. I can no longer see his eyes, but I can feel them on me still. My breathing quickens. So does his. I can feel a warmth spreading through my stomach. I mustn't run away. I mustn't start talking to dispel the awkwardness.

It's here and now.

I swallow hard and take a step towards him. He doesn't

move. His face is lit up each time he inhales on his cigarette. He caresses my face with his eyes. Why doesn't he touch me?

Another inhalation. A loooong inhalation. Sweet torture. The excitement builds, every inch of my skin can't wait to feel his. His eyes are burning with longing. I've never wanted anyone so much. His hand on my cheek. Soft and tender. I close my eyes. His hand slides to the back of my neck and up into my hair. My whole body is a-shudder. He brings my face up to his, I can feel his breath on my skin. My legs are shaking. Lightly, as light as a feather, he brushes his lips over mine. Then I feel his tongue. Holy fuck, his tongue. It's in my mouth, toying with me. I give an involuntary moan, I want him to make love to me, here, right now, straight away.

I slip my hand against his back, his skin is warm, I pull him to me. He's breathing harder and harder, I dig my fingers into his muscles, he's kissing my neck. My knees are going to give way.

'Come on,' he says hoarsely, taking my hand.

I follow him to his studio with my heart beating in my ears. He closes the door and I stand there in the dark on legs of jelly. He steps behind me, lifts up my hair and kisses the back of my neck, slowly, languorously. I lean against the wall; I don't want this ever to end. He lifts my arms and takes off my pyjama top, his lips travel down my spine, growing more ardent. I moan as he slides his hands around on to my breasts, which quiver in response, he cups them, caresses them, then presses his body against my back. All I can think of are his fingers playing with my nipples, his erection against my buttocks, his tongue next to my ear, his hips rocking and taking my breath away. I turn around and unbutton his jeans.

Here and now.

Chapter 85

It's a long time since I've woken up in a man's bed. He's still asleep.

I've had some harsh awakenings in strangers' beds, wondering what the hell I was doing there, feeling dirty for giving my body to them, as if it were worthless, like it didn't belong to me any more. I would sneak out quietly, gathering up my knickers, bra, dress and handbag, but trying to leave behind some of my distress. It always ended up finding me, and it had always grown a bit.

I don't feel like sneaking out quietly this morning. In fact, I feel like making loads of noise to wake him so we can start all over again.

I cough.

He snores.

I blow on his face.

He wrinkles his nose but doesn't wake up.

I kick him in the shin.

He wakes with a start.

'Did you have a bad dream?' I ask him, smiling innocently.

His eyes are all sleepy. He pulls me to him and I rest my head on his chest.

'Sleep well?' I ask.

'Like a baby. Although I'm a bit disappointed . . .'

I sit up immediately. I hope he's not talking about my performance. He lifts the duvet and glances under it.

'Yup, really disappointed,' he says again. 'I thought I was sleeping with Snuggles . . .'

We spend the morning in bed, then our rumbling stomachs remind us there's an outside world. I go into the refectory ten minutes after him, but the junkies' table can't be fooled that easily. Five smiling faces watch me. Luckily, Clara spent the night at Greg's place so they're not here; otherwise, I'd be outed.

My phone rings just as I'm tucking into a plate of beetroot. It's a message from Marion.

Hey, gorgeous! So, you'll get an official call tomorrow and you have to pretend to be surprised, but I couldn't wait to tell you. I spent the evening with Jacques Martin and he wants you for the job. Welcome back to Paris, babe!

Chapter 86

Clara and I are both slumped on her sofa with one eye on a reality-TV show, chatting about one thing and another, when I spot it. On the ceiling, just overhead. Motionless. Huge. Deformed. Terrifying.

I'm paralysed with horror. Even if I weren't, I wouldn't move. It would jump on to me, for sure.

'Clara,' I manage. 'Clara, there's a spider up there.'

She looks up and emits a sound halfway between a squeal and a wheeze.

'Shush, it'll hear you. Whatever you do, don't move.'

She makes the sign of the cross. We can't take our eyes off the ceiling. The monstrous creature is watching us. I'm sure it's smiling at us.

'It looks like a tarantula,' whispers Clara.

'Or a crab.'

'You know what they say: "Spider at dawn, don't be forlorn. Spider at night, it's a bitch." '

We roar with laughter. Without making a move or a sound. If spiders have out-takes, we'll be going viral.

'Right, we need to move,' says Clara. 'If we stay here, it'll go and hide somewhere. I can't go on living here, knowing there's a spider in my studio.'

'Okay, but then what do we do? Would you be up to catching it and putting it outside?'

She stares at me flatly. I think I can detect pity in her eyes.

'You're completely bonkers!' she says. 'We just need to thump it, that's all. Do you think the vacuum thingy's long enough?'

I don't answer.

'You don't mean it!' she wails. 'I know you've got a problem with death, but it's a spider! You must have killed dozens of them in your life, just by swallowing them in your sleep.'

'Maybe it's just come to find something for its babies to eat . . .'

'Then I'll set the flipping studio on fire and they can all die together.'

There's a chance the spider can hear us, because the dark spot on the ceiling is moving. Without a second thought, my body propels itself off the sofa, leaps to the door and flies down the stairs. Clara is already outside when I get there.

'I prefer living outside, anyway,' she says with a shrug.

An hour later, we still haven't found the courage to go back upstairs. We have no cigarettes, no phones, no coats; in other words, we're on the brink of despair.

'There's something I want to tell you, Julia,' Clara says solemnly.

'What? Have you killed a spider?' I snigger.

'Stop it, it's something really difficult. Well, it's nothing serious, but every time I try to talk to you about it, I feel like crying.'

'Okay, you're scaring me now . . .'

She takes a deep breath then launches into her speech.

'I'm going to move in with Greg. We want to give it a try. I'll leave my stuff here for a while, just in case, but I'll stay there every night. I'd rather leave first than watch you go. And anyway, you saw his bath!'

She doesn't wait for me to reply before throwing her arms around me.

She was right. Spider at night, it's a bitch.

Chapter 87

I told her I was happy for her and that I hoped she'd be happy with Greg.

I told her I only had two weeks left here, anyway, before going back to Paris.

I told her I wasn't sad – no, really, I promise.

I didn't tell her I felt like crying.

I didn't tell her my brain had scheduled the end for 10 October, and I wasn't ready.

I didn't tell her that her leaving made my own departure real.

Clara's sleeping on my sofa. She chose my company over that of a spider last night. That's friendship for you.

Meanwhile, I can't sleep at all. Thoughts are bustling around inside my head, keeping me awake. I remember arriving here, completely lost but sure of one thing: I needed to be alone. I remember when I first met Clara, with that dye in her hair. She's so different from anyone else I've known. Clara doesn't beat about the bush, she doesn't dress things up, wear kid gloves or use any kind of filter. She gets right to the point: *bish, bash, bosh!* It threw me at first. It shook up all the broken pieces inside me. I remember our evenings together, laughing uncontrollably, being scared of things, confiding in each other. By applying to work at a retirement home, I'd been looking for peace and quiet, some answers and maybe even a feeling of calm, and I didn't expect to find this. Friendship. Trust. Other people.

Tomorrow evening, I'll be the only inhabitant on the first floor of the annexe. Clara won't be just the other side of the wall, I won't ever see her leaning on her balcony again when I go out for a cigarette, I won't hear her singing off-key when she's getting ready in the morning, I won't be able knock on her door when I need to laugh. I think I'd rather she'd told me sooner. I could have prepared for this, we could have spent an evening together, with me knowing it was the last time and banking all those final memories.

I hear the springs of my sofa creak. Then a grumpy sigh. Then Clara's voice.

'It's impossible to sleep on your sofa, it's even softer than my ex's dick!'

Or you could say that those words aren't bad as a final memento.

Chapter 88

From: Raphael Marin-Goncalves
Subject: Saturday night

It was great. I can't stop thinking about it. I can't wait to
see you again.
  Raph xxx

Tickling feeling in my tummy.

From: Julia Rimini
Subject: Re: Saturday night

Yes, it was really great. I can't wait either.
  Julia xxx
  PS Snuggles sends his love.

October

'The deeper that sorrow carves into your being,
the more joy you can contain'

– Kahlil Gibran

Chapter 89

Once a month, the minibus loads up with pensioners and heads for the public swimming pool. The order of the day is aqua-gym. When Greg asked whether I'd like to join them, I chuckled. But he was serious.

'Come on, you need to make the most of the time you have left here!'

Sneaky git.

I was planning to update some files, nothing that couldn't wait, so I agreed, just so long as I didn't have to join in. He asked whether I'd be bored waiting for an hour and a half, and I said I felt perfectly capable of floating motionless in the warm water of the trainer pool for three days without experiencing a whisper of boredom.

So that's what I'm doing. Floating. Muffled by the water in my ears, the aqua-gym instructor's voice lulls me. 'Draw the water towards you with your hands . . . That's it, very good. Now faster, like a little dog . . . No, Gustave, there's no need to bark.' I'm nearing a state of rapture when a hand presses on my forehead. Water floods into my nostrils, mouth and eyes: tsunami alert. I cough and splutter and Greg watches me, laughing at his prank.

'Come on, let's have a go on the slide,' he suggests.

I can't explain why, but my befuddled brain encourages me to go with him. It's only when I'm at the top of the steps that I realise this slide isn't the sort of sweet little thing with three steps that you have as a toddler. No, the pool's slide is a huge blue contraption with corners, and it spits you out into the children's pool. I'm cold, I'm breathing like an asthmatic bulldog after climbing the steps, and I've got vertigo.

Two options: either I climb back down, which means my legs need to stop shaking, or I launch myself into the mouth of the slide. That's what Greg does, taking with him the last vestiges of my courage.

I cast an eye over the group of residents: they've stopped what they're doing and are watching us. They must have fond memories of the only time before now that I joined in their exercise class. I need to get on with this or I'll look like a sissy.

I stand myself on the edge of the slide, adjust my swimming costume and take a deep breath, then put one foot on the plastic. I thought I'd have time to prepare myself but, oh no, the water sends me flying and whisks me away like a tree trunk in a torrent. With every corner, I feel I'm going to end up on Pluto. I try to straighten myself and sit up, but the speed presses my back against the walls of the tube and I can feel my abdominals and my perineum giving up. I don't even have the strength to scream. I've just decided to stop struggling and accept my sad fate when I'm ejected from the tube. I think tenderly of dwarves projected out of cannons. And then, a black hole. Or rather, a blue grave.

I open my eyes. I'm alive. The group of residents is standing, peering at me. I think I can see respect in their eyes. What they saw was a gutsy woman who didn't waver for a moment before leaping into danger and who has emerged victorious. Greg asks if I'd like to go again, but I say no, the slide's too tame, and I step out of the pool with my head held high, almost with a hand on my heart, with legs going like castanets and a costume that thinks it's a G-string.

Chapter 90

From: Raphael Marin-Goncalves
Subject: News

Hi Julia,

How are you?

It's all go here, I've had a couple of job interviews, without any success, and the landlord is refusing to hold off on the rent while I look for work. I really need to spend all my time on job-hunting, so I won't be able to come down next weekend, as planned, which is so dis-appointing . . . I'd really like to see you.

I've just realised this means that, next time I visit, you won't be there. I'd like to go on seeing you. I know it won't be easy, with you in Paris and me in London, but if it's okay with you, could we give it a go?

Anyway, how's my grandmother? I don't know if she misses me – she doesn't say that sort of thing – but I definitely miss her.

See you soon, I hope!

Raphael xx

How to find Love in the Little Things

From: Julia Rimini
Subject: Oh, the disappointment

Hi Raphael,

I think your grandmother misses you terribly. She'll be devastated not to see you this weekend, particularly because she's feeling a bit low. Having you here would probably have cheered her up. Never mind, she'll just have to cry herself to death all alone in her bed AND YOU'LL BE MILES AWAY.

I hope you end up on the street and lose all your teeth.

Farewell
Julia

Chapter 91

I was in Anne-Marie's office, sorting out an administrative issue to do with the end of my contract, when Clara came to find us: the residents wanted to see us both.

They have all congregated in the lounge, and are sitting in a half-circle, as they did on the first day when I was introduced to them. At the time, I wondered how I'd remember all their names. Right now, I wonder how I'll ever forget them.

My first thought is that they want to tell us about a new idea for Louise and Gustave's wedding, which happens about a thousand times every hour. It's in a few days' time, and all the residents have taken it into their heads to help organise it. But I realise that's not what this is when I notice a banner they've hung on the wall.

DON'T TAKE OUR JULIA!

Clara is first to speak, reading from a speech she holds in both hands.

'We are all here together to protest against the departure of Julia Rimini, psychologist at Ocean View retirement home. Here are our reasons . . .'

Elisabeth stands up from her chair:

'Because she gives up her time to make other people happy.'

She sits down and Pierre stands:

'Because she doesn't just nod her head, she's genuinely interested in us.'

My tears give me fair warning: *We're on our way!* they say.

Now it's Lucienne's turn to speak:

'Because she likes *Plus belle la vie.*'

Then Mohamed:

'Because she can tell when something's wrong.'

And Arlette:

'Because she speaks slowly and clearly.'

I segue from laughter to tears; my emotions have taken control of my body. I'm so touched by their thoughts, their words.

Jules stands up next:

'Because she just loves swimming in freezing water.'

Next, it's Rosa:

'Because my grandson really likes her.'

This is one of those moments I never want to forget. Sometimes, I wish I had a film camera screwed to my forehead, to immortalise wonderful little snippets of my life so I can watch them when I'm feeling down. One after another, the residents explain why they don't want me to leave. Even Leon:

'Because I like the other psychologist even less.'

Gustave comes next:

'Because I've never met anyone who knows worse jokes than mine.'

And lastly, Louise:

'Because she's the granddaughter we all wish we had.'

I'm not crying, I'm one huge tear on two legs. I don't know what moves me most, the things they're saying about me, the catch I can hear in their voices, the fact that they organised this for me or the realisation that I mean as much to them as they do to me.

Clara's cheeks are flooded. She goes back to her script in a quavering voice.

'For all these reasons, and so many more, they'd take too long to list, we refuse to let Julia go. We hope our wishes will be taken seriously. Otherwise, we are seriously contemplating a morning-bath strike.'

All eyes turn to Anne-Marie, who is standing, dumbstruck, beside me. She draws the pencil out of her curls and toys with it nervously.

'I hear your request and, believe me, I understand it. But I'm terribly sorry, there's nothing I can do. Julia will be leaving on 10 October.'

I wipe my nose on the sleeve of my sweatshirt. I'd like to make a long speech, tell them how moved I am, how much I care about every one of them. But I only manage to get six words out:

'You oldies are breaking my heart.'

Chapter 92

From: Raph
Subject: Question

Julia,
Will you still want me when all my teeth have fallen out?
Raph

Chapter 93

Elisabeth, Louise and Rosa have vanished. I was the last person to see them.

They were on their usual bench this morning. I smiled when I realised Rosa had found a place for herself in Team Granny. When I asked what plans they had for the day, they mentioned a pottery workshop, and that was that. Thinking back, nothing struck me as unusual, apart from the sports bag on Louise's lap.

The whole staff is mobilised to find them, and the other residents are joining in as back-up. Anne-Marie thinks she should call the police as a precaution, but I ask her to wait a few minutes while I go to talk to Gustave and Pierre, who are sitting on their partners' favourite bench.

'I'm sure you know where they are.'

They shake their heads. Like two little boys denying they've eaten the chocolate when the stuff's smeared all over their faces.

'Oh, well, we'll just have to let their families know. They're going to be very worried . . .' I say, walking away.

'Wait!' Pierre calls. 'I'll tell you where they are.'

Gustave scowls at his accomplice.

'I'm glad we never robbed a bank together.'

An hour later, after telling Anne-Marie and reassuring the other residents, I park up by one of Biarritz's most beautiful landmarks, the outcrop of rock called the Rocher de la Vierge, and start to walk along the footbridge over the sea.

There's no one there except for three women sitting on folding chairs, facing out across the Atlantic. I can't see their faces, but one is a redhead, one a brunette and one a blonde, and all three have long hair – they're not my grannies. I go over, anyway; you never know, they might have seen them. The blonde turns around just as I reach them. I give a little cry. The other two turn around, and I almost choke with laughter. They make quite a sight, my three runaways, with their mischievous smiles and trying-to-be-innocent eyes under synthetic wigs.

'What on earth is going on?' I ask when I've caught my breath.

'This is my hen party,' Louise says proudly. 'I'm saying goodbye to my youth.'

I laugh all the more, and they join in.

'And what are the wigs for?'

'We didn't want to dress up as nurses,' Elisabeth explains. 'So we've dressed as young women.'

'But what have you been up to all day?'

'We haven't moved from this spot, except for going to get sandwiches,' Louise says. 'We'd have liked to do the rounds of the nightclubs, but we thought a day looking out to sea would be more sensible.'

'Why didn't you tell anyone? You *are* allowed out!'

'The adrenaline buzz,' Rosa replies. 'Organising our little escapade and picturing you all looking for us made us feel like naughty little girls.'

I nod.

'All right, then, girls. Time to go now – it's getting cold. Shall I take you home to your parents?'

'Absolutely not! We've brought our coats . . . We won't let you stop us seeing the sunset – I mean, *really*!'

There are three of them and there's one of me. I don't want to take a thrashing. I sit down beside them, on a rock. The sun is almost touching the horizon.

Rosa takes her purse from her pocket and produces an old photograph. It's of a woman and a little boy posing in front of a sunset here at the Rocher de la Vierge.

'That's my Raphael and me, a long time ago. We used to come here a lot; it was our place. "Can we go and see the lady on the rock?" he always used to say. Wasn't he sweet?'

I take the photo from her.

'He was *very* sweet. If he'd been in my class, I'd have shared my packed lunch with him.'

All three old girls chuckle.

'It's not too late for that . . .' Louise says.

'Julia,' Rosa goes on, 'I think you'd be a good person for Raphael.'

I laugh out loud. They don't like it, and look at me as if I've just said something blasphemous.

'If Clara were here, she'd say you were all bonkers!' I retort. 'Raphael and I hardly know each other. I don't even know if he really wants to be with me . . .'

'What about you?' Louise interjects. 'Are you sure you *don't* want to be with him?'

These women are mad.

'I have no idea. Yes . . . no . . . I don't know! I like being with him, I think about him when he's not here, but to go from that to saying I want to spend my life with him . . . What are you like? You're getting me to talk about my love-life, and I'm not used to it!'

'Well, we'll talk to you about it, then,' chips in Elisabeth. 'You're leaving in a few days, and we won't be able to give you the benefit of our experience.'

The other two nod their heads. Guru grannies.

'You can't stand back and get any perspective on this,' says Louise, 'but we've been watching you for several months. It would be a mistake to let this relationship slip through your fingers.'

'I have to admit,' says Rosa, 'there's an element of self-ishness here for me. I'd rather know he was with you than with that horrible English girl who broke his heart.'

She definitely belongs in Team Granny, this one. As if talk of an ex would make me react.

To react or not to react.

'If you really like him,' Louise says, 'don't let him walk on by. You shouldn't turn your back on love.'

'But I'm not turning my back on anything! I'm just not rushing into anything, that's all. Don't forget, he lives in London and I'll soon be in Paris – not ideal for the start of a relationship.'

'We've already had this conversation,' Elisabeth

replies. 'Life together is a path dotted with pitfalls. But it's worth it! If this young man is the right one, you'll overcome them all and, when you're our age, you can give advice to youngsters who are so sure of themselves.'

'And I'll be able to die happy,' Rosa announces nonchalantly.

The sun is dipping below the horizon. All that's left of it is a smudge of orange disappearing before our very eyes. I'll never tire of watching it.

'One day we'll all be gone,' Louise tells me. 'Us, you, all the people we know . . . the sun will still be entrancing people, but we won't be here. Time goes by, and we go along with it. It's often too late when people realise they've missed the life they could have had. Don't miss your chance, dear little Julia.'

'We're not saying this to be a nuisance,' Elisabeth adds. 'Quite the opposite, it's because we really care for you.'

I stand up and clap my hands together.

'Right, off we go, or I'll be throwing myself in the sea next! Thank you for this delightful interlude. I'm feeling much better now.'

The three old ladies get to their feet, fold their chairs and load them into my arms. I bring up the rear, watching them walk across the footbridge in their wigs, their wavering little steps clanking on the metal structure. I'm suddenly painfully aware that this is one of the last times I'll see them. Please don't turn to look at me.

Chapter 94

Jules is celebrating his ninety-ninth birthday.

His family and the residents have all gathered in the day room for the occasion. He wanted to wait till next year and have a big party for his hundredth birthday, but he's changed his mind.

'At our age,' he explained, 'we have to celebrate every birthday as if it were the last. We should even celebrate every day.'

Jules is the oldest resident at Ocean View and yet he seems one of the youngest. He doesn't wear glasses, walks unaided and still has the lively mind of a young man, if you can ignore his rambling.

'Nearly a hundred – it takes quite a lot of strength to get through that many years . . .' Lucienne murmurs.

'You're right,' agrees Mina. 'He's in good shape for his age. It's wonderful!'

I smile to think they're only ten years younger than him but think of him as much older. We're all old in somebody's eyes. I was twenty-three the first time a child referred to me as 'the nice lady'. It was nearly the death of me.

Greg arranges the candles on the chocolate cake. It's

been made to Jules's mother's recipe; he's treated to the same one every year.

'There are more candles than cake!' Gustave muses.

We could have put two candles shaped like nines on the cake, but we thought it was more symbolic and visual to have a candle for every year of his life. Jules puffs out his thin cheeks, blows on the flames, has to make several attempts, splutters a little, asks for help from his great-grandson and eventually blows them all out. Ninety-nine candles, ninety-nine years. A lifetime.

'Spee-eech! Spee-eech! Spee-eech!' Elisabeth chants, clapping in time, then leans towards me and adds quietly, 'He says the same thing every year, word for word. But it's such a lovely speech that we ask for it again.'

The old man stands up and clears his throat. His body is shaking with emotion, a frail house of cards threatening to collapse, but when his daughter gestures for him to sit down, he ignores her. He intends to stay on his feet.

'When I went to bed last night, I was twenty years old. When I woke up this morning, I was ninety-nine. Even when it's long, life feels very short. When I was a child, my grandmother – who seemed terribly old to me but was much younger than I am now – always used to say: "Life is short, my boy, and we get just the one, so you should only spend your time on things that are really worth it." I've cherished that thought like a jewel all my life. We don't have time to do justice to everything that makes up a life. We have to make choices. Should I favour work or love? My children or my free time? Reading or fishing? What is really worthwhile? Some of the answers are obvious, others less so. I've made mistakes – of course I have – but I've always tried to listen to my heart rather than my mind.'

He pauses and drinks a mouthful of water. Everyone is listening to his words, as if for the first time.

'At regular intervals through my life,' he goes on, 'I've wondered whether I'd feel satisfied if it ended then. That's the secret: asking whether the child we once were would be proud of us now. I'm no longer in a position to be making plans for life, more to be taking stock. When I look at all the smiles around me, smiles of people I hold dear, I have no regrets. I know I made the right choices.'

The applause begins before he's said the last word. He's clearly not the only one here who knows the speech by heart. One by one, Jules's guests give him a hug and wish him a happy birthday. His gaunt cheeks knock against mine, and he smiles and moves on to the next person, completely unaware of the lesson he's just taught me.

I don't want to come to the end of my life regretting the fact that I've been ruled by fear. That's not what I pictured when I was a little girl. It's time to make the right choices.

Chapter 95

The black cab drops me in the London borough of Islington, outside the address Rosa gave me. I stand outside the small door to the building for a few minutes, not sure whether I should ring the bell or run away. The first option seems more sensible, considering I don't know anyone here except Raphael.

I haven't warned him. I'm here on a whim. At first, it seemed like such a good idea to turn up – *Hiya, it's me! Seeing as you couldn't come over, I thought I'd surprise you* – but the doubts started creeping in on the plane and completely overwhelmed me in the taxi. What if he's not here? What if he doesn't want to see me? What if he lives with his wife, their three children and a parrot?

I press the buzzer for the intercom. A click, and the door opens. I climb the stairs, looking for flat 2b. When I find the door, I clutch the handle of my suitcase with one clammy hand and knock with the other.

A tall, red-haired guy opens the door. Either Raphael has changed a lot or it's not him . . .

'Hello,' he says, in English.

'Hello, I'm looking for Raphael,' I say, with an accent that leaves no room for doubt about my nationality.

'Oh, you're French!' he exclaims in French. 'I'm Laurent, his flatmate. Come in, I'll go and get him.'

I stand in the hall while he heads off down a corridor and knocks at a door. I hope this doesn't take long – I'm turning to jelly at the thought of his reaction.

'Julia?'

Raphael bursts out of the room and looms in front of me, wild-eyed.

'Has something happened to my grandmother?'

'No, no, nothing at all! I'm the one something's happened to: I think I've gone completely mad. I convinced myself it was a good idea to come and surprise you. I should have called . . .'

He smiles, and I start solidifying again.

'It *was* a good idea. It's wonderful to see you! Is that for me?' he asks, pointing to a small, wrapped parcel in my hand.

I nod and hand it to him. He opens it, watched by his flatmate, who's leaning on the door-frame, observing us. When Raphael takes the present out of the box, he laughs out loud.

'With that, I'll still like you even when you've lost all your teeth,' I say.

He pretends to put the dentures into his mouth, and Laurent nods his head with mischievous complicity.

'You lied about her. You said she was cool, but she's really, really cool.'

I've been validated. With this hurdle overcome, the

two 'Frenchies' show me into their living room and take my coat. I look around the room.

'Do you like it?' Laurent asks.

'It's very tastefully decorated.'

I'm not lying, it *is* very tastefully decorated . . . if you're into a nerdy-ten-year-old look. Clearly satisfied, my hosts show me to the black leather sofa, where I sit down between a Lego spaceship and a display cabinet full of miniature cars. I should have brought my cat-head slippers.

Chapter 96

We spend the weekend visiting all the London sights: Buckingham Palace, Parliament Square, Madame Tussauds, the British Museum, the London Eye, moving from one place to the next on foot, stopping only to grab a burger or a coffee.

That's what I'll tell anyone who asks about my time in London. The truth is, we don't get out of bed the whole weekend. Laurent offered to leave us alone by going to spend a couple of days with his girlfriend. We made a show of saying, 'No, no, that's very kind, you needn't do that'; he insisted; we rejected his offer less forcefully – 'Oh, no, we couldn't let you' – he packed a bag and was gone, not before advising us that the kitchen table was 'very comfortable'.

We prefer the bed, though. A mattress on the floor, I should say. Laurent has barely shut the door before Raphael launches himself at me and kisses me as if he's just been released from prison. I lose my blouse on the sofa, my bra in the middle of the living room, my jeans in the corridor, my knickers in the doorway to the bedroom, and my head in bed. All through the weekend we repeat this performance to make sure there was no mistake and it really is that fantastic. It is. And we talk, too, a lot.

We make love, he tells me about his work, we make love, I confide in him about my father's death, we make love, he talks about his plans, we make love, I tell him about mine. He really listens. When I talked to Marc, I often had the uncomfortable feeling he was just waiting for me to stop so he could talk about himself. He didn't always wait till I'd finished, to be honest. I was his mirror. But Raphael takes an interest, asks me questions, sympathises, laughs at my jokes. I feel I can trust him, so I tell him about my feelings, about Nannynoo, getting away from it all so I could take stock, Mum, the reasons I'm at Ocean View. He talks about his parents, his grandmother, his ex, himself. He's as gorgeous to listen to as he is to look at. I'm not bored for a nanosecond; I could spend days in this room, making love, talking and eating. My thighs wouldn't come out of it very well, though.

'Hey, I've got an idea,' he says, as we're tucking into the last pizza from the freezer. 'Usually when people are getting to know each other, they try to paint a rosy picture of themselves. What if we did the opposite?'

'How do you mean?'

'What if we listed our flaws? Then there'll be no surprises – we'll know what to expect.'

I giggle, thinking he's joking. He's serious.

'You do know it'll take much more than a weekend for me to list my faults?' I warn.

'I'm at my leisure.'

By the time we've finished the pizza, he knows I'm lazy, a whinger, that I like trashy magazines, I'm an Olympic-level procrastinator, I have one leg longer than the other and one ear higher than the other (the one perhaps explaining the other), I get car sick, I only like vegetables when they're smothered in cheese, my hair is magnetically drawn to plugholes, I smoke too much, I like having the last word, I overspend, I'm a black-belt neurotic, I laugh at my own jokes, I have all Celine Dion's records, I always need the loo just when it's time to leave, I don't take my make-up off every evening, I can't help myself telling people how a film ends . . . and two or three other things that spill out of my mouth before it strikes me they could be detrimental.

He, on the other hand, says he can sometimes be hypocritical and occasionally has breath like a fennec fox in the morning. Oh, and he snores, too, now and then.

'Is that it?'

'That's it.'

'I think you forgot to say you're modest.'

He pulls me to him, laughing, and kisses me. I have absolutely no desire to know any more of his faults at this precise moment.

'Shall we try out the kitchen table?'

He holds my hand all the way in the taxi back to the airport on Sunday evening. I close my eyes and rest my head on his shoulder. Maybe Marion is right. Maybe good things can happen to me, too.

Chapter 97

Bernadette is a hairdresser. She comes to do the residents' hair once a week. Today, it's me at the mercy of her scissors.

This morning, like every other, the first people I greeted were Team Granny. Stationed on their bench, the three women said hello to me in their usual kindly way.

'You can't have had much sleep during your weekend in London.' Elisabeth started the assault.

'It's actually your hair that looks really tired,' Rosa agreed.

'Surely you're not planning to come to my wedding with your hair like that?' Louise asked anxiously.

In three days' time, my contract comes to an end. In four days' time, Louise and Gustave are getting married and I'm leaving my apartment and heading to Paris. Today, I'm dealing with my hair.

Rosa is here with me. While her black dye takes, Bernadette asks me what I'd like. I tell her I'd just like a trim, but please not too short, you know, just shoulder length would be perfect; no thanks, I don't want a shampoo and set; no thanks, I'm not keen to have a perm; no thanks, I don't need lowlights, or highlights either; thanks, no; don't touch my fringe or I'll thump you.

'Are we not doing anything about the grey hairs?' she asks, inspecting my roots.

She's not very nice, this Bernadette.

'I don't have any grey hairs.'

'Oh, but you do! And not just the one. You may not notice them, but other people do. Shall I do your roots?'

Still reeling from the shock of this terrible news, I consider it.

'I'm sure some little lowlights would really suit you,' Rosa chips in.

'Absolutely!' Bernadette coos. 'It would bring this slightly down-in-the-mouth brown to life . . .'

You'll be down in the mouth if you keep this up.

'Look,' she says, taking a folder from her bag. 'I can really see you like this.'

The model in the picture has a long, glossy bob.

'Could you do that for me?'

'Of course I can! I'm a hairdresser!'

I don't take my eyes off the mirror as she busies away overhead.

'So, Rosa,' I say, 'are you still searching away on the goggle?'

'Do you mean on Google? I go online every day.'

'You go on the internet?' Bernadette asks admiringly.

'I don't understand any of it. My son tried to explain it, but I gave up. What do you do there?'

'I meet men.'

Bernadette stops what she's doing for a few seconds. I ask her if everything's okay . . . I'd like – insofar as it's possible – to avoid being scalped. She nods slowly and goes back to work.

'Well, then? Have you found love?' I ask.

'Still not, but I've found something very special: companionship. There's nothing worse than feeling lonely. I've met several men who are also trying to escape loneliness and are only interested in chatting.'

'But they're not even real!' exclaims Bernadette. 'I mean, they're not as good as real people.'

'Am I not real, then? I promise you, there are real people behind the screens. It may seem strange to you, but when my friends here go back to their studios, I feel alone. It does me a lot of good chatting to people who take an interest in me. You know, when my husband died, I was tempted to cut myself off, isolate myself, but it doesn't do any good at all – in fact, it's awful. Other people are important. It's better to open the door too wide than slam it in their face.'

They keep up their debate, while my thoughts drift to my mother. I slammed the door in her face. That's exactly what I did. Since my weekend with her, we've called each other regularly, I've been back home twice and we feel like mother and daughter, just like before. One Saturday, my sister and my nephew came. The four of us cooked together, we laughed, went for a walk, looked at old photos and didn't even cry. It felt like happiness, that day. It felt like family when I thought my family no longer existed. My sister hoped I'd take the opportunity to tell my mother the truth. I couldn't do it. I wasn't ready. Rosa's words make me realise that I am now. I'm going to open the door to her. I just have to find the right moment and hope she'll forgive me.

'Do you like it?' Bernadette asks, picking up the hairdryer.

I look at myself. Then at the girl in the picture. Back at myself. Back at the picture. Back to me. I can see absolutely no difference from what my hair was like before, and no similarity at all to what I asked for. But I'm polite, so I go into ecstasies, pay and leave a tip. For my trouble, Bernadette gives me one last charming comment:

'Shame you're leaving – you'll have to find someone in Paris to take care of your grey hairs.'

Chapter 98

It's my last day of work at Ocean View.

It's the last time I'll have my morning cup of coffee on the balcony looking out over the sea.

It's the last time I'll head downstairs, mentally going through the day's appointments.

It's the last time I'll stop and chat with Team Granny for a few minutes.

It's the last time I'll knock at these doors knowing there's someone on the other side waiting to confide in me, tell me their feelings.

It's the last time I'll sigh when I see the day's menu.

It's the last time I'll see these walls, these corridors, this furniture, these windows, those trees, and all the faces that have become so familiar.

When I arrived here eight months ago, I would never have believed this place would become my home.

The day hurtles by, as if time can't wait to be over and done with. I lock up my office, for the last time. It's four o'clock: it's over. The day is ending earlier than usual because a farewell drink has been planned.

'Julia!' Clara calls from the end of the corridor. 'Are you coming? We're waiting for you.'

They're all waiting in the refectory. I've been trying to find an excuse to avoid this since breakfast. I don't feel like it, but I definitely don't have a choice, so I put a fake smile on my face and step into complete and utter silence. They stand looking at me with gloomy faces. I feel like I'm at my own funeral.

True to character, Gustave asks if I like salmon, Ella. I give an exaggerated laugh and others join in; we know it's not funny but, if we don't laugh, we'll cry. We wouldn't want our last memory of each other to be blurred by tears.

They each come to talk to me in turn. They come out with stock phrases – 'Still warm for the time of year, isn't it?'; 'We'll be celebrating tomorrow'; 'The nibbles are delicious' – but the words don't sound the same as usual. They're gentle, they linger, they're paired with a probing look or a hand on my arm. Words wrapped in affection and filled with emotion.

There's a box on the table that I'm told to open.

'It's a little present so you never forget us.'

The box is full of Polaroids. One for each resident, one for each colleague. They pose, serious, mischievous or self-conscious, so that I can take a little bit of them away with me. On the back of the photos, they've each written a note.

'Thank you for everything.'

'I'm happy to have known you.'

'I hope you have the wonderful life you deserve.'

'You've given me a lot.'

'I'll miss you.'

My eyesight starts to swim as I look through them. They say things that are sabotaging my efforts not to break down. The residents' eyes are all trained on me, studying my reactions.

'A little speech?' suggests Isabelle.

I remember the detached, professional speech I gave to introduce myself on the first day. It felt like an insurmountable task. It's even worse today. When all's said and done, it's easier to talk in front of people you don't know. I cough to brighten my voice. My bottom lip is wobbling.

'The day I came to Ocean View, I kept wondering what I was doing here. Now, I know: I was here to meet all of you. You say I've given you a lot. I'm glad I have, but the truth is you've given me so much more. You've really made me a better person. You with your terrible jokes, Gustave; you with your wisdom, Elisabeth . . .'

My throat tightens. I take a deep breath and keep going.

'You with your gentleness, Louise; you with your humour, Lucienne; you with your wonderful outlook on life, Jules; you with your directness and your friendship, Clara; you with your generosity, Anne-Marie; you with your breath-of-fresh-air attitude, Isabelle; you with your kindness, Greg . . . you've all enriched who I am. I've learned life lessons here. Ocean View isn't a home for the elderly, it's a place for people with a story, a philosophy, a personality and an individuality, and that's what makes you all so endearing. I'm going to miss you so much . . .'

Some of the eyes start to glisten. If they start, I won't be able to keep up the fight. I sob, and the tears flow. My parting gift is my face distorted by sadness. A hand settles on my shoulder. Gustave.

'You have a good cry, you'll wee less,' he says gently.

Greg comes over.

'We've planned a little outing for the last day. Go and get your swimming costume and meet us in the car park.'

An hour later, most of the residents and staff are shivering, their near-naked bodies offered up to the fresh October wind.

'You're all bonkers,' I say.

'This is how we started, so this is how we have to end!' explains Elisabeth.

'Hmm, yes, but this time you won't abandon me!'

On the signal to go, we form a long line, hold hands and throw ourselves into the waves. The water is icy, and we shriek, but keep going until we're in over our waists.

'Fucking hell, it's cold!' Clara squeals.

'You're absolutely right! Fuck me!' Elisabeth agrees, to her husband's consternation.

'Are you having a heart attack, my darling?'

We laugh and splash each other, and the cold deadens everything – our limbs and our heartache. I take a mental snapshot of this moment. Gustave huddled up to

Louise; Isabelle, who suggests we all wee to warm the water; Leon, swimming a few metres away from everyone; Greg launching Clara into the waves; Rosa giggling like a little girl, Elisabeth waving hello to her friend Marilyn up in heaven; Lucienne jumping the waves . . . A snapshot so I never forget.

Chapter 99

I get my outfit ready for tomorrow – a petrol-blue jump-
suit and yellow shoes – and I've kept my washbag and
make-up in the bathroom. Everything else is in bags,
some of which are already in my car. After the wedding
tomorrow, I'll set off for Paris.

Taking the photos off the wall, putting my clothes in a
suitcase, throwing away anything I don't need, removing
everything that made this studio my home . . . none of it
was easy. So, as a counterbalance, I make a list of all the
positive things about going back to Paris.

1. Marion's sofa is comfortable. Not as comfortable
   as the bed here, but probably better than a
   pavement.
2. I'll have only an hour's commute to work. That's
   sixty times more than here, granted, but less
   than people who have to travel three hours.
3. The view over Place de la Nation is nice.
   Not as good as the Atlantic, but better than
   a wall.
4.

*

I'm struggling to find a fourth plus point when the door opens without anyone knocking. Clara and Greg appear laden with sweets, biscuits, treats and a bottle.

'Don't tell me you thought we'd let you go without one last social,' says Clara.

I'm so happy to see them I'd say yes if they suggested a threesome.

'Wow, this place feels empty!' Greg says, looking round my studio. 'Are you okay? Not finding this too hard?'

'A bit, but I'll be fine. I'll come and visit you.'

'I should hope so!' replies Clara. 'Don't go thinking you can get rid of us that easily.'

We spend the evening forcing ourselves to nibble on things and behaving as if this were just another one of our socials. They tell me about their life together and ask about Raphael, and I talk about my plans for Paris: nothing would betray the fact that this is our last night together – if our cheerfulness didn't have a false ring to it.

As they leave, somewhere around midnight, Clara turns appearances on their head. She hugs me to her, in tears, and stays there a long time.

'I really love you,' she whispers.

'Me, too,' I manage, between sniffs.

Greg has tears in his eyes, too. I tell him his acting was better in that ad he did. He gives me a hug.

'We'll miss you.'

They disappear down the stairs, and I close the door on the silence. Dejection makes itself comfortable in my brain. I'm devastated. I feel as if I'm being torn away from the first place where I've felt at home. I don't want to go to Paris, I don't want to work with people who'll spend the whole time talking about their hair, I don't want anything else. Even the prospect of tomorrow's wedding doesn't succeed in cheering me. I go out on to the balcony and light a cigarette. What the hell am I doing, for God's sake? So was all this for nothing? I retreat into my comfort zone, cursing the whole world for what's happening to me. Seeing only negatives. For months, I've admired these people who keep smiling as they weather storms. People who can see the beam of sunlight breaking through the clouds. It's about time I followed their example.

I'm sad. I'm going to miss them. But most importantly, I'm lucky they ever came into my life.

Chapter 100

I hear them laughing just as I stub out my cigarette. It's Friday – they probably need to unwind a bit before the wedding. Good timing: so do I.

Gustave, Louise, Elisabeth, Pierre, Rosa and one other person are sitting around the garden table. As I get closer, I see Leon dragging on the joint. Panicking at the sight of me, he throws it at Rosa. The others play up to this.

'I promise, we can explain everything!' says Gustave. 'Leon made us do it!'

The accused flushes scarlet.

'But n-no,' he stammers. 'I didn't do anything! This is only the second time I've been, but *they* meet up regularly.'

'Gustave's telling the truth,' Elisabeth says quickly. 'Leon has threatened us with terrible things if we don't come and smoke the cannabis he grows in the vegetable plot.'

Leon's eyes are about to pop out of their sockets. He looks from one to the other of his fellow residents, in search of some compassion. I decide to put an end to his suffering by grabbing the joint and taking a long, confident toke on it.

'Don't worry, Leon. If you smoked regularly, it would be obvious. You'd be way more chilled.'

The other five laugh. Leon does, too, eventually. I sit

down with them and hold on to the joint. I'll need plenty to get to sleep.

'By the way, Leon,' Rosa asks, 'have you changed your mind about tomorrow?'

'Not at all. I won't come.'

No one insists. I almost feel sorry for him, isolated in his sour contempt.

'That's a shame,' I say. 'It could have been an opportunity for you to open up to the others a bit. I'll never understand you . . . You're surrounded by lovely people but you seem to do everything in your power to end your days alone.'

He sits in silence for a while, while I drag on the joint and hand it to Elisabeth.

'You're still just as naïve,' he says eventually. 'Please stop thinking there's a sweet old man hiding inside me, you'll be giving everyone a break. I don't give a damn about other people, I don't give a damn about ending my days alone, I'm very happy as I am and I won't change. If you don't understand that, I recommend you retake your degree. And with that, I wish you goodnight.'

He gets up and walks away. Rosa shrugs.

'Shame he's about as appealing as a tax assessment. He could be quite the charmer.'

It's two o'clock in the morning when we decide to go to bed.

'May I remind you we've got a wedding to go to in the morning,' says Louise. 'Our wedding!'

While the others head straight back to their studios, Gustave insists on seeing me to the door of the annexe. I feel like I'm floating, as if on a cloud.

'My daughter called,' he says.

'Really? Will she come tomorrow?'

'No, she won't. She's come to a radical decision: she never wants to see me again. She wanted to explain her reasons. Part of me is relieved. I won't judge, it's all too painful for her. She has her reasons.'

'Her reasons?' I cry. 'I can't think what she has to hold against you – you're the personification of kindness!'

'I've made mistakes. I'm not perfect. There's one she just can't forgive me for. I understand her. I can't forgive myself either.'

'What on earth did you do to her to make her resent you this much?'

He sighs.

'She was twenty when our son had his accident. She'd just gone off for a holiday with her fiancé's family. He was in a coma for three days before he died. My wife wanted to tell her, but I didn't have the heart to ruin her holiday. She didn't have the chance to say goodbye to her own brother because of me.'

'I don't know what to say, Gustave. You did what you thought was best at the time . . .'

'If I had my life over again, I'd do it differently. I'd tell her the truth straight away. The people we love deserve the truth.'

He leans over his walking frame and places a kiss on my cheek.

'Goodnight, Julia. See you tomorrow for the big day!'

I climb the steps as best I can, my legs are made of cotton wool and my head is full of the stuff. There's just one thing going round on a loop in my mind: 'The people we love deserve the truth.'

I don't even wait till I'm inside before writing the text.

I'm ready to reveal all. Meet in the car park @ 10 tomorrow. Love you.

And I send it to my sister.

Chapter 101

From: Raphael Marin-Goncalves
Subject: Today

Hi Julia,

I've been thinking about you all day, I hope it went okay. I can't wait to hold you in my arms.

Thinking of you.

Lots of kisses

Raphael

From: Julia Rimini
Subject: Re: Today

Thanks, Raphael, your support means a lot to me.

It was tough, but nothing compared to what I have to go through tomorrow. You know, the thing I told you about last time . . . I've made up my mind. I'm going to tell them everything. I so wish you could have been here.

Can't wait till next month to see you.

Hugs and kisses

Julia

Chapter 102

I must get to sleep. I'll be needing all my strength at ten o'clock tomorrow. But I just can't.

I've been tossing and turning in bed for ages – hours. I try to concentrate on my breathing, my toes, sheep jumping over a gate, but it's no good: thoughts invite themselves in, ideas muscle in. So I get up, take a sheet of paper and a pen, and I let the ink set my feelings free.

A letter to my 80-year-old self

Dear 80-year-old Julia,

It's 32-year-old Julia here. I don't know whether you'll read this letter someday but, if you do, I can see you smiling at the memory of this night: me writing to you in my Snuggles pyjamas and my head at boiling point. I can't imagine I'll ever be 80 but, just in case, I felt like talking to you.

I hope you're well. I'm trying to picture what you look like. It's not easy . . . Do you have lines on either side of your mouth, like Dad or Mum's laughter lines? Have you given up worrying about your roots? And what about this body I've so abused with cigarettes and fast food? Is it still in working order? To be honest, it doesn't matter much. The only question that matters, the one that's stopping me sleeping is: Are you happy?

I hope you are. I hope you look back with gratitude and ahead with enthusiasm. I hope that what I've learned these last few months has stayed with you your whole life.

I hope you still feel a sense of wonder when you see the sea, a child's smile, the shape of a cloud or a beautiful film.

I hope you live somewhere that you love. In your own home, or somewhere else, so long as it feels right. If Ocean View still exists, Studio 8 has a fantastic view, even if a grumpy old man once lived there . . .

I hope you have loved ones around you. I hope with all my heart that you have children, that they're well and that you see them now. Sometimes, I'd just like to jump into the future for a few minutes and then come back to where I am. The most worrying thing is not knowing. I hope your beloved sister is still with you and you have girls' nights with Clara and Marion. If you like, there are some delightful plants in the vegetable plot at Ocean View.

I hope you've experienced love. The true sort of love you always dreamed of. With Raphael, perhaps. Or someone else, so long as you go to bed every evening feeling grateful that you were lucky enough to meet him. A tall man called Pierre taught me that a long time ago.

I hope you've shaken off your fears and are more serene. I'm working at it, you know, but I'm still a long way from managing not to anticipate everything and stress about everything. I hope you've shrugged off all your fears along the path you've taken.

I hope you treasure your memories and know how precious they are. I'm trying to make lovely ones for you every day.

It's 10 October 2015. I'm at a crossroads. I hope I don't get this wrong. I hope, one day, you'll tell me I made the right choice.

Take care and see you soon.

Julia.

I put down the pen, fold the piece of paper, put it into my purse, slip into bed and fall asleep as if I've been knocked out.

Chapter 103

Ten o'clock. This is it.

The moment I've been putting off for almost a year has come.

Carole is waiting for me by the door to the annexe. I lead her off to the far end of the gardens, to the bench that looks out to sea. The waves are pounding relentlessly. My heart's not far off the same state.

'Are you sure you want to do this today?' she asks me.

'I think so.'

'It'll be fine.'

'I hope so. I'm scared.'

'What are you scared of?'

'Of not being understood. Of being a disappointment.'

'It's likely to be a bit unsettling, but I'm not worried at all. In a few minutes' time, you'll be in the arms of someone you love, feeling completely at peace. Shall we go?'

'Let's go.'

We walk along the corridors till we come to the blue door. My heart's beating so quickly I can no longer feel it. Actually, I can't feel anything any more.

Carole knocks on the door.

'Come in!'

She opens the door.

Standing in the middle of the day room is my mother. She stares at me with her mouth open wide, one arm frozen in mid-air and a veil in her hand.

'What are *you* doing here?' she asks.

I can't bring myself to answer. Next to her, in her pretty white dress, Louise gives me a big smile. My tears spill, just as I throw myself into her arms.

'Oh, Nannynoo!'

I bury my face in her neck, it smells of Chanel N° 5 and my childhood. She strokes my hair with her shaking hand.

'Hello, my darling. You took your time . . .'

Chapter 104

Mum has slipped away, encouraged by Carole, who told her that I would explain later. My eyes thanked my sister silently: I needed to be alone with Nannynoo.

I'm crying shamelessly, loudly, my back racked with spasms. Like a five-year-old. On the receiving end, my grandmother is more dignified, but her face is streaming with tears.

'Thank goodness I don't have my make-up on yet!' she says, trying to ease the tension. 'Shall I make you a hot chocolate?'

I shake my head. I couldn't drink it.

'Did you know who I was?' I ask between sobs.

She takes me over to the sofa, where we both sit down, then she takes my hands in hers.

'I didn't recognise you straight away. The day you arrived, it struck me that you had the same name as one of my granddaughters, but that's all. If your mum had taken your father's name, it might have been easier, but I'd forgotten his name so I didn't make the connection.'

She strokes my hands gently.

'I felt something every time I saw you,' she continues. 'I felt comfortable, and I could tell you did, too. But

I thought it was just, you know, an affinity. And then there was the photo . . .'

'Don't say you recognised me on that family photo!' I say, tilting my chin towards the picture on the sideboard. 'I was seventeen, more than a stone lighter, and I had waist-length black hair. I'm unrecognisable!'

She smiles. My tears are starting to subside. Now I'm having to stop myself snuggling in her arms, which I've missed so much.

'Not in that one,' she says. 'Do you remember one time when you came to see me here and I was heading off for your Uncle Daniel's sixtieth birthday?'

'I remember it well. You'd put all your jewellery on – you were radiant! I so wanted to go with you, but I couldn't; I'd have ruined everything. As usual, I declined, and told Mum I had to stay in Paris because of work.'

She nods.

'Your mother wanted to give Daniel a personalised present. She needed a photo of each member of the family and remembered that I had a beautiful one of you. Obviously, I've forgotten, but your mum tells me I took it on the beach, two or three years ago.'

I remember the occasion. I'd come down to spend a weekend with my parents and had made the most of a bright spell between squalls of rain to go for a walk on the beach with Nannynoo. I'd teased her when she produced a disposable camera. She pressed the button just as I burst out laughing. I've never seen the result.

She carries on with her explanations. I could listen to

her for hours, like when she used to tell me fairy tales before my afternoon nap. Just one more story, Nannynoo, pleeeease!

'Your mother looked through my albums for the photo. I have several of them here in the sideboard, but I haven't had the heart to go through them since my stroke. When she took it out and showed it to me, I thought I was going to faint. It was you, Julia. You were my granddaughter!'

My eyes can't contain my tears again.

'Your Technicolor Dreamgirl . . . Didn't Mum notice anything?'

'I immediately realised she wasn't in the know, so I didn't say anything. It wasn't for me to tell her. I just thought you must have your reasons and the time would come . . .'

I squeeze her hands a little bit harder.

'I knew she came to see you every Sunday, so I'd make myself scarce. I was always afraid I'd bump into her in the corridor. I'll go and talk to her soon. But first I want to explain why I did this.'

And so I explain.

When my mother called me a year ago to tell me Nannynoo had had a stroke, I decided to come down on the spot . . . until Mum said she'd lost forty years of memories. I thought about it for days, couldn't sleep for nights on end, I clicked on 'reserve tickets' hundreds of times before giving up. The truth is, I was terrified. The memories I shared with Nannynoo were some of the most precious things I have. Knowing she'd forgotten all our shared experiences, all our Wednesdays, all our cuddles, and that she'd forgotten me, it was just too much. I was trying to get over losing my father; I was in remission and frightened of having a relapse.

'I didn't want to be a stranger to you,' I say between my tears. 'I couldn't bear it. Then I saw this job offer: to be the therapist in your retirement home. I didn't even hesitate, although I wasn't at all sure it was the right thing to do. I missed you too much, and it was an opportunity to be with you, but without being your granddaughter.'

She smiles that smile I love so much. I can't hold back any longer: I burrow into her arms and curl up against this woman I was so afraid I'd lost. She looks surprised.

'We always cuddled like this when I came to see you. It was part of our Wednesday ritual.'

She puts her arms around me and hugs me close to her heart.

'I'm relying on you to fill me in on all our memories. And we're going to make plenty more for ourselves, my darling.'

We've been in each other's arms several minutes when someone knocks at the door.

'Come in!' calls Nannynoo, who, like me, seems to be in no hurry to relax our embrace.

Gustave appears, looking elegant in a grey suit with a rose in his buttonhole.

'Is my bride-to-be ready?' he asks, before seeing us.

'My little one has finally revealed her secret,' Nanny-noo tells him.

He nods his head, smiling.

'Well, there we are! She'll finally be able to call me Grandpa!'

Chapter 105

My mother drives to the town hall. I'm in the passenger seat, in my wedding shoes.

'Are you angry with me, Mum?'

'No . . . but I think I need a bit more time to understand. You said you couldn't come to your grandmother's wedding, so it was a shock seeing you. Then Carole told me you've been here all along . . .'

She's trying to hide it, but I can hear the sadness in her voice. I look down. I've hurt her.

'I'm so sorry, Mum. It wasn't that I didn't want to see you. I needed to be alone, to get back to being me, and be close to Nannynoo. So it could be like before. And I didn't want you to worry. I was out of my depth. I hope you can forgive me . . .'

'I'm not angry, my love. You handled things as best you could. That's what we've all done. No one can judge us for that. You're doing better now, that's the important thing. I'm sad I haven't been able to make the most of you being here before you go.'

'I'll come and see you a lot, I promise. And you can come to me, too; we can explore Paris together. It'll be great!'

Silence descends on us for several long minutes. Out the corner of my eye, I see her turn to look at me a few times. At one point, she even opens her mouth and closes it again. I know what she wants to say. The words are stuck in her throat. They must be burning her, but they won't come out.

I remember what Nannynoo told me. Here and now.

Not waiting for special occasions to say those three words to the people who matter.

Now's the time.

I open my mouth and, in a shaky voice, I say those important words to the person who matters the most.

'I love you, Mummy.'

My eyes stay on the road ahead. Can't ask too much of me in one go.

Chapter 106

The town hall is packed full.

All Nannynoo's family is here. *My* family. My mother, my sister, my nephew, my uncles and aunts, my cousins. Gustave has never looked so serious; maybe he doesn't need to wear his clown costume any more. When he walks past me to get to his front-row chair, he whispers in my ear:

'So many people are welcoming me into your family. It's making my head spin, but I'm loving it already! And there I was, thinking I no longer had a family . . .'

My mother doesn't let go of my hand for a minute. I won't run away again, Mum. Earlier, she did my hair for me, then looked me right in the eye for a long time. Carole took a picture of us at that exact moment, then my nephew took the camera from her.

'I'm going to take a picture of all three of you!' he announced, in his sweet little voice. He took four photos, all of them either out of focus or on a slant, imperfect but true. One day, I'll hold them in my wrinkled hands and I'll remember that magic moment when the three of us were together: my mother, my sister and myself. And in each of us there was something of Dad.

The residents are here, too. All of them except for

Leon, and Mina, who isn't feeling well. They brought out dresses and suits they thought they might never wear again, they've been to the hairdresser or the barber, proud to tell everyone they were going to a wedding. Their eyes are lit up with the distinctive sparkle of special occasions, a combination of pride, happiness and tiredness. They are sitting in the back rows so as not to get in the way of the family. But then . . . even though they don't have the same surname, they have no relations in common and no old memories to share, what I see sitting there at the back of the town hall is definitely a family.

The staff are here, too, and they thought they'd never see this day: an Ocean View wedding – now that's an original activity. Greg and Clara shoot fervent looks at each other. I wouldn't be surprised to be invited to their wedding before long. Let's hope the DJ doesn't play anything from *Dirty Dancing*.

Music rings out around the town hall and Isabelle is first to clap. Frank Michael starts to sing.

'Ooh,' says Lucienne, looking around agitatedly. 'I like Frank Michael. Where is he?'

'He's in the speakers,' says Clara, bringing Lucienne's dreams crashing down.

All eyes turn to the door. Louise is about to make her entrance, on my uncle's arm. When the celebrant asked whether they'd like the basic ceremony or something more traditional with music and decorations, they immediately agreed they wanted 'the whole shebang'.

I see my uncle first, then Nannynoo's frail outline. I barely recognise her under her long white veil. She walks up the aisle with an assured step, her tear-filled eyes fixed on an emotional Gustave. My own tears spill over. I thought she'd gone, I was almost convinced that, without her memories, she'd only ever be a stranger inside my grandmother's body. By living alongside her without being her granddaughter, I've learned to see her in another light. I've come to know the woman she is. I've discovered Louise. She's a different Nannynoo, it's a new relationship, but she's there, alive and happy. I can snuggle in her arms, I can listen to her voice, I can drink her hot chocolate. I can carry our memories in me for the two of us. And now we can start making new ones.

'Louise Marguerite Dutiss, do you take Gustave Marius Jacques Champagne as your husband?'

'I do!'

'Gustave Marius Jacques Champagne, do you take Louise Marguerite Dutiss as your wife?'

'I do, until death us do part, but I warn you, I don't want any children.'

'I now pronounce you husband and wife. You may kiss the bride.'

While they oblige with very genuine pleasure, the room fills with applause. Next, all the guests congratulate the newly-weds. When my turn comes, Nannynoo hugs me to her for a long time then cranes her head back to look at me.

'I'm proud to have a granddaughter as generous and brave as you. My Technicolor Dreamgirl . . .'

I'm very pleased I'm wearing waterproof mascara.

Nannynoo and Gustave are last to emerge, under a shower of rose petals and snapping cameras. I've moved a little further away, to film the scene on my phone. A message pops up on the screen. It's from Raphael.

Do you think my grandmother misses me?

I smile. I was right about Pomponnette all along.

I'm sure she does. She wishes you were here.

New message.

Tell her to look across the street.

Chapter 107

'You came . . .'

'Of course I came! I wish I could have been here this morning for your big moment, but there wasn't an earlier flight. Did it go well?'

'Better than well. Thank you for being here . . .'

He takes me in his arms and I kiss him.

'When are you heading to Paris?'

'This evening, after the reception.'

'Do you have any room in your car?' he asks.

'A bit, why?'

'I've got a job interview in Paris on Monday, and I thought I could be useful as a co-pilot. In case you come across any sharks . . .'

I don't know how to reply except with an idiotic smile. How thrilled he must be to come face to face with the Cheshire Cat.

'Right, are you going to introduce me to your family, then?'

I take his hand and we cross the street to the clusters of people. My heart is dancing for joy.

Mind you, I'll have to check with Google whether it hurts if you explode with happiness.

Epilogue

Six months later

Hi Dad.

I've brought you a new orchid. The last one had completely wilted.

I'm really sorry I didn't come to see you last month, I didn't come down to Biarritz – Mum and Carole came to see me in Paris. We had a great weekend. You should have seen the three of us, like real tourists, the Arc de Triomphe, the Champs-Élysées, a *bateau-mouche* . . . It was perfect, up until Mum got it into her head she wanted to go up the Eiffel Tower. We tried to put her off, but you know what she's like. Once up there, she told us we were right. That was just before she had a panic attack because of how high we were.

We missed you, even though you were with us. We talked about you. We talk about you more and more – we even laugh sometimes about our memories. Like that time you thought Madame Broca was pregnant and asked her how far gone she was, and she said, 'About 10 kilos!'

Do you know something, Dad? The memories I miss the most are the ones we'll never have. But I'm getting better, I promise.

My work's still not very exciting but my colleagues are really nice and the pay's good. I miss Ocean View, especially the residents . . . I'm glad I manage to get to Biarritz at least once a month, and they welcome me every time like their own granddaughter – all of them. I can't remember if I told you, but they made a petition to get me back, and Lea, who I was filling in for, found it. She didn't take it very well, apparently, and she's threatening to have another baby. So the residents gave her a bumper bag of pregnancy tests! I cried laughing when they told me that, their faces all sweet and innocent. I hope she uses them soon.

In other news, Nannynoo and Gustave have taken the leap: they've moved in together. The building work went on for several weeks, but it was worth it: they have a brand-new, bigger studio. The other couple there, Elisabeth and Pierre, liked it so much that the director offered to completely renovate theirs. I'm sure you can imagine how all the others reacted to that . . . As you can probably guess, the whole of Ocean View is now going to be overhauled. It's expensive, so the residents have offered to contribute to the cost. Let's hope no one touches the vegetable plot – I can think of five residents who'd never get over it!

I'm going for dinner this evening with Greg and Clara – you know, my friends, who are getting married. They've got a puppy and they're really keen for me to see him. He's a French bulldog and he's got one of those permanently grumpy faces. So they've called him Leon! I can't wait to see them.

But before that, there's someone I'd like you to meet. My Raphael. He's waiting in the car till I call him over. I've been telling you about him for long enough . . . This is a big deal for me; I wanted to be sure. It took me a long time to break down all my barriers, but I'm there now, and I'm no longer in any doubt. I'm worthy of him. We've started looking at apartments together. We haven't fallen for anything yet, but even though I love Marion, I'm looking forward to leaving her sofa behind and letting her coo away in peace with Issa. And Raphael's had more than enough of his little garret. I'm sure you're going to like him. Look, he's coming over.

Do you remember, you always used to say, 'You'll understand when you're grown up,' and it was always guaranteed to annoy me. You were right, Dad. I hope you're proud of me. I think it's happened now. I've grown up.

Acknowledgements

I won't go as far as to liken a book to a baby but, all the same, just over a year ago when I sent my first novel off in to the big, wide world, I felt a bit like a mother whose child was leaving home. I was happy, proud, excited, but also unbelievably apprehensive. Would it be well received? What if it wasn't any good? What if no one liked it?

But, as if you sensed how I was feeling, you were quick to reassure me – with photos, you let me know how my book was getting on. There it was in your homes: you were lending it to your loved ones, it was with you at significant moments, it was allowing you to escape everything, and it made you have a good time. I'd said in an interview a few months earlier: 'I believe that if I go to bed every night knowing that I'm making people happy, that does me good too'. You all do me good.

Writing a book was my childhood dream. I'd always imagined the incredible emotion of seeing my name on a book cover, in a book shop. I wasn't wrong – each time is still as strong as the first. But the most powerful feelings came from your messages. Every single word moved me, made me laugh, gave me butterflies in my stomach. As I

439

reached the final full stop of my first novel, I felt a real mix of happiness and sadness. Sad to leave the characters who'd been with me every day for months, happy to have told their story. I feel the same thing today as I introduce Julia, Clara, Louise, Raphael, Gustave, Leon and the others here. I get a bit misty-eyed when I talk about them, like they really exist. They're real to me. And I know that they'll be just fine with you. And so it's to you, dear readers, that I say my first thank you. Thank you for living this adventure with me. It's great to be with you.

Thank you to my son. You make me see the world through your young eyes. Thank you for coming to lie next to me from time to time while I'm writing, your little head resting on my knee. I don't think I ever write as well as I do as when you're there. I want to write you a beautiful world.

Thank you, A., for teaching me that happiness shouldn't wait for tomorrow and that you need to look for it every day in the little things. You are always with me. Thank you, my love, for always believing in me, even – and especially – when I didn't believe in myself. Thank you for the stars in your eyes when you talk about me, thank you for being my first reader, for encouraging me, for being so accommodating, so patient, for giving me ideas, for looking after *everything* when I'm buried in my writing, for listening to me talk about my characters for hours, as if we really know them. Thank you for making my life so beautiful.

Thank you to my dear family for sharing my joy.

Maman, Papa, Marie, Mamie, Papy, Mimi, my cousins, uncles and aunts . . . Thank you for your encouragement, for the press cuttings on the fridge, the stars in your eyes, the magazines bought en masse, your pride, your interest, your opinions, your sincere delight. Thank you, especially, for always letting me believe it. I'm incredibly lucky to have been born into so much love.

Thank you, Papy, for running like the wind to catch up with that beautiful young woman on the Avenue de Paris in Tunis. Thank you, Mamie, for accepting his invitation, although it seemed like madness. Thank you for being my grandparents. I love you so much.

Thank you, Mamie Arlette, for allowing me to tell your story. You forget us a little more each day, but Helmut will always be in your thoughts now. I hope that you're right, that he's waiting for you and that you'll finally be happy with him.

Thank you, Mutti, for lending your names to this sweet couple.

Thank you to Constance, my fairy godmother – there's a lot of you in this book. And you always know how to kick-start me when I fall by the wayside.

Thank you to my early readers for your suggestions, your encouragement, your friendship and for always being there: Arnold, at any time, a thousand times, Maman and Mamie, the first ones; Marie, *ma puce*; Mimi and your crazy laughter; Faustine, *ma paupiette*; Alexia and all your corrections; Emma and your moral support; my little Maïne, always rooting for me; Serena, Sophie,

Cynthia, my Bertignac *chéries*; Constance and Camille, always there . . . It's invaluable to get your opinions, to hear your laughter, to read your expressions. Thank you for sharing this adventure with me. I can't wait to make you read the next one!

Thank you, Alexandrine, for sending me that email, one Friday. Thank you for your passion, your advice, for always being around for me. Thank you for allowing me to boast: 'My editor, at Fayard!'

Thank you, Claire, for being one of the first people to believe in this book and for always being there to bring back my inspiration when it does a bunk.

Thank you to Jean-Claude for whispering some very fine words to me, and to Seb for making me howl with laughter with his werewolf story, one evening on a terrace.

Thank you Fayard and Le Livre de Poche (Alexandrine, Sophie, Sophie, Véronique, Audrey, Constance, Marie, Pauline, Carole, Ariane, Agathe, Sylvie, David and the others who I can't wait to meet) for your trust, your energy and your enthusiasm.

Thank you to the sales teams and bookshops who allow my stories to meet their readers.

Thank you to my characters for insisting on being written and for being with me through everything, night and day, for all these months. I will miss you.